Beautifully
BROKEN CONTROL

THE
SUTTER LAKE
SERIES

CATHERINE
COWLES

BEAUTIFULLY BROKEN CONTROL
Copyright © 2019 by The PageSmith LLC. All rights reserved.

Editor: Susan Barnes
Copy Editor: Chelle Olson
Proofreading: Julie Deaton and Janice Owen
Paperback Formatting: Stacey Blake, Champagne Book Design
Cover Design: Hang Le

Dedication

For Trisha, my favorite ballerina. Thank you for your friendship and for encouraging me to take the crazy leap into authordom.

And, as always, for my dad. I carry you with me on every step of this journey. Eternally grateful to be your daughter.

Prologue

Kennedy

A SINGLE BEAD OF SWEAT ROLLED DOWN MY STERNUM, and my hand shook as I tried to wipe it away.

"Don't." The tech guy's stern voice whipped through the small cargo van, making me jump.

"Geez, Whitley, would you calm down already?" Agent Carnes gave me a reassuring smile that did nothing to ease the rapid beat of my heart.

Agent Whitley turned his scowl from me to Carnes. "This case has been years in the making, and she's going to blow it by covering the mic with her hand because she's twirling her hair or some other stupid shit."

I winced, slowly lowering my hands to my lap and resting them carefully on my Chanel bag. The purse was a lie, just like the rest of my life. The pale pink tufted leather had made me so happy when my mother had gifted it to me for my birthday, reminding me of the pointe shoes I loved so much. Now, just the feel of it made me sick to my stomach.

"Kennedy?"

My gaze jumped from the purse to Agent Carnes. "Hmm?"

Unease filled his expression. "You good on the plan?"

I swallowed hard, my tongue sticking to the roof of my mouth. "Yes." The slight tremor in my voice revealed me to be as much of a liar as my bag was.

Carnes scooted a bit closer, leaning his elbows on his knees as he stared at me without speaking for a moment. He sighed. "Look, I know this isn't easy. But think about all the people you'll be helping." I said nothing, simply bit down on my bottom lip to stop its trembling. Carnes went in for the kill. "Think about your *brother*."

The FBI had done their research. They knew the exact strings to pull to get me to do their bidding. My eyes traveled to the wall of monitors on the opposite side of the van, my gaze going a bit unfocused. It seemed impossible that what lay before me was real. It was as if, at any moment, I might wake up, and this would all be one epically long nightmare. "Tell me you're sure."

"Kennedy, you've seen the evidence. We could arrest your father right now, but we want a slam dunk. For that, we need a confession. You can get us that."

I had seen the evidence. Hundreds of pages of documents I could barely wrap my head around. Spreadsheets and figures that meant the life I'd been living for the past twenty years had never really been mine. My father had stolen it all.

My hands pressed into the hard seat beneath me, the edges biting into my palms. "And if I do this, Preston is safe, right?"

Carnes reached out and patted my hand. "You signed the agreement. If you get a confession, your brother won't even be arrested." My hold on the seat tightened. "We truly don't think he even knows about the Ponzi scheme, but you know how these things go...innocent people can get caught in the crossfire..."

The agent let his words hang in the air. The threat they'd

been lauding over my head for weeks. Get the confession they needed, or my brother could end up in jail. My dad was going away either way. And as much as it killed me to even think the thought, it looked like he deserved it. My breath hitched. But my brother...he was good, and kind, and he didn't deserve any of the shitstorm this was going to rain down on him.

I let out a slow breath and raised my head. "I'm ready."

Carnes clapped his hands together. "Good. Remember, we'll be able to hear everything. Just get him talking."

I nodded and rose, squeezing by the asshole agent at the recording controls and slipping through the small opening Carnes had given me. My heart rate picked up its pace as I climbed out of the van and made my way through the parking garage. I passed by the Mercedes Coupe my father had gotten me as a high school graduation present, and my stomach roiled. How many people's paychecks had been stolen to pay for that car?

The backs of my eyes burned as though the tears building there were made of acid. *Hold it together, Kennedy. Do it for Pres.* My hand shook as I pulled the building pass out of my purse and held it to the card reader. The elevator doors opened, and I hit the button for the top floor. Of course, it was the penthouse office. Nothing but the best for Davis Barrington.

My mind swirled around that thought as the elevator climbed. Was it that desperate need for the best that had sent Dad down this path? One where he took and took, knowing he'd never be able to give it all back?

My gaze drifted down to the damn purse again. I had the sudden urge to rip it from my body and send it hurtling from the top floor of my father's Wall Street high-rise. But I couldn't stop there. I'd have to strip off every piece of clothing I had on. Scrub off the perfectly executed makeup. Undo the expertly applied highlights in my hair.

And what would be left? A burn danced along my sternum, one I desperately wanted to rub away. I squeezed my eyes closed. I wasn't just a pretty canvas. I was a dancer who expressed myself through movement. I was a friend who always listened when someone needed an ear. I was a student. A sister.

My breath hitched on the last thought, and the elevator doors slid open. A sister was maybe the most important thing of all. Preston had looked out for me from the day I was born, it was time for me to return the favor.

The office was quiet, the lighting low. The minimum requirements for corporate Manhattan on a Saturday. I wove through the cubicles, by the fishbowl conference rooms, past a plaque that held my brother's name, finally stopping at the gold plate that held my father's.

I took a deep breath, raised my hand, and knocked.

"Come in."

I pushed the door open and took a tentative step inside.

My father sat with floor-to-ceiling windows behind him, the cityscape as his backdrop, and grinned at the sight of me. "Little Princess, what are you doing here?"

The nickname almost brought me to my knees. He'd read me the book as a little girl. We'd even taken a trip to India because of it, I'd been so enamored with the tale. And like everything else in my life that I'd ever wanted, he'd given it to me. He'd always been a good father. Even when we didn't understand each other, I always knew he loved me.

I couldn't reconcile the two images in my mind. The father who read me my favorite stories before bed, and the man who had stolen over a billion dollars from unsuspecting investors. None of the jumbled discord dancing in my head made sense.

Concern flashed in my dad's expression. "What's wrong?" He rose.

I shook my head, lowering myself into a chair opposite his

desk. "Nothing, I—" My gaze flicked down to the microphone I knew lay taped between my breasts. I couldn't do this. My hand reached up, seemingly of its own accord, twisting the fabric of my blouse, muffling the sounds in the room.

I met my father's gaze. "Actually, there is something."

Dad lowered himself into his leather desk chair. "Lay it on me."

My whole body seemed to shake as I watched the man who had banished the monsters hiding under my bed. "Do you steal money from your clients?" The words tripped out of my mouth of their own accord, boldly spilling into the space between us.

My father's mouth opened and closed like a fish trying to escape a hook. "What are you talking about? Of course, not. Why would you think such a thing?" My heart cracked as he rubbed the spot behind his left ear. It was his tell. My brother always thought I was bullshitting, but from the time when I was ten and asked for a puppy for Christmas, I'd known this was his giveaway. He'd looked me dead in the eyes while rubbing that spot and said I wasn't old enough for a dog of my own yet. That bundle of brown and white fur Christmas morning had told me otherwise. Every time he lied to Mom about eating a salad at the club, he'd rub that same spot, and I'd know he'd had the steak.

I gripped my blouse tighter, tears welling in my eyes. "Please, don't lie to me."

A coldness that I'd never seen before filled his eyes. "Investing is a complicated business, Kennedy. I've built a good life for our family. You should be grateful for that."

"I don't want a life that was stolen from other people." My voice shook as I spoke.

My father scoffed. "Oh, really? And you'd be just fine in a public school? No car or fancy dance lessons?"

My hand trembled as I tried to keep my hold on the fabric surrounding the microphone. "I could make it work."

"Bullshit!" His hand banged on the desk, startling me into releasing my hold on the mic. I didn't move to cover it up again. "I have slaved for this company. For this family. The least you could do is show me a little respect."

"So, you did it?" I could barely get the words out, the truth of them burning my vocal cords.

"I *borrowed* some money from clients. There's a difference."

I wondered if my father believed the words he said; if they were lies he told himself every day. "So, you're going to pay everything back?"

"Of course." He rubbed that same spot behind his ear. He'd never pay a dime back. His gaze turned shrewd. "You never said how these questions came about."

My blood heated. His selfishness, that unquenchable thirst for more, was going to destroy our family and so many others. I swallowed down the rage thrumming through me, did my best to not let it shine through in my voice. "I saw an email I shouldn't have." It was what Agent Carnes had told me to say, and it wasn't as if my father guarded his computer or phone. I'd used both in the past week.

My father's voice turned gentle, but the tone was a lie, just like the rest of our lives. "I promise you, Little Princess, this is nothing for you to be worried about. I've got everything under control."

I forced the tension in my face to ease, tried to give him a small smile. "I'm so glad. I just wanted to make sure."

Dad gave me his own forced smile. "Of course. You know you can come to me with anything."

He rose and I followed suit. As he wrapped his arms around me, pulling me to him, I was struck by the audacity of the situation. I wanted nothing more than comfort and security from the man who had ripped all my comfort and security away. Because the FBI had told me the reality of the situation. At the rate the hedge fund was currently earning, it would take my father over a century to pay back everything he'd stolen. And as soon as the truth came out, it would be a physical impossibility.

I let my fingers sift through my dog's silky fur. Tried to focus on my breathing, and the cool night air as I stared out my open window. None of it worked. A knock sounded on my bedroom door, and I quickly swiped at the wetness under my eyes. "Come in."

A face as familiar as my own appeared in the opening. My brother stepped through, closing the door behind him. "Twinkle Toes."

I forced a small smile. "Hey, what are you doing here?"

Preston crossed to me, lowering himself onto the opposite end of the window seat so that he faced me head-on. My chest spasmed, anxiety drumming a quick rhythm against my ribs. Ever since I'd walked out of my father's office, gotten in my car, and drove away, it was as if I were waiting for a nuclear bomb to detonate. Waiting to watch the radioactive material infect people far and wide. And clinging to hope that amidst all the destruction, my brother would be safe.

He gave my dog, Chuck, a little pat, and Chuck let out a snore. "Gotta take a break from city life every now and then. And I wanted to make sure you and Mom weren't at each other's throats with this gala next weekend."

I swallowed hard. When I'd returned home from college a month ago, I'd thought the worst thing I'd have to face was my mother's critique of my wardrobe, or her trying to push me on one of her friend's *eligible* sons. I'd had no idea that my entire life would come crumbling down around me. "It's fine."

Preston's gaze narrowed on me, taking in every detail of my face. "No, it's not. You've been crying."

My heart rate picked up its pace, but I urged my expression to remain blank and gestured to the open window. "Allergies."

"Liar." He shook his head but grinned. "You've always been the absolute worst at it."

I'd gotten a hell of a lot better. Something twisted deep inside me. Guilt. So much that I was drowning in it. I wanted to tell him the truth. But it was against the deal I'd signed with the feds. And the truth…it was going to kill Preston. I closed my eyes against the renewed threat of tears.

I loved my brother. He hadn't just been my protector. He'd also been my champion. He distracted Mom when she was being too critical. He helped me escape when the pressure of expectations from both my parents got to be too much. He whispered in my ear that I should follow my dream of opening a ballet studio instead of obeying Dad's wishes to go into accounting or law.

When Preston learned the truth, it would rip his world apart. He'd worked alongside my father for five years, idolized him, did everything he could to follow in Dad's footsteps. And the whole time, he was unknowingly helping to facilitate the robbery.

Preston squeezed my foot. "Tell me what's going on, Twinkle Toes."

My gaze met his, my throat suddenly dry. Screw the feds, he deserved to know. "The FBI came to see me."

"What?" Preston's mouth opened and closed a few times before he continued. "Why? Are you okay?"

The concern in his gaze made choppy waves of guilt churn in my stomach. Guilt that heated with anger swirling beneath it. It all swam together with a healthy dose of fear mixed in. And it was all my father's doing. "Dad's stealing from his clients."

Preston released his hold on my foot. "What are you talking about?"

"They got a tip from some colleagues, returns that didn't add up. They've got a mountain of evidence, Pres." My voice dropped to a hoarse whisper. "He's taken over a billion dollars."

The pile of papers the FBI had set in front of me flashed in my mind. Evidence that had proven that my privileged and pampered life was stolen. Every dance lesson, family trip, and semester of private school. It was never mine. It belonged to the hundreds of people who had entrusted their life savings to my father.

Vomit crawled up the back of my throat. I knew now that it was so much worse than that. Families were going to find out that their entire livelihoods had been wiped out. Even worse, he'd robbed from his poorest clients to convince his richest of his investment prowess.

Preston's jaw ticked. "They made a mistake. It's probably a jealous competitor trying to cut us down at the knees. I work there every day. I'd know if something fishy were going on. And come on, Dad isn't exactly a criminal mastermind."

But that's exactly what our father was. "He stole from people, Pres. People's lives are going to be ruined when they find out. They won't be able to make their house payments or retire when they thought they could."

"Kennedy." Preston's voice cracked like a whip. "You can't say stuff like that." He leaned in closer. "To anyone. Even a whisper of something like this could tank the fund. I know you're not interested in business, but this is my dream. I'm going to take the firm to the next level, and that won't happen if whispers and rumors are flying around."

Preston stood, pulling me up and towards my door. "Come on, let's go talk to Dad. He'll clear this up."

My eyes closed as though if by doing so, I could keep out the pain. The doorbell rang. I heard our housekeeper's quick steps against the marble floor. The sound of the huge oak door opening. "FBI, ma'am, we have a warrant to search the premises."

Preston released his hold on my hand as if he'd been burned, his head whipping from the FBI at the door and back to me again. "What did you do?"

Tears crested over my bottom lids. "The only thing I could live with."

"You didn't even give him a chance to explain?"

My hands fisted in my shirt. "I did. He admitted it, Pres."

The sheer shock and betrayal on my brother's face sliced at my heart. "And what about me? Did I even cross your mind?"

My tears were flowing freely now, streaming down my face. "I did it *for* you." Preston looked as if I'd slapped him. My voice hiccupped. "They-they promised you immunity if I got Dad to confess."

Preston shook his head, his eyes wide. He looked at me as if he didn't know me at all. "This is all a mistake. Dad will clear it up. But it won't matter. It'll all be too late because of what *you* did." His shoulders slumped. "I've only ever been there for you." He opened his mouth as if to say something but stopped, shaking his head again and heading for the stairs instead.

It was as if he had punched through my chest and dug his fingers into my still-beating heart. "Pres, I'm so sorry."

He whirled on me. "You're *sorry*? You just ruined your family's lives. What's wrong with you?"

I raced forward, gripping his sleeve, my movements desperate as I pleaded for him to understand. "I did it to protect you! To protect all the people Dad has hurt, to stop them from losing more. It was the only way." Preston stared at me as if I were a stranger. That fire deep in my belly burned brighter. How could he not see? How could he not care about all the innocent people our father had destroyed in his quest for *more*?

Preston ripped his arm from my grasp. "Next time you think about protecting me, do me a favor and stay the fuck out of my life." Disgust filled his eyes. "I can't even look at you."

Preston stormed down the stairs, and I crumpled to the floor. "It was the right thing. I did the right thing." I whispered the words over and over as I rocked back and forth, tears streaming down my face. I'd done the right thing, the only thing I could live with. But I wasn't sure I could live with the hatred in my brother's eyes either.

My hand shook as I took the paper cup of water Agent Carnes handed me. He was all kindness and concern now. He'd gotten what he wanted, but I think he felt a little guilty for talking me into an action that had blown my family apart.

My phone buzzed in my purse under the chair for what seemed like the millionth time. I couldn't bring myself to pull it out. "I take it the news got out?" My phone had started ringing two hours ago and hadn't stopped since.

Carnes grimaced as he took a seat in the chair opposite me at his desk. "It's not good."

I set the paper cup on the oak surface. "Can you get any of it back? The money he stole?" The hope in my voice felt juvenile, even to my own ears.

"Not enough."

Tears filled my eyes. "How much do people know?"

Carnes looked out of his office window at the sun starting to rise on the horizon. "There's a leak in the department." My heart-beat stuttered. "They know everything."

"Okay." Maybe it was better this way. I knew the whole world would find out eventually. This was just ripping off the Band-Aid. All the pain in one night. I had to face it. I pulled my cell out and looked at the screen. A friend had texted me a news article. *Is it true?* I scanned the article, and my heart stopped, my entire body locked, only my eyes moved to dart to Carnes' face. "Is this real?" I turned the phone around so he could see the article.

Carnes winced, the lines in his face deepening. "Yes. One of your father's clients committed suicide tonight."

A burning sensation started up in my chest. So bright and strong, it stole my breath. I tried to suck in air, but the action didn't seem to work. All it garnered me was a gasping sound, no relief, no oxygen.

Carnes gripped my shoulder. "Breathe, Kennedy, just breathe. Slowly now."

I tried, but it mostly came in short pants. "Is. This. My. Fault?" Sure, my father had built the bomb that had detonated tonight, but wasn't I the one who had launched it?

"No. There's only one person who's at fault."

The man who'd read me *A Little Princess* more times than I could count had made someone want to end their life. And all I could think about was what I could have done differently.

Carnes squeezed my shoulder, bringing my gaze back to him. "Your father was never going to be able to dig himself out of this hole. It was only a matter of time before it all came crumbling down around him."

My body began to shake as the sobs came. Violent and all-encompassing. So many things flashed through my mind. So much privilege. Tuition to one of the most expensive universities, as many ballet lessons as I wanted, my favorite pointe shoes, our trips to Paris, and St. Barts. I'd loved it all. But none of it was worth a human life.

"It's going to be okay." Carnes handed me the cup of water again. "Not right away. But, eventually."

I didn't believe a word he said, but I did my best to get my ragged, hiccupping breath under control, to staunch the tears that seemed to have an endless pool to draw from. "What's next?" My voice shook as I asked, but the sobs stayed quiet.

"You might have to testify, but I honestly doubt it. There's no hiding what he did. Your father kept his company small for a reason. His employees had access to some of the data, but only his second in command had access to all of it. Your brother's in the clear."

My breath came out in one big, trembling whoosh. Preston was safe. He'd forgive me eventually. "Okay."

Carnes rose. "I believe you're free to go."

I pressed my lips together as I stood, my legs just a little bit shaky. A combination of adrenaline and a sleepless night. "Thank you."

Carnes shook his head. "We should be thanking you. Not many people would have done what you did in your place." He paused for a moment, rubbing a hand over his stubbled jaw. "I'm sorry you and your family got caught in the crossfire."

I didn't say a word in reply because what was there to say to that? Agents kept telling me I'd done the right thing, but it didn't change how empty I felt inside.

Carnes opened his office door and led me through a maze of desks towards a small waiting area. My mother rose as she saw us, her face pale, but her hair still in that perfect chignon she wore, not a strand out of place. Her movements were graceful. Like always.

She seemed to glide towards me. Some sort of slow-motion Grace Kelly. Her hand came out of nowhere, and the crack of flesh against flesh echoed in the room. I wasn't sure what had shocked me more, the sound or the stinging burn in my cheek.

Carnes moved quickly then, grabbing my mother by her arm. "Mrs. Barrington, that's enough."

She tore her arm from Carnes' grasp, but her eyes never strayed from mine. "You're a disgrace. You get your things and get out of my house. I don't want to see your face again." Her jerky movements had a single lock of hair falling free of her perfect updo.

I swallowed hard, not giving in to the urge to rub at my

cheek. I'd expected hatred from her. What killed me was Preston merely looking on, hurt filling his features. The one person I could always count on in this life was no longer my ally. Tears pricked at the backs of my eyes, but I forced them down.

I kept my head level, not allowing it to dip in shame the way I wanted, but not meeting the stunned gazes of everyone looking on either. I pulled the door open and stepped into the hall. I found a quiet corner and let my head fall against the wall. I tilted my face so my still-stinging cheek rested against the cool plaster.

I would get through this. I had to. I pushed up, twisted so my back rested against the wall, and dug in my purse for my phone. Dozens of missed calls and texts. But they'd all stopped about thirty minutes ago. Right around the time news of the suicide had hit.

I swallowed hard. My thumb hovered over my best friend Heather's number. I tapped it. The phone rang and rang until her voicemail picked up. I hung up and tried again. No answer. I repeated the actions with two other friends with the same result. My phone dinged with a text.

Heather: *I can't talk, my parents said it's not a good idea. Hope you're okay.*

A startled laugh escaped me, one that turned into a strangled sob. No one was going to stand by me in this. No one in my world would even give me a chance to share my side of the story. I was totally and completely alone.

A voice cleared behind me, and I turned to see Agent Carnes. "Why don't I give you a lift home? Do you have somewhere you can stay for a while?"

I looked down at my phone and then back at him. "I'm thinking a hotel in another town might be the best bet for now." I had a bit of cash in my own personal checking account. The small salary I'd been paid this summer for my internship. Birthday and

Christmas money my grandmother gave me each year. I'd started the account when I was sixteen. A little something that was just mine. It would cover me for a while.

Carnes and I were silent as we rode the elevator down to the ground floor. As we stepped out, I could see a throng of reporters out front. My chest seized.

Carnes guided me in the opposite direction. "My SUV's out back." The tension in my torso released just a bit, and I nodded. "You might want to go farther than just one town over." My phone buzzed in my hand. "Maybe change your phone number. Just make sure I have the new one."

I nodded again. I felt like one of those bobblehead dolls, my head seeming to move of its own accord, unable to stop. Carnes pushed open a back door. I was assaulted by jeers and camera flashes. "Shit. I might need backup."

The thought of waiting longer, with more time to think about what faced me, had my stomach roiling. There was no way to avoid it. I wanted out of here, and the quickest way out was through. "No. It's fine."

"All right." Carnes did his best to push people aside. "Make a path, or I'll have agents down here arresting you." That helped a bit, but not much.

I ducked my head and waded through the bodies. People yelling, screaming horrible things that I would never forget. I felt something warm and liquid hit the side of my face. Spit. I wiped it off and kept moving, holding on to the back of Carnes' sports jacket as he cut through the sea of people.

"*You.*" The voice was softer than the rest, full of pain.

I took in the woman just ahead of me, her face ravaged with grief and rage.

"Murderer." With the single word, she lunged.

I thought she was going to strike me. Twice in one night. But this time, I yearned for it. The bloom of a blow across my other cheek. I wondered if the physical pain would distract from the emotional. Instead, a thick liquid hit me.

The crowd leapt back. All but the woman and me. I wiped at my eyes, my hand coming away red. Corn syrup and food coloring. I recognized the combination from my days in high school theatre.

"Now, the whole world can see the blood on your hands." The woman hissed the words before disappearing into the crowd.

I flinched as a camera flash went off, the crowd quiet enough that I could hear the click of one shutter, then another, and another.

"Fuck! Come on. Let's go." Carnes ushered me towards an SUV, pulling out a blanket and placing it on the seat before I slid inside.

Tears streaked down my face, but I couldn't even wipe them away, my hands were covered in the sticky red substance. The burning sensation between my breasts was back. It didn't matter that it was my father who had acted, I was still guilty. And I didn't blame them for thinking it.

I had to get away. Far, far away. But a little voice inside me told me that I'd never escape the guilt.

CHAPTER
One

TWO YEARS LATER

THE FEEL OF THE SUN ON MY FACE, PUPPY SNORES, AND *Easy Mac*. I scrawled the words on a tiny scrap of paper. My formal script had eased a bit. The stiff, tight lines easing into a loopy, irregular pattern. I folded the paper in half and placed it in the jar. Tightening the lid, I rose and put the container back on the bookshelf.

Soon, I'd need a new jar. My eyes scanned the seven others on the shelf, each one with the word *gratitude* painted on the front. It was a practice I'd taken up during my darkest days. Those when I felt like there was not even a glimmer of hope to be had.

I'd blown through most of my reserves to make my way west. I'd landed in Portland, but it had taken me less than a year to realize that I'd never make it in a big city. With the prices on apartments, food, everyday living expenses, I'd known I needed to find a smaller town.

But I'd waited too long. My checking account down to the piddliest amount, I'd done what any person at their wits' end would do: I left it up to chance. I pulled up a bus schedule at the library and studied how far one hundred dollars would get me.

I had three options. I played eeny, meeny, miny, moe. And when I landed on Sutter Lake, I'd herded my dog back into his carrier and prayed that no one on the bus would notice him.

Looking back on it now, I realized that it was insane. I could've ended up in a town with only a mini-mart and a gas station. Instead, I'd ended up in a place that was just what I needed. The peacefulness of the lake. The vastness of the forest surrounding the town. The quaint shops dotting the streets.

Chuck and I had made it. And I was grateful every day that fate had landed me in Sutter Lake. I had a job and a place to stay. I was safe, warm, and mostly happy.

Chuck let out an especially loud snore from the couch, and I laughed. I bent down and ruffled his floppy, brown ears. He opened one eye. "You gonna be okay while I'm gone?"

He let out another snore, even though he was technically awake, a little bit of drool slipping from his mouth.

I grinned. "I'm taking that as a yes."

I straightened from my crouch. Crossing to the bathroom, I paused for a moment in front of the mirror. My auburn hair was swept up in a loose bun atop my head today, and my green eyes seemed to stand out in stark contrast to my pale skin, the freckles scattered across my nose no longer hidden under perfectly applied foundation.

I smoothed out invisible wrinkles in my shirt. The material was wearing a bit at one of the seams, but I could still get at least another month out of it. Thankfully, there was a wonderful Goodwill store down the street that had all sorts of hidden gems.

I turned away from the mirror. I still wasn't quite used to my new appearance. So long, pearls and designer blouses. Hello, t-shirts, jeans, and sneakers. But there was still a small part of me looking over my shoulder, waiting to hear my mother's disdainful tone whip out about what I was wearing or my lack of makeup. It never came.

I slipped my phone into the back pocket of my jeans and headed for the door of my studio. "Don't get into trouble while I'm gone."

Chuck just kept snoring away. I hadn't figured out if he truly was going deaf or if he just had selective hearing.

I locked the door and jogged down the stairs just as the back door of the building opened, and a dark head appeared. "Morning, J."

The olive-skinned beauty smiled up at me. "Morning, Kenz."

I loved seeing that bright smile on her face. She'd been through so much, but things had turned around for her. And that gave me hope for my own future. "How are Noah and Tuck?"

She chuckled as she headed into the kitchen and hung her bag on a hook. "I left them practicing a fight sequence from *The Karate Kid*, so I'd say they're doing fine."

I let out a laugh. "I'm sure Noah's putting Tuck through his paces."

Jensen went to the sink and began washing her hands. "I swear that man is a ten-year-old at heart."

I smiled as I stuck my hands under the warm water after her. "So, what's on the list this morning?"

"It's going to be a doozy today. We've got a couple of special orders on top of the regular fare."

I nodded, drying my hands on a towel and reaching for my apron. You'd think a job in a tea shop would be a pretty easy gig, but I worked myself to the bone most days. I was sure it didn't help that I still hadn't quite gotten used to the baking aspect of the job. "What do you need first?"

Jensen wrapped the strings of her apron around her waist. "Why don't you grab all the ingredients for scones."

"Got it." I moved quickly through the now-familiar space,

pulling things from the pantry and fridge, lining them up on one of the counters. I could prep the ingredients no problem, but something happened when I tried to put them all together. My forays into baking always ended in disaster.

Jensen kept me on anyway, that was just the kind of woman she was. Always reaching out a hand to those in need. Doing whatever she could to help. Like giving me a place to live, pretty much for free, above the Tea Kettle. So, I'd do whatever I could to be the best employee possible, even if I lacked the necessary baking skills.

We worked mostly in silence for the first hour, moving in the coordinated pattern we'd perfected over the past few months. Then Jensen eased on the music—low at first, then louder. By the time customers arrived, we'd be energized and ready to go.

A timer dinged, and J moved to one of the ovens, removing perfectly golden-brown scones. She glanced over her shoulder at me. "Want one?"

I grinned. "Like you even have to ask." The perks of working at a tea shop with a bakery meant my choice of treats whenever I wanted.

J quickly but methodically moved the scones to a cooling rack. "Give them a minute or two to cool."

I measured out flour for our next batch. "You know that's torture. I've been smelling them for half an hour."

Jensen laughed. "You're going to burn your tongue again."

I grimaced. Patience had never been my virtue. And I *had* burned myself on more than one baked good in this kitchen. "Fine."

There was a knock on the glass of the front door. Both Jensen and I peeked our heads out of the kitchen. The smile that overtook Jensen's face was sheer joy. She crossed to the front, unlocking the door and pulling it open. "What are you guys doing here?"

Noah bounded into the shop. "Hi, Mom!" Then he ran for the kitchen. He grinned at me and then eyed the scones. "They ready to eat yet?"

"Hey, bud." I gave his hair a ruffle. "Give them just another minute or two."

Tuck pulled Jensen into his arms. "We wanted to see if you would feed us before we headed off for our days." He gave her a wicked grin. "We're growing boys, you know." Jensen let out a soft laugh. "And I needed a little more of this." His mouth took hers in a slow kiss that should've scorched the paint off the walls.

I averted my eyes. I loved that my friend had this, that she'd built a family after enduring so much. Noah had a father figure now, and Jensen had someone who would do anything to make sure the life she lived was the most beautiful one she could imagine.

A flutter of jealousy flitted through my chest, lighting a faint burn along my sternum. I rubbed at the spot. Maybe, one day. One day, I could find that, too. Build my own family.

Since the one I'd been born into would rather I hadn't been born at all.

CHAPTER
Two

Cain

M Y GAZE WENT UNFOCUSED AS THE COFFIN LOWERED into the ground. I thought that the finality of the moment might stir something within me. Sympathy. Sadness. Anything that wasn't a distant numbness. If I searched hard enough, I knew I'd find the rage. It had turned to a low, simmering fury over the years, but it would never be gone entirely.

"I'm sorry her life was such a hard one."

I blinked rapidly, the priest coming into focus in front of me, the only person present other than the men lowering the woman who had given birth to me into the ground. My jaw tightened, making a faint clicking sound in my ear. "The harshness was of her own making."

The priest gave me a sad smile, one that had me resisting the urge to clench my fists. He'd been prying since the moment I'd called to arrange a burial. Wanting to know details of my mother's life, tidbits he could share at the service. He'd been in for a shock. I was the only one in attendance, and there were no sweet stories to share. The woman had drunk and drugged herself into an early grave, only after she'd ruined the lives of those who wanted nothing more than her love.

I extended a hand. "Thank you for performing the service."

The priest's grip, like the rest of his demeanor, was full of sympathy. "If you need to talk, my son, you know where I'll be. My door is always open."

"I'm not your *son*." I ripped my hand from his grasp and had a sudden urge to deck the old man. God, I needed to get a grip. The memories were battering at the door to my brain, and I wasn't sure how long I could hold them off. I gave my head a little shake. "I'm sorry, Father."

I didn't wait for an answer, simply turned on my heel and strode towards my car. The skies gave an ominous rumble that was so very fitting. The city spread out before me as I crossed the hillside graveyard. I hadn't even known she was in Portland. The social worker from the hospital had informed me that she'd been here for years before being admitted months ago for liver failure. She wasn't a candidate for a transplant.

She'd known she was dying and hadn't called. I guessed I could be grateful for that small mercy. She didn't force me to refuse to see a dying woman. Because that's precisely what I would've done.

And while I hadn't seen her once in this city that I'd claimed as my own, I now saw her everywhere. At the café where I picked up my coffee each morning. On the treadmill down the row from me at the gym. Hell, I'd sworn I saw her walking into a conference room at my office the other day.

I beeped the locks to my Aston Martin and pulled open the door. I slid inside just as the first few drops of rain began to fall. I let my head slump against the headrest, my fingers squeezing the bridge of my nose where I could feel pressure building.

Images flashed in my mind. Dark brown hair gleaming in the sunlight. A laugh carried across the breeze. *Cain, come on!*

Hurry! Kiara let out another giggle. *I want to go swimming before it gets dark.* I shook my head, trying to clear the image, but it was too late. My chest tightened as my fingers started to go numb. *No.* I refused to go back there.

My phone buzzed in my suit pocket. The pressure in my chest crept higher but lessened a fraction as I saw the screen. I hit the button to accept. "Walker." My voice sounded hoarse even to my own ears, and I cleared my throat.

"Hey, Cain. How the hell are you?"

The sound of a friend's voice, one who was more like a brother, eased something in me just a bit. I stared out at the headstones gone blurry with rain, unsure what the hell to say. I cleared my throat again. "I'm fine." I flexed and clenched my hands, trying to get some feeling back in my fingers.

"Cain—"

Walker could hear something in my tone, knew that my answer was total bullshit. I hurried on. "How are you? Taylor?"

He paused for just a moment before speaking. "We're good." I could hear the smile in Walker's voice, as though it were utterly impossible for him not to have a cheesy grin plastered on his face when he spoke of his fiancée. "I'm actually calling to see if you can make it to our engagement party."

"At the ranch?"

"Yup. Taylor wants something simple and outdoors."

He'd know I was a wreck the second he saw me. So would Tuck. That's what happened when your friends knew your darkest demons. But maybe that wasn't a bad thing. They'd helped me fight off the darkness before. And it wasn't nearly as bad this time, but I couldn't allow it to get its hooks in. Gears turned in my brain, an idea that was only slightly insane coming to light. "I can make that happen."

Walker chuckled. "I haven't even told you when it is. Hell, we haven't even set an exact date yet. That's why I'm calling, we want to make sure the most important people in our lives can be there."

My chest tightened at his words. I picked up a coin from the cupholder, flipping it over and over in my fingers, relishing the feeling that had finally returned to them. "What would you think about me buying a place in Sutter Lake? Someplace I could use as a vacation home. Somewhere to get away."

There was silence on Walker's end of the line for a few seconds. "I'd be thrilled, but you've always sworn that the city was the only place you'd ever call home."

It was true. After the childhood I'd spent in rural Oregon, I'd wanted to build a life that was the polar opposite. That meant cities and high-rises, not small towns and wide-open spaces. But now, I was desperate. I needed an escape. A place where I could be around people I trusted, who knew my demons. And that list was short. So short, it only included two names: Walker Cole and Tucker Harris. They'd been with me through my darkest days, and I trusted them both with my life.

"I need a getaway. Some distance from Portland." My city was tainted now. My mother had infected it like everything else. I cleared my throat, trying to keep my tone light. "Why not Sutter Lake?"

Walker's voice grew serious. "What's going on?"

Of course, Walker saw through it all. I watched the rain track in rivulets down my windshield. "I just buried Karen."

"Where are you? I'll grab Tuck, and we'll start driving. Be to you as soon as we can."

Walk knew better than anyone all the toxic crap this event was bound to bring up. "That's not necessary." There was silence on the other end of the line again. "You've got my word. I'm fine. Just let me wrap things up here, and then I'll head to Sutter Lake."

"When are you coming?"

I thought through everything I needed to do before I could leave. "Tomorrow."

Walker let out a chuckle, but it sounded forced. "I should've known you wouldn't mess around. What can I do to help?"

"I'll need a realtor, someone who can handle a higher-end sale."

The sound of Walker tapping on his keyboard came across the line. "There's only one company in town that handles that kind of business. I'm emailing you their info now."

I put him on speaker and pulled up my inbox. "Got it."

"You know my mom is going to want you at dinner as soon as you arrive."

The corners of my mouth turned up for the first time since I'd gotten the call from the hospital a week ago. The Cole family was everything I *didn't* have growing up. Warm, welcoming, full of life, and willing to include anyone in their mishmash brood. "How about the day after tomorrow?"

"I can probably hold her off till then."

I chuckled. "Looking forward to it."

"Me, too. It's been too long, Cain."

It had been. I'd let far too many months go by without seeing my brothers. "It has. But now I'll be around so much, you'll get sick of me."

Walker's tone remained serious. "Travel safe."

"Will do." I checked my watch. "I've got to run, Walk. I'll see you soon."

"Soon, brother."

The elevator doors opened, and my mask slid into place. I strode in the direction of my office, giving simple nods of acknowledgment to any employees who greeted me. I had even less time for niceties than normal.

My assistant rose as I approached our wing, a smile on her face. "Welcome back. I sent your messages to your device, ranked in order of importance."

"Thank you, Rachel. Will you grab Jake and meet me in my office?"

She gave a quick nod. "Of course." Concern flitted across Rachel's features, but she said nothing more, simply turned in the direction of Jake's office.

I pushed open the double doors to my suite and headed for my safe, holding my forefinger to a fingerprint reader and then punching in an eight-digit code. I removed my personal laptop and the handful of files that rested there.

My gaze caught on a photo, worn with age. She'd been young, but so vibrant, beautiful, full of promise until all of the possibilities that lay in front of her were cut down. I shook my head as though the action could clear away the memories. The pain. But nothing ever would.

I crossed back to my desk, placing all the items in my bag, careful to slip the photo between two other files. Protected. Even though I hadn't been able to do that in life. A knock sounded. "Come in." I eased into my desk chair.

My second in command strode through the doors, followed closely by Rachel. Jake lowered himself into one of the chairs opposite me while Rachel remained standing. "So, what's up? You finally going to tell us why you've been such a moody bastard for the past week?" Jake asked as he rolled up one of the cuffs of his shirt.

I swallowed back the urge to put Jake in his place. Sometimes, he forgot that this was my company, and he worked for *me*. I understood why. Jake and Rachel had been with me since the days the company only had five employees, and we were renting space in a warehouse. But, sometimes, it pissed me the hell off. "I'm going to be working remotely for a while."

Jake's movements stilled. "Why? We've got at least five projects that are in critical phases right now. Not to mention prospective client meetings. And what about the program prototype? Aren't you supposed to be close to finishing?"

"There's nothing on those projects that I can't do from another location, and you're the schmoozer, not me. Those prospective client meetings will probably go a lot smoother without me in attendance." It was true. Jake had always handled the interpersonal part of the business, the small talk. I'd taken care of the tech, the strategy. It worked well that way.

Rachel cleared her throat. "Would you like me to come with you? So you have someone to manage wherever you set up your mobile office."

The thought of Rachel hovering had my jaw clenching, but I forced a smile. "The last thing you want is to hang out with a moody bugger like me." She opened her mouth to argue, and I hurried on. "Plus, I need you to be my point person here."

Rachel nodded slowly. "Okay, but let me know if you change your mind."

"I will."

Jake studied me. "Where are you going?"

I flipped the coin over and over in my pocket. I had no excuse for not telling them. "Sutter Lake."

Jake blinked. "That tiny town in the middle of nowhere?"

"That's the one."

Jake's eyes narrowed. "Why?"

I leaned forward, just a bit. I owed him no explanations. He might've been with me from the beginning, but this was my company. My life. But I'd called on him to cover more than a couple of meetings this week, and he didn't deserve to have his head bitten off on top of the extra work I'd dumped on his plate. "I'm ready for a change of scenery. And I think it's time for a little vacation."

Jake ran a hand through his hair. "What's really going on, Cain? I can let you off the hook for the client meetings and project management, but the prototype? That's the future of our company."

A muscle in my cheek ticked. "This is my company, Jake. I know how important the prototype is, but I think you're forgetting who's steering this ship." The program was one that would cement our company as the leader in security systems for the next decade. I had a firm hold on the concept, but the execution had been evading me. The last thing I needed was Jake bearing down on me, adding to the weight already crushing my shoulders. Just another reason to get the hell out of Portland for a while.

A muscle in Jake's cheek ticked. "Am I your VP, or not?" I didn't respond, and he pushed on. "It's my job to make sure we bring your vision to fruition, but I can't do that without your help."

I let out a long breath. He had a point. "I'll make sure you have what you need for the program by the end of the summer." The set of Jake's shoulders eased just a bit. "But I need this break."

Jake jerked his chin. "Thank you." He grinned. "Now, do you really need to go to bumfuck nowhere to do whatever it is that you're planning on doing? Soul-searching or some shit?"

I chuckled, the tension between my shoulder blades easing a bit. "I'm leaving tomorrow."

Rachel stepped forward. "Do you need me to prepare anything for you, Cain?"

Jake rolled his eyes. "Stop kissing his ass, Rachel. You're already the highest-paid assistant known to man."

Rachel scowled at him and opened her mouth for what I was sure would be a verbal smackdown. I held up a hand. "Now, children."

They both scowled at me. I laughed. I'd missed this. The back and forth that we so often had when the company was just getting started. The camaraderie. Somewhere along the way, as the company grew, we'd lost some of that. Once I got my shit together, I'd figure out how to get us back there.

I placed my hands on my desk as I rose. "I'm trusting you to hold down the fort while I'm gone."

Jake headed for the door, holding up a hand in a backwards wave. "Strippers and booze on Fridays."

Rachel let out a huff. "You're really going to leave me with him?"

I grinned. "If it gets too bad, let me know, and I'll have a talk with him."

Rachel nodded, her gaze zeroing in on my face. "Is everything okay, Cain?"

I swallowed, fighting the mounting dryness in my throat. I thought about the nightmares that had awoken me in a cold sweat every night since I'd gotten the call about Karen. Her ghost haunting every corner of my city. The flashbacks. The fear that I was going to lose my hold on the control I'd gained. "Everything's fine. I just need a vacation."

What I needed was to feel like I could breathe.

CHAPTER
Three

Kennedy

MY PHONE BUZZED IN MY POCKET AS I WIPED THE last of the fingerprints from the glass bakery case. I tossed the rag on the counter and pulled out my cell. An alert danced across the screen. *Davis Barrington granted early parole hearing.*

My heart thudded so hard, my ribs seemed to rattle. I slid my thumb across the screen, and the news article popped up. I had told myself time and again that I should simply turn off the alerts, that reading updates on my father and all the people he'd hurt would only cause me more pain. But it felt like something that I needed to face. To bear.

My eyes skimmed the text. My father had, in fact, been granted a hearing for parole less than two years into his sentence. Apparently, he had enough money left to grease palms somewhere. My gaze caught on a photo, a woman who couldn't be much older than I was. A woman whose face would be forever ingrained in my mind, the twisted pain of her features right before she doused me in fake blood. *"My father wasn't one of Mr. Barrington's wealthy clients. We were a working-class family, but*

Barrington promised he would invest my dad's savings and get him early retirement. Instead, he stole it all, and my father hanged himself the day the truth came out."

Acidic tears stung my eyes, but I forced myself to further commit the woman's features to memory. The pain in that ravaged face. No amount of prison time or payment of restitution would ever be enough. There were now four people who were dead because of my father. Four human beings who had taken their lives out of desperation.

The bell over the door rang, and I hurriedly wiped under my eyes. "Hey, Walker," I greeted, forcing as much cheer into my voice as possible.

"Hey, Kennedy. My sister around?"

Jensen poked her head out of the kitchen. "I'm here. We're just getting ready to close up for the day."

Walker rounded the counter and wrapped his sister in a hug, ruffling her hair. Jensen struggled out of his hold. "What's got you in such a good mood?"

Walker grinned. "Cain's coming to town."

Jensen smiled. "That's great. We haven't seen him in forever. How long's he staying?"

"He's buying a place here, so for the foreseeable future."

Jensen's mouth fell open just a bit. "He's moving here?"

"Well, he's buying a vacation home. Not sure how much time he'll actually spend in it."

Jensen laughed. "Ah, to have money to burn."

Her words had that spot between my shoulder blades tightening. I forced myself to return my focus to the bakery case. I ran the rag across each shelf, searching for every tiny speck of food I could find.

Walker chuckled. "Mom's going to put on a big spread Wednesday night to welcome him to town."

Jensen hit a few buttons on the register, pulling out the cash drawer and a deposit envelope. "Of course, she is. I don't think Tuck and I have any plans, so we're there."

"Good." Walker rubbed his hands together like a little kid. "Gang's back together."

Jensen let out a snort of laughter. "Just as long as you three aren't calling me at three a.m. to bail you out of jail."

A small smile curved my mouth as I moved to the back counter. I wondered what it would be like to have friends like that. Those who knew your whole history and always gave you the warmest welcome home. I'd never known that kind of relationship. Instead, I'd known so-called friends who dropped me like a contagious disease the moment things got hard. I longed for the kind of bond Walker clearly had with Tuck and this Cain, but that sort of friendship required total honesty, and I simply wasn't brave enough for that. I'd been hurt too many times before.

One of the first things I'd done when I got to Portland was to start the process of changing my last name. The whole ordeal had wiped out what little remained of my savings, but it was necessary. I didn't want anyone from my past to find me, and I didn't want to see the looks of disgust from the people in my present if they found out the truth. That meant hiring a lawyer to plead my case in the courts for my name change to remain sealed. Thankfully, they had agreed.

I fiercely protected the freedom my new name had afforded me. I had a driver's license, but that was it. No credit cards. No bank account. Even my cell phone was one of those pay-as-you-go deals. I would do everything I could to prevent the ghosts of my past from resurfacing.

"Kenz."

Jensen's voice shook me from my thoughts. "Sorry, what?"

A little furrow appeared between her brows. "I asked if you could come to dinner on Wednesday."

I searched for an excuse, but I wasn't quick enough.

Jensen's lips tipped up. "You can."

I twisted the rag in my fingers. "I don't know, J. It sounds like a family thing."

She wrapped an arm around me. "You're family."

My cheeks heated. I wasn't. I was the hanger-on. The awkward addition that people felt bad for. "It's really fine. I've been working a ton, and it'll be nice to just have a night off to relax."

J gave my shoulder a squeeze. "Nope. No arguments. I'll pick you up at five." She paused. "Plus, Cain's hot. Maybe you two will hit it off."

My body stiffened.

"Jensen," Walker warned.

J released her hold on me and shrugged. "What? I'm stupidly happy and in love. Is it so wrong I want everyone else to be, too?"

My face got hotter. "That's not really something I'm looking for right now, J." Lie. Total and complete lie. I wanted a partner, a family, somewhere to belong. I longed for it more than my next breath.

Walker cleared his throat. "It's not a good idea."

J studied her brother. "He's had girlfriends. I've seen him with them in the papers when he goes to all those fancy shindigs."

Walker shook his head. "Yeah, but have you seen those women more than once or twice?"

Jensen began putting the cash from the register into a zippered pouch. "He just needs to meet the right woman. One who's not after his money."

Well, I certainly wouldn't be after that. I knew the one thing money did above all others. It corrupted.

"Little J, you need to let that alone." Walker pinned Jensen with a hard stare. "You know why."

Jensen's shoulders slumped. "Oh, fine. I won't meddle."

"Thank you." He brushed a kiss to the top of his sister's head. "I gotta head back to the station, but I'll see you ladies Wednesday night."

I lifted a hand in a wave. It would be fine. It was just one dinner.

"See you next week, Annabeth." I waved to the golden-haired girl as her mother helped her into their minivan. I double-checked the door on the small ballet studio and headed for my bike. Dance had been one of the few things my mother and I had agreed on when I was growing up. And I was especially grateful for all the lessons now because it gave me an extra bit of employment.

I slid my bag off my shoulder and placed it in my bike basket, careful not to squish the baked goods we had left over from the Kettle that day. I strapped down my bag, my fingers dusting against the satin of my pointe shoes. I winced at the new tear that had appeared in the middle of today's advanced class. I'd need to stitch that up before my session tomorrow.

I swung onto the bike and headed out of the parking lot. Late spring meant the smell of pine trees and no need for a jacket. I let my eyes close just for a moment as my bike coasted down the street, the sky still bright with early evening sun. I was so lucky to have landed in this place.

My eyes opened as the road dipped, and I headed downhill. The warm breeze felt heavenly now, but the trek back up would be killer. It was every night I rode this route.

I tapped on my brakes, slowing to make the turn into the Sutter Lake community center. The center held my destination for the evening: Hope House. Volunteering was something I'd done most of my life, but typically because it was a requirement of whatever private school I attended. It wasn't that I didn't enjoy offering my time, or wasn't impacted by those I served, I just didn't think much about how they had gotten to a place in their lives where they needed help.

I cringed. I'd been so naïve. It wasn't until I saw up close and personal the true devastation that my father's greed wrought that I realized the *why* behind so much of it. The reason we needed homeless shelters and so many other programs was often because some people took way more than their share. Now, I was doing all I could to help balance those scales.

But in that act, I'd fallen in love with the process. Helping others find what they needed to get back on their feet lit a fire inside me that I'd never felt before. A sense of purpose and something else I couldn't quite name. I looked up at the center as I slowed. It was a bit run-down and could be so much more if we had the staff and funds to make it shine. Maybe one day.

I slid off my bike, taking a minute to lock it to the rack in front of the shelter's double doors before slinging my bag over my shoulder and grabbing the baked goods from my basket. Heading inside, I felt a small twinge in my back. I'd been pushing it pretty hard lately, but every commitment I had was too important to let slide.

"Hey, Kennedy!" Doug's bright voice greeted from the space that served as both rec room and cafeteria.

I headed in the direction of the program director's voice. "Hey, Doug. How are you?"

"Doing great." He reached out for my bag of goodies from the Kettle. "Here, let me take those."

"Thank you." I released my hold on the bag and started towards the kitchen.

Doug followed. "How was ballet today?"

I smiled at the memory of my last class. The eight-year-olds I taught on Mondays always reminded me why I'd fallen in love with dance in the first place. They would come in wearing leotards and tutus, and when they spun in front of the mirror, they could be anyone their imagination dreamed up. "It was great."

He set the bag down on one of the counters. "You know, the Portland Ballet is putting on *Swan Lake* next month. Maybe we could go?"

I swallowed, my throat suddenly dry. Doug was a great guy, I valued his friendship and all he did for the shelter, but I felt no spark there. "I don't know. I'm pretty busy these days."

Doug reached out a hand and squeezed my shoulder. "You work too hard. Everyone deserves a break now and then."

A throat cleared, and Doug dropped his hand. I breathed a sigh of relief at the sight of Anna. "You ready to get started?" she asked, her eyes flicking back and forth between Doug and me.

I bent to put my bag in one of the cubbies. "Yup. Just let me wash my hands."

Doug shuffled his feet. "I've got some paperwork to finish up but give me a holler when you guys are ready to serve the meal, I'll come out and help."

Anna gave Doug a mock salute. "Will do, boss man."

Doug chuckled, shaking his head and moving towards his office.

"Girl, at some point, you're going to have to just come out and tell him you're not interested."

My stomach twisted. "He's only being friendly."

Anna shook her head and began chopping vegetables. "Friendly is, 'here, let me carry that bag.' Not, 'let me take you to Portland to go to some fancy-schmancy ballet,' something that will probably cost him hundreds of dollars." She raised her brows at me to punctuate her point.

I turned on the faucet and dunked my hands beneath the spray. "He's a friend, a good one. I think he'll eventually get the message I'm not interested in more." I truly believed he would.

It wasn't like he was creepy about his advances; he just had a schoolboy crush. He'd get over it.

Anna grunted and continued her chopping. "Whatever you say."

I reached for a towel to dry my hands. "So, how were things around here today?"

"Oh, the usual. Folks bickering over what chores they were assigned. Cal trying to steal food between mealtimes. Lizzie spilled paint all over one of the rec tables." Anna dumped the carrot she'd been chopping into a large pot on the stove.

I raised my brows at her. "Thank goodness they've got you to keep this place running."

Anna pointed her knife at me, and her face broke out into a grin. "And don't you forget it."

Anna was a shelter hybrid. She'd moved in as a guest, and like all those who stayed here, she had been required to work to help keep the place running. But, unlike the others who typically used the shelter as a brief stop on their way to something more permanent, Anna had stayed. Now, she pretty much ran the show. Doug might have the director plaque on his door, but everyone knew it was Anna who really called the shots.

We worked together in a mostly silent rhythm, broken only by Anna assigning me tasks, ones she knew were within my skill set where I wouldn't accidentally set the kitchen on fire. This was my favorite part of the day. The one time the guilt released its hold, just a bit. The one time I didn't feel like a drain on the world around me, but instead like I gave something back. The one time a feeling of worth truly seeped into my bones and settled there.

I just wished it would stay a little bit longer.

CHAPTER
Four

Cain

THERE WAS A POP AS THE DOOR TO MY JET OPENED, A release of pressure mirrored in my chest. Relief at getting some distance from Portland, having some privacy to deal with every demon this past week had raised, and simply having a moment to breathe.

I rose from my seat, grabbing my briefcase. The flight attendant stepped into the aisle, looking up at me through fluttering lashes. "Is there anything else I can do for you, Mr. Hale? Anything at all?"

I fought the sneer that wanted to surface. Her movements felt desperate and grasping and seemed to grate against my skin. "No, thank you. I'll just be on my way."

A flicker of annoyance passed over the woman's face. "Of course, sir." She stepped out of my path.

I headed down the aisle, careful to keep my distance as I passed the woman. I ducked through the door and stepped out into the sunshine, inhaling deeply. The runway was surrounded by forest. The fresh pine scent filling my lungs had my muscles easing. This was precisely what I needed, some distance from the ghosts haunting me in Portland, and some good old-fashioned peace and quiet.

"Mr. Hale, sir."

I blinked against the sun to see a man wearing slacks and a button-down, standing near an SUV. "Mr. Fields?"

The man strode towards me, extending his hand. "I have your vehicle all ready for you." He inclined his head to the Range Rover behind him. "All the requirements are to your specifications. And if you have any issues, please contact me directly."

I nodded, shaking the man's hand. "Thank you. I appreciate you bringing it to the airstrip."

Fields grinned. "Happy to do so."

Of course, he was happy. I'd taken a top-of-the-line Range Rover off his hands and paid cash for it. "Keys?"

Fields handed them over. "Will you be needing anything else?"

"That's all." I beeped the locks so the porter could stow my bags in the back.

Fields gave a nod. "It was wonderful doing business with you." He turned and walked to a waiting vehicle. I instantly liked him. No polite chit-chat. No wasting of my time. Simply gave me what I asked for and left. I'd use him again if I decided I needed another toy out here, something that went fast.

"All of your bags are stowed, Mr. Hale. Can I do anything else for you?" The porter barely made eye contact with me when he asked.

"That'll be all. Thank you." I reached out, handing him a bill.

His eyes bulged as he took in the president on the paper. "Thank you, sir."

I climbed into the Rover and pressed the button to start the engine, glancing at the clock. I had fifteen minutes before I needed to meet the realtor at the first property. I plugged the address into the navigation system and headed out.

The tiny Sutter Lake airport, more designed for hobby pilots and skydiving, sat on the edge of town. As I made the turn onto Main Street, I grinned. I hadn't been here in a year or two, but nothing had changed. The streets were immaculately kept with baskets of bright flowers hanging from antique lamp posts. The storefronts all looked as though they belonged on the set of an old western film. And people milled about with smiles on their faces.

It was the perfect, picturesque small town. But I knew better than most that small, idyllic places sometimes held the darkest secrets. Sutter Lake was no different. They'd had their share of heartache lately, and my friends had not come out unscathed. But they had come out alive, and so had the women they loved. And that's what was important.

I made it through downtown in approximately ninety seconds. I grimaced, thinking of all the things from the city I wouldn't have access to. It would be worth it for a little peace.

Soon, the paved roads turned to gravel, and I wound around until my GPS told me to turn onto a private drive. The gate was wide open, and I didn't see any security system in place. That would be the first thing that would have to change if I bought the home.

My vehicle climbed the gravel drive, and as I crested a hill, the full picture of the property came into view. The house was large, a well-designed mix of wood and stone. This could work. What wouldn't, was the vast array of outbuildings. Barns and what I assumed were storage sheds for machinery.

My jaw made a clicking noise as it clenched, the sound that always belied my frustration. I didn't want to run a farm or a ranch or anything of the sort. I wanted privacy. I'd made that clear when I spoke with the realtor. Privacy meant no staff. No one nosing around to deal with land or animal maintenance.

I shut off the Rover and climbed out. A woman stood on the

front steps of the house. Her blonde hair was perfectly curled, her makeup expertly done. She wore a figure-hugging dress paired with cowboy boots and a cat-that-got-the-canary smile. "Mr. Hale, I'm Kelly. So lovely to meet you in person. What do you think? It's perfect, right?"

I scowled. "No."

Her smile faltered. "No?"

I strode towards her. "No. Privacy."

A look of bafflement overtook her face. "This ranch is ten thousand acres. You can't get much more *private* than that."

I shook my head. She didn't get it. "I need a property that doesn't require a massive staff for maintenance." I gestured around us. "Fields that need tending, animals. No."

The realtor blinked up at me for a moment, then straightened her shoulders. "All right, then." She pulled a tablet from the purse on her shoulder and began tapping on the screen. "Let me just adjust our plan for the afternoon."

I waited in silence as she scrolled. I wondered if I'd be able to find a place here. I hadn't really thought through everything that went into these country homes. Was there even anything here that wasn't full of crops and livestock?

Kelly's head snapped up, her smile from earlier back in place. "I've got the perfect place. I just sent the address to your phone. It's currently vacant, so we can view it now."

I tilted my head to show my assent but said nothing, simply headed back to my SUV. My GPS led me back towards town, but instead of heading through it, the navigation system sent me skirting around and towards the body of water Sutter Lake had been named for. My jaw tightened again. This woman had better not be showing me a house on a lake that would be full of people during the summer.

Instead of leading me towards Sutter Lake, my GPS sent me skirting around again. I paused as I got to a large, well-designed gate, the sign overhead reading: *Termonn*. There was a code box to the side. My phone beeped.

Kelly: *The code is #3975.*

I lowered the window and punched the keys. The gate swung open. This was better. I would easily be able to update that system with additional security. Gravel crunched under my tires as I inhaled more pine air. Trees lined the drive, creating a tunnel-like effect. It was beautiful.

The house was a ways back from the gate, which would give me more time to prepare if someone breached the entrance. As I rounded a curve, the sight of the house stole my breath for a moment. It was the perfect mix of stone, glass, and wood. And all of that glass meant unobstructed views from just about every room in the house.

I pulled to a stop, shutting off my SUV and hopping out. I'd rounded the side of the house before I heard Kelly's door shut. The home sat on a lake, but as I scanned the shoreline, I saw only a single dock. This body of water wasn't as large as Sutter, but it was substantial.

"This is Termonn Lake. The property includes the waterfront and the surrounding two hundred acres. It has eight bedrooms..."

Kelly continued to talk, but I zoned out, merely staring at the lake. It was quiet here, so very still, only the call of some birds overhead, and the leaves rustling in the wind. The land surrounding the house and the lake was all forest, requiring no maintenance on my part. It was perfect. "I'll take it."

Kelly was still speaking, but her words stuttered at my declaration. "You haven't even seen the inside."

I stayed focused on the lake, thoughts of how much Kiara had loved swimming filling my mind. She would've loved this house. I gave my head a little shake to clear it. "You can show me, but it doesn't matter. I'll take it."

"You don't even know how much it costs."

I turned to Kelly. "How much?"

She looked down at her tablet. "Eight million."

I scanned the house, the deck, the drive. "Eight bedrooms and nine baths?"

"Yes, sir."

My gaze returned to Kelly. "Offer seven point two. Cash."

She grinned. "You know this market."

I simply gave a single nod. I wasn't an idiot. Just because I had money didn't mean I wanted to waste it. I'd researched the properties around central Oregon, and I knew what was a worthwhile investment and what wasn't.

Kelly took a step closer, that smile of hers turning just a bit sultry. "I'll make the offer today, but I'm almost positive they'll take it. The property has been on the market for almost a year." She got even closer, not touching me but barely a breath away. "Tomorrow, we should go out and celebrate. I'll show you the town."

I stepped to the side, creating some distance between us but gave her a grin to soothe the sting of my rejection. "That's a real tempting offer, but I've got plans."

She arched a brow. "Another night, then?"

"I just might take you up on that." I searched for a flicker of interest but came up empty. My jaw tightened. I couldn't put my finger on why, but I just couldn't get excited about burning up the sheets with Kelly. She was gorgeous, but I felt nothing. I gave my head a quick shake. The *why* didn't matter.

I held out a hand towards the deck. "Why don't you show me my new house?"

CHAPTER
Five

Kennedy

"KENNEDY, I'M SO GLAD YOU COULD COME." JENSEN'S mom, Sarah, wrapped me in a warm hug.

Every time she did this, tears stung the backs of my eyes, and my throat began to burn. She was easy with her affection. Warm and welcoming. So very different from my mother. It was strange how a person could long for something they never had. "Thank you for inviting me."

She ushered me further through the large but warm ranch house. The men were gathered in a living area that was open to the kitchen and dining room, all of them clustered on couches, laughing and ribbing one another. Jensen's grandmother, Irma, and Taylor were in their usual spots, sipping wine at the bar in the kitchen. "You know you're welcome anytime. I wish you'd come every week."

"That's very kind of you." I swallowed the emotion clogging my throat.

"Kenz, I'm getting us wine." Jensen lifted up a bottle. "White okay?"

"Yes, thank you."

Taylor reached out a hand, pulling me to her for a hug. "Hey, girlie."

"Hey, Tay. How are plans for the engagement party going?"

She grinned up at me as I hopped onto a stool. "I think we're pretty much done. We're going casual and plan to have it right in the backyard." She inclined her head towards the outside.

I took the glass of wine that Jensen handed me. "That sounds perfect."

Irma peeked out from around Taylor, the lines on her face deepening as a mischievous smile spread. "What I can't wait for is the bachelorette party. I'm calling it now. I'm in charge of the strippers!"

"Grams," Jensen chided, but she couldn't hold in her laughter.

I took a sip of the crisp, white wine. "If Irma's in charge, we better all start saving for bail money."

Taylor eyed her fiancé in the living room. "I think I've got us covered in that department."

I chuckled. "Perks of marrying a cop."

The doorbell rang, and Sarah straightened, wiping her hands on her apron. "Oh, good, that must be Cain." Her smile was huge. "It's been so long since I've seen my boy."

I looked at Jensen as Sarah headed to the door. "Does she adopt everyone who comes her way?"

Jensen set her wine glass down on the counter. "Pretty much."

Taylor's gaze followed Sarah before she glanced back to J. "So, what's this guy's story? I haven't heard much from Walker. All I know is that he, Tuck, and Cain went to college together and that they're close."

Something unidentifiable flickered across Jensen's face before her features smoothed out. "He's a real good guy. He comes across a bit distant at times, but he's got a great heart. You'll like him."

Taylor set down her wine, as well. "Well, he found Tessa

when she was kidnapped, so he's already on my list of favorite people."

Tessa was one of the girls I knew the least. She had been gone almost the entire time I'd lived in Sutter Lake, accompanying her boyfriend on a US tour for his latest album. But I knew from just a few encounters she was really kind. I eyed J. "How did he find her?"

There was a sparkle in Jensen's eyes. "Didn't I tell you? He's kind of a crazy hacker. He can dig up anything on anyone."

My stomach twisted. *He could find out anything about anyone.* I let out a breath, giving my head a little shake. So what if he could. There was nothing for him to discover about me, even if he was interested enough to look. Kennedy Charles was a blank slate, an empty canvas. One of these days, I'd start filling it in.

Irma shot to her feet. "Quick, someone call 9-1-1. I'm going into cardiac arrest with all this hotness."

Jensen let out a snort of laughter, smacking her grandmother's arm. "You're incorrigible."

"I know a fine man-meat sandwich when I see it."

I looked up to see Walker, Tuck, and a man who had to be Cain in a huddle of hugs and back slaps. As the dark-haired man pulled out of Tuck's hold, I sucked in a sharp breath. And then I couldn't seem to take in any air at all.

Cain was tall, with broad shoulders encased in what could only be a custom-made button-down that skimmed his muscular chest and arms before tucking into dark-wash jeans that hugged his hips perfectly. But it was his face that held me captive. No, his eyes. They were a shade of blue I'd never seen on a human being. So dark, you might think they were brown. And they were locked on me.

My fingers began to tingle, and I realized that I hadn't taken another breath. I forced my gaze away, taking in air and grinning at my shoes. Apparently, Irma wasn't the only one affected by the hotness in the room. *Get a grip, Kenz.*

Taylor let out a low whistle next to me. "That man is something."

Jensen laughed. "Yeah, I called the three of them the trio of terror when they were in college."

"I bet." Taylor took a sip of wine. "I'm looking forward to summer when they're all shirtless at the lake."

Jensen wadded up her napkin and threw it at Taylor. "Gross. One of those guys is my brother."

Taylor shrugged. "Just keep your gaze focused on the other two."

Jensen's lip quirked. "Not a bad plan." She looked at me. "He's hot, right?"

I felt heat hit my cheeks. "They're all handsome."

Taylor scoffed. "Understatement of the century."

Jensen rose from her stool. "Cain, get over here."

My heart picked up its pace. It was fine. He was just a man. Handsome, sure, but nothing to be intimidated by. I forced my gaze up just as Cain wrapped Jensen in a hug.

"Little J," he whispered into her hair. "It's so good to see you."

Jensen pulled back. "I've missed you."

"Hey, hands off my girl." Tuck strode forward, pulling Jensen into his arms. "You've got your pick of women. They follow you around like lost puppies. Go find another one and stay away from mine."

Of course, Cain had a trail of women. My gaze traveled over him quickly, more assessing than appreciative now. The perfectly tailored outfit. The expertly cut and styled hair. I knew men like this. And I wanted nothing to do with any of them.

Jensen elbowed Tuck in the gut. "Like you were much better."

He bent down, sweeping his lips across hers. "But you tamed me."

Jensen snorted but gave him another quick kiss. "And now your ass is mine," she whispered.

"Ew, gross. Enough with the gushy stuff." Noah's face screwed up as he spoke. He looked to Cain. "They're always doing that."

Cain chuckled, the sound so deep and rich, I swore I felt its vibrations against my skin. "It is pretty gross, little man. Don't worry, you can come hang out with me if it ever gets to be too much."

Noah threw his hands in the air. "Thank goodness."

Jensen reached out a hand and ruffled his hair. "Just remember who feeds you pancakes, bud."

"I'll come back for pancakes."

Walker stepped forward, wrapping an arm around Taylor. "Cain, this is my fiancée, Taylor."

Cain reached out a hand, his expression just a touch more formal now. "It's a pleasure to finally meet you."

Taylor took his hand in hers. "You, too. I've only heard mysterious tidbits about you, so you're basically Batman in my mind."

That chuckle was back, and it made me shiver this time. "No bat cave, I'm afraid. Though maybe I should look into that."

"You should," Noah piped in. "I could help."

"Sounds like a plan."

Jensen gestured in my direction, and my stomach twisted. "Cain, this is my friend, Kennedy. She works at the Kettle with me."

Cain's dark blue depths moved in my direction, scanning my face as though committing it to memory and assessing me for weaknesses all at the same time. He reached out a hand. "It's nice to meet you, Kennedy."

I hesitated a brief second before moving to accept the shake, but my delay registered for Cain, and his eyes flared just a bit. I hurried to place my hand in his. It was warm, his palm a mix of smooth and rough. My mind wandered, trying to think of what could cause the roughness when the man probably spent all day behind a mahogany desk. The warmth from his hand spread up my arm, burning a path on its way. I released my grasp immediately. "It's nice to meet you, too."

I stepped back, letting the conversation swirl around me, a dull cacophony of noise with only direct questions cutting through. But every so often, I felt Cain's eyes on me. Curious. Probing. What he didn't know was that there was nothing for him to find. I was nothing. No one. And for now, that's just what I needed to be.

CHAPTER
Six

Cain

"**A**LL RIGHT! PEANUT BUTTER PIE!" NOAH SHOT HIS small fist in the air as Sarah rose from the table.

She smiled at her grandson. "You know I save it for special occasions." She turned kind eyes to me. "And Cain settling in Sutter Lake for a spell is definitely a special occasion."

Heat crept up the back of my neck. "Your peanut butter pie is worth it alone."

"Right?" Noah sidled up next to my chair, keeping his voice low. "Maybe you could leave and come back a few times so we get more peanut butter pie."

I chuckled. "I'll see what I can do, bud."

"Here, let me help you with that." The voice that called out was neither soft nor loud but held a melodious quality. Kennedy rose from her chair, heading to the kitchen island to help Sarah plate the pie. Her movements were graceful and fluid, as though she might simply dip into a pirouette or some other fancy spin at any moment. My eyes couldn't help but follow her. She seemed to have an ability to weave a spell around everyone, and that alone had me on edge.

"So, how are you holding up?"

Walker's question was low enough that only I could hear, and I forced my gaze away from Kennedy. I gave the rest of the table a quick assessment, but everyone else was engaged in conversation, and Noah had taken off towards the kitchen. "You didn't tell anyone?" I'd honestly expected to be greeted by Sarah, expressing devastation for my loss, and heartfelt wishes of sympathy from everyone else. I was so damn glad I hadn't been.

Walker shook his head. "No, only Tuck knows." Because the three of us shared it all. They knew every detail from when my life had fallen apart and never judged me for it.

"Thanks." I let out a slow breath. "I'm fine." Walker arched a brow, and I fought the urge to loosen my collar. "I wish I felt something at her loss, but I don't. It just stirred up a lot of old memories. And I needed to get away from the city. Knowing she'd been there all these years...it messed with my mind. I just—I needed some peace and quiet to get my head straight."

Walker gave my shoulder a squeeze. "I'm glad you came here to do that. You know Tuck and I have your back, always."

I nodded, swallowing the emotion that was crawling up my throat. A flash of red hair caught my attention as Kennedy leaned over to place a slice of pie in front of Jensen. A graceful movement that reminded me of an impressionist painting, all long, graceful lines, and rounded curves.

It didn't escape my notice that she started serving at the opposite end of the table from where I sat. The woman seemed to be avoiding me. She'd hesitated in shaking my hand. Waited to see where I sat and then took the seat farthest away. Now, this. She finally made her way to me, carefully placing the slice of pie in front of me without saying anything. A hint of rose filled my senses as she straightened, her hair swaying.

"Thank you." I tried to meet her gaze, but she avoided eye contact, simply nodded and moved on.

Kennedy settled in her chair as Sarah poured tea and coffee, engaging Jensen in conversation. The redhead expertly poured a dash of milk into her tea before adding a single cube of sugar. No splashes or spills.

It was as she raised her cup from the saucer that I realized what had been scratching at the back of my brain. Everything about Kennedy read: perfectly poised. Not in the way she spoke, but in the way she moved and acted. The kind of manners and grace that was either bred into a woman over decades—or carefully practiced. But I'd learned over dinner that Kennedy worked at the Kettle and lived in the minuscule apartment above the shop. If I hadn't known that, I would've guessed she was from a world of privilege.

Kennedy was gorgeous, almost hypnotic in her unique beauty. But, somehow, all the pieces of her puzzle didn't fit together. And the knowledge of that had me too damn curious for my own good.

Faint rays of sunshine still lit the sky as I headed to my SUV, but the air had just a hint of a bite to it. That was spring in the mountains. I glanced at Walker. "Thanks for the warm welcome."

He gave my back a slap. "Anytime, brother." He paused with me at my vehicle, looking out to the fields and then back to me.

"What is it?" You didn't know someone as long as I'd known Walker without recognizing their tells. The little ticks that told you they were worried or angry or, like now, had something they wanted to say but were holding back.

"Kennedy."

My body began to stiffen, but I forced it to relax. I was the master of giving nothing away, and this situation should be no different. "What about her?"

Walker shifted on his feet. "She's young."

"Looks it." I didn't know how young, but I'd find out soon enough.

Walker's jaw hardened. "Be careful."

I bristled at that. But he wasn't wrong to warn me off. She had an innocence that radiated from her in waves. And I had no plans to change that, but I was curious. That...something I couldn't put my finger on kept niggling at me as though she were playing at something she wasn't. I shook my head and gave Walker a grin. "I've got no plans to defile Jensen's protégé. You can rest easy."

The set of Walker's shoulders eased. "Good. You want free and easy, there are plenty of women around here who are down for that, just like you are. But I get the sense that's not Kenz."

"Kenz?" The nickname curled around my tongue. It fit her.

"That's what Jensen calls her, said Kennedy was too formal. Guess it's catching on."

I nodded. "I gotta get back to the resort, but let's grab a drink tomorrow. Hopefully, we'll be celebrating my closing on that property."

Walker grinned. "I hope it works out. Shoot me a text tomorrow, and we'll figure out a time."

"Sounds good." I beeped my locks and opened my door, but paused before I climbed in. "Walker?" He paused in his trek back to the ranch house, turning to face me. "I'm happy for you." The words made a burn take flight in my chest.

The smile that spread across his face was one that could only belong to a man who was a total goner for his woman. "Thanks, Cain. You'll—" He cut himself off before he could finish the sentence. He knew better than to tell me that I'd find that. "I'm glad you're here."

"I am, too." I gave a jerk of my chin and climbed into my SUV. The drive back to the resort I was staying at a few miles outside of town was quiet. Only the sounds of gravel under my tires to keep me company.

Gravel turned to pavement as I pulled into the resort. I hopped out of my Rover, leaving the door open for the valet. I ignored any polite smiles from fellow guests and staff as I headed straight for my suite.

The familiar itch at the back of my brain was back. Something that said I needed to know more about the girl from dinner. I slipped my keycard into the lock, fingers drumming against my thigh as I waited for the light to turn green. I pushed open the door and headed straight for the safe. Keying in the code, I removed my laptop.

I strode to the desk, setting my computer down and settling into the chair. I opened the laptop, typing in my security codes. I launched a browser and got to work. An hour went by in record time. An hour, and almost nothing to show for it.

I stared at the image on my screen. Auburn hair, freckles dusting the tops of her cheeks and nose, creamy white complexion below, and startling green eyes. There was no denying she was beautiful. Beautiful in a way that would stop a man in his tracks and make him do a whole lot of stupid shit just to get her to turn that smile his way.

But there was also no denying that she was a ghost. The only photo I could find of her was the one on her driver's license. Other than that one single piece of ID, the woman didn't exist. No bank account. No credit cards. No lease. No car.

There was nothing else, good or bad, that I could find. Anywhere. While some would say that was a good thing, I knew the truth. It was nothing but bad. People didn't erase a life unless they had something to hide.

One dinner and I knew my friends were taken by her. It was no surprise. Sarah and Jensen had the most tender hearts of anyone I knew. They were forever rescuing strays, both animal and human. Hell, that's why I was there, wasn't it?

But they often didn't think about the risks involved. Walker used to be good about checking that stuff out, but it seemed Taylor had softened him, made him just a touch less cynical about the world. I was happy for my brother, but it just meant that I needed to look out for the friends in my life who were more like family.

And that's just what I'd do.

I glanced up at the sign that read *The Tea Kettle* as I headed up the stone walk to Jensen's tea shop. She'd done a great job with the place, and it looked better than ever. It wasn't my taste, but I knew plenty of people who loved that shabby chic, mismatched look, and she'd created that in spades. Worn, wooden tables with an array of chairs in all shapes and sizes. Different jars holding mixed wildflowers dotted the tables, and all sorts of knickknacks decorated the walls. A bell jingled as I pushed open the door, and my gaze zeroed in on the woman behind the counter.

Mid-morning sunlight kissed her hair, making the red in the strands appear that much more vibrant. And that russet tone seemed to make the green in her eyes glow. I gave my head a little shake. "Good morning."

Kennedy startled a bit at my voice, apparently lost in thought as she placed scones in the bakery case. She straightened, licking her bow-shaped lips. "Morning. What can I get you?"

I looked up at the chalkboard above Kennedy's head. Jensen had added to the menu. "I'll take the breakfast sandwich with bacon."

Kennedy jotted that down on a notepad. "Anything to drink?"

"Do you have orange juice?"

She nodded. "Let me just run this back to the kitchen, and then I'll ring you up." She disappeared before I could agree or not.

"Coming right up, bigshot," Jensen called from the kitchen.

I chuckled. "Thanks, Little J."

Kennedy emerged from the back, wiping her hands on her apron. I studied her as she hit a few keys on the register. "That'll be eleven fifty."

I pulled a twenty out of my wallet and handed it to her. "Keep the change."

She scowled at the bill. "That's too much."

My focus on her narrowed. What game was she playing? "Shouldn't I be the one to decide what sort of tip is warranted? I am the customer, after all."

Kennedy's mouth pressed into a firm line before she spoke. "Of course. I'll bring your meal out to you as soon as it's ready." She ducked down to pull an orange juice out of the fridge. "Here's your juice." She set it on the counter instead of handing it to me.

"Thank you." I stayed near the register. "So, how long have you lived in Sutter Lake?"

Her gaze met mine and held. "A few months."

"And before that?"

She licked her lips again. A cue she was unsure about something. I just wasn't sure what. "Portland." Her gaze drifted away from mine as she said the word. A lie. Or not the whole truth.

"Hmmm." I let the sound out slowly, not moving my gaze from her. She started to squirm. Good.

"Can I get you anything else?" Kennedy didn't meet my eyes as she spoke.

"Nope." I still didn't move. "So, where'd you grow up?"

Kennedy's entire body seized as though someone had sent an electric shock through her. "What's with the twenty questions?"

I searched her face, looking for answers I knew she wouldn't give, but shrugged at the same time. "Just trying to get to know the folks in my new home."

Her skeptical expression told me that she wasn't buying it for a minute. "Okay. I'm twenty-two years old, I have a dog who snores louder than a freight train, I hate Brussel sprouts, and my favorite color is purple. What about you?"

I leaned a hip against the counter. "I'm thirty-six, no pets but I'd like a dog someday, I hate creamed corn, and my favorite color is green." The shade of green of her eyes flashed in my mind, and my jaw tightened. "Now, why don't you tell me something real?"

Kennedy's knuckles bleached white as she gripped the counter. "What are you talking about?"

"You're very good at avoiding questions you don't want to answer. Have Jensen and Walker even noticed they don't know the first thing about you?"

Kennedy's creamy white complexion bleached of any color, and I had the sudden urge to steady her, worried that she might faint. Her spine straightened, and I let out a breath I hadn't realized I'd been holding. "What they know is really none of your business, is it?"

My fists tightened at my sides, but I kept my tone casual. "They're my family. It's certainly my business."

"Bullshit," she hissed, color rising to her cheeks.

I grinned. It looked as if I'd finally tripped a trigger. That was good. When people got frustrated or angry, they stopped keeping a leash on their tongues. My grin turned just a bit heated. "What? Is asking questions a crime like large tips?"

Her fingers wrapped around the strings of her apron, twisting and tightening. "I know your type. All custom-tailoring and hundred-thousand-dollar cars. Thinking money can buy you anything. Well, let me tell you this. A ten-dollar tip doesn't buy you the right to stick your nose in my business. No amount of money would. I don't know why you're asking so many questions. I don't care to know. Keep your distance from me, and I'll return the favor."

The grin had slipped from my face. There was pain in her eyes. It was deep and raw and...*fuck*. I might have read the situation totally wrong. Maybe it wasn't my friends who needed protecting. Maybe it was Kennedy. I cleared my throat. "I'm sorr—"

She cut me off by holding up a hand. "It's fine. Just grab a table. I'll bring you your food when it's ready." She turned on her heel and strode into the kitchen.

Well, shit.

CHAPTER
Seven

Kennedy

MY PHONE BUZZED IN MY BIKE BASKET AS I WAS chaining it to the rack in front of the ballet studio. *Unknown number*. A trickle of unease slid down my spine. I tapped the screen. "Hello?"

"Hello. Is this Kennedy Barrington?"

My stomach churned, and I could feel the beat of my pulse in my neck. "No. I'm sorry, you must have the wrong number." The tremble in my voice was barely audible, but I knew it was there. I just hoped the person on the other end of the line didn't hear it.

"I apologize for the inconvenience."

I swallowed, the movement sticking as my throat had gone dry. "No problem."

I hit *end* on the screen. My hand shook as I placed the phone back into my bag. Memories assaulted me as I zipped the top closed. Memories from before I'd gotten smart, changed my last name, and got a new phone number.

I grabbed my phone off the rickety table in my minuscule studio apartment. "Hello?"

"Is this Kennedy?"

"It is. Who am I speaking with?" I went back to emptying the small grocery bag.

"You're a murderer. Your whole family is. You'll pay. One day, you'll get what's coming to you. I'll make sure of it."

I'd dropped the phone as if I'd been burned, the screen shattering. I'd made an appointment with a lawyer the next day. And slowly began the process of erasing my life.

But there was something so incredibly freeing about being a blank canvas. I could decide who I wanted to be. I could try things on. Pick them up and put them down. What did Kennedy Charles wear? What music did she listen to? What books did she read? What did she like to do in her free time?

Who was I kidding? There was no free time. I worked myself to the bone. Mostly for distraction. Because as soon as I was still for too long, the guilt got louder. Most of the time, it was low background noise. But if I got too quiet, sat with my thoughts for too long, it became a thundering drum.

And now, someone who knew about the person I used to be had my number. I flashed back to earlier that morning. All of Cain's questions. Did he know the truth? In the moment, I hadn't been able to tell if he was fucking with me or flirting—or maybe a little bit of both. But now I wondered if he knew about my past.

I let out a slow breath. *You're okay. You're safe.* I mouthed the words over and over to myself until my heart rate calmed. Just because someone had found a phone number didn't mean that someone was going to show up and throw fake blood on me again. Or worse. I'd go to the convenience store tomorrow and pick up a new cell with a new number. I'd had this one for too long anyhow. Everything would be fine.

"Miss Kennedy!" Annabeth ran across the parking lot, her mother following closely behind. She hit my legs with an *oomph* and grinned up at me, one tooth missing.

I gave her a squeeze. "How are you today, Miss A?"

Her grin got wider. "I'm great! It's ballet day."

"That it is." I flicked one of her pigtails over her shoulder as she let me go. When I looked up, I saw a sheen of tears in her mother's eyes. "Annabeth, why don't you run inside and practice your positions? I'll be right in."

She nodded and ran for the studio. I looked back to Patrice. "Are you all right?"

She wiped a finger under her eyes. "Sorry. I'm fine. It's just, Jim lost his job. Cutbacks. Things are going to be tight for a while. I don't think we'll be able to manage these ballet lessons."

My heart clenched. Annabeth was my most gung-ho student. She loved every second of her classes. I reached out and took Patrice's hand. "Don't worry about paying. I'll work something out with Seraphina. You just do what you need to for your family."

The wetness was back in Patrice's eyes. "I can't let you do that."

"Nonsense. Of course, you can." I squeezed her shoulder. "We all need a hand sometimes. It's okay to take it." I did a quick mental calculation. I could swing it. My grocery budget would be a little tight, but I could make it work.

Patrice pulled me into a hug. "You are such a good soul."

A war of sensations erupted in my chest. Warmth, gratitude, pride. Pain, guilt, and fear. I had to hold on to the reminder that I could be whoever I wanted to be now. And the person I wanted to be was generous. She made sure everyone around her had whatever they needed.

Patrice released me, and I gave her a warm smile. "I'm happy to help. Let me know if there's anything else I can do."

Patrice nodded, her lips pressed together in an attempt to hold back another rush of tears. "Thank you. I'll see you after class."

"See you then." I lifted a hand in a wave as I headed inside.

"You're late." Seraphina's words cracked in the echoey space.

I glanced at the clock on the wall. I was literally one minute late. "I'm sorry. I was talking to Annabeth's mother."

"I saw. What was that all about?"

My gaze traveled to the studio space where Annabeth was diligently practicing her positions. "Her husband lost his job, and they won't be able to pay for ballet lessons anymore."

Seraphina grimaced. "Then what is she doing here?" Seraphina gestured to the young girl in the studio, the movement causing the gauzy sleeves of her blouse to billow.

Seraphina was not the warm and fuzzy type. Why she had decided to open a ballet studio to teach children was beyond me. I got the sense that she was someone who had been turned bitter by a dream left unfulfilled. She often spoke of her time in New York, though I wasn't sure how much of it was true. I knew for sure that Seraphina wasn't her real name. Her driver's license read *Sally*. But who was I to judge? It wasn't like Kennedy Charles was my birth name either.

I twisted the strap of my bag in my fingers. "Just take her class fees out of my pay."

Seraphina's gaze narrowed on me. "I'm not giving you a discount."

Of course, she wasn't. "That's fine."

"All right. Now, get to work. I don't pay you to chit-chat." She turned on her heel and glided towards her office.

I let out a breath. One problem solved. Hopefully, the rest would stay at bay, and I would be left to my blank-canvas life.

CHAPTER
Eight

Cain

MY PHONE BUZZED IN MY POCKET AS I EASED MY FEET into the icy-cold lake water. Pulling out my cell, I grimaced at the screen. Not even seventy-two hours of peace. "Hello, Rachel."

"Cain." Her voice was a hushed whisper, and there was an urgency to the single word she spoke.

"What's wrong?" God, I didn't want to fly back to Portland already.

There was the sound of a door shutting before Rachel continued speaking. "I think someone was nosing around your office."

My spine stiffened. "What makes you say that?"

"I've been placing non-urgent files that need your attention in there. I figured you could handle them whenever you returned, or I'd bring them out to you. Anyway, when I went to add another file to the stack this afternoon, they were all out of order."

"Are you sure?"

Rachel scoffed. "Cain, please."

Of course, she was sure. Rachel was one of the most organized people I had ever met. There was always a method to her madness. "Start locking my office." I should've made that arrangement as soon as I'd known I'd be gone for an extended period of time.

Rachel was silent for a moment. "Maybe you should think about coming back."

I looked out at the lake around me and flexed my feet in the soothing water. It was the first bit of peace I'd felt in years. "I won't be returning anytime soon."

"You like it there." Rachel's voice gentled. She'd always taken her job as my assistant to the extreme, seeing it as her responsibility to look out for me.

"I do. But you're right that we need to take precautions." My office was on a floor that housed only a handful of others, and everyone with access had the highest security clearance. "Did you ask Jake if he went in there, looking for something?" He never asked permission and always messed up whatever system Rachel had going.

She let out a huff. "I did. He swears he wasn't in there. But there's something else." I said nothing, letting the silence encourage Rachel to continue. "Pete said someone tried to hack our systems yesterday."

My grip on the phone tightened. That wasn't anything new. Corporate espionage and trying to sneak in through back doors was just the name of the game when you were at the top. There were whispers in the community that I was working on a new program, one that would revolutionize security systems at every level. If my competitors got their hands on that before we made it to market, it could be a death blow to everything I'd built with Halo.

Rachel pressed on in that same hushed tone. "He's been working on it all morning. He said whoever it was knew what they were doing. They almost got in."

My jaw made that familiar clicking noise as my teeth ground

together. This was not good. We hadn't had a close call like this...
ever. Why the hell hadn't he notified me immediately? "Have him
call me, *now*. And I'll check out the system from here." I pushed
to my feet, losing the calming presence the water had brought.
"And I want you to keep your eyes and ears open. Call me if you
notice anyone acting suspicious."

"Of course, Cain. Let me know if I can do anything else."

"Thank you. I'm glad I can always count on you to look out
for me and Halo." I hit end on the call and muttered a curse.
There was always someone out to get you. It was a reminder I
didn't need.

The sun shone over the lake as I took a pull of the ice-cold soda
water. "You guys bring the perfect housewarming gifts." I twisted
my head to the side, popping my neck and trying to release some
of the stress of the day.

Tuck chuckled. "Had to make sure you were stocked with
your essentials of choice."

Walker popped the cap off his beer. "Thank God you at least
have a fridge."

I looked over my shoulder at the house behind us. The very
empty house. "I sent my designer photos last night. She said she'd
have the furniture here by the end of the week."

Tuck spun a cap between his fingers. "What're you going to
do in the meantime?"

"I picked up an air mattress and a few other essentials at the
hardware store." I looked at my friends. "Does that store carry
everything? I swear one aisle had power tools, and the next
bedding."

Walker grinned. "Welcome back to small-town life."

It had been so long since I'd lived that life, I guessed I'd forgotten. "It'll be a bit of an adjustment."

Tuck let out a snort. "We'll see how long you last, city boy."

I glared in his direction. "I'll last just fine." I gestured to the space around me. "Especially with all this."

Tuck stared out at the dock. "It's not too shabby."

My phone beeped from where it sat next to me on the deck. I swiped it up and tapped the notification. It was the camera I'd installed at the gate. I flipped it around so Walker could see the screen. "This your friend Liam?"

Walker nodded. "That's him."

Tuck dissolved into laughter. "Only you wouldn't recognize a multi-platinum musician whose face has been plastered everywhere for almost the last decade."

I hit the option to open the gate and set my phone down. "What can I say? I don't keep up with the gossip magazines like you do."

Tuck threw his beer cap at me, and I chuckled. The crunch of tires on gravel sounded, and then I heard a door opening and closing. Tuck cupped his hands around the sides of his mouth. "We're back here, Hollywood."

"On my way, asshole." The voice sounded from the front of the house. In a few moments, a man appeared from the side of the house. He was casually dressed, but the way his hair was artfully disheveled screamed *creative* of some sort.

"Hey, man," Walker greeted, holding out a hand for a slap but not rising to his feet. "Liam, this is our friend, Cain. Cain, Liam."

I pushed to standing, holding out my hand for a shake. "Nice to meet you."

Liam took my palm in a firm grip, one that held as he spoke. "You, too. Thank you for everything you did for Tessa and me. I'll never be able to repay you."

I shook my head. "No repayment necessary." When Liam's girlfriend, Tessa, had been kidnapped by her psycho ex, I'd been able to locate the house where he was holding her. And while I appreciated the gratitude, it wasn't necessary.

Liam bent and picked up a beer. "Heard lots about you from these two, so it's nice to finally meet you in person."

"It was obviously all lies," Tuck called as he lay back on the deck, hands laced behind his head.

I shook my head. "Better than all the truths I know about you."

Tuck jolted back to sitting. "You keep your trap shut around Jensen."

My grin was just a little bit evil. "I don't know, I've got a couple of doozies she might be interested in."

Tuck shot to his feet and dashed towards me, trying to get me in a headlock. Walker reached out and grabbed the back of Tuck's shirt, yanking him back. "Enough already, children."

Liam shook his head and looked out at the lake, taking it all in. "This place is amazing."

"It doesn't suck," Walker said, following Liam's gaze.

Tuck straightened his tee. "I know where we'll be hanging out all summer."

I flipped the ball cap off Tuck's head. "Sure, just invite yourself."

Tuck grinned. "Thank you. I will."

Liam ignored the bickering, clearly already used to the dynamic that always seemed to surround Tuck. "What I want to know is who did your security system. That setup at the gate was great."

A flicker of pride lanced through my chest. It had been too long since I was hands-on. I used to do that kind of stuff all the time, but as my company grew, I was no longer in charge of the minutia of gadgetry. I had to stay focused on the big-picture stuff. "I did."

Liam's brows rose. "Really?"

I nodded. "I used to do that kind of stuff a lot when I was

just getting started. But my company grew, and then I didn't have time for it as much. But I wanted a solid system here." My gaze traveled over the land around us. "I'm only getting started. There's a lot of ground to cover."

Liam rubbed a hand over his jaw. "Think you'd be willing to draw something up for me? I'm looking at property around here, and security is a big concern."

Tuck snorted. "You've been looking for the past year, and nothing meets your standards. You'll be living in Walker's guest cabin until you and Tessa are old and gray."

Liam's eyes narrowed on Tuck. "It just so happens, I think I found the perfect spot."

Walker's eyes widened. "Really? That's amazing."

"Don't say anything yet. Tessa doesn't know. I'm waiting to make sure nothing falls through with the sale. I was going to surprise her before we have to head back out on tour next week."

Walker slapped Liam on the back. "Pleased for you, man."

I was always a bit cautious of newcomers in my circle, but I got a good vibe from Liam right off. "I'd be happy to look at property specs and consult with whoever you use for a system install."

"Thanks, man. Gotta do whatever I can to make things safe for my girl."

That familiar ugly sensation twisted in my gut. I shook it off. There was nothing I respected more than trying to keep the ones you loved safe, and I'd do whatever I could to help. "No problem. It's good to flex those muscles again."

"Okay, enough of all this boring security talk." Tuck rubbed his hands together with an expression that hinted at all sorts of trouble. "Let's discuss all the parties we're going to throw here this summer."

My body stiffened. "No parties." The two words came out more harshly than I'd intended.

Tuck's eyes narrowed on me. "What's going on, Cain? I know you've got that loner Bruce Wayne vibe going for you, but this is more."

Walker's gaze turned to me, as well. "Everything okay?"

I sighed and sat back down on the deck steps. The earlier call had reminded me of how careful I needed to be right now. Still, I knew it would come off as paranoid to someone who wasn't entrenched in my industry. But Tuck and Walker were the two people I trusted most in this world. My gaze traveled to Liam.

Liam noticed my stare. "I can take a walk if you need to speak privately."

Walker held up a hand and turned to me. "I'd trust him with my life."

Walker knew me. My trust issues. Everything. He wouldn't say something like that lightly. "I've got some security concerns at my company right now. I'm working on a new project, and I have to be extra careful." I blew out a harsh breath, uneasy thinking of someone being in my office. "And there might be an insider helping them out."

Tuck eased down onto the steps a few feet away, and the other guys followed. "That sucks, man."

"And it's not just that. There have been multiple cyber-attacks against the company system over the past couple of weeks. Someone wants to know how we do things."

Walker picked up his beer. "Shouldn't that give you a little more information? You know it's not someone who's developing your systems because then they could just sell the stuff outright."

I shook my head. "I only have one developer assigned to each project. So, if a specific program hit the open market or ended up in another company's hands, I'd know exactly who was responsible. This is more widespread than that."

"Do you know who the company is that's behind it all?" Tuck asked, stealing another beer from the six-pack.

"I've got a pretty good idea." A few months ago, a new firm had emerged on the scene. Based in Seattle, no one knew who was at the helm of Raider Industries. At first, they were scooping up all the companies I simply didn't have time for, the smaller fish. But now, they were going after my clients. And it was starting to look as if they might have recruited help. I filled the guys in on everything I knew about my competition.

Liam took a pull from his beer. "That seriously sucks, man. I've got some contacts in LA, solid investigators if you want to put someone on this."

I'd thought about that. But no one I hired would know these people better than I did. I needed to be the one to hunt the asshole down. "Thanks, but I think I need to be at the helm for this."

"I get it. Just let me know if you change your mind." I nodded in assent.

Walker leaned forward, his elbows going to his knees. "We'll help. Whatever you need."

I didn't know what I'd done in a past life to deserve these friends, but whatever it was, I was grateful. "Appreciate it. Mostly it just means making this place a fortress. No one I don't know comes onto this property. I need a safe space to work." I glanced at Tuck. "Which means, no parties."

Tuck winced. "Uh, Jensen and Sarah are already planning some sort of housewarming something or other for you, so you might want to talk to them."

I sighed. "The fewer people that know what's going on, the better."

Walker drummed his fingers together. "Why don't we say just family? We can call in an order for food but tell the girls to pick it up, no caterers or staff on the premises."

I considered it. I guessed just those at dinner the other night, plus Liam and Tessa would be okay. Red hair and green eyes flashed in my brain. "That's fine. But no staff. And I pay for everything."

Tuck chuckled. "You might have a fight on your hands there. Sarah's determined to welcome you properly."

I groaned. "Fine. Tell her that she and J can be in charge of dessert." I paused for a moment, trying to think of the best way to put what I wanted to say next. "And have J invite Kennedy."

Walker stiffened next to me, but Tuck chuckled. "Got your eye on someone already, huh?"

"Tuck," Walker warned.

Tuck threw up his hands. "What? I want our boy to get himself some. What's wrong with that?"

Liam just laughed, and Walker and Tuck continued to bicker like the two old men they were in spirit. I finally let out a piercing whistle. "Enough already. It's not like that." Tuck arched a brow as if to say *bullshit*. "Don't get me wrong, she's beautiful, but she's too young for me, and I'm not looking for anything serious right now."

Walker studied me carefully. "What is it, then?"

I began to draw circles in the condensation on my glass. "I get the sense that she's running from something."

Liam immediately straightened, and I wanted to curse. Of course, this would bring up things for him. "You think she's running from an ex?"

Tuck's face no longer held any hints of humor. "She's not skittish. Doesn't seem to be afraid of men."

I tore at another piece of the label. "Honestly, at first, I thought she was taking you guys for a ride. I know Jensen lets her live in that apartment basically for free. I thought she might be conning you."

"Cain—" Walker started, but I held up a hand, silencing him.

"I don't think that anymore. I went into the Kettle the other morning and asked her some questions."

Tuck groaned. "You were a total asshole, weren't you?"

I winced at the memory. "Some of my less than favorable qualities might have made an appearance."

Tuck shook his head. "Jesus. Your paranoia knows no bounds."

My shoulders straightened. "I wasn't totally wrong. She's lying about something."

"What do you mean?" Walker asked, cop hat firmly in place now.

I tried to think about how I could explain this to them. Convince them that I wasn't totally out of my mind about Kennedy. "She was super guarded about her past."

"Maybe she just didn't want to tell a relative stranger her life story," Tuck argued. "She is a single woman living alone. And she doesn't really know you."

I set my glass down on the deck. "Fair enough. Do any of you know where she's from?"

Walker looked to me. "She moved here from Portland."

"Yeah, but where is she *from*?" I looked around at the men beside me, none of them having an answer. "She's lived in Jensen's shop for like six months, been over to the ranch countless times, and you don't really know anything about her. She's hiding something. And I don't think it's an attempt to con you out of money or anything else. I think she's running from something."

"Fuck." Walker scrubbed a hand over his cheek. "When you put it like that, you might be right."

I met Walker's stare. "I am."

Tuck got to his feet. "I'll make sure J brings her to the party. We'll figure out what's going on. And if she needs protecting, we'll be there."

These were good men, and whether Kennedy knew it or not, she was lucky to have them in her corner.

CHAPTER
Nine

Kennedy

"I DON'T THINK SO. THANKS FOR THE INVITE, THOUGH."
What I wanted to say was "*hell, no,*" but I didn't think
that was appropriate.

Jensen leaned on the counter, giving me her best version of
puppy-dog eyes. "Please, Kenz. He'll only let me invite the people
from dinner the other night, and Tessa and Liam. I really want
Cain to get to know some good people."

My brow furrowed. "Why?" It wasn't like the guy couldn't afford food and drinks for more people.

Jensen pressed her lips together, seeming to choose her words
carefully. "Cain doesn't let a lot of people in. He's super private
and doesn't trust easily. He's so used to people just using him for
his money and connections. I want him to know what it's like to
have a community of people who aren't users."

A flicker of sympathy flitted through me. I knew a little
about what that was like, and it wasn't fun. It didn't change that
I wanted nothing to do with the man. He was dangerous for me.
Someone who saw too much, maybe already knew it all. I met
Jensen's hopeful gaze. "Chuck and I have plans to curl up and

read tonight. I'm researching some of the programming other community centers have and how they do their fundraising, hoping to get some ideas for the shelter."

J's eyes narrowed on me. "Kenz, Chuck will be snoring by five p.m. And you can research tomorrow night. *Please?* Do it for me?"

She didn't fight fair. Jensen had done so much for me since I'd moved to Sutter Lake. I could suffer through one party for her. I'd just avoid the guest of honor. "Okay. I'll go."

Jensen let out a little squeal as she clapped her hands together and jumped. She threw her arms around me. "Thank you. Plus, free food. I'm picking it up in an hour. Taylor and Walker will swing by and pick you up at five."

Nerves churned in my belly. "What's the dress?"

"Dress?" A little line of confusion appeared between J's brows.

"What should I wear?" I didn't have very many options, so I hoped it was casual.

"Oh. You can wear anything, this isn't fancy."

That didn't really help, but I'd figure something out. "Okay, I'll be ready for Taylor and Walker at five." I was curious about the property Cain had bought. J had said it was on its own private lake and that Tuck had told her the view was breathtaking. I could always escape to the outdoors if needed.

"Perfect." Jensen glanced at her watch. "All right. I'm off to pick up Noah, get cleaned up, and grab the food. I'll see you in a couple of hours."

"See you." I followed Jensen towards the back door, checking to make sure she'd locked it behind her, and then headed upstairs. I unlocked my apartment door and pushed it open. Chuck lay across the folded quilt at the foot of my bed, snoring away.

I crouched by the bed. "Chuck," I called in a gentle singsong. He didn't stir. Today he was apparently deaf as a doornail. He let out an especially loud snore, one that seemed to shake his whole body. I laughed and rubbed behind his ears the way he liked. His eyes fluttered open.

"Hey, buddy. You have a good day?" He didn't lift his head but let his tongue flick out and lap at my face. "I missed you, too. Come on. I gotta take you out."

Chuck groaned but slowly rose to his feet. My little man was getting old. I carefully lifted him off the bed. I'd gotten some stairs so that he could climb up and down, but he seemed to prefer it when I picked him up.

I took him out for a quick potty break and then dashed back up to survey my clothing options. I stood in front of my small closet, hands braced on either side of the door. "What do you think?" Chuck looked up from where he sat at my feet as if to say, *"how the hell should I know?"*

My eyes scanned the contents of the closet. So different from years past when my walk-in was full of dresses and shoes for every occasion. There was a brief flicker of longing at the memory. I hadn't enjoyed the ridiculous number of events my parents required me to attend, but I did miss the beautiful dresses, especially the ones with fabric that seemed to float around me as I danced.

I shook my head, trying to clear the image as guilt gnawed at my belly. So many things I hadn't needed. Now, my closet was mostly filled with jeans, tees, a few flannels, and a couple of sweaters. I had a handful of dance outfits and sweats stacking the shelves on the side. I had to admit, my casual wardrobe was a nice change most of the time, but I didn't exactly have a lot of party options.

My hands reached out and pushed hangers aside until I found what I was looking for. My lone sundress. I'd found it at a second-hand shop in Portland. And even though I'd had no use for it, I couldn't resist it. I'd felt guilty about the purchase for days after and probably would've returned it if the shop hadn't had a no-refund policy. But it was perfect for today.

I pulled it out and hung in on the back of the closet door. I looked down at Chuck. "Hopefully, this works." He lay down on the floor. "Thanks for your vote of confidence."

I glanced at the clock in the kitchen. "Shit. I gotta get going." Chuck didn't move. If people could hear how much I talked to my dog, I'd probably be committed. But he'd been my constant companion for so long, the one being I could trust with anything.

I hurried into the bathroom and hopped into the shower. I made quick work of getting cleaned up, toweling off, and donning a robe. I opened the medicine cabinet and pulled out the few items of makeup I had. A little eyeliner, some mascara, and a dash of blush. That would have to be good enough.

I took a few minutes to weave strands of hair into an intricate braid around the crown of my head before dashing out of the bathroom for my dress and a pair of panties. I sighed as I slipped the fabric over my head. It was that perfect feel of worn cotton.

I straightened the dress, smoothing out the wrinkles, and then headed back towards the bathroom and the mirror that hung on the outside of the door. My appearance was almost startling. The pale blush pink of the dress accented my complexion perfectly, and the deeper hue of the small rosebuds that made up the straps and lined the neck seemed to make the green of my eyes pop. It was the perfect dress.

My phone buzzed on my bed, and I made a dash for it.

Taylor: *We're here. In the back lot.*

Me: *Be right down.*

I glanced around my small studio. There was one thing I didn't have. A purse. *Crud. Oh, well.* The dress had pockets. That would have to be good enough. I grabbed my keys and phone and bent to give Chuck one more rub. "You be good." He let out a cross between a snort and a grunt, and I laughed.

I hurried out, locking the door behind me, and then headed down the stairs. As soon as I was out the back door, Walker was climbing out of his truck and opening the passenger door for me.

"Thank you." I climbed in, grateful for my height since the truck was ridiculously high.

Walker hopped in. "You look beautiful, Kennedy."

I felt my cheeks start to heat.

Taylor grinned at me through the rearview mirror. "No, she looks smokin'. Get it, girl."

I let out a startled laugh. "That wasn't really what I was going for, but this is the only dress I have." I was relieved to see that Taylor was dressed similarly in a flouncy skirt and sleeveless blouse.

"Well, thank God it is because you look gorg."

"Thank you. So do you. I love that skirt."

Taylor brushed her hands over the vibrant fabric. "You can borrow it anytime."

My laughter returned. "Uh, Tay. I think that might be a little too short on me." Taylor was basically a pixie, meaning she and Walker were about the cutest couple ever. Her, a petite spitfire, and him all tall, dark, and handsome.

She shrugged. "It'd show off those long legs of yours, though."

"Yeah, and probably half my butt."

Taylor snickered. "You certainly wouldn't be hurting for dates."

"All right, already," Walker griped as he turned to take the road out of town towards Sutter Lake. "Enough about legs and butts and skirts."

I reached forward and patted his shoulder. "Sorry about that, buddy."

He shook his head. "I hate being outnumbered."

Taylor giggled. "I love it when you're outnumbered."

"Short-stack," he warned.

"Bigfoot," she warned back. But the heat in her eyes spoke of love and passion.

Longing flared to life in my chest again. To have someone to lovingly bicker with. To share a language only the two of you spoke. To have a partner. And maybe, one day, a family again. I let my gaze go unfocused as I stared out the window at the passing fields. *One day.*

It wasn't long before we were turning off the road and pulling to a stop at an intimidating gate. No one would be getting in here without the owner's consent. My gaze flicked up to the single word in scrawling script above the entry. *Termonn.* Gaelic for sanctuary. I wondered if Cain had chosen it. He didn't look Irish. Walker rolled down his window, pressed a button, and waved at what must've been a camera. My stomach tightened. A few seconds later, the gates swung open.

Walker wove his truck down a curved gravel drive. When I caught my first glimpse of the house, I let out a little gasp. It was beautiful. Wood and stone and glass for days. Gorgeous, but way too big for one man. What was he going to do with all that space?

Taylor let out a low whistle. "Not too shabby."

Walker chuckled. "Wait until you see the view."

That's what I was hungry for, the lake. But I reined in my desire to forgo the party entirely and head straight for the water. I'd make nice first.

We climbed out of the truck as the front door opened, and Sarah appeared with Noah. Noah bounded down the steps. "This place is awesome! Cain has his own dock, and he said he's going to get a boat and that I can come over and go tubing anytime I want."

At least the man was generous with what he had. That was something. Sarah pulled me in for a hug as Noah bounced around us. "I'm so glad you came."

"It was nice of you to invite me."

Sarah gave my shoulders a squeeze as she released me. "Of course. You're one of the family."

That low background noise of guilt hummed a little louder. I wasn't. Because they didn't know who I really was. What I'd been a part of. I wasn't sure they'd want to claim me as one of theirs if they did. And I didn't think I could withstand the look of disappointment in their eyes if they ever found out. I shook it off and followed the group up the stone steps.

The house was no less impressive inside. There was a massive stone fireplace circled by one of the largest sectionals I'd ever seen. I was surprised it wasn't fancy leather but more a distressed linen. It looked incredibly comfortable—the perfect place to curl up with a good book on a stormy day. But it was the windows that stole the show. The entire back of the house was glass. It felt like the lake and the forest were a part of the home. It was magical.

"It's breathtaking, huh?" Jensen leaned her shoulder into mine.

"That view is pretty spectacular."

"That it is. Come on." She gestured towards a bar that was stocked with more alcohol and soda than a party ten times this size could consume. "Let's get you a drink."

I swallowed. "Thanks."

"What are you in the mood for?"

My gaze traveled over the bar, settling on an old favorite. A tiny smile pulled at my lips. "I'll take one of these." I grabbed the small glass bottle of Perrier out of the bucket of ice.

Jensen's head gave a little jerk. "There's grade-A hooch here, Kenz. And you're going for fizzy water?"

I grinned at her. "This is my favorite, and I never get it for myself." It wasn't a necessity, and Perrier was so dang expensive, I just couldn't justify it.

J shook her head. "Whatever floats your boat."

My eyes traveled over the room. It looked like everyone was here. I couldn't help the way my gaze seemed to catch on Cain. His dark hair gleamed in the sunlight as he bent to talk with Noah. I forced myself to look away and back to Jensen. "I'm going to take this out onto the back deck to check out the view."

"Sounds like a plan. I'm going to check on all the food, make sure it's reheating properly."

I turned back to her. "Do you need any help?"

Jensen waved me off. "No, I'm good. Go get a look at that view before the sun sets."

I headed outside, and as soon as the fresh mountain air hit my lungs, I began to relax. I leaned against the railing of the deck, breathing deeply. Magic. There really was no other way to describe this place. The wind rustled leaves, and a frog croaked as the sun, low in the sky, seemed to make the water shimmer.

"It's beautiful, isn't it?"

I jolted at the low voice and spun to see Cain. I swallowed hard. "It is. Congratulations."

"Thank you. I'm glad you could come. I wanted to apologize if I came on a little strong the other day. I can be nosy."

My palms dampened. "Is that what it was? Nosiness?"

Cain studied me, seeming to search my face. He shrugged, the movement letting the defined muscles beneath another of those expertly tailored shirts show. "I'm protective of my friends. I didn't know anything about you."

My eyes widened. "You thought I was going to hurt your friends."

He took a sip of what looked like either a vodka soda or a gin and tonic. "I'm not sure exactly what I thought, but I know I was wrong."

The muscles that had tightened across my shoulder blades when he first appeared relaxed just a bit. He had no idea who

I was. My history. My family. He figured there was something off about me. And he was right, so how could I be mad at that? "You're forgiven."

Cain arched a brow. "Easy as that?"

I shrugged a shoulder. "I'm not really one for grudges."

"Good to know." He turned, gesturing to the house. "So, what do you think?"

I followed his movement. "It's gorgeous. But it's a lot of house for just one person."

Cain swirled the ice in his glass. "I like my space."

I let out a small laugh. "Well, you'll certainly have that." My gaze traveled over all the windows, settling on the ones right in front of us, ones that looked into the kitchen. There was food everywhere. So much that it would take the dozen or so of us here a month to eat it all. "Why did you get so much?" My voice came out choked.

Cain's brow furrowed. "So much what?"

"Food."

He laughed. "Well, it is a party."

An uncomfortable heat rolled through my body. "What are you going to do with the leftovers?"

Cain studied me, but I couldn't find it in me to care. "I guess I'll send leftovers home with whoever wants them, keep some for myself, and throw out the rest."

My hands tightened into fists. "That's incredibly wasteful." The words were out of my mouth before I could stop them. "I'm so sorry. That was rude and none of my business. If you'll excuse me."

I dashed around Cain before he could say a word and headed down the deck steps. The grass tickled my toes as I made my way to the dock. It was older but looked sturdy enough. I sat down on the end, slipping off my sandals so I could dip my toes into the frigid water.

I needed the cold right then. Needed it to cool my temper and my embarrassment. I let my head drop into my hands. What was I thinking? What Cain wanted to do with his money was none of my business.

The dock swayed as someone sat next to me. I couldn't look. I saw only rolled-up slacks and male feet dipping into the water next to me. "You're not wrong, you know. It is wasteful."

I said nothing but dropped my hands, keeping my gaze on the water. "Jensen said you volunteer at the local shelter. Why don't I drop the leftovers by there tomorrow, along with a donation?"

"It's not always about money, you know." What was wrong with me? It was like I couldn't keep my mouth shut around this man. But I'd seen money thrown at so many problems before. When you seemed to have an endless supply, what did it really cost you? I swallowed down my frustration.

"What do you mean?"

I shook my head. "Sorry. I didn't mean anything. That would be great, and the shelter can always use donations."

Cain reached out and, with a single finger, turned my face towards him. The contact was gentle and rough at the same time, sending tingles up the side of my face. "No. Tell me the truth."

I swallowed, my gaze locked with his as he released his hold on me. "You should spend some time there." *Shut up, Kennedy.* "Get to know the people you're helping. See how important food is to them."

Clarity seemed to dawn for Cain. "Sounds fair enough. When can I start?"

Like the genius I was, I'd somehow convinced the man I'd been determined to stay away from to volunteer at the place I spent most of my evenings. *Smooth move, Kennedy.*

CHAPTER
Ten

Cain

I SHUT THE DOOR TO MY SUV, THE NOISE ECHOING OFF THE mostly empty parking lot. But the sound did nothing to attract Kennedy's attention. She stood, head bent, gaze focused intently on her phone. Too focused. She didn't seem to be aware of anything around her. Foolish. Dangerous.

I cleared my throat. "Kennedy."

She jumped, a hand flying to her chest. "Whoa. You scared me."

I fought the scowl that wanted to surface. "You weren't paying attention." My gaze flicked to her cell, and she quickly shoved it into her bag.

"Sorry. Just lost in thought, I guess." She inclined her head towards the doors of the community center. "You ready to go in?"

She started towards the building before I'd said a single word, but I reached out a hand, grasping her elbow as gently as possible. It was a mistake. Her skin was the smoothest thing I'd ever felt. It seemed to burn my fingertips, sear my palm. "Are you okay?"

Kennedy nodded quickly. "Fine. Why?"

The way her eyes drifted away told me that she was lying. My jaw made that familiar clicking noise as it tightened. "You were so focused on your phone, you wouldn't have noticed a herd of elephants until they were trampling you."

Her berry-red lips quirked. "A herd of elephants? I don't think those are native to Oregon."

"That's not the point. It's dangerous not to be aware of your surroundings."

The small smile fell from her face, and I hated myself just a little bit for being the cause. "Sutter Lake is safe."

"Bad things can happen anywhere." Hell, there'd been a serial killer hunting in the area mere months ago.

Kennedy straightened. "You're right. Bad stuff happens everywhere, but I'm not going to live my life assuming it's waiting around every corner."

"I'm not asking you to do that. I'm asking you to be careful." I struggled to keep my tone even, to not allow the anger and frustration pulsing through me to show.

She sighed. "I'm careful. Promise. Come on, we need to go, or we're going to be late."

She wasn't careful enough. My hands clenched and flexed. I had no control over Kennedy, or how she lived her life, how she protected herself. Why did that burn so much when I barely knew the woman?

Kennedy pushed open the door, and I hurried to catch up. "The shelter is currently housed in the community center, but they're trying to raise enough funds to build their own separate space." I took in the space that looked mostly like a school cafeteria. "This is where residents eat, have activities, and where events are held."

"How often do you volunteer here?"

Kennedy turned to face me, the action causing her hair to swing and catch the early evening light, the red flaming for just a moment. "Usually, five nights a week."

That was a lot. Between her work at the Kettle and this, I wondered when she got any time for herself. "That's generous of you."

Something flitted across her expression, too quick for me to identify for certain, but it looked a lot like pain. "I get a lot out of it in return."

My palms itched to reach out to her. To comfort. And I had no idea why. "Why don't you introduce me around?"

"Sounds good."

A back door swung open, and a man appeared. He wore khakis and a blue polo shirt. He smiled wide the minute he saw Kennedy, but the expression turned forced as soon as he spotted me. "Kenz, who do you have here?"

Kennedy returned his smile. Hers was warm, and something in my gut twisted at the familiarity. "Doug, this is Cain. He's new to town and wants to help out. Cain, this is Hope House's director, Doug."

I reached out a hand to shake Doug's. His grip attempted to dominate, to show who was in charge. I simply kept mine steady, not giving in to his games. He took it as a victory, smirking slightly. I fought the urge to roll my eyes. "Nice to meet you, Doug."

"You, as well. I hope you don't mind, but I'll need to make a copy of your driver's license. We do basic background checks on all of our volunteers."

I pulled my wallet from my back pocket and handed him my ID. "Here you go."

There was a flicker of disappointment in his expression, as though he thought I might throw a temper tantrum. "I'll go run this now." His gaze flicked back to Kennedy. "Have you thought any more about *Swan Lake*? If we're going to go, I should get tickets."

Kennedy's fingers twisted in the strap of her bag. "I can't right now. Things are just too busy. Thanks for inviting me, though."

Doug's forced smile was back. "Of course. We'll go another time." He turned on his heel and headed down another hall. Kennedy's shoulders slumped slightly.

"*Swan Lake*, huh?" Why did her denial make me so damn happy?

Her body gave a little jolt as though she'd forgotten I was even there. "Yeah, he knows I love ballet."

I edged just a bit closer. "Why aren't you going with him, then?" I couldn't help probing, I wanted to know more, to see how her mind worked, to find out who—and what—Doug was to her. I should've restrained myself, but my control always seemed to slip a bit around Kennedy.

She nibbled on the corner of her lip. "I'm really busy right now." Kennedy paused and then blew out a breath. "And I don't want to give him the wrong impression. I'm not interested in being anything but friends."

My muscles loosened even more. "Then you did the right thing."

"I hope so."

The same door swung open again. This time, a woman who looked to be in her mid-twenties emerged. She was curvy and wore an apron, her blonde hair up in a bun. "There you are. I was starting to worry you got kidnapped by a roving band of hooligans." Her steps faltered as she took me in. "Well, hello, Mr. Tall Dark and Handsome. No wonder you're late. I would be too if this was who I was with."

Kennedy laughed. "Anna, this is Cain. Cain, this is Anna. She really runs the show around here."

I extended a hand. "It's lovely to meet you."

Anna began to fan herself exaggeratedly as she turned to Kennedy. "Where did you find him, and does he have a twin brother who wants to run away with me?"

Kennedy shook her head but kept grinning. "You're awful.

Cain is a college friend of Walker's and Tuck's. He just bought a house here."

Anna turned back to me, eyes a bit more assessing now. "Hmmmm. And what's your story, handsome? Why'd you move to Sutter Lake?"

I liked her instantly, and not just for her easy compliments. It was her unhindered honesty. There was no pretense, no hidden agenda. Everything was right out in the open. "I needed a change of scenery." That was true enough.

"From where?" The inquisition was apparently on.

"Portland."

Her gaze narrowed slightly. "You running from something?"

"Maybe."

Anna's eyes widened as though surprised by my honesty. She opened her mouth to ask another question, but Kennedy jumped in. "All right. I think that's enough questioning for one day. Can we show him the ropes?"

Anna's hands went to her hips. "He as helpless as you in the kitchen?"

Kennedy's cheeks blushed the prettiest shade of pink I'd ever seen. "I have no idea."

Anna turned back to me, pinning me with her no-bullshit stare. "You know your ass from your elbow in the kitchen?"

I chuckled. "Well, I hope I'm not using either in this kitchen."

Anna shook her head. "Too charming for your own good."

"I like it that way." She scowled at me, and I held up a hand. "I can handle the basics." I'd had no choice but to learn. When you were eight, and your mom was passed out drunk more often than not, you learned how to feed yourself.

"I'll be the judge of that." Anna spun on her heel and headed for what I assumed was the kitchen. "Hurry up, you two. Time's a-wasting."

Kennedy stifled a giggle. "Believe it or not, that was her warm welcome."

I chuckled as we followed in Anna's wake. "I'd hate to see her cold one."

Kennedy pushed open a swinging door, the red of her hair catching in the lights as she glanced over her shoulder. "Just wait till you see her put the smackdown on someone."

"I heard that," Anna called from the sink as she washed her hands.

"I wasn't trying to hide it."

Anna snapped the towel she'd been using to dry her hands in Kennedy's direction. "You watch it, missy."

I chuckled low. There was something special about Anna and Kennedy's relationship. And that tightness in my chest relaxed just a fraction at the knowledge that Kennedy had someone looking out for her here. "Tell me what I can do."

"Wash your hands first," Anna instructed.

I dipped my hands under the spray, alternating with Kennedy. She handed me the soap, her wet fingers brushing mine, reminding me of slick bodies and a whole different scenario. I pushed the thoughts from my head, soaping up my hands, rinsing, and then reaching for a towel. "Ready and reporting for duty, ma'am."

Anna pointed her spoon in my direction. "Now that's the kind of attitude I can get behind." She turned to Kennedy. "I think I should require everyone to call me ma'am."

Kennedy chuckled. "Good luck with that."

"No respect, I tell you. Come on, handsome. You're gonna help me with the meatloaf, while Kenz works on the salad. Try not to cut off a finger, would you?"

Kennedy groaned. "It was one time, and I didn't even need stitches."

Anna shook her head as she led me farther into the space. "That girl is a walking disaster in the kitchen."

I glanced over to where Kennedy was now carefully slicing an onion. "Is she going to be okay?"

The assessing stare was back. "You trying to get in her pants?"

"What?" My head jerked.

"You heard me, pretty boy."

"No, ma'am."

Anna let out a snort. "Yeah, right. She's gorgeous and has that delicate bird thing going on." She pointed her spoon at me again. "Kenz doesn't need some playboy messing with her head."

"I'm not—"

Anna cut me off before I could finish my sentence. "Of course, you are. You're hot. From the looks of it, you got money. There's no way you aren't used to getting exactly what you want."

She wasn't wrong. I couldn't remember the last time a woman had turned me down, but it didn't change the fact that I had no plans to pursue Kennedy. "She's not for me."

Anna's eyes flared. "She's not?"

"No. She's not. We're friends. That's it." We weren't even friends. But I wanted us to be. She needed someone to look out for her. Deserved it.

A delighted shriek filled the air, and I turned to see a girl who couldn't be more than three or four leap into Kennedy's outstretched arms. "Kennie!"

"Lizzie girl. I missed you." Kennedy nuzzled the little girl's neck, blowing a raspberry there. The tightness in my chest was back, but this time, it was a vise. "What have you been up to today?"

"Mom took me to pre-school, and then I've just been waiting for you. Can we have another ballet class? Can we?"

Kennedy bent, gently setting the girl on her feet. "You know it, sister. Why don't you show me how you've been practicing the positions while I finish up this salad?"

Lizzie nodded, her face taking on a serious expression as she concentrated on contorting her legs into a series of movements. Kennedy praised and encouraged the whole time. If there was any correction, it was gentle and kind, always accompanied by praise when Lizzie got it right.

"Not interested in her, my ass." The words were uttered under Anna's breath, but I heard them clear as day.

I shook myself out of my Kennedy-induced stupor and turned back to Anna. "What can I do?"

"You make a mean meatloaf." Kennedy grinned up at me as I held the community center door open for her.

"It happens to be one of my specialties." There had been a burning sensation in my chest as I'd made the dish. Low and simmering as memories assaulted me. All the times I'd made it before. Who I made it for. But the second I'd seen little Lizzie take a bite and smile hugely, it had all been worth it.

A hand brushed my arm, the contact oddly calming. "Are you okay?"

"What?" I blinked away the cobwebs and met Kennedy's concerned stare. "Sorry, just got lost in thought. All that meatloaf praise going to my head."

Kennedy dropped her hand and gave a light laugh, but it didn't quite ring true. "Well, you did an amazing job. I know I kind of backed you into coming, and it was really nice of you to do so. And to write that check."

"I'm happy to help in any way I can." My eyes bored into hers, urging her to hear that the promise was true for her, as well. She stayed silent. "I'd like to come back. Would that be okay?"

Surprise flickered across Kennedy's face. "Of course. When?"

"When are you coming back?"

"Tomorrow."

I twirled keys around my finger. "Then, tomorrow it is."

Kennedy's fingers twisted in her bag's strap again, an action I'd already learned meant that she was unsure about something. "You don't have to. I don't want to think I guilted you into something you don't want to do just because I couldn't keep my mouth shut."

I reached out, my hand covering hers, stilling her movements. "You didn't. You spoke your truth. I can only admire that." I paused for a moment, unsure if I could share what I wanted to. "The truth is, you reminded me about some pretty important things."

I stared up at the community center. "I give a lot of money to organizations like this one, but I can't tell you the last time I walked through one of their doors." The truth of that hit like a punch to the gut. When I'd started to gain success with my company, I'd given money and time. I'd even made it a requirement for my employees to volunteer, gave them paid time to do it. But slowly, that had fallen away. The monetary donations grew, and the time spent disappeared.

Kennedy squeezed my hand, bringing my attention back to her. "We all lose sight sometimes. Of what's truly important. Of all the people around us who are suffering. That doesn't mean we can't recalibrate. Reset our compass so we're facing the right direction again."

I cleared my throat and let go of Kennedy's hand. "Where's your car? I'll walk you to it."

She inclined her head towards a bike rack with one lone ten-speed chained to its metal posts. "My wheels are right here."

My body locked. "You're going to ride your bike home at eight o'clock at night?" Sure, the sky was still faintly light, but anything could happen to her. And if it did, no one would know until she didn't show up for work the next day. My heart rate sped up, and my palms dampened, my mind running away with itself at all that could happen to her in those ten hours.

"Cain, I ride my bike everywhere. It's totally safe."

I blinked rapidly, trying to clear my vision of all the images that were assaulting me. "It's not safe."

Kennedy grumbled something under her breath. "I see you've got the same overprotective streak as Tuck and Walker."

Tuck and Walker had nothing on me, but I didn't tell her that. I simply walked over to her bike. "What's the code?"

Kennedy didn't move. "Why?"

"So I can unlock your chain, put your bike in the back of my SUV, and take you home."

"No." She crossed her arms over her chest on the single word.

"No?"

"That's right. No. It's a two-letter word I'm sure you're not used to hearing much, but one I say often. I'm absolutely fine riding my bike. I've been doing it for years."

I let out a long breath, trying to remain calm, to keep the demons at bay. When I looked up at her, I knew there was an air of desperation in my gaze. "Please."

She opened her mouth, then shut it again. "Why?"

I swallowed. The movement felt like sandpaper rubbing against my throat. "I just need to know you're safe."

Kennedy studied me for a moment. "Okay."

The air came out of my lungs in a whoosh. "Thank you."

She unlocked her bike, shaking her head the whole time. "I should sit in the back and make you be my chauffeur."

I chuckled. "You're welcome to." She could put me in a damn driving cap if she wanted. Whatever it took to make sure she got home safely.

I loaded the bike into the back of my Range Rover, and we climbed in. The drive to the Kettle was mostly silent. I didn't even turn on music, just rolled down the windows and let the cool air and the songs of the crickets calm my frayed nerves. It was all the ghosts burying Karen had brought up. That was why I was on edge. It had to be. With time and distance, things would ease, go back to normal. I just had to wait it out.

I turned into the back alley behind the Kettle and pulled to a stop outside the back door. I hopped out before Kennedy could argue and grabbed her bike from the back. She took it quickly from me and rolled it over to a post where she chained it up. She shuffled her feet. "Thanks, uh, for the ride."

I chuckled. "You don't have to thank me for a ride you didn't want in the first place. Thanks for humoring me."

Kennedy grinned as she unlocked the door. A door that only had a simple deadbolt and a knob lock. "Well, as you can see, I'm safe from all bandits."

Our gazes locked, held. Some foreign energy crackling between us. "Stay that way."

"I will."

She would. I'd make sure of it.

CHAPTER
Eleven

Kennedy

THE WATER IN THE KETTLE WAS JUST STARTING TO HUM when the back door opened. "Morning," Jensen called as she strode in. Her movements were automatic as she hung her purse on a hook, slipped her sunglasses into her bag, pulled on an apron, and headed for the sink to wash up.

There was something comforting about the familiarity. The routine we both had. There was safety in the predictable. "Morning, J."

She dried her hands on a towel. "You got enough water there for two?"

"Of course." I poured the liquid over the loose-leaf tea in intricate strainers. Soon, the scent of the cherry blossom green tea filled my senses. I handed Jensen her mug. "Here you go."

She inhaled deeply. "You are an angel. Never leave me."

I chuckled. "You're stuck with me."

"Thank God." Jensen blew on her tea. "So, how did Cain do at Hope House?"

My grip on the mug tightened ever so slightly. "He was great. Everyone loved him. Even Anna."

Jensen's brows rose. "If he won over Anna, he must have been on his A-game."

"Well, he made a pretty delicious meatloaf." There were a million questions I wanted to ask Jensen about Cain. So much about him didn't add up. And then there was his minor freak-out at me riding my bike home. I would've fought him on it, but I'd seen the panic in his eyes. I swallowed a sip of tea. "What's his story?"

Jensen cupped a hand around her mug and was silent for a moment. "It's not mine to tell. I'll just say that he's been through a lot and didn't have the best home life growing up." Something in my chest tightened. "You didn't like him very much when you first met him, did you?"

I set my mug down on the counter. God, I was the worst kind of snob. Judging someone for simply having money, not allowing their actions to speak for themselves. "I haven't had the best experiences with people who have a lot of money."

Jensen studied me. "Whatever happened, I'm sorry."

That familiar burn of guilt along my sternum was back. I was hiding things from one of the kindest human beings I'd ever met. She didn't deserve it, but I didn't know how to tell her the truth. "I shouldn't have judged Cain on the size of his wallet."

A wicked grin spread over Jensen's face. "No, you should judge him on the size of his—"

"Jensen!" We both dissolved into laughter. "What are we? Twelve?"

She shrugged, wiping at tears that had gathered under her eyes. "Gotta find the laughter where you can." Her expression grew a bit more serious. "I'm glad you're giving him a second chance."

"Me, too." A frisson of something I hadn't felt in a long time slid through me. A light electrical pulse, a hum beneath my skin. I ignored it and got to work.

The bell over the door jingled, and I looked up from wiping down a table. Gleaming dark hair, piercing dark blue eyes, and a t-shirt that fit way too well based on the slight uptick in my heart rate.

"Hey, Kenz."

The sound of my nickname coming out of Cain's mouth for the first time felt way too intimate, and his gentle smile might as well have kicked me in the stomach. "Hi." The greeting came out as more of a squeak. I cleared my throat. "What are you doing here?"

"I offered to put in a security system for Jensen."

My brows pulled together. Jensen hadn't uttered a word about wanting an alarm to me. "Did something happen?"

Cain shook his head. "No, nothing like that. I offered."

Pieces came together in my mind. Cain's overprotectiveness last night. The way he had studied the locks on the door when he dropped me off. "Cain, that's not necessary."

He shrugged. "It's fun for me. And we can't have you kidnapped by bandits."

There was a forced levity in his tone that I couldn't quite understand, but I let him off the hook. Fresh starts and all that. "What do you need to get started?"

The set of Cain's shoulders seemed to ease a bit. "Just need to unlock the back door so I can grab my stuff out of my SUV."

I gestured towards the back door. "Help yourself."

Jensen appeared from the kitchen. "Oh, you're here." She crossed to us and wrapped Cain in a quick hug. He stiffened just a bit as though not used to the familiar gesture, but if Jensen noticed his hesitation, she didn't show it. "I've been meaning to get an alarm in here forever. There just never seems to be the time."

"No problem. I'm happy to help."

J turned to me. "Can you hold down the fort for a bit? I want to walk through the building with Cain."

"Of course." The lunch rush was over, and we were headed into wind-down time, so I doubted I'd be overrun with customers.

They started towards the back door, but Jensen paused and turned back. "Oh, and is it okay if we go into the studio? I just want to show him all the windows up there."

"*No*" was on the tip of my tongue. It wasn't like I had anything to hide, but there was something so personal about my space and the idea of Cain in it. I couldn't explain it, but it was like I wasn't ready. I gave my head a little shake. That was ridiculous. "Of course. Just make sure Chuck doesn't pull a Houdini."

"Thanks. We'll be careful and quick."

"Take your time." I returned to my task. Slowly and methodically wiping down all the tables, refilling pitchers of honey and jars of sugar on each one, and trying to ignore the deep voice that occasionally filtered down from above.

Footsteps sounded on the stairs, and I looked up to see Jensen. She glanced at the clock on the wall. "Shoot. I took longer than I thought. Sorry. Get out of here. I know you have ballet."

I wiped my hands on the towel and set it behind the counter. "I've got plenty of time. Don't worry about it."

"No, you don't. At least, let me handle Chuck's walk."

I grinned. "You know that would make his day. Thank you." Chuck loved Jensen, probably because she snuck him bacon from the savory scones she made each morning.

"No problem. Now, skedaddle." She shooed me on.

"Sir, yes, sir." I jogged up the steps, laughing as I went, but came to a screeching halt at my open door. Cain was crouched, examining the lock. "What are you doing?"

He looked up. "Putting in an alarm. This lock is actually pretty good. I don't think it needs to be replaced, but there will be sensors on all your windows, a keypad on this inside wall here. I could do motion sensors, but you have a dog." He inclined his head towards my bed, where Chuck was snoring away. "Though I don't get the sense he moves much."

"I don't need an alarm." It was such a waste.

"Sure, you do."

"Cain. It's not like someone is going to drag a ladder over here and climb up two stories to try and break in and steal... what? My five books?" I gestured to the handful of worn paperbacks on my shelf.

Cain's jaw tightened. "There are bad people in this world. It's better to be safe."

I fought the urge to throw something at him. I didn't need any of this. My stomach twisted as I took in all the gadgets strewn across the floor. How much money did all of this cost? Hundreds of dollars, at least. Maybe thousands. My mouth went dry. How many more worthwhile things could that money be spent on?

I squeezed my eyes closed. It wasn't my money. I couldn't decide how it was spent. "Fine. I need to grab a bag and go, so please don't set the alarm until I know how to use it. The last thing I need is to wake up the entire town when I don't know how to shut the damn thing off." I crossed to my closet, footsteps a bit heavier than necessary, and reached for my dance bag.

"Where are you going?"

I tossed a leotard and my pointe shoes into the bag, not looking up. "I'm teaching a class in twenty minutes."

"A class?" Cain's voice was closer now. I still didn't look up.

I threw in a sweatshirt for my bike ride home. "Yup. I teach ballet."

Cain let out an exasperated sigh. "How many jobs do you have?"

I straightened and turned. "Two. Why? Is it a crime to work hard?"

"Of course, not." He opened his mouth to say something else, but then seemed to think better of it. "Are you riding your bike?"

"Yup." I lifted the bag over my shoulder and headed for the door.

"Hold on a sec."

I turned to face Cain, annoyance tingling under my skin now. "Yes?"

He looked sheepish now, almost a little hesitant. "I have a friend who owns a dealership near here. I think he'd lend you a car until you're ready to buy one."

My jaw fell open. If there had been a fly nearby, it would've flown right in. "Lend me a car?"

Cain's expression brightened, mistaking my dumbfounded shock for excitement. "Yeah, I can give him a call in a few. I'm sure he could have one here by tomorrow."

My hands tightened around the strap of my dance bag, and I did my best to keep my voice calm and even. "What have I said or done that has given you the impression that I want a vehicle?"

He looked almost a little bewildered now. Adorably so, but I pushed that down. "You don't have one."

"Did it ever occur to you that I don't have a car because I don't want one?" And I didn't. I could've scrounged together the money for one, but it would've been a waste. I didn't *need* one, and I was done with being wasteful. "I am perfectly capable of providing everything that I need for myself. I don't need you sweeping in here, thinking you're some white knight who's going to fix everything for the poor Cinderella. I've got everything I need. So, just stop."

I didn't give him a chance to say another word. I didn't trust myself not to do something incredibly stupid, like throw one of his ridiculously expensive gadgets at the wall. I turned on my heel and stormed out.

I jogged down the stairs and was met by Jensen. "What was all that about?"

I held up a hand. "I can't right now. I'll talk to you about it tomorrow."

Jensen nodded slowly. "Okay. Ride carefully, you're upset."

I pulled her into a quick hug. "Thank you." Tears threatened behind those words. I held them back until I was riding away. My emotions were all over the place. Anger. Frustration. Guilt. Shame. I let myself cry it out; the wind stinging my face where the tears tracked down my cheeks. I'd let it out as much as I could, and then I'd bottle it back up. Just like I always did.

CHAPTER
Twelve

Cain

"F UCK."

Jensen's face appeared in the doorway. "What the hell happened?"

I swiped a hand over my face. "I might've overstepped my boundaries." That was a giant-ass understatement.

Jensen glanced around at the array of sensors, wires, keypads, and other gadgetry. "Uh, Cain? I said you could put some sensors in here, but you didn't need to wire Fort Knox."

I sat down on the end of Kennedy's bed. "I got a little carried away."

J took a seat on the couch opposite me. "What's all this about?"

Jensen knew my story—the broad strokes anyway. The finer details were mine to carry, and mine alone. "Something triggered me last night." Jensen stayed quiet, letting me get to it in my own time. "Kenz was going to ride that damn bike home after eight at night, and my thoughts just started spinning, and I couldn't seem to get a hold of them. Each scenario that flashed through my brain was worse than the one before."

"And that's why you drove her home?" Jensen's voice was gentle, holding not even a hint of judgment.

I nodded. "When I dropped her off, I saw that there were only basic locks on the back door, and my mind started cycling again. How easy it would be to break in. That no one would be around to hear Kennedy scream if something happened." I forced my eyes closed, trying to block out the images, the memories. A wet, rough tongue licked at my hand. My lids flew open to see a brown and white face looking up at me as if to say, *"it's okay."* I gave the dog a scratch behind the ears. He started to drool.

"Cain." My gaze rose to meet Jensen's. "Is this about Kiara?"

I don't think Jensen had ever spoken her name out loud to me. Maybe at the funeral, but that time was all a blur. "It always is." The grin I gave her was sad more than anything else.

"It wasn't your fault."

Fire licked at the back of my throat. I'd heard the words a million times before, and never once had I believed them. "I knew my mom was a basket case. I shouldn't have left Kiara with her." I rose and began to pace. "But I just had to go to college, use that fancy scholarship."

"You had an opportunity to make a better life. For you and your sister. Can you tell me for one second that you were going to leave Kiara and never look back?"

I ran a hand through my hair. Of course, I wasn't. I'd had a plan. *We'd* had a plan. I studied my ass off in high school, worked nights and weekends, saving every penny I could for my and Kiara's college funds. God knew my mother wasn't saving anything, it all went to her booze and a premium cable TV package.

Then, I'd gotten a scholarship to Portland University. One of the best criminal justice programs on the west coast and their computer programming department hadn't sucked either. Kiara and I had made a new plan. I'd go to college, keep working and saving so that we'd have enough to send her to university when she graduated two years later.

I'd checked in with her every day. She'd never said a word about Mom slipping from drinking into drugs. Not a single hint that Mom had started bringing sketchy guys back to the house for parties. My little sister, who was better than I would ever be, kept silent so I could have my fucking dream.

But what good was that fucking dream when she'd lain dying hours away? My breaths started to come quicker. I couldn't seem to hold on to the air.

Jensen rose and crossed to me. "Breathe, Cain. Just breathe."

I watched J's chest rise and fall and copied the movements. *Fuck.* I'd thought I had put these panic attacks to rest. It had been so long since my entire life had crumbled around me. I'd learned to control it all—my fears, my anxiety. I'd built a life where I didn't have to feel any of those things, and that was the way I liked it. Then, my mom had to invade my city. Even in death, she was able to ignite the pain of all the wounds she'd inflicted over the years.

Jensen pulled me in for a hard hug. "I know my hugs make you feel awkward and uncomfortable, but you're just going to have to suck it up. You're loved, Cain Hale, and there's nothing you can do to change that."

The burn in my throat was back. "I'm going to tell Tuck you hugged me for so long."

J laughed into my neck. "Good. It'll keep him on his toes." She slowly released me. "You going to be okay?"

I nodded. God, I hated that J had gotten this glimpse into all the insanity that swirled in my mind. But there was nothing I could do about it now. "I'm going to dial back the security in here."

Jensen grinned. "Probably a good idea." Her brow furrowed. "Was this what got Kenz all upset?"

I scrubbed a hand over my jaw. "This was part of it, but I think the kicker was when I told her I had a friend who owned a car dealership who could loan her a car."

Jensen dropped her face into her hands and slowly shook her head. When she looked up, I could tell she was trying desperately to hold in her laughter. "You don't have a friend who owns a dealership here."

My lips pressed together in a firm line. "I could have a friend you don't know about."

J couldn't hold her laughter in any longer. "But you don't. You were going to buy her a freaking car, weren't you?"

Heat crept up the back of my neck. "Don't be crazy." I paused as Jensen arched a brow at me. "I was going to lease one."

Jensen's laughter grew until tears rolled down her face. "Oh, Cain. You picked the wrong girl."

"What do you mean?"

J straightened, her laughter subsiding. "She's not charmed by expensive gifts. In fact, I'd say they have the opposite effect. I mean, look around you."

My gaze traveled over the space that was Kennedy's. Everything about it said simple and homey. The two-seater table in the kitchen had an old jar she'd turned into a vase by tying a ribbon around it and filling it with the wildflowers from the field behind the Kettle. The bookcase held worn paperbacks, a photo of her and a blond young man from at least ten years ago that burned my gut, and more jars. These jars were painted with the word *gratitude*. There were a few that were full of slips of paper, and one that was three-quarters of the way there.

The quilt on her bed was worn and housed a snoring-again dog, though the pup looked to be purebred, looks could be deceiving. The door to her closet was still open, and there were hardly any clothes inside. Fewer than any other woman's wardrobe I'd seen.

"She likes to live simply."

Jensen's words brought my gaze back to her. "I'm getting that."

She patted my arm. "Give her a chance to get to know you. Are you going back to Hope House?"

I'd planned on it, but I wasn't sure Kennedy would greet me with open arms now. "Tonight."

"Good."

"I'm not interested in her like that." The lie tasted bitter on my tongue. "I just want to be her friend." Now, I sounded like a five-year-old. Great. I shoved a hand through my hair.

Jensen's lips twitched. "Whatever you say, bigshot." She glanced down at the mess around us. "Now, what are you going to do about all of this?"

I grimaced. "I still want to put a system in here, but I promise I won't go overboard."

"Sounds like a plan. I have to go pick up Noah, but here's an extra set of keys. Lock up on your way out?"

I caught the keys as she tossed them to me. "No problem. And I'll swing back by tomorrow morning to finish setting things up and to walk you through the system."

"Thanks, Cain." Jensen looked as if she were fighting the urge to hug me again. "You're a good man."

Her words seared my skin, but I said nothing. She shook her head. "I'll see you tomorrow."

I buckled down and got to work, doing everything I could to push the lingering memories from my mind. I focused on wires and sensors. There was so much out of my control, but giving Kennedy a safe home was something I could do, paying things forward just a bit.

My phone buzzed in my pocket. Pulling it out, I gave the screen a quick glance. "Hale."

"It's Jake."

His tone told me all I needed to know. "What's wrong?"

"We lost the Criterion account to Raider."

I sucked in air. They weren't one of our biggest, but it was still a blow. "What did they say?"

"They're making cutbacks, and another company offered tech and software similar to ours at a more affordable price."

My grip on my phone tightened. "Were you able to figure out the price break?"

"Twenty percent less than our starting packages."

It didn't add up. Either Raider was cutting corners on their equipment, or they were paying their employees next to nothing. Unless they had succeeded in getting their hands on some of our software. If they'd stolen that and didn't have to pay anyone to develop their own, they just might be able to offer those prices. "I want a full diagnostic on our systems."

"What? Why? What we need is a game plan to make some cuts so we can compete with Raider's pricing structure."

I began packing up the last of my gear on the floor. "Run the diagnostic. I'm almost positive they got in and stole some software. Tell Pete I want a report in an hour. Call my cell."

"Fine. But we need to discuss a game plan."

We needed a game plan, all right, but I wouldn't be discussing it with him. For all I knew, he or someone else in-house could've given someone a back door into our system. Anyone on the alpha team could have. Right now, there wasn't a single person at my own damn company that I could trust.

CHAPTER
Thirteen

Kennedy

LATE. I WAS SO FREAKING LATE. AND IT WAS ALL CAIN Hale's fault. It had been years since I'd been that frustrated with someone. The more space I got from my outburst, the more I wondered if I'd overreacted. But second-guessing myself just pissed me off more.

I had started over. And the gift of erasing my past, of being a blank canvas, was that I got to decide what my life looked like. I got to choose whether I drove a car or rode a bike or...hell, if I trained a donkey and trotted all over town. It was my choice, and mine alone.

I drew up short as I entered the rec room space of the shelter. Lizzie was sitting on a chair, her back to Cain, legs swinging. She chatted up a storm as he braided her hair. And it wasn't an awkward, uneven design either. He was weaving her hair into two intricate French braids without a single strand out of place.

What the heck? Nothing about this man added up. And yet again, I had to swallow my judgmental assumptions.

I slowly walked towards the duo, listening as Lizzie recounted the trip to a farm her preschool had taken that day. "They had *three* pigs and more chickens than I could count. There were horses, and I reeeeeally wanted to ride one, but my teacher said no because I didn't have pah-mission."

Cain nodded along with her chatter. "I would've wanted to ride one, too."

Lizzie gave a little jolt in her chair, twisting to face him. "Maybe we can find a horse to ride together!"

Cain expertly followed her jerky motions, moving his hands so there was no pull on her hair, but he didn't lose his hold on her braid either. "I think that sounds like a great plan. I'll see what I can find." He tied a bright pink rubber band around her pigtail.

"Kennie!" Lizzie leaped up and ran straight for me.

The collision knocked me back a step and startled a laugh out of me. "Hey, you."

"Look what Cain did! Look at my braids!" She twirled in a circle, her pigtails swinging out around her.

"You are stylin', Lizzie." I tugged on one of the braids as she came to a stop. "I love them." My gaze tangled with Cain's over Lizzie's head. "This is pretty impressive."

Cain rubbed at the back of his neck. "Better at braids than meddling where I shouldn't, apparently."

My lips twitched. "It's good to recognize where your calling lies."

Cain's shoulders eased a fraction, and he pushed to his feet. "I'll try to remember that."

Lizzie's head swung back and forth as if she were watching a tennis match. "What's meddlin'?"

Cain chuckled. "It's when you stick your nose in something that's none of your business."

Lizzie nodded as if she had a deep understanding of the issue. "My mom says I do that a whole lot. But I just want to know what's going on."

"I have the same problem, Lizzie." Cain turned to me. "Is it okay that I'm here?"

My cheeks heated as guilt flooded me. "Of course. You're always welcome." Anyone who could put this kind of look on Lizzie's face would be.

He gave me a small smile. "I'm not sure Doug agrees." He inclined his head to where the director stood in the corner with a clipboard and a scowl.

"He'll get used to you."

"I'm not so sure about that."

Anna poked her head out from the kitchen. "Hey, lovebirds, get with the program. This chili isn't going to cook itself, and I need to see if that meatloaf was a fluke or if Handsome there is the next top chef."

I couldn't hold in my laugh, but Lizzie gasped. "Are you guys boyfriend and girlfriend?"

I gave a quick shake of my head. "No, honey. We're just"—I paused for a second—"friends." It wasn't entirely true, but maybe we could be.

Lizzie looked to Cain. "You should ask her to be your girlfriend. Tommy asked me to be his girlfriend, and now we're getting married."

Cain's brows furrowed. "Who's Tommy?"

I tugged on his arm. "Come on, oh, overprotective one. We've got chili to cook."

Cain looked behind him at a giggling Lizzie as I pulled him towards the kitchen. "But I need Tommy's last name if I'm going to run a background check."

The night had flown by. The shelter was a full house, with one of our residents getting a cake to celebrate his new job, and a youth group serving dinner. Everything was madness and mayhem in the best possible way. Nights like these filled my soul. Gave me hope.

There were good people in the world. Ones who would do anything to help someone struggling. And there was always time for a second chance at life. I saw it every time one of the residents graduated out of temporary housing with a job and a real home. It reminded me that anything was possible for me, too.

Cain pulled the door open for me, and the cool air hit me in a blast. I pulled my sweatshirt out of my bag. "Just when you think summer's around the corner."

"It's that mountain air." Cain shuffled his feet as he waited for me to unlock my bike. "Can we talk?"

My stomach flipped. "Sure. Want to give me a ride home?"

Cain chuckled, the sound seeming to slide over my skin, a wave of invisible vibrations. "You know I do."

I grinned into the night. "Bandits are always afoot."

He took my bike from my hold and steered it towards his SUV. "There could be a herd of rabid deer."

"Heaven forbid those guys get me."

In a matter of minutes, we were settled in Cain's vehicle and heading towards the Kettle. Cain shifted in his seat, the leather creaking in the silence. "I'm sorry I overstepped. I did get a system in your apartment, but I dialed back the setup."

I let out a breath. "Thank you."

"And I hear you about the car. I just—" He shifted again, adjusting his hold on the steering wheel. "I have a need to fix things."

My body stiffened. "I don't need to be fixed, Cain. I'm doing just fine. Better than." If he knew the wreckage I'd come from, maybe he'd be able to see. Money, *things*, they didn't always solve everything. Sometimes, they made it so much worse.

Cain winced. "I know *you* don't need to be fixed. I just saw a situation that could be improved. I have the ability to do it, so why not help?"

"Improved for *you*. My bike, my life…it's how I want it."

He ran a hand through his hair, distressing it into artful waves. "I'm getting that."

I studied him in the darkness, trying to see past his careful words. There was something below the surface. The *why* of it all. "Where does this come from?"

Cain gripped the wheel tighter, his knuckles bleaching white. "I lost someone I cared about."

My chest constricted in a painful squeeze. "I'm sorry."

He shook his head. "I just wanted to make sure you were safe. And, sometimes, I can go a bit overboard with all of that stuff."

There were so many questions I wanted to ask. But I knew if I asked a single one, I'd be inviting the same. And that was a door I simply couldn't open. "Thanks for telling me." He nodded into the dark. My voice was as gentle as I could make it. "But I'm not giving up my bike."

The hands on the wheel tightened again. "Will you let me drive you home after Hope House, at least?"

What harm would that do? Cain wasn't going to be around forever. He'd take his vacation here for a season, and then he'd head back to Portland. To his real life. This was simply a break from reality for him. "For now."

Cain's lips twitched. "I'll take it."

CHAPTER
Fourteen

Cain

I PULLED TO A STOP BEHIND THE KETTLE. THE URGE TO check out the whole building before Kennedy went inside was so strong. The security system wasn't in place yet. I beat it back, my eyes scanning the windows. No movement. Everything was fine.

"Why did you come to Sutter Lake?"

The question caught me off guard. I thought for sure Kenz would have asked something about who I'd lost. How? What had happened? But she'd let me off the hook. I studied her face, searching for what, I wasn't sure. "I needed to get away. Needed some peace and quiet to deal with a few things." It was a bit of a cop-out answer, and I knew it. I had the urge to give her more, but I couldn't give her anything that would lead to discussions of Kiara. "And someone's attacking my company from the inside. I don't know who I can trust. It helps to have a place away from all that to work on a project that's the future of Halo—my company. One that, if it fell into my competition's hands, would sink me."

Kennedy's eyes flared as if she were shocked that I'd given her so much information. But unless she was the best actress I'd ever met, this was not someone I needed to worry about revealing my secrets. "I'm sorry you're dealing with all of that."

"Me, too." Paul had done the survey of our system, and someone had, in fact, been let in through backdoor means. Three different programs had been compromised. Tonight, I'd work on the system remotely, shoring up our defenses and reworking things so every entry point would require two employees to access it. Well, for everyone but me.

"Is there anything I can do?" Kennedy's voice was kind, honest, true.

I grinned at her. "You can let me drive you home."

She rolled her eyes. "I already agreed."

I shrugged. "It helps."

"Well, then I best be getting you that driving cap."

I chuckled. "I'm officially warned."

We hopped out of the SUV, and I lifted her bike out so she could lock it up again. "Here." I handed her the set of keys Jensen had given me. "Jensen gave me these so I could lock up."

Her eyes narrowed in mock assessment. "You didn't paw through my underwear drawer, did you?"

My laughter deepened. "No, but your dog did drool on me."

Pink hit her cheeks. "Sorry about that. He's got overactive salivary glands."

"Is that the technical diagnosis?"

She smiled, and it felt like a physical blow. I thought I'd seen her smile before, at Jensen or Lizzie or Anna, but I hadn't. Nothing like this. It was full and unabashed and so damn beautiful it almost hurt to look at her. "It means he likes you. He gifted you with his drool."

I swallowed hard, trying to clear my throat. "I'll try to remember that."

Kennedy's feet shuffled against the pavement. "I need to head up. I've got an early day tomorrow."

"I'll be by in the morning to finish the system and show you how it works."

"No sensors that are going to blow me or Chuck up if we step on the wrong floorboard, right?"

"Chuck?" Who the hell was Chuck?

She laughed. "Mr. Drool."

The tension that had seeped into my muscles eased. "You and Mr. Drool are safe from spontaneous combustion."

Kennedy swept a hand over her brow. "Phew."

"Goodnight, Kenz."

Her gaze met mine. "Goodnight, Cain."

I watched as she unlocked the door, waited until I heard the deadbolt slide back into place, and even longer until I saw a light come on upstairs. She was home. Safe.

I climbed into my Rover and hit a button on my console. "Call Murphy."

It rang a few times before someone answered. "Cain, how are you? It's been too long."

I headed down the alley and turned towards home. "I'm sorry for calling so late."

"It's not even nine. And you know you can call anytime you need."

I did. And that, in and of itself, was a gift. "Something happened."

"Are you all right?" The sound of a door closing came across the line.

"I'm fine. I just...something triggered me." More like some*one*.

"Walk me through it."

I started with what had brought me to Sutter Lake, all that had happened at my company, being back with Tuck and Walker, and finally meeting Kennedy. "I don't know. I just get the impression that she's hiding from something, and when

I saw her getting ready to ride that bike home all by herself, it flipped something in me."

Murphy cleared his throat. The sound was so familiar, one I'd heard session after session. "How long has it been since you spent any real time in a small town or any place similar to where you grew up?"

"Not more than a couple of days since I buried Kiara." There was that burn at the back of my throat again at the mention of her name.

"I want to acknowledge that in and of itself. Places hold power, memories, reminders. I think it says a lot that you're facing all of that. Especially given everything that burying your mother must have brought up."

I blew out a harsh breath. "But I'm losing it. I wanted to wire this girl's—someone I barely know, by the way—apartment like it was the Pentagon. I wanted to buy her a car. I've only known her for a couple of weeks."

Something tapped in the background, most likely a pen against Murphy's desk. "Kiara had a bike that she rode everywhere. Didn't she?"

My jaw turned to granite, so rock-hard I thought it might crack. Visions assailed me. A teal bike with a woven basket. I'd even gotten one of those silly bells to put on it. I couldn't afford to buy her a car, so I'd gotten her a damn bike. "She did." My voice was ragged, as though I'd just smoked a full pack of cigarettes.

"Places *and* items hold power, Cain. Cut yourself some slack. I think you're doing remarkably well." Murphy paused for a moment, seeming to choose his words carefully. "I don't think it would hurt to start up our sessions again, however. We can do them over the phone."

I swallowed hard. "I don't want this to turn into another situation like Janie."

"It won't. You'd just lost your sister, Cain. It was understandable that you fixated on keeping the other woman in your life safe."

I let out a laugh that was nothing but ugly. Dr. Murphy was always letting me off the hook, trying to get me to be more forgiving of myself. But he hadn't smothered his girlfriend so much that she'd cheated. And he hadn't beaten the guy she'd cheated with to the point of unconsciousness.

Memories assaulted me. The sheer panic every time Janie had left my sight. The incessant phone calls to make sure she was all right. Finding her at that frat house. Totally and completely losing it.

Miraculously, the guy hadn't pressed charges, and I hadn't been kicked out of school. A murdered sister bought you some leeway, apparently. But Janie had transferred schools, leaving me with only the knowledge that I had ruined the last good thing in my life.

If it weren't for Walker and Tuck, I didn't think I would have made it. I would've drowned at the bottom of a bottle of whiskey. They'd found Dr. Murphy. For the first three months, one of them had driven me to Murphy's office three days a week, knowing that if they didn't, I wouldn't have gone.

It wasn't that I was against seeking help. I'd known I needed it. Desperately. It was just that everything felt like too much effort. I was moving through life with an extra five hundred pounds on my back. The weight of guilt and shame and sorrow.

Slowly, things began to change. The weight shifted. There were days when it still felt as if it would drag me down, but there were others where it only felt like a suitcase I was dragging behind me. That was the thing about grief, it was ever-changing. The most hopeful thing of all was the knowledge that no state I found myself in was final.

"Cain." Murphy's voice jolted me back into the present

moment. "You've come so far. But your coping mechanism has always been to cut out anything that might cause you to stumble, to struggle."

I bristled at that. I wasn't afraid of a challenge. I'd built Halo from the ground up, started with no more than five hundred dollars in my pocket, and the determination to succeed. That didn't mean I wasn't terrified to fail, but I let every failure teach me, fuel me, spur me on.

"I'm not talking about business or your boxing or any other task that you've set your mind to accomplishing, Cain. You are one of the smartest and most hardworking people I know." My shoulders eased a bit. "I'm talking about emotionally."

The tension in my muscles ramped right back up. "I'm being cautious."

Murphy sighed. "Drinking was a crutch. You're not an addict, but you cut it out entirely. Caring for another woman caused you fear, so you cut out women altogether."

I punched in the code to my gate a little more forcefully than necessary. "I haven't exactly been celibate, Doc."

"Fine. You avoid any women you have the potential to care about."

"I have female friends. Jensen and Sarah." I didn't know why I was arguing, he was right.

"Both of whom you have no sexual interest in, am I right?" I stayed silent. "I'm right. I've got your first assignment."

I threw my SUV into park in front of my house. "You and your damn assignments. I didn't miss those one bit."

Murphy chuckled. "I want you to find reasons to be around Kennedy. And I want you to live in the uncomfortable feelings that come up. Breathe into them. But don't do anything to get them to go away. Don't try to manage them."

I hissed out a breath. "I'm volunteering at the shelter with her."

"That's perfect. Start keeping a journal. Track what comes up. And we'll talk in a few days."

"I'm worried I won't be able to control it. That I'll lose it again." Just saying the words made me feel so incredibly weak.

"You called me for help *before* things got bad. You're so much stronger now. Wiser. Whether we like it or not, grief is sometimes our greatest teacher."

I'd give back every ounce of wisdom and strength if I could just have one more afternoon at the pond with Kiara. One more trip to the ice cream parlor. One more movie night where we laughed ourselves sick. "I have to go." The raggedness in my voice was back.

"Okay. Be kind to yourself, Cain."

"Talk soon, Doc." I hung up and headed straight for the garage, thanking the universe that my gym equipment had been delivered with my furniture. I didn't bother changing. Simply unbuttoned my shirt and hung in on a weight rack. I slipped on the boxing gloves and began slow, testing jabs on the bag.

The hits picked up speed, force. I lost myself in the rhythm. In the sounds. I let out everything I'd kept so tightly bottled up for the past twenty-four hours. I unleashed all the ugliness I held inside, the self-hatred, the pain, focused it all on the bag.

I didn't stop until I could barely hold up my arms. My chest heaved, and sweat poured off me in waves. But the pain. There was barely a dent in that.

CHAPTER
Fifteen

Kennedy

THE GRASS TICKLED MY TOES AS I ARCHED MY ACHING feet. I was so very glad to have this afternoon off from dance and not just because it meant a trip to the park with Chuck. Dancing in pointe shoes that needed to be replaced meant that I'd bruised a toenail pretty badly.

I was used to dancing through pain, but this was just stupid. I needed new shoes. I opened up my notebook and wrote down my upcoming expenses, wincing when I remembered to add the cost of Annabeth's classes for the month. I could take some of the end-of-the-day baked goods home with me, but that meant less for the shelter.

I nibbled on the end of my pen. Maybe I could offer to take over one of Seraphina's classes for extra hours. If I got the cheap pointe shoes, it would all work out. I scratched between Chuck's ears. "We'll figure it out."

I pulled out a piece of paper from the notebook and tore it into five strips. "A little reminder never hurt anyone." Chuck let out a snore of agreement.

I paused for a moment before I began writing, tapping the

pen to my lips. *Sunshine afternoons at the park with Chuck.* I folded the slip and tucked it into the back of my journal so I could place it in my jar when I got home, then repeated the process.

The perfect marionberry muffin. The ability to help Annabeth stay in dance class. I looked around, my gaze settling on the worn library hardback. *Rereading an old favorite. Lizzie's smile when Cain braided her hair.*

My thoughts began to wander, dark blue eyes flashing in my mind. I shook my head. "Not for you, girl." I needed to date someone like Doug. My stomach turned at the thought. That wasn't fair to Doug, but there was simply no spark there. No fire. Nothing that drew me to him in a way that felt effortlessly magnetic.

I flipped my journal closed and picked up the mini tennis ball. "Want to play?"

Chuck perked right up. You'd never know he was a senior citizen. He hopped up and down, letting out a playful growl. I laughed and let the ball fly, throwing it as far as I could. Chuck took off like a rocket.

There was something about his brown floppy ears flapping in the wind like they were wings that might help him take flight that put the biggest dopey grin on my face. He dropped the drool-soaked ball in my lap, and I groaned. "Really, Chuck?" He only barked his demand that I throw it again. I, of course, obeyed.

On the way back, he was side-tracked by a woman with a dog who looked like Chuck's twin. She waved. "How do you get him to fetch? I can barely get Louie off the couch."

I grinned. "Chuck sleeps about twenty out of twenty-four hours. But bring out a tennis ball, and he's a different dog."

She returned my smile and walked a few steps closer. "Did you get him around here? My husband and I are looking for another Cavalier breeder because ours retired."

I forced my muscles to stay relaxed. It was a normal question. "No, nowhere near here, unfortunately."

"Drat." Chuck came back and dropped the ball into my lap yet again. "Louie, learn from him, would you?" The dog just looked up at his owner with a happy pant, and the woman sighed. "I'm Laura, by the way."

I gave a little wave. "Kennedy. It's nice to meet you."

"You, too. Well, we'll let you get back to fetch, but I'm sure we'll see you around. Maybe we can have a doggie playdate."

"That'd be fun." As I watched Laura and Louie walk off, I realized I'd meant what I said. It would be fun. I wasn't as hesitant to let others in as I once was. Sure, I was careful, but I had friends now. A community.

My phone buzzed next to me, and I glanced down. *Davis Barrington has been granted parole.* A lead weight settled in my belly. Less than two years in prison and my father was going free. Those acid tears gathered at the backs of my eyes again. Emotions all over the map swirled within me.

I squeezed my eyes closed, pulling my knees to my chest as I let my head fall. I couldn't imagine what a life in prison, even one for white-collar crimes, would be like. But I knew none of it was pleasant. I didn't want my father hurt or in pain, but I also longed for justice for his victims. Who decided what was just, though? I knew it wasn't less than two years in prison before walking free. Yet there was a bit of relief that my dad would be safe now. How did I come to terms with the emotions warring inside me?

How could you love someone and hate them at the same time? I loved my father, but I hated what he'd become. What he'd turned me into. A face I couldn't look at in the mirror. A liar. A thief. The reason that four people were dead. How did I live with what my own life had cost others?

"Why are you scowling?" I looked back down to the onion I was chopping so I didn't accidentally cut off a finger. My head hadn't exactly been in the game since learning that my father was about to walk free.

Anna's scowl deepened. "I'm not scowling."

My lips twitched. "It just got worse."

"Whatever." She poured a can of tomatoes into a large pot.

"Come on, tell me."

"There's a new resident, and I don't trust him."

My laughter deepened. "You're paranoid." Anna got this way about every new resident. She trusted no one until they passed her test. What that test was, I had no idea. I could just tell when someone had made the cut.

Anna pelted a carrot at me as the kitchen door swung open. "What's going on in here?"

That deep voice skittered across my skin, leaving chill bumps in its wake. "Just Anna thinking the new resident is one of your bandits."

Cain's expression grew serious as he looked to Anna. "You don't like someone?"

"It's not a matter of like, it's a matter of trust. This one"— she pointed at me with the can opener in her hand—"is far too trusting."

I rolled my eyes. "No, I'm just not paranoid like the two of you." I knew there were plenty of bad people in the world. And I knew better than most that they could be closer than you ever would've guessed.

Cain leaned against the counter. "Get me his full name, and I'll run him."

Anna opened her mouth to agree, but I waved a hand between them. "Oh, no, you don't. Doug runs a background check on anyone who comes through that door. This poor man deserves his privacy. He doesn't need you two playing Charlie's Angels."

Cain's lips twitched in a way that had my eyes zeroing right in on his mouth. "I hope I'm Charlie."

"No, you're the one who wears the low-cut catsuit."

He shook his head and crossed to the sink, sticking his hands under the spray. "So, angels, what's on the menu tonight?"

Anna grinned. "Spaghetti, garlic bread, and salad."

"One of my favorites." He wiped his hands on a towel.

My gaze followed the movement, focusing on his knuckles. They were bruised. What had he—? "Oh, shit!" I dropped the knife on the cutting board, but it was too late. Blood seeped from my finger where it had a nice, long gash. "Shit, shit, shit."

Cain was in front of me in a flash. "Kenz, what—? Oh, fuck." He instantly pressed the towel to my wound. "Here, sit down on the stool." He ushered me back to the seat. "Anna, do you have a first-aid kit?"

She was one step ahead of him and unzipped a kit on the island in the middle of the kitchen. "I told you to be careful. When will you learn?" She pulled out some sort of antibacterial spray, gauze, and tape.

Cain carefully removed the towel. "This might need stitches."

I shook my head fiercely. "No stitches."

He probed the wound, and I winced. "Scared of needles?"

"Something like that." I was scared of an emergency room bill when I didn't have health insurance.

Cain continued assessing the wound. "Anna, do you have super glue in the office?"

"What in the devil for?"

"Just trust me."

"All right." She headed for the office.

Cain met my gaze. "It hurt?"

I swallowed hard. "It doesn't feel like puppy kisses."

"We'll get you fixed up." He shook the bottle of antibacterial spray and coated my finger. I sucked in a breath. "Shit. I didn't think it would hurt, or I would've warned you." He blew gently on my hand.

"Sometimes, it's better not to know the hurt's coming."

Cain's eyes met mine again, the dark blue in them almost seeming to glow. "Never can prepare for pain, I guess."

"I found some!" Anna jogged back into the kitchen. "Jeez, you two look like you're about to make out. How can you make almost slicing off a finger look sexy?"

I choked on my laugh, but Cain just held out a hand for the glue. Anna huffed. "'Thank you, Anna, for running your sweet ass to the office and back. I really appreciate it.' Is that too much to ask?"

Cain shot Anna a grin that would've melted the panties off a nun. "Thank you, gorgeous." He made an exaggerated motion of checking out her backside. "And that ass is sweet."

Anna began fanning herself. "Boy, you are lethal."

"Glad you know it." He focused back on my hand, pinching the sides of the wound together.

I squeezed my eyes closed. "Is that really necessary?"

"If you refuse to go to the hospital like a sane person, then yes, it is."

I felt something liquid and cool hit my finger. It stung but only slightly. Then there was more blowing air. I kept my eyes firmly closed.

Cain squeezed my hand. "All done."

I cracked open a single eyelid. My cut was sealed closed, and the glue was dry. "How'd you know to do that?"

A shadow passed over his eyes, and I was immediately sorry I'd asked. "Secrets of a misspent youth." He said the words with a smile, but it was forced. A lie. I hated that smile just a little bit. "Since I'm the doctor on record in this case, you're going to have to let me examine your hand once in a while, make sure it's not infected."

I rolled my eyes and tried to remove my hand from his grasp, but Cain held firm. "That's the deal, or I throw you over my shoulder and drive you to the nearest hospital right now."

I threw up my free hand. "Oh, fine." I muttered something about overprotective alpha males under my breath.

Cain ignored me and placed the offending knife and bloodied cutting board in the sink. "And I think you're done with knives for a while."

"What else am I supposed to do around here?" The things I was allowed to help with in the kitchen had become a dwindling list.

Anna pressed her lips together, trying to hold in her laughter. "You can do the dishes."

Cain looked to Anna. "Maybe we should get her one of those metal gloves some chefs wear."

Anna grinned. "We're probably better off just getting her a full body suit made out of the stuff."

Cain shook a finger at her in agreement. "Not a bad idea."

I let some sort of annoyed growl escape. "I hope you both sit on an extra-prickly cactus." They dissolved into laughter. "You can make dinner yourselves. I'm going to hang out with Lizzie."

CHAPTER
Sixteen

Cain

I PUSHED THROUGH THE KITCHEN DOOR AND OUT TO THE rec room to tell Kenz we were ready to serve dinner. What I saw halted me in my tracks: Kennedy executing a series of spins, jumps, and contortions. How was it possible for a body to even bend like that? Her hair, not tied back, flew around her, the red in it catching in the gleam of the overhead lights. She was breathtaking. Graceful. Powerful. And something so unique, I couldn't find a word to capture it.

As she came to a halt on the other end of the room, Lizzie jumped up and down, clapping and squealing. "Kennie! I want to do that! Can you teach me? Can you?"

Kennedy laughed as Lizzie sailed towards her. "I sure can. But it's going to take a lot of practice. Think you can do that?"

Lizzie nodded in earnest. "I'll practice every day after preschool."

Kennedy wrapped her in a hug. "You'll get there in no time."

"That was impressive." My voice seemed to catch in my throat as I spoke, as though I'd forgotten how to talk.

Kennedy started at the sound. "I didn't see you there."

"You were pretty focused. That was amazing, Kenz. Where'd you learn to dance like that?"

A flicker of shadow passed over her eyes, and her shoulders seemed to tense. "I studied ballet for a long time."

It was a non-answer. Obviously, she'd studied. You didn't get to be that good without endless hours of classes and practice. But I'd gone on a few dates with a ballerina, and I knew that those kinds of classes, the ones that taught at such a high level, didn't come cheap.

I wanted to push. To force her to give me more. To find out what had caused that shadow, to make sure there wasn't a threat of whatever it was returning. I pushed it down. *Live in the uncomfortable.* I said it over and over in my mind. I didn't want to push Kennedy away. I didn't want to scare her off. The thought alone should've sent me running for the hills, but it didn't.

"Well, it's damn impressive."

Lizzie pointed at me. "You said a bad word."

I looked down at the little pixie standing in front of me. "You're right. Never say what I do."

She giggled. "It's okay. I'm no snitch." Kennedy and I burst into laughter. "What? What's so funny?"

Kennedy ruffled Lizzie's hair. "You are, gorgeous girl. And making people laugh is a gift. Cherish it."

Lizzie beamed with pride. Kennedy was so good with her, and I found myself yearning to watch her teach. I couldn't imagine anyone being made for something more. My mind continued to spin, picturing her teaching her own little ones.

I cleared my throat, trying to get my runaway thoughts under control. What the hell was wrong with me? "I came out to tell you, dinner is ready to be served."

Kennedy arched an eyebrow at me. "Oh, and am I allowed to touch it?"

I chuckled. "I might have to tape potholders to your hands so you don't burn yourself."

She rolled her eyes. "Just wrap me in Bubble Wrap, why don't you?"

"Now, that's an idea." I looked down at Lizzie. "Do you have any Bubble Wrap?" She just giggled and shook her head.

Kennedy moved towards her shoes in the corner, and as she went to slip them on, I saw that one of her toenails was almost black. "What happened?" My voice came out more harshly than I intended, but it couldn't be helped.

Her brow furrowed. "What do you mean?"

I gestured to her foot. "Your toenail?"

"Oh, that's nothing. Just a bruise."

She made it sound as if she'd just bumped it, but it was more. "How did it happen?"

Kennedy slipped on her shoes and shrugged. "I danced with shoes that need replacing. It happens."

My jaw tightened, that familiar clicking sound in my ears. "Why haven't you replaced them?"

"I just haven't had time. But I'm going to go get some new ones this weekend."

"What are you going to dance on in the meantime?"

She winced, and I knew she was going to use the same shoes that had injured her in the first place. I opened my mouth to say that I'd get her some damn shoes tomorrow, but she held up a hand to silence me. "I don't have to go up on pointe in my classes for the next two days, it'll be fine. And Jensen is going into Pine Ridge this weekend, so I'll just tag along and get my shoes then."

I nodded, and we headed for the kitchen. Dinner prep went off without a hitch. Or *mostly* without a hitch. I'd noticed the new resident—Jay, he'd introduced himself as—watching Kennedy a few times. I couldn't blame the man, she was beautiful, but I didn't have to like it. I'd introduced myself to him, hoping to get a last name so I could run him, but all I'd gotten was: Jay. I'd just have to keep a close eye on him for now.

"You're really good with Lizzie."

I was jolted back to the present moment by Kennedy's voice. "She's a great kid, which makes it easy." I hadn't been around kids much since college and hadn't realized how much I missed the dynamic. I'd always been more of a father to Kiara than a brother, and I missed that. Having someone to care for, guide, make laugh.

Just like always, the warm memories of all the good times my sister and I shared were followed by an assault of horrible ones. The knowledge of what had happened to her. The understanding that it'd likely happened because I wasn't there.

Kennedy touched my shoulder gently, a silent question in her gaze.

"Sorry. Just lost in thought." More like lost in a nightmare.

"Okay." She didn't sound as if she believed me.

"Cain, you have to go. We need you there."

I let out an exasperated growl as I paced in front of the community center. "Why is this so important, Jake?"

"We need to show everyone that it's business as usual, even though we lost the Criterion account. Attending the gala will give us a chance to ease frayed nerves. Plus, I want an update on the new program, and I know your paranoid ass isn't going to give that to me over the phone."

He was right about that, but there wasn't exactly a lot to update him on, my progress had been minuscule. I eased onto a bench, closing my eyes and tipping my face up to the sky. "I hate these things."

The sound of papers ruffling came over the line. "I know you do, but you always make it through alive."

I grunted. I couldn't explain it, but ever since receiving the news of Karen's passing, it was as if my shields didn't work as well as they usually did. The reserves I had to deal with all the crap in my life seemed non-existent. I felt like one raw nerve. And that made me feel weak as hell. But the thought of going to this event, having to don that mask I wore as protection, had my chest constricting in a painful squeeze. "I'll see what I can do."

"Thank you. Talk soon."

I hit end on the call and set the phone down on the bench. I rubbed the spot between my pecs, trying desperately to get the tension to release. It only got tighter. *Fuck.* Going to this gala would be a disaster.

"Cain?" Kennedy's melodic voice cut through the evening air.

"Hey. Sorry I disappeared on you guys, I had to take a call."

She sat down next to me on the bench, tucking one leg under her and turning to face me. "Not a great call, I take it."

I shook my head, staring out at the forest beyond the parking lot. I had the sudden urge to run into the trees and get lost in there, never to return again.

Soft fingers wrapped around my biceps, the touch reassuring, a promise that I wasn't alone. "I know we don't know each other that well, but I'm here if you want to talk."

My gaze traveled back to the woman next to me. She was a storm wrapped in beauty and grace. She held fierceness and gentleness in equal measure, and it eased something in me. It was her tender kindness in that moment that had some of the pressure in my chest releasing. "I have to go to an event in Portland. It's bad timing on every level. I hate these kinds of things in general, and I just don't have a lot stored up right now to handle it."

Understanding lit Kennedy's features. "I'm sorry. Can I do anything?"

"Go with me." The words were out of my mouth before I could stop them, but as soon as I heard them, I knew they were true.

She blinked rapidly. "Why me?"

This was one of those make or break moments. If I held back,

I'd lose the small chance I had of her agreement. "You ease something in me. I can't explain it." Our gazes locked. "I don't trust many people, but I trust you. Don't make me do this alone."

She released her hold on my arm, and I missed it instantly. "How long would we have to stay?"

"Not long. Just enough time to shake a few hands, pose for a few pictures, and then we can hop in the jet back here."

"No pictures."

My gut clenched. She was hiding from something. "No pictures."

Kennedy nibbled on her bottom lip. "I assume this is black-tie?" I nodded. "I don't have anything to wear."

"Don't worry about that. Just get me your sizes, and I'll have my personal shopper send over some options."

She shook her head. "No, don't do that. I'll ask Jensen. I bet she has something I can borrow."

I squeezed my hands into fists but stayed silent. I didn't want her borrowing from Jensen. I wanted to do something nice for her. Spoil her for once. But Kennedy didn't want a damn thing from me. Why did that burn so much?

CHAPTER
Seventeen

Kennedy

"THE EMERALD ONE. PROMISE ME YOU'LL WEAR THE emerald one." Jensen was practically bouncing on her toes as she spoke.

The emerald gown was beautiful. It skimmed my body perfectly and made my eyes look like the green gemstones themselves. It was also daringly low-cut. "I don't know."

Jensen grabbed my hands, pulling me to her. "Kenz. That dress was made for you. You have to wear it."

I rolled my eyes. "It was not made for me. It's your dress."

"Not anymore, it's not. I'm leaving it with you and never taking it back."

"Jensen, no. I don't want it. It's yours."

She sighed. "Fine. I'll take it back on one condition." I arched a brow as if to ask *what*? "That you wear it first."

I pulled my hands from her grasp. "Oh, fine."

Jensen let out some sort of girlie shriek that was so unlike her I couldn't help but laugh. "Okay. I'm taking the others home with me, then." I opened my mouth to argue, but shut it quickly, knowing it would do me no good. "You've got my straightener and curling iron. I've got Chuck. Need anything else?"

"No, you've covered all my bases." I met her gaze. "Thank you. For everything. I'm so glad I ended up in Sutter Lake and at the Kettle."

Jensen pointed a finger at me. "Don't you dare make me cry. Because if I cry, then you'll cry. And we can't have you looking all puffy and splotchy for your big date."

Her final words sent any emotion running. "It's not a date. I'm just a friend doing a favor."

"Suuuuure, you are." Jensen grinned wickedly at me.

"Stop that."

Jensen tried to hold in a laugh and failed. "I think you're good for him." She sobered. "He's got wounds, so cut him some slack if he's a little much at times."

I wanted to ask what those wounds were. All I knew was that he'd lost someone. But, who? How? I had millions of questions swirling in my mind, but I held them back. I wouldn't want someone prying into my life by asking others about my greatest traumas. I had to give Cain the same respect.

"I'll cut him some slack." I pulled J into a tight hug. When I released her, I bent to scratch behind Chuck's ears. "You be good."

Jensen hooked the leash to Chuck's collar. "He's always good. And Noah is thrilled to have a dog for the night. He's been begging me and Tuck for a puppy, and I think we're going to have to give in."

"Oh, you should. Every kid needs a puppy."

She draped the excess dresses over her arm. "He lives on a ranch. He's surrounded by every kind of animal, why does he need to add a dog who's gonna poop and pee all over my house until it's potty trained."

I let out a laugh. "It'll be worth it."

Jensen just shook her head. "Try and have fun tonight, okay?"

"I'll do my best. Tell Noah and Tuck 'hey' for me."

"Will do. See you tomorrow."

"Tomorrow." I opened the door for J and waited until I heard the back door shut and lock before closing my own. "Fun. Just have fun." Yeah, right.

I glanced at the clock in my kitchen. Shit. I needed to get moving. I was already showered, but my hair and makeup needed some serious work. I got to it.

My eyes locked on my reflection in the mirror. It was an image I hadn't seen in a long time, one I wasn't exactly happy to see again. If I were honest with myself, I didn't like the person I used to be all that much. Going along with just about every dictate set out by my parents, even the ones disguised as a suggestion. Closing my eyes to all the suffering that had been going on in the world around me. That girl had been nothing but a carefully crafted façade. An expertly painted canvas with little heart.

But I had heart now. I was growing to like the woman I was becoming. I might still know how to expertly paint a canvas, but there was life behind it. Purpose. And the woman I was working my way to being. She would have Cain's back. So, that's just what I was going to do.

My hands shook slightly as I brought the locket up to clasp around my neck. It was the one piece of jewelry I'd taken with me when I left. A gift from my grandmother, my father's mother, someone who probably hated me now.

She'd never been a warm woman. She was couched in proper etiquette and cold distance. But she'd given me this one gift that had spoken to me. A gold locket with a dancer in mid-spin. It wasn't fancy, but I'd loved it from the moment she'd given it to me for my thirteenth birthday. My mother had always scowled when she saw me wearing it. Called it *juvenile*, but she couldn't remove it as she had the other items in my wardrobe that she found displeasing because it was a gift from the matriarch of our family. Even she didn't dare cross Helen Barrington.

There was a knock at my door. Apparently, Jensen had told

Cain to keep an extra set of keys. I took a deep breath and crossed to the sound, pulling the door open. It was a good thing I'd taken that deep breath because I could no longer get air into my lungs.

Cain. In the most expertly tailored tux I'd ever seen. It was unique, just like him. A mixture of playing by the rules and pushing the boundaries. The fabric was a blue so dark, it was nearly black, though not quite. A color that matched his eyes almost perfectly. And the cut… It skimmed his broad shoulders and chest in a way that hinted at the muscle beneath.

My cheeks heated as I saw Cain's eyes skim down my body. I swore the gaze felt like the lightest touch of fingertips and ignited a shiver I couldn't contain. "You look incredible, Kenz. Scratch that, incredible isn't good enough. Transcendent. That's how you look."

"Thank you. I just need to grab my purse." Well, Jensen's purse, but he didn't need to know that. I snagged the clutch, a wrap, and a pair of flip-flops for the flight home and then took an inventory of my studio apartment. I felt like I was forgetting something, but maybe it was simply that I was leaving my safe and predictable life behind for a night. *It's only one night.* I could do it for one night. I took a slow, measured breath and turned. "Ready."

"Let's go."

Cain offered his arm as we headed down the stairs, and I was glad for it. I hadn't worn a shoe with a heel in over two years, and I was still getting my sea legs back. "I'll never know how you ladies can wear those things without breaking an ankle."

I laughed. "Well, it's been a minute since I've worn ones this high. I might break an ankle before the night is over, or trip and end up on my ass."

Cain paused at the foot of the stairs, his eyes boring into mine. "I won't let you fall."

That handful of words held so much more than their surface

meaning as his eyes burned with an unnamed emotion. "Thank you." The gratitude came out as a whisper, but I couldn't help the hope it contained.

He squeezed my hand. "Let's get this show on the road."

We headed for the airport in silence. It was only a five-minute drive, but each second seemed to ratchet up my anxiety another level. I could do this. Cain needed a friend, someone he could trust, to face a sea of people who could house the traitor trying to hurt his company.

When Cain talked about Halo, I could tell it was about more than money for him. He'd created something that he was proud of. And he didn't want to lose it. Someone from the inside selling him out had cut at his heart. He hadn't used those words, but the expression on his face as he'd talked said as much.

Cain pulled right onto the airstrip, parking mere feet away from the jet awaiting us. "Stay put. I'll come and get your door."

I nodded, my palms turning clammy. I watched as he rounded the SUV. So confident, so self-assured, as if he could bend the world to his will with only the crook of a finger. There was none of the vulnerability I'd seen a few nights ago. He seemed ready to face what lay ahead while I was a quaking mess.

He opened my door and held out a hand. I slipped my fingertips into his roughened palm. The texture was comforting, a reminder that he wasn't the typical wealthy elite, someone who would never deign to partake in an activity that might damage his hands. He was different. He was Cain.

He led me up to the plane and ushered me aboard. We took seats opposite each other, and I immediately gazed out the window as I gripped the armrests of the seat.

"Nervous flyer?"

"No." It wasn't the flight that had me terrified. It was leaving behind my safe and secure existence here in Sutter Lake to reenter the den of wolves.

CHAPTER
Eighteen

Cain

SOMETHING WAS OFF. I WATCHED KENNEDY CLOSELY AS WE took off. She simply stared blankly out the window. No comments about the sleek jet or making fun of me for using it. Just a quiet numbness. I hated everything about it.

"We don't have to go. I can tell the pilot to turn around. We'll go back to Sutter Lake, and I'll take you for ice cream instead." I would've done just about anything to get that look off her face.

Kennedy turned back to face me and gave her head a little shake. "No. I want to go." I arched a brow at her, and she let out a tiny laugh. That was better. "Okay *want* might be too strong a word. But I think we should go."

"Okay. But just say the word if you want to leave. Or maybe we should come up with some sort of secret signal." I reached up and gave the lobe of my ear two quick tugs. "Something like that?"

Her laughter deepened, filling the cabin of the plane. It was fast becoming my favorite sound. "I'll keep that in mind."

A stewardess entered the cabin. "Can I get you anything to drink?"

Kennedy shook her head. "No, thank you. I don't trust myself not to spill on my dress."

The stewardess gave her a kind smile. "Just let me know if you change your mind. And for you, sir?"

I liked this flight attendant, no eye-batting or come-ons, just thorough and impeccable service. I was going to offer her a full-time job. "I'm fine, thank you."

She nodded and headed back to the front of the plane.

Kennedy folded her hands in her lap. "So, who am I going to be meeting tonight?"

"I'm not entirely sure. My driver and assistant will pick us up at the airport. The vice president of my company will be at the event. A number of people we do business with or who use our tech in their day-to-day operations."

"What made you want to start Halo?"

It had been some time since anyone had asked me that question. I always gave a canned response that was mostly a lie, but there was something that made me want to give Kennedy more. "After I went through that loss I mentioned, I became pretty obsessed with security. I'd always thought to go into law enforcement, maybe try for the FBI because I've always been good with computers. Something about the way they work just always clicked in my mind. But after everything that happened, I wanted a more hands-on impact. Something that was truly preventative. I knew I could make equipment and software that was top-of-the-line, but I also knew I could make the everyday stuff significantly more affordable."

Kennedy nodded slowly. I saw her desire to ask more questions, to delve deeper, but she held back. I was grateful for that. I just didn't have it in me to tell her about Kiara. I hadn't told anyone new about her since walking into Dr. Murphy's office a decade and a half ago.

"Alarm companies all over the world use our equipment, but

we also work one-on-one with larger individual clients, designing systems specifically for them."

"And what you're working on right now, what's that for?"

I hadn't been doing much on that project at all. I'd hoped Sutter Lake would provide me some quiet and time to focus on my new program, but I'd been distracted by the mysterious beauty in front of me. "It's a program that we'd use for all our individually designed systems."

"It sounds like you love what you do."

"I do. Most of the time."

Kennedy grinned at me. "It's a job. It's impossible to love it all the time."

"What about you? Are you happy at the Kettle and teaching ballet?"

Her smile turned soft. "I am. Both jobs give me a sense of purpose." She started to say something more but stopped herself.

"What is it?"

Kennedy gave her head a little shake. "I have this crazy dream of rebuilding the community center, creating all sorts of new programming." She let out a breath. "But I'm not sure how that would even be possible. Maybe one day."

"You're pretty amazing, you know that?"

Kennedy's eyes widened as her cheeks flushed. "Uh, thank you."

I chuckled. "Okay, no more compliments tonight. I promise."

The pilot announced our descent into Portland, and before long, we were pulling to a stop on the tarmac. I unbuckled my seat belt and rose. As Kennedy did the same, I noticed her fingers trembling slightly.

My jaw clenched, and I reached out to take her hand in mine. I gave it a little squeeze. "Just remember, you can call it at any time."

"I'll be fine."

"Okay." I helped her out of the plane and led her towards a waiting SUV. As we approached, the driver rounded the vehicle, and Rachel stepped out of the passenger side.

She strode towards me, reaching out and giving my arm a quick squeeze. "Missed you, Cain."

I gave her a quick smile. "Thanks for holding down the fort while I'm away." I took a step back. "Rachel, Vince, this is Kennedy."

A look of shock swept over Rachel's features before she hid it. I wanted to laugh. It wasn't exactly typical for me to fly in with a date. "Nice to meet you."

"You, too. It's lovely to meet you both," Kennedy said as she made her way to the door Vince held open.

He grinned at her. "You, too, ma'am." He turned to me. "There are a few items that were messengered to the house. Would you like me to have them stored in the plane?"

I climbed into the SUV behind Kenz. "That would be great."

Rachel followed suit, hopping into the front. "Here are some files for you to look over." She looked briefly at Kennedy as though unsure if she should continue speaking.

I waved a hand for her to continue. "You can say anything in front of Kennedy."

Rachel's eyes flared. "O-okay. There's a file in there with the list of employees we were discussing."

I nodded. "I'll look at them tomorrow. The system update is in place and working?"

"It is. Though I have to be honest with you, some people balked at needing another employee for access."

"Tough shit." My hands fisted at my sides. "Our company is under attack, and if any of them have a problem with doing something that's just a little inconvenient to protect it, they are welcome to leave."

"Understood."

Kennedy placed a hand on my knee, squeezing gently. The simple touch calmed me somehow. The knowledge that I wouldn't be walking into this den of thieves on my own helped. I covered her hand with mine and breathed deeply. I had everything under control.

Me, too.

I had arranged for us to enter the gala through a back door, knowing that Kennedy didn't want her photograph taken. A harried-looking event staff member met us there. "Right this way, Mr. Hale, Ms. Charles."

I placed a hand on the small of Kennedy's back, the heat of her seeping into my palm and making it tingle. "Thank you for meeting us back here."

"Of course, Mr. Hale. Thank you for your generous donation."

Kennedy dipped her head to whisper to me. "I didn't even ask. What organization is the gala for?"

I swallowed thickly. "A rape crisis center here in Portland."

She paused her forward movement for a moment. "I'm really glad we're here, then."

"Me, too."

The ballroom of the hotel was full but not over-crowded. As always, I spotted many familiar faces, and even more I didn't know. I hated this kind of thing. That something for good was turned into a chance to hob-knob and make deals. The focus should be on the center, but that was never going to be the case. At least, I knew they'd walk away with a few million by the end of the night.

"Cain," a voice called from my right. Drew Wright, a long-time client, appeared through the crowd. "I wasn't sure if you were going to make it. The rumor mill's been working overtime. Something about you running away to the mountains."

I chuckled. "Thank God for private planes, they can bring you in from anywhere. How are things?"

"Great. The missus and I just got back from a couple of weeks in St. Barts. You been to the island this year?"

"No, there's only so many sandy beaches and five-star resorts I can take. I was getting a little sick of the same ol', same ol'."

Drew grinned. "Only you would get tired of a private villa on the ocean."

From the corner of my eye, I saw Kennedy's expression turn sour. I hadn't thought about the fact that she would hate the persona I put on at these events. And didn't that just turn my stomach? I wanted to be a man she'd be proud to stand next to, not someone she was ashamed of.

"And who do we have here?" Drew eyed Kennedy in a way that made me want to deck him.

I wrapped an arm around her, pulling her to my side. "Drew Wright, this is Kennedy Charles. Kennedy, Drew."

Kennedy took Drew's hand in a polite shake. "Nice to meet you."

"You, too, darlin'. How'd you meet this one?" He stuck a thumb out towards me.

She smiled politely. "Mutual friends."

"I know these friends?"

I jumped in before Drew could push any further. "I don't think so. I've got to get this lovely lady a drink, but I'll find you later."

"You do that. I've got a proposition to discuss with you."

I nodded and ushered Kennedy forward with my hand on the small of her back. This time it wasn't heat I felt but tension. "Sorry about that."

"About what?" Her voice was tight.

"Being a bit of a douche canoe."

She spun to face me. I thought my comment would at least

earn me a little laugh, but no such luck. Instead, there was fire in Kennedy's green eyes. "If you know that's how you're acting, why do it?"

She deserved the truth. "Honestly? It's habit. It's how I get through these events. I don't know if this will make any sense, but I play a character when I come to these things. It's like putting on a suit of armor before doing battle. If I play someone else, then everything I have to deal with doesn't touch the real me." I'd never told a soul that, not even Walker or Tuck. Only Kennedy.

Her shoulders that had been rigid with tension dropped a hair. "I get it. More than you know. I just don't like the character you play very much."

I gave her arm a squeeze. "I don't like him very much either. So, why don't I throw him away for the night?"

"Think you can do that?"

"With you by my side? No problem."

Kennedy melted into my side as we headed for the bar. The tension was gone, and the warmth was back. She seemed to fit perfectly against me, her long, willowy frame melding to the hard planes of my chest. With the four-inch stilettos, she was the perfect height that if I dipped my head, I'd be able to kiss her neck... *Fuck.* I did not need to be thinking about that.

"What can I get you, ma'am? Sir?" I was jolted back to the present moment by the bartender's voice.

Kennedy placed her purse on the bar. "Do you have Perrier?"

"We do. Would you like a lemon in that?"

"Lime, please."

"Of course. Sir?"

"Soda water with lime in a rocks glass."

The bartender nodded and turned to prepare our drinks. Kennedy looked up at me. "Do you not drink?"

I shook my head. "No." Alcohol had been such a part of that

downward spiral in college, I wouldn't risk it again. I wanted all my faculties about me at all times. "You?"

She smiled up at me. "I do. Perrier is just my favorite drink."

I tucked a strand of hair behind her ear. "I'll have to remember that."

The bartender returned with our drinks, and we headed out to brave the crowds. The way Kennedy handled my business associates, you would've thought she'd been doing this her whole life. She could talk about anything: current events, their children, art, and she even seemed to have a keen mind for business. I couldn't help but wonder what else was hiding just beneath the surface.

I gave her hand a gentle tug, and she glanced up. "Dance with me?"

"I thought you'd never ask."

"I've clearly been neglecting my date." I led her towards the dance floor as a string quartet played some classical piece I didn't recognize, and then pulled Kennedy into my arms. "I'm afraid you've got me beat on the dancing front."

"It's not about executing the perfect steps. It's about enjoying the journey."

"I'll try to remember that." I inhaled deeply as I held her body closer to mine. Her hair smelled of roses and something I couldn't quite name. I'd never been one to notice a woman's perfume, but I knew without a doubt that her scent would be burned into my memory forever.

We were silent as we swayed. I could've made a better attempt at fancy footwork, but I wanted to simply lose myself in the moment. Her body pressed against mine. The closest it had ever been. An excuse to touch her was all I wanted. But it still wasn't enough. I was greedy for Kennedy. I think I'd always want more.

The song was over far too quickly, and as the last strains of a cello lifted up into the air, a hand clamped on my shoulder. "Cain."

I turned and met Jake with a shake and slap on the back. "Jake, this is Kennedy. Kennedy, this is my VP, Jake."

I hadn't been sure how well Kennedy would handle meeting company employees when she knew one of them was stabbing me in the back. Still, each time, she kept her cool, a mask perfectly in place. That façade made me twitchy. She was too damn good at it. "Nice to meet you, Jake."

"You, as well. Would you mind if I borrowed Cain for a moment?"

I opened my mouth to protest, but she responded before I did. "Of course, not." She looked at me. "I'm going to find the ladies' room. I'll meet you at the bar when you're done."

I nodded, but my chest began to constrict as she walked away, that familiar panic setting in. She was in a room of sharks, and I didn't want her out of my sight for even a second.

Jake gripped my shoulder. "What's that all about?"

I cleared my throat. "What do you mean?"

"You fall in love in the last few weeks? I've never seen you look at a woman that way in all my life."

My jaw tightened, and that familiar clicking noise sounded in my ear. "She's a friend."

He let out a low whistle. "That's one hell of a friend. Is she why you're behind on the project?"

My gaze grew steely now. Jake was my VP. A vice president in *my* privately held company. He answered to me. "The speed with which I complete something is none of your concern."

He held up his hands in mock-apology. "We have clients who are hungry for it, that's all."

My gaze narrowed further. "And why the hell do they even know about it? I told you not to mention it to anyone."

Jake flushed. "We were losing people or on the verge of losing them, and I just wanted to make sure they had a reason to stick around. You might not believe this, Cain, but I care about Halo. I don't want to see it go under."

I knew Jake cared about Halo, he'd put almost as much sweat equity into the company as I had, and I would always be grateful. But the second one of my people didn't follow orders, they became a liability. "I'm going to give you this warning only once. You disobey a direct order again, and you're out."

Jake's jaw fell open, but I didn't have time to hear what he had to say. I needed to find Kennedy.

CHAPTER
Nineteen

Kennedy

I PUSHED OPEN THE BATHROOM DOOR, GRATEFUL TO BE free of the small space. The women inside had been awful. Analyzing what everyone had been wearing, who had dared to don something from last season, who'd gotten a new piece of jewelry from a husband who felt guilty for cheating. The whole thing made me feel nauseous. So many memories of similar functions flew through my mind. How had I lasted in that world for so long?

"Well, look who we have here."

I blinked rapidly, trying to clear what had to be a mirage. But no matter how many times I opened and closed my eyes, the image before was the same. "Preston." The single word came out as a hoarse whisper.

"Looks like my baby sister had the same idea as I did. Flee the east coast where our name means pariah and start somewhere new." He looked me up and down. "I see you've found yourself someone to keep you in the lifestyle you're accustomed to."

The words stung, but it was the disgust in his eyes that

killed, a pain that reached into my chest and clawed at my heart. When I didn't have to face Preston, the daily reminder, I could live in my land of deluded hope. That the two years that had passed would've dulled his hatred.

I'd tried calling him about a month after the arrest. He'd never picked up. I kept it up, leaving messages, trying to explain why I'd done what I did, to tell him I loved him. Eventually, he changed his number. It was the straw that broke me. While I had alerts about my father, I never looked for Preston. It was too painful; the wound still too raw. Sometimes, I imagined he was looking for me, hoping to make amends, to forgive me. Apparently, that wasn't the case. "What are you doing here, Pres?"

His jaw tightened at the familiar nickname. "I live in Seattle now. I'm here with some business associates."

I wanted to ask about our mother, grandmother, even Father. They might hate me now, but there was always a part of me that would love them. I held my tongue. "I'm glad you made a fresh start."

He let out a snort of derision. "You're glad I made a fresh start. Why would you care? You had no problem ruining my life. I almost went to jail, Kennedy. All because you couldn't give Dad a chance to fix his mistakes."

As harsh as his words were, as deep as they cut, they also gave me peace. I'd been right not to share what I'd found with Preston. He was under my father's spell too deeply and would've believed anything he said.

"I'm so sorry I hurt you, Pres. I was trying to do what was right. The only thing I could live with." My eyes begged him to understand, to see things from my perspective. "I was so scared when the FBI showed me all their evidence. I knew my entire life had been a lie. Preston, we lived our charmed lives off others' hard work. Don't you see how wrong that was?"

A muscle in his cheek began to flutter. "Dad made a mistake. The market was sliding, and he didn't want to let his clients down. That meant borrowing from some other accounts. And it also meant we had to live as if nothing was wrong. Why can't you get that?"

Borrowing. How could it be borrowing when you never once paid back even a dime? How was it borrowing when it had been going on for years? Preston was living in denial. "It had been going on for too long for that to be true."

"Must be nice to sit up there on your high horse. Newsflash, Twinkle Toes, people hate you just as much as the rest of us."

That familiar burn lit my sternum. I knew they did. And they had a right to. It didn't matter that I hadn't known what was going on, I'd still stolen from them. And I wasn't sure if I'd ever be able to forgive myself for that.

A hand gripped my shoulder. "Everything okay, Kenz?"

I jolted at the touch, and my vision began to tunnel. This was the beginning of the end. Soon, the fresh start I'd created for myself, my safe space, would crumble because everyone was going to learn the truth. Tears burned the backs of my eyes, and I couldn't seem to get any words out.

Preston scoffed. "So, this is the guy you've conned into supporting you?"

Cain's hand tightened on my shoulder as he pulled me closer to him and away from Preston.

Preston began to laugh. "I wouldn't be so quick to protect her. She'll bleed you dry and then tank your business with lies."

"Who are you, and what the hell is wrong with you?"

"She hasn't told you, has she?" Preston's laughter intensified. "Of course, she hasn't. No one in business would want her within one hundred miles of them. I'm Preston Barrington. I'll let her fill in the rest." And with that, he side-stepped us both and strode back towards the party.

I was full-on shaking now. Trying so hard to push my emotions down. To keep the lid on. Because I knew the moment I let them out, they'd never stop.

Cain turned me towards him, his hands cupping my face gently—oh, so gently. "Kennedy. Look at me." My gaze went to his eyes, but I didn't really see him. "Who was that? Who is he to you?"

"My brother," I whispered. "That was my brother."

CHAPTER
Twenty

Cain

KENNEDY WAS LOST IN HER OWN WORLD. SO LOST, SHE barely noticed as I guided her out of the ballroom and into the waiting SUV. She said not a single word as we drove to the airport. Didn't blink at the fact that I kept her hand in mine, our fingers twined.

I didn't want to let her go. I had no idea what fucked-up history she had with her family, but I'd find out. And, in the meantime, I somehow felt that if I kept a hold of her hand, I could keep her safe. Nothing in this world could touch her if I was holding her.

When we reached the plane, I helped her out of the vehicle and led her towards the jet. I ignored the single seats and sat us on a bench seat so I wouldn't have to let her go. I didn't think I could if I tried.

As the plane began to taxi, Kennedy started to whisper. "Chuck. Jensen lending me a dress. Dancing. Unlimited Perrier."

"Baby. What are you talking about?" None of what she said made sense.

"Things I'm grateful for."

My brow furrowed. "Things you're grateful for?" At least, she was speaking now, even if none of it made much sense.

She began to tremble. "I'm listing the things I'm grateful for today. Even on the worst days, there's something to be grateful for." Her voice hitched on the last word, and then she dissolved into sobs.

I held her to me as the plane lifted into the air. *Fuck this.* I unbuckled her seat belt and lifted her onto my lap as her body became wracked with sobs. I wanted to murder her brother. I couldn't imagine Kennedy doing anything to warrant this kind of punishment.

I rocked her back and forth, pressing my lips to her hair, whispering over and over that it would be all right. Until Kennedy went limp in my arms. I didn't move her. I simply held her as though I could fix it all.

The flight attendant appeared in the aisle, looking concerned. "Is she all right?" I shook my head. "Is there anything I can do? I know she's asleep now, but I'll ready a glass of water and some aspirin for when she wakes up. I bet she's going to have a headache."

I was so hiring this woman. "That would be great. If she doesn't wake before we land, I'll take it in the car with me."

She nodded. "Just call for me if she wakes up."

Kennedy didn't wake. Not even when the plane landed. She only let out a low moan. The flight crew helped me navigate the steps and unloaded everything Vince and Rachel had left for me on board. The flight attendant placed the drink and medicine in the cupholder as I laid Kennedy in the passenger seat of my Range Rover. I carefully buckled her in and then gently closed the door.

I turned to the flight crew. "Thank you, for everything. I'll be sending bonuses to you all, along with job offers."

They all blinked, but it was the woman who spoke. "Thank you, sir. I hope she's feeling better soon."

I gave a jerk of my head and rounded my vehicle. With only a moment's hesitation, I headed for home. My home. I wasn't leaving Kennedy alone, and there was way more space at my place.

As we pulled up to my front door, Kennedy stirred, blinking rapidly. "Where are we?"

I brushed the hair back from her face. "We're at my place." She blinked some more but said nothing. "I want you to stay here tonight." She opened her mouth to reply, but I held up a hand. "Please, don't argue. If I have to take you home, I'll just end up sleeping on your couch." I paused for a moment, holding her gaze with mine. "I need to make sure you're okay."

Kennedy nodded slowly.

I fought the urge to reach out and pull her to me again. To wrap her in my arms and never let her go. "Thank you."

I grabbed the important items from the back seat, and we headed inside. "I'll grab you some stuff you can sleep in and show you to a guest room." Kennedy nodded again and followed me through the hallways until I stopped at an open door. "Here you go. There's a bathroom through that door. Do you want to shower or have a bath?"

"Yes." The word came out on a croak, her voice raw from crying.

"Everything you need should be in the bathroom. I'll go grab you some clothes and leave them on the bed."

"Thank you." Her voice sounded…dead. Devoid of any emotion. And it had me wishing I'd decked her brother when I had the chance.

"Be right back."

She shuffled towards the bathroom as I headed for the master suite two doors down. I knew I'd be sleeping with my door open, if I slept at all, listening for any sounds of her movement. I set down the various files and packages I'd gotten from Vince and Rachel on a chair in the corner. I'd go through it all tomorrow.

It took me a bit to find something that had any chance of fitting Kennedy. I finally opted for a tee, boxer briefs, and a pair of sweatpants that had a drawstring. I lifted the pile along with the water and aspirin I'd forgotten about and headed down the hall. I faltered at the door. Kennedy stood in the center of the room, her hair wrapped in a towel, body clad in only one of the terry-cloth robes that had been in the bathroom. A wrap that was gaping open in the front just a bit. I swallowed, hard. "Here you go. Sorry it took so long. I had trouble finding something I thought might fit you."

Her lips flickered as though they were trying to smile but couldn't quite make it happen. "Thank you."

"And here's some aspirin." I set the packet of pills and the drink down on her bedside table. "I thought you might have a headache." I cleared my throat as I stuffed my hands into my pockets. "Is there anything else you need? Something else to drink? A snack?"

Kennedy bent to pick up the clothes at the end of the bed. "I think I just want to go to sleep."

"I'll leave you to it, then."

As I headed for the door, Kennedy's voice stopped me. "Thanks for not asking any questions."

"Get some rest." What I didn't say was that there would be plenty of time to talk in the future. And we would be talking. But I'd do my research first.

I headed for my room, going straight to the wall safe I'd put in and opening it up. I pulled out my laptop and set it on my bed. I quickly showered, pulling on the only pair of flannel sleep pants I owned, something I didn't think I'd ever worn before. But it seemed like a dangerous idea to sleep in the nude like I usually did. What if Kennedy needed me in the middle of the night? My chest constricted, but I forced the thought from my mind.

I settled myself against the array of pillows on my bed and

pulled the computer onto my lap. My fingers drummed as I waited for the security checks to complete. As soon as they did, I opened a browser. The first thing that came to mind was that Kennedy and her brother didn't share the same last name. They could be half-siblings, I supposed. But there was something about the last name *Barrington* that tickled the back of my brain.

I entered *Preston Barrington* into my search engine and hit the motherload. No wonder the last name had sounded familiar. Davis Barrington had been arrested and convicted for turning his hedge fund into a Ponzi scheme. It had been all over the papers two years ago.

But why had Preston said that Kennedy would tank my business? My eyes skimmed over an article about the case. *Davis Barrington was arrested yesterday on various charges, all centering around the misappropriation of funds from his investment company. The real twist of the story comes from who helped the FBI make the arrest. His twenty-year-old daughter, Kennedy Barrington, allegedly got a confession on tape for the law enforcement agency. Many believe she was complicit in the crimes but simply knew her father would soon be caught and decided to save herself.*

I exited out of the article. Everything made a hell of a lot more sense now. How jumpy Kennedy had been when I'd asked questions about her past. Her aversion to anything she perceived as waste. She was drowning in guilt. For something she'd had no part in.

My fingers flew over the keyboard again, my brain working out all the potential ways for this to cause Kennedy harm. I'd only followed the case in a cursory way and had no idea who all the players were. Davis had been sentenced to ten years in a federal penitentiary but had recently been granted parole.

My chest squeezed. Kennedy had one of the most tender hearts I'd ever known. What had it done to her to know that she'd put her father away and that he was getting out after only two years?

The majority of the hedge fund employees had been found innocent, including Kennedy's brother, but their careers had been tanked. They'd never work in New York finance again. I searched out Preston, he was the figure I was most concerned about right now.

After a deep background dive, I found that he too had changed his name. He now went by Preston Williams. But his identity switch was easier to find. Apparently, it hadn't been sealed by the courts as I assumed Kennedy's was. Preston worked for a new financial startup in Seattle, but it appeared he was more of a silent partner. His name and photo were featured nowhere on their site. The only connection I'd found was when I hacked into the man's bank account and saw the direct deposits.

My back molars ground together. Preston wasn't exactly hurting for cash. He had a couple million sitting in his savings account alone. So, why was he so angry with his sister? Because of the lost prestige?

My mind circled everything that had happened from every angle I could think of, and I kept coming back to Kennedy's sealed name change. Why had that been necessary? I plugged her old name into my search engine.

The first photo that popped up was what must have been a graduation photo. She wore pearls around her neck and dangling from her ears, along with the black draping that was typical of those private prep school photos. Her hair was swept back in a perfect bun at the base of her neck.

I barely recognized her. The smile on her face was forced, and her eyes didn't have the sparkle they held now. She looked as if she were playing a part that had been miscast. No wonder she'd bristled at the persona I'd put on earlier in the evening.

I minimized the photo. I couldn't look at it anymore. The next article I opened had me sitting up in bed. *Kennedy Barrington Attacked Leaving FBI*, the headline read. My eyes skimmed the text, speeding ahead to get to the information I needed, but then came to a dead stop on the photo. The woman who was one of the kindest I knew was covered in what looked like blood. My heart stopped until I read the caption. *Attacker throws fake blood on Barrington.*

No wonder she'd run. Started over. I would've done the same. My heart ached for the woman I knew now. How alone she must've felt.

I pushed those feelings aside and forced myself to go into threat assessment mode. I did something I hadn't done since I was a senior in college. I hacked into the FBI's database.

My focus tunneled. All I saw was a series of ones and zeroes until I got to where I needed to go. Then all I saw were names and reports, most of it useless until I came to one by an Agent Carnes. Apparently, he'd been Kennedy's point of contact, the one who had first approached her for help.

I fought the urge to clench my hands as I read through the transcript of that first meeting. They'd basically threatened to arrest her brother if Kennedy didn't help. My eyes scanned down the screen. The report listed a slew of threats made against Kennedy, including four or five people who had been harassing her, making those threats directly to her, even after she'd moved across the country.

It appeared as if Carnes had grown protective of Kennedy. Maybe it was guilt for using her as a pawn in his case, or perhaps he wasn't as bad a guy as that first meeting suggested. Regardless, he'd pushed for Kennedy to file restraining orders against the harassers. She'd refused, stating: "these people have lost enough. I'm not going to take any more from them." Instead, she'd opted to change her name and basically erase herself from existence.

I knew now that she'd moved to a small town in Oregon where

she avoided having her photograph taken and encountering any-one who might recognize her. She paid for the sins of her father by taking as little as humanly possible and giving more than I could fathom in return. It wasn't an existence that was sustainable. She was punishing herself. And it had to stop.

CHAPTER
Twenty-One

Kennedy

MY WAKE-UP CALL CAME IN THE FORM OF A pounding head and something that smelled like bacon. I pushed up in bed, my hands going to my temples and attempting to rub some relief in there. I tried to blink away the scratchiness behind my eyelids. No luck.

I sniffed the air. It was definitely bacon I smelled. I swung my legs out of bed and stood. The idea of hiding away in this room forever was tempting, but I'd have to face Cain at some point. It might as well be with bacon.

I padded towards the bathroom and winced at my reflection. My eyes were swollen and bloodshot, my hair was a rat's nest, and there were creases along the side of my face from my pillow—all of it a reminder from the night before.

I closed my eyes against the image of Preston's face, twisted in anger, in hurt. My brother. My protector. And now, he was nothing. No, it was worse than nothing. There had been hatred in his gaze. Those green eyes flashed over and over in my mind.

I inhaled deeply, forcing my lids open. I wouldn't let myself wallow. I refused. I'd come too far. *The most comfortable bed I'd ever slept in. Someone who cared enough to not let me go home alone. Chuck. Bacon.* There was always something to be grateful for. Always.

I released my hold on the sink and gave the cabinets a quick search, finding that the bathroom was, of course, fully stocked. I brushed my teeth, washed my face, and attempted to get a brush through my hair. There was nothing else I could do to prolong seeing Cain.

I tiptoed out of my room and headed down the hall towards the kitchen and the smells of breakfast. Cain looked up from the island at the sound of my footsteps. "Hey."

I twisted my hands in front of me. "Good morning."

He patted a stool next to him. "Hop on up here. I bribed one of the busboys from the bakery and cafe to bring us out some breakfast."

I took in the spread in front of me. Eggs, bacon, pancakes, and donuts. "This looks great."

"Definitely worth the bribe since I'm overdue for a grocery shop. You sleep okay?" An edge of concern slipped into his tone with his question.

I slid onto the stool. "I did. That bed is super comfortable."

Cain chuckled. "I'll be sure to tell my decorator."

I nibbled on a strip of bacon and waited. I was sure the questions were coming, so I needed to stay braced for them. Cain simply poured me a glass of orange juice and went back to his own eggs. "What time do you have to be at work?"

I jolted at the totally normal question. "I, uh, actually don't work today. Just volunteer at the shelter tonight." Jensen had started closing the Kettle on Sundays so she could have time with her family. I loved that she'd found that—balance, peace.

"Do you need to pick up Chuck from her?"

"She offered to bring him to me since I don't have a car, but if you have time to swing by there, I'd love to save her the trip." I forked a bite of egg, relaxing just a bit.

"Not a problem. We can go get him after we finish breakfast."

"Thank you." We continued to eat in silence. I wanted to apologize for last night, but I also didn't want to give Cain an opening to ask more questions about what had happened with my family. So, I opted for silence.

When I finished eating, I cleared my plate, rinsing it and placing it in the dishwasher. "Do you mind if I wear this home? I'd rather not put on a formal gown first thing in the morning."

Cain chuckled. "Of course."

"I'll wash it and get it back to you ASAP."

He rose, bringing his own dish to the sink and standing just a breath away from me. "Don't worry about it. I've got more where those came from."

I fingered the hem of the tee. It was perfectly worn and had a hint of the cologne Cain wore. I didn't want to give it back. But I would. "Thank you."

Cain turned to face me, one hip leaning against the counter. "You don't have to thank me for everything. I like doing things for you."

My nose twitched. "Well, I like thanking you."

Cain shook his head, grinning. "Fair enough. Ready to go get your pup?"

"Yup. Let me grab my purse and dress." I hadn't been away from Chuck overnight in years, and after last night, I was more than ready for some puppy cuddles.

By the time I'd retrieved my belongings from the guest room, Cain was waiting for me in the entryway. Thankfully, I'd brought my flip-flops on the plane, so I wasn't wearing sweatpants and stiletto heels. However, I still looked ridiculous, wearing clothes that were about six sizes too big.

Cain grinned at me. "You look like someone shrunk you but not your clothes."

I scowled at him. "You do realize that when we show up at

Jensen's, she and Tuck are going to get the total wrong impression of what went down here, right?"

He blanched just a bit. "Fuck."

"Yeah, buddy." I patted his arm and headed out the front door.

The drive to Cole Ranch was peaceful. We rolled down the windows and let the warm breeze flow through the SUV. I let my arm drape out the window, my hand riding the wave of air.

Cain keyed in the gate code at the ranch, and we wound around until we reached the guest cottage. Sixty seconds after we pulled in, Noah came bounding out of the front door, Jensen and Tuck on his heels. "Kenz, Cain!" He wrapped his arms around me in a warm hug. "Chuck and I had the best time. We played fetch, and I gave him peanut butter treats, and he slept on my bed."

Jensen lifted her brows at me as she took in my outfit. "I think we wore him out because he's been sleeping on the couch all morning. Looks like you're worn out, too."

I squirmed in place. "It was late when we got back, so I just crashed in one of Cain's guest rooms."

"Guest room, huh?" Jensen didn't look like she believed me one bit.

"Wilder…" Tuck's single word was a warning as he pulled her into his side. "Don't meddle."

She stuck out her tongue at him. "I'll meddle if I want to. I'm a great meddler. Look at Taylor and Walker, and Liam and Tessa. Someone should give me a meddling medal."

Tuck just shook his head. "You two crazy kids have fun at that fancy shindig?"

I stiffened. I should've had an answer prepared. Of course, they'd ask. I tried to force a smile, but before I could say a word, Cain jumped in. "I don't know if I'd call it *fun*,"—he looked at me—"but at least I didn't have to face the piranhas alone."

My heart did a stutter-step. There was nothing but honesty

in Cain's voice. He was grateful he hadn't had to face that scene alone. Even after I'd ended the night in the most dramatic fashion imaginable, he was still thankful I'd gone with him.

"Noah, why don't you go get Chuck for Kenz?" Jensen ushered her son inside. Noah nodded and ran back into the house.

"Thank you so much for watching him, J."

"Are you kidding? He kept Noah entertained for hours. I think it's official that we need a dog."

Tuck brushed his lips against her temple. "Told you."

"Yeah, yeah." She shoved at his chest playfully.

I knew then that I'd have to tell them the truth. Jensen, at least. She'd employed me when I had basically no skills, given me a place to live, and welcomed me into her home. She deserved to know who it was that she'd done those things for. Even if it meant I'd lose the safe place I'd built for myself. I didn't think she'd fire me, but she was guaranteed to look at me differently. How could she not? Tears clogged my throat as the memories of the stares and jeers from the crowd behind the FBI building filled my mind. I gave my head a little shake, trying to clear them.

Noah appeared with Chuck on his leash. The second he saw me, my pup rushed towards me. I crouched so I could meet his leap with open arms. I couldn't help the little laugh that escaped me as he bathed my face in kisses. "I missed you too, buddy." I hauled him up into my arms, soaking in his unconditional love. "Okay, we're ready."

Cain had a smile on his face that said he was desperately trying to hold in a laugh. "Then let's head out."

"Thanks again, you guys. J, I'll see you tomorrow."

"Later, Kenz. Cain." She waved as we hopped into the car.

Chuck settled in my lap, head resting on my arm and the center console, and immediately began snoring. This time, Cain couldn't hold in his laughter. "I wish I had that dog's capacity for sleep."

"Cut him some slack. He's an old man." I stroked Chuck's silky fur.

"He's spoiled. If there's such a thing as multiple lives, I hope I come back as that dog."

I grinned. "You should only be so lucky."

Cain guided the SUV out of the ranch and back towards town. Before long, we were pulling up to the back of the Kettle. As I lifted Chuck, I winced. "Uh, Cain?"

"Yeah?"

"Do you have any paper towels in your car?"

His brow furrowed. "I don't think so, why?"

I pressed my lips together before answering. "My dog might've drooled a bit."

Cain glanced down at the substantial puddle on the center console and let out a bark of laughter. "I think you need to get that dog some medical attention."

I cuddled Chuck to my chest. "Don't listen to him, baby. You're perfectly fine."

"Sure, he is." Cain pushed his door open. "Come on, I'll follow you up and steal a few paper towels from you."

I opened my own door and got out with Chuck in tow. "I guess that's the least I could do."

We headed inside. Once I'd unlocked my door and keyed in the alarm code, Cain was already inside and studying my space. He'd been in here before, for hours, but he still seemed riveted. He pointed to my gratitude jars. "What are those?"

I nibbled on the corner of my lip. "Where I keep the things I'm grateful for."

He gave me a gentle smile. "Do you ever read through them?"

I nodded. "If I'm having a bad day or just need a reminder of all the good there is in the world. I'll take one off the shelf and pick out some papers at random."

Cain edged closer to me, gaze searching my face. "Does it help?" He stopped just a breath away from me.

I licked my lips. "Always."

He tucked a strand of hair behind my ear, his hand stalling there, slipping to my neck. "I just might have to try that."

"You should." I didn't breathe, couldn't as his gaze zeroed in on my mouth.

Chuck let out a loud snore, and Cain dropped his hold on me as if he'd been burned. "I've got to go. I'll see you later."

He was gone before I had a second to process what had happened. And he hadn't even gotten the towels he needed. That's how eager he was to get away from me. It hurt in a way I hadn't expected. I thought my brother's disgust was the worst pain I'd feel. But I'd been wrong.

CHAPTER
Twenty-Two

Cain

"**H**OW'S THE LIVING IN DISCOMFORT GOING?"

My hands tightened on the wheel as I heard the smile in Dr. Murphy's voice. "Not fucking good." I'd spent the day working on my new program for Halo and trying desperately to distract myself from the temptation that was Kennedy. It had been a failure. I'd made almost no progress, and all I seemed to be able to see were Kennedy's lips.

I'd almost kissed her. I'd almost taken that mouth, consequences be damned. But she didn't deserve the demons I wrestled with. She'd been through too much already.

"Talk to me." The trace of humor had left Murphy's voice.

I blew out a long breath as I rounded a curve in the road. "I almost kissed her today."

"And that would be so bad, why?"

"You know why. I've wanted to swing by the Kettle at least ten times today to check on her. Just to make sure she was safe."

"But did you?"

My jaw clenched. "No. I didn't."

"Cain, the urge will probably always be there. You lost

someone close to you in an incredibly violent manner. Someone you saw yourself as the protector of."

"I was her fucking protector!" The words tore from me with a vehemence I couldn't control.

"But that wasn't your job."

Emotion burned the back of my throat. "I promised her I'd always look out for her."

"And you did. But your mother should've been looking out for *both* of you. She didn't. And she let someone into her life she shouldn't have."

"Don't. Just, don't. I don't have it in me to talk about that today." I couldn't handle the truth of what had happened to Kiara on top of the disaster that was work and trying to sort through everything in my head about Kennedy. Everyone had their breaking point, and this was mine.

"Okay, Cain. We don't have to talk about it. But I want you to give yourself some credit. Whether or not you decide to pursue Kennedy, you care about her. She triggers those protective instincts in you, but you haven't gone overboard. It's fine, healthy even, to want to make sure she's safe."

"Okay, Doc."

Murphy sighed. "It's all right to let yourself care for someone, Cain."

"I know." And I did. In theory. It was the practice part I struggled with. Because the second I thought about kissing Kennedy, I imagined how it would feel to lose her. The problem was, I didn't think I was strong enough to walk away and let someone else have her either. It was a purgatory of my own making.

I cleared my throat as I pulled into a parking spot outside the community center. "I have to go. I'm at the shelter. I just wanted to check in real quick."

"I'm glad you did. Keep calling, okay?"

"Will do." I hit end on the call and climbed out of my SUV. The air was warm, the seasons' turn to early summer officially upon us. I needed to get a boat. The lake was calling me. I pushed open the door to the community center and came face-to-face with Anna.

"What's going on with Kenz?"

"What do you mean?" Worry pricked at my skin as though it were suddenly too tight for my body. "Is she okay?"

I started to head towards the rec room and kitchen, but Anna took hold of my arm. "Cool it, cowboy. Nothing is wrong." Her face scrunched. "But something *is* wrong. You get what I mean?"

The tension running through my body eased a bit. I did get it. Kennedy had come face-to-face with her past last night. Of course, it was messing with her head. "It's not my story to tell. But she'll be okay."

Anna's eyes narrowed at me. "Spill."

"I can't. I'm not going to betray her trust that way, not even to you."

Anna let out what almost sounded like a growl. "Fine. Tell me what to do then."

I couldn't help the smile that tipped my lips. I was so glad Kennedy had this kind of friend in her life. "Just be there for her. But act normal. I'm hoping she'll open up on her own time and not because we forced her." But I knew I could only go along with that plan for so long. Soon, I'd have to start some gentle pushing.

"All right." She turned and headed towards the rec room. "Hurry up, pretty boy. I got potatoes that aren't going to peel themselves."

I chuckled and followed behind her. That laugh died on my lips as I saw Kennedy talking with Doug. He was close. Too close. I strode towards them. "Hey, guys. What's up?"

Doug dropped his hold on Kennedy's arm. "We were just chatting about the Portland ballet."

My jaw clenched. "Didn't she already tell you she didn't want to go?"

"Cain!" Kennedy's outrage was clear in her tone, but I didn't give a fuck.

Doug cleared his throat as his face reddened. "Actually, she said she was too busy to attend *Swan Lake*, but we were discussing shows later in the season."

"She's not interested, buddy. Get a clue."

"God, you're an asshole. Kennedy, we'll talk later when he's not around." And with that, Doug turned and headed for his office. What a catch.

"What the hell is your problem, Cain? That was cruel." The anger had Kennedy's eyes blazing with green fire.

"Am I wrong? Do you want to go on a date with him?"

"That's not the point, nor is it your business."

"I'll take that as a no. I was just saving you the awkward dance for the next three months."

Kennedy's spine straightened as she rose to her full height. "Maybe I did want to say yes. At least if Doug leaned in like he was going to kiss me, he'd finish the job and not run away like a scared child." With that parting shot, she headed for the kitchen.

Well, shit.

CHAPTER
Twenty-Three

Kennedy

HIS LIPS WERE JUST OUT OF REACH, HIS HANDS STOPPING *a breath away from my skin. I panted. Strained. But I couldn't move. Couldn't reach him.* My alarm sounded.

I jolted up in bed, out of breath as if I'd just sprinted around the block. I pushed the hair back from my face as I hit my alarm. *Shit.*

I couldn't escape Cain, even in my dreams. He'd avoided me the rest of the night at Hope House, opting to help with the kids instead of in the kitchen. That didn't mean he wasn't haunting me, though. I'd had to watch as he played beauty parlor with three girls as we'd served dessert. He'd even let them try to put little braids in his hair.

I rubbed my hands over my face. Cain had a good heart, but he could also drive me crazy. What did he want from me? I blew out a breath, sending my hair fluttering around my face. I wasn't going to find out today. Or maybe ever. And I needed to focus on the important things.

Like telling Jensen the truth. It was time. Just the thought had my stomach roiling. I reached over and scratched between

Chuck's ears. "We'll be okay. No matter what happens, we'll be okay."

I repeated that over and over as I got ready, hoping the repetition would help me to believe it. But I'd lied to Jensen, and a lie of omission wasn't any better than an outright one. I bit my bottom lip as my gaze traveled over the studio apartment I'd made my home. I had no idea where Chuck and I would go if Jensen kicked us out. I didn't exactly have money saved up for a security deposit. No prospects for another job. And it wasn't like Seraphina would hire me on full-time.

"One thing at a time." I armed my security system, locked the door, and headed downstairs. I got the water going in a kettle and set out two mugs. The familiar routine helped. Grounded me.

Sounds of the lock at the back door coming unlatched met my ears. "Morning, Kenz."

My palms went damp the second I heard Jensen's words. "Morning." My voice cracked on the second syllable.

I stayed focused on the tea. Tea I could handle. "Honey?"

"You know it." The sounds of Jensen putting away her belongings and washing her hands filled the kitchen. I still didn't look her way. I simply set the mug next to the sink and hurried back to my own cup. I took my time pouring the honey first, then added just a dash of almond milk.

"Soooooo…" Jensen let the word drag out. "Is there a reason you're quiet as a mouse this morning? Wait! Did you sleep with Cain?"

I choked on the sip of tea I'd just taken, spluttering and coughing as J patted my back. She filled a glass of water and handed it to me. "Shit, sorry." Her lips tipped up. "I can't tell if that's a yes or a no."

"It's a no. A definite no." I wheezed out the words.

Two little lines appeared in Jensen's brow. "Then why so quiet? Everything okay?"

This was it. The perfect moment. But how did I start? How did one explain that you had been involved in stealing the livelihoods of hundreds of people? If even indirectly. That you had destroyed families? *You're a murderer!* The words of that woman echoed in my head.

I closed my eyes and gave my head a little shake, trying to flick the memory free, get the words out. It never worked, but I tried just the same. "I saw my brother when I was in Portland."

Jensen leaned a hip against the counter. "I didn't even know you had a brother."

I looked up and met Jensen's gaze; it was kind and cautious as though she knew whatever I had to say would be hard for me. "He probably wishes that I didn't."

"Want to tell me why?"

I rolled my lips together, biting down on the bottom one, and then I nodded. "I haven't told you everything about me. About my past. Some important things."

Jensen reached out, laying her hand over mine on the counter, squeezing it gently and then releasing. "I don't think it was a requirement of the job or my friendship that you reveal every detail of your past." She paused, giving me a gentle smile. "I would've asked a lot more questions in the interview."

I wanted to smile. Tried to get my lips to mirror Jensen's movement, but they wouldn't obey. "I changed my last name. For most of my life, it was Barrington, not Charles." I took in a slow breath, somehow hoping the air would steel me. "My father is Davis Barrington."

Jensen's brow furrowed. "The name sounds vaguely familiar."

I twisted my hands in front of me, locking them together so tightly, they began to tingle. "Ponzi scheme."

J's eyes widened. "Oh, Kenz." There wasn't judgment in her voice. No disgust or even mistrust. Only sympathy. "I think I remember most of the story. You helped the FBI, right?"

I nodded. "I got a confession for them." I began unloading, unpacking my past and laying it bare before her. I told her about Preston, what a wonderful brother he'd been, and the night it all changed.

I told her about all the extravagances of growing up in the Barrington household. The things I hated and the stuff I loved. I told her about my father and how I never would've thought his betrayal possible until the moment I saw the proof in front of me. In that moment, everything had clicked into place, and I'd wondered how I hadn't seen it sooner.

But maybe I hadn't wanted to. Perhaps I had been happy hiding my head in the sand because I got all the ballet lessons, the custom pointe shoes, and the nicest leotards. Along with the swankiest vacations, and the best schools. Maybe I'd been lying to myself all along.

"Kenz." I was jolted back to the present moment by Jensen's voice. "You don't blame yourself, do you? None of this was your fault."

Tears pricked at the backs of my eyes. "I might not have stolen the money outright. But I lived off it. For over twenty years, I lived on the stolen lives of others. Do you know how that feels to know that? To know that people died because I got ballet lessons, and trips to St. Barts, and as many shoes as I wanted?"

It was the first time I'd said the words out loud, the ugly truth of them. Four people had died, taken their own lives because my family had wanted more. How did I live with that?

Jensen pulled me into a hard hug and didn't let go even though I remained stiff in her arms. "I can't imagine what that feels like, and it makes me want to kick your father in the balls for putting you in that position. But it wasn't your fault. You didn't know."

I understood on a logical level, but it didn't change how I *felt*. It was as if the destruction my family had wrought had seeped into my bones, and I didn't know if I'd ever be able to get it out. "I can't change how I feel," I whispered into Jensen's shoulder.

She rubbed soothing circles on my back. "I know. But, one day, it will change. Life is a cycle. It ebbs and flows." She seemed to trace that cycle along my back, pushing her fingers into peaks and valleys as she kept moving them in a circle. "There are moments that are so hard, you'll think they've broken you, and you'll never recover. But it's those moments that make you appreciate the goodness, the sweetness, something so beautiful it will almost seem painful to take it all in."

Jensen slowed her hand's path, pausing, pressing her fingertips into my shoulder. "But there's one thing I know for sure. The kind of guilt you've been feeling, it's nothing but a lie. As women, we take so much on. It's one of our gifts, to feel what others do, and deeply. It's a gift to be able to sit in those emotions with another, to hold it with them. To feel what others experience and have it spur you to make changes in the world. I see that in you. But you can't take it all on. You have to let it pass through you. Kennedy, you can't hold the pain of the whole world. You'll drown under the weight.

"Your father stole your choice from you. He didn't allow you or the rest of your family to decide whether you were okay with living off stolen money. I *know* what your choice would've been. There is no doubt in my mind. You are a good person, one of the best. And one day, you'll believe that, too. But until you do, I'll be here to remind you."

I let out a little sniffle as she released me. "So, you're not firing me?"

Jensen let out a bark of laughter. "If I didn't fire you the first three times you almost set my kitchen on fire, I'm not going to fire you because your father's an asshole." She paused, her mouth quirking. "The fact that you had no idea what you were doing in the kitchen makes a little more sense now."

A laugh of my own escaped me. "I wasn't really allowed in the kitchen at home. When I went to college, my roommate had to show me how to make Easy Mac. She thought I was an alien."

Jensen wrapped an arm around me. The feel of it was better than anything I'd ever experienced before. Warmth, comfort, and affection, all given freely, even after I'd told her the ugly truth. All of it. "It's going to be okay."

I nodded. "You can tell Walker and Tuck. Your parents. I don't want to live with this secret hanging over my head anymore, but I don't know that I have the energy to go through it another half-dozen times."

J turned to face me. "Are you sure? This is no one's business but yours."

I squeezed her hand. "I don't want to feel like I'm living a lie. I don't want to wonder if people want to be my friend or not if they knew the truth. I don't want that weight."

"I get that. But if anyone doesn't want you in their life because of something your father did, then they deserve a swift kick where the sun don't shine."

I grinned at Jensen. "You'll never know how often I thank my lucky stars I landed in Sutter Lake, in your tea shop. That you took a chance on me. Thank you."

Jensen's eyes began to water, and she shook a finger at me. "Oh no, you don't. You are not going to make me cry, you evil woman."

I chuckled. "It's just that emotional ebb and flow you were talking about."

She shoved at my shoulder. "That's what I get for sharing my Zen wisdom with you. You throw it back in my face."

We spent the rest of the morning laughing as we prepped. We didn't venture into serious terrain at all, just enjoyed the simple pleasure of each other's company. It was perfect.

I arched a foot, wincing just a bit as I slipped it back into my sneaker. The new pointe shoes I'd gotten were murdering my feet. There wasn't a ton I missed from my old life, but my fancy pointe shoes were one. They had been so much easier to break in.

At least, I had new ones. I was no longer at risk of twisting an ankle or splitting a toenail because I was dancing on dead shoes. That was enough to be grateful for.

I yawned as I placed my dance bag in the basket on my bike. The day had taken more out of me than I'd realized. Mostly the talk with Jensen. I didn't think I'd ever felt this light, even before I'd realized I was living a nightmare. But I was spent. The worry and anxiety of how the conversation would go, having to talk through it all, it had used up all my reserves.

"Just a few hours at the shelter. You can do it." I threw a leg over my bike. I'd get a burst of energy as soon as I saw Anna and Lizzie. *And Cain.* A little voice in my head whispered the last part. I promptly ignored that voice.

I headed away from the dance studio and towards the community center. The air was so warm, I didn't even need a long-sleeve shirt. Summer was officially here, and I'd finally get to fully enjoy the lake for which the town had been named. Jensen had already told me we'd go out tubing on her family's boat, and I couldn't wait.

I turned and headed down the familiar hill, the wind picking up my hair and swirling it behind me. I squeezed the brakes to slow my speed a touch, but there was no resistance. I pressed harder. Nothing.

My heart hammered against my ribs as I scanned the sidewalk in front of me. The bottom of the hill was fast approaching, and there were only two options: fly into traffic or send myself into an empty lot of gravel, dirt, and weeds.

I tried the brakes again, squeezing as hard as I could. There wasn't even the slightest catch. I turned the handlebars, doing my best to aim for the empty lot. The second my tire hit the gravel, it skidded, and I was airborne. Everything was a blur. A kaleidoscope of colors that ended in shuddering pain and then nothing but darkness.

CHAPTER
Twenty-Four

Cain

I NAVIGATED THE COUNTRY ROADS, HEADING TOWARDS THE community center. I shouldn't even be going. I'd made even less progress on the program today than I had yesterday. What I should be doing is picking up a six-pack of energy drinks and pulling an all-nighter. Sometimes, that was just what it took. The slightly manic feel the lack of sleep brought on occasionally meant a breakthrough.

But I wasn't doing what I should. This program could cement my company's future, and still, I was driving to Hope House. To Kennedy. The pull of her was almost impossible to understand. She snuck up like a damn riptide. The tug was gentle at first, but before long, I couldn't break away, no matter how hard I tried.

I rolled to a four-way stop just around the corner from the community center. A flash of color caught my attention, and I saw someone flying down the hill opposite me. Not just someone, Kennedy. And she was going way too fast. What the hell was wrong with her?

Her head jerked in panicked movements, taking in

everything around her. Could she not stop? *Fuck.* Blood roared in my ears as I watched in time that seemed to move both too fast and in slow-motion. She steered into an empty field of sorts, her bike hitting some gravel and pitching her over the handlebars. Kennedy flipped in the air, making almost a full rotation before her body hit the ground in a sickening crumple.

I didn't think, I just moved. I jumped out of my SUV and ran across the intersection, ignoring the honking cars. She wasn't trying to get up, wasn't moving at all. I couldn't even see a flicker of a hand or foot. This wasn't happening.

I skidded to a halt, crouching beside Kennedy's fallen form. I didn't think I breathed as I carefully slipped her hair away from her neck, pressing two fingers there. A pulse. Nothing had ever felt as good as that flickering bump against my fingers.

I pulled my phone from my pocket and tapped 9-1-1.

"9-1-1, what is your emergency?"

"There's been a bike accident on the corner of"—I had to look up to find the street names—"Crest View and Main. The woman is unconscious. She has a pulse. I don't know what I should do. She's on her side. Her face…it's in the dirt. Should I roll her to her back? I don't want to hurt her."

"Sir, an ambulance is en route, don't move her, we don't know if there's a spinal injury."

I closed my eyes as though that would erase the possibility. Kennedy, my beautiful dancer, not being able to walk? No. I refused to believe it. A small moan sounded, and my eyes flew open. "Kennedy? Kenz? Can you hear me?"

She let out another moan and rolled to her back. My hand went to her shoulder. "Don't move, they don't want you to move, baby."

"What happened?"

I started to answer, but a man jogged up. "Is she okay? Did you call an ambulance?"

"No, she's not *okay*," I gritted out. "An ambulance is on its way." I could faintly hear the sirens in the distance now.

"How can I help? Do you want me to move your car?"

I glanced over my shoulder to see that people were driving around it, but it was still somewhat blocking traffic. "Sure, the keys are inside." I didn't give a fuck about my Rover, all I cared about was Kenz. My gaze focused back on her. "What hurts?"

She squinted up at me. "Cain?" The confusion in her voice was apparent. Not good.

"It's me. I'm here. You're safe. Can you tell me what hurts?" I made an inventory of her the best I could. The right side of her face was all scraped, blood trickling down to her chin, but I knew it could've been so much worse if she hadn't been wearing a helmet. The purple plastic had a large crack down the side, and I winced, thinking of how much force it would take to do that. Her shirt was torn and stained red on the right, and her pants were covered in dirt.

"Everything. It all hurts." Her voice came out as a hoarse whisper, but as it did, her feet moved. It was a small, testing action as if to see if her legs hurt, but it was movement nonetheless.

The sirens were closer now. "Try not to move. The ambulance is here. They're going to help you."

"No. No ambulance. Please." Her eyes were wide now, almost panicked.

"Kenz, you need the damn hospital, and they are going to get you there."

She winced at my tone. "I don't have health insurance."

I let out a slew of curses. "It doesn't matter. I've got you." Kennedy blinked up at me, then opened her mouth to say something else. "Don't. Do not even think about telling me to send the ambulance away. They are going to help you, and you are going to let them."

Her fingers reached out, feeling for mine. "Okay."

My entire body sagged. "Thank you."

"Sir." An EMT ran up, another following him, a backboard between them. "Can you tell us what happened?"

I walked them through everything I could, and then they got to work, forcing me to take a step back. But I stayed as close as I was allowed.

A throat cleared behind me. "Um, here are your keys. I parked it right over there."

I didn't even bother to look. I didn't give a damn. "Can you do me a favor?"

"Sure."

My gaze focused on Kenz as they rolled her onto the backboard. "Can you take the keys to the police station? Give them to Walker Cole and tell him where you parked it?"

"Of course. No problem. You know her or something?"

"Yeah, I know her." I still didn't look at the man. He was nice enough, doing me a favor, but you could tell he was one of those gawker hangers-on that got a thrill out of emergencies.

"Okay. I'll go do that now."

"Thanks."

The EMTs lifted the backboard, carrying it towards a gurney. "You riding with us?" one of them asked.

"I am."

"Stay back until we load her in."

I watched as they worked. I'd only felt this powerless one other time. A time that, if I thought about it now, I'd lose it, and I wasn't sure I'd ever recover. *Focus on Kennedy.* She's here, she's okay. They're helping her.

"You can hop in, sir."

I was climbing into the rig before the EMT had even finished his sentence. "How's she doing?" I gave the EMT more of my attention now. He looked like he was barely out of high school.

"I'm fine, Cain. Just a little banged up."

My head snapped in Kennedy's direction. "You are not fine. You flipped off your bike, going at least twenty miles an hour and were knocked unconscious. So, if the next words out of your mouth have anything to do with not needing to go to the hospital, I swear I will have a suit made out of Bubble Wrap for you and force you to wear it."

Kennedy's mouth stretched into a smile, which instantly turned to a wince, the action pulling at the torn skin on the side of her face. "No Bubble Wrap for me." She forced levity into her tone, but I could hear the pain underlying it.

I took hold of her hand. "We're going to get you fixed up." I turned to the EMT. "Right?"

He nodded quickly. "We'll be to the hospital as quick as we can."

The sirens flipped on as we pulled into traffic. "How long does it usually take?"

"About twenty minutes."

My jaw clenched. That was a hell of a trek in a true emergency. My mind whirled with contingency plans. Maybe I could put a helipad on my lake property and have a pilot on standby, perhaps employ a nurse.

Kennedy's hand squeezed mine. "Cain. I'm fine. I promise."

The feel of her hand in mine was soothing. The rhythmic series of squeezes. It eased something in me. Slowed the pace of my mind. Stilled the cycles it so easily descended into. How could a single delicate hand do all that?

I lifted her hand to my mouth and pressed my lips to the back of it. "You're right. You're going to be fine."

My phone buzzed in my back pocket, and I lifted a hip off the seat to pull it out. Walker's name flashed on the screen. I hit accept. "Hey, Walk."

"What the hell happened?"

"Kennedy took a spill off her bike. She's going to be fine, but I wouldn't be surprised if she has a concussion. We're on our way to the hospital."

"I'll head there as soon as I pick up your SUV."

Kennedy squeezed my hand again, bringing my attention back to her. "Tell them not to come. There's no reason." She obviously knew what our friends' immediate reaction would be. I must have looked doubtful because she pushed on. "I don't want a bunch of people there."

"What's going on?" Walker barked in my ear.

"Sorry. Kennedy says not to come."

"Tough shit."

I grinned. "She doesn't want to be fawned over right now, Walk. It's just going to stress her out to know you're all in the waiting room. I'll call you as soon as we know what's going on, and you and the rest of the gang can come check on her as soon as we're home."

Walker blew out an audible breath across the line. "I want regular updates. The girls are going to be worried sick."

I winced. All the women in Walker's circle were natural-born nurturers, and therefore, worriers. It manifested in different ways, but they all cared deeply and fiercely. "Do what you can to keep them settled."

"Updates will help."

"You got it. I need to go."

"Okay. Take care of her, brother."

"You know I will."

Walker grunted, and we both hung up.

"Success?" Kennedy asked hopefully.

I rubbed my thumb over the back of her hand. "With Walker, yes. Hopefully, he'll be able to keep the others at bay." I paused, studying her face. "But they care about you, Kennedy. They want to make sure you're okay."

Tears gathered in her eyes, and I scrambled forward, cupping the side of her face that wasn't marred with scratches and cuts. "Baby, no. What's wrong?"

Kennedy tried to swallow the tears back, to get them under control, but a few slipped free. "It's been so long since I've felt that. Not since—" Her breath started to hiccup as she held back the sob.

"It's okay. Everything's going to be okay." I pressed the side of my face against hers. "You're not alone." Her body gave a shudder, and she sucked in a breath that I knew was pain-induced. "Try to relax. You're going to hurt yourself if you don't."

Kennedy gave a small nod, and I straightened, daring the EMT to say something with my eyes. Wisely, he said nothing.

The sirens ceased as we pulled to a stop. Within seconds, the back doors were open, and the EMTs were pulling Kennedy from the ambulance. We'd made it. Kennedy was going to get help, and everything would be fine. So why couldn't I get the fist that had my heart in a vise to relax?

CHAPTER
Twenty-five

Kennedy

THERE HAD BEEN BLOODWORK AND X-RAYS AND, AT Cain's insistence, even an MRI. My cuts had been doctored by a nurse, and an IV inserted. Finally, I had been returned to my bay in the ER. I scowled at Cain as the gurney was locked into place.

"Why are you scowling at me?"

"Was the MRI really necessary?"

He scooted his chair closer to my bed. "Yes. There is plenty you can't see on an x-ray."

I rolled my eyes and then winced. God, even my eyeballs hurt. I felt like I needed to submerge my entire body in ice and not come out for days.

"What hurts?" Cain slipped his hand into mine.

There had been a lot of touching in the past few hours. Touching and terms of endearment and things that made my already scrambled brain scramble even more. What was going on? I didn't dare ask because I didn't want to risk it going away. "Pretty much everything hurts."

"Where the hell is that doctor?" Cain growled. "You need pain meds."

I squeezed his hand. "They have to read the x-rays and MRI before they give me anything, you know that." The nurse had told him so. Repeatedly.

Cain let out a little huff of air. "Well, they could hurry up about it."

"I'm sure they're going as fast as they can. Just relax, would you? You're stressing me out."

"Sorry." Cain's focus moved from the daggers he was staring at the curtain to me, gentling. "Sorry." He let out a long breath. "Do you know what happened? How you lost control?"

I hadn't had a moment to really think about it. The whole thing was a bit fuzzy—thankfully so—but I remembered when the first lick of panic had set in. "My brakes. They wouldn't work."

Cain let out another growl. "Probably because that bike is older than Irma."

I pressed my lips together to hold in my laugh, knowing it would only hurt. "I'm going to tell her you said that."

"You wouldn't."

"Try and send me for one more test, and you'll see."

Cain's thumb traced a pattern over the back of my hand. "No more tests." He paused. "Unless the doctor says you need them."

I groaned, but before I could say anything, the curtain pulled back, and a woman in a white lab coat appeared. She had a warm face, one that instantly put me at ease. Her tumble of curls was piled high atop her head, and she held what I assumed was my chart. "Ms. Charles, I'm Dr. Moseley. How are you feeling?"

"I'm doing okay, thanks."

"She's in pain," Cain immediately cut in.

Dr. Moseley gave me a gentle smile. "That's understandable, you took quite a tumble. As soon as I examine you, I'll get a nurse in here with some pain meds." She crossed to the bed, taking out a penlight. "The x-rays and MRI are clear, but I want to check you for a concussion. Are you nauseous at all?"

I bit down on my bottom lip. "Maybe a little."

"What about dizzy?"

"Not really, but I haven't stood up or anything."

The doctor nodded. "Okay, I'm just going to shine this in your eyes to check your pupils."

She flashed the light over my irises, and I winced.

"Is that uncomfortable?"

My hands fisted the blanket. "It's not exactly rainbows and butterflies."

Dr. Moseley chuckled. "I won't put you through that again. It's safe to say you have a mild concussion." She reached down and pressed the nurse call button. "I'm going to have them give you an intravenous pain medication now, and I'll write you a prescription for an oral medication you can have filled at your pharmacy." The doctor glanced over at Cain. "Will you be taking care of her?"

I opened my mouth to say I could take care of myself, but Cain beat me to it. "Yes, she'll be staying with me until she's well."

Dr. Moseley placed the penlight back in her pocket. "Perfect. You'll need to wake her every few hours for the next twenty-four. If she shows any worsening symptoms—vomiting, memory loss, inability to stand—bring her back to the hospital immediately. But I don't think that will be an issue."

She looked back to me. "Mostly, you're going to be very sore for the next week or two. I'm ordering lots of rest and no work or strenuous activity for the next seven days. I want you to follow up with your primary care doctor then."

I winced. "Are you sure I have to miss work for a whole week? Wouldn't a couple of days be enough?"

"Kennedy…" My name was a warning. I ignored Cain and looked hopefully at the doctor.

"I'm sorry, Ms. Charles, but it's important you let your body heal. If you push yourself too much, too soon, the recovery could last much longer."

I blew out a breath, sending the wisps of hair around my face flying. "Okay."

She patted the side of my bed. "Take it as a forced vacation."

A nurse strode into the room, syringe in hand. "I've got the meds you ordered, Dr. Moseley."

"Thank you, Sean." She took the syringe from him and deftly inserted it into the IV tube. At least I didn't have to get poked again. "That should take effect very quickly. I'll get your discharge papers, and you'll be good to go."

"Thank you." I reached out to shake her hand.

"Anytime. But try to stay upright on that bike."

"I'll be doing my best, trust me."

The medical staff left, and Cain rose. "I need to make a call. Will you be all right? It'll be quick."

"I'm fine. I'll just be here waiting for those sweet, sweet drugs to kick in."

His lips twitched. "You hopped up on painkillers could be interesting…" I stuck out my tongue at him, and he chuckled as he headed for the hall.

I ran my hands over the rough blanket. What would've happened if Cain hadn't seen my fall? I would've had to go through this whole ordeal alone. I prided myself on how strong I'd gotten over the past two years. Steel forged in fire. But in this moment, I was so very grateful to not be alone in this. Not to be going back to an empty studio. To have someone to lean on.

A faint fog flitted over me. Ah, thank you, pain meds. I leaned my head back on the bed and let my eyes close.

"Kenz, open those eyes for me."

I let out a little moan but obeyed. Cain was leaning over me. "The car is out front, and I have all your discharge paperwork."

"How long was I out?" I gave my body a testing stretch. Things didn't hurt quite as bad as they had before.

"Only forty-five minutes." He reached out a hand. "Here, let me help you up."

The getting to sitting had some pain flaring back to life, but I did my best to hide it. "Thank you." The breathlessness in my voice gave the pain away.

The same male nurse from before appeared with a wheelchair. "Your chariot awaits, madame."

Cain scowled at the nurse, and I grinned. "Thank you." I eased into the chair, and we headed for the exit. "Wait. Cain, we don't have a car." I hadn't even thought of that when I told him to tell Walker not to come to the hospital.

"I got a car service." Of course, he did. "I'll have them swing by your apartment to pick up Chuck and some of your belongings. I had Jensen pack you a bag."

I blinked up at him. "You've been busy."

He shrugged as the sliding doors opened, and a black town car appeared. The driver got out and circled to open the door. Cain helped me out of the wheelchair and held my hands as I lowered myself into the vehicle, wincing as I went.

In a matter of seconds, Cain was settled in the car next to me, and we were heading back to Sutter Lake. I glanced over at Cain. There was tension behind his eyes, a furrow of worry between his brows that had a swarm of guilt rolling around in my belly. I laid my hand over his. I wanted to tell him that I was fine for the five-hundredth time that day, but I knew he wouldn't be able to hear me. Whoever he'd lost—it had marked him. Created a lens through which he viewed the world.

I knew a little something about lenses that changed the way you saw things. They were always a mixed bag. Some good, some bad, just like life in general. But Cain's, it seemed to twist things into those old, dark fairytales, the real ones, not the Disney versions, where everything was a potential threat. I hated that for him. But I was sure that same lens also made him the fierce protector and amazing friend that he was. You couldn't have one without the other. But maybe, just maybe you could heal a bit of the first.

CHAPTER
Twenty-Six

Cain

I PULLED THE COVERS UP AROUND KENNEDY; SHE WAS already out like a light. The ride home, picking up her belongings, even just changing into her pajamas, had taken everything out of her. My hands lingered by her shoulders, holding tight to the blanket. I bent slowly, dipping low, my chest constricting with each minuscule movement. I gently pressed my lips to her forehead and simply breathed her in. The scents of the hospital were already fading, replaced by the hint of rose from her hair, and that thing I still hadn't been able to name.

I stayed frozen in place, just soaking her in. I needed this. The assurance that life flowed freely through her still. Kennedy would make a full recovery. She would dance and twirl with Lizzie and her students, she would laugh with Anna at her attempts to help in the kitchen. She had a full life ahead of her.

My phone buzzed in my pocket. I pulled it out and saw a security alert on the screen. Walker waved at the camera. I hit the button to let him in and headed for the door. I reached the front steps just as he pulled to a stop, Tuck trailing behind him in his truck.

Walker hopped out of my Range Rover as he popped the hatch. "How's she doing?"

"She's sleeping. Hopefully, she'll be doing a lot of that over the next few days."

"What did the doctor say?" Tuck asked as he climbed out of his own vehicle.

"Mild concussion. No work or strenuous activity for the next week."

Walker pulled Kennedy's bike out of the back of my SUV. I scowled at the thing. It had survived the wreck a hell of a lot better than Kennedy had. "You couldn't throw that thing in a dumpster?"

Walker shook his head. "I took a look at it when I got there. She must've ridden through some oil. It was on her front and back tires. That's why the brakes didn't work." I said nothing, just kept scowling. "I already cleaned it off. It's good as new."

"Doesn't matter. She won't be riding it."

Walker's brows rose, a flicker of humor passing over his expression. "She won't be?"

My hand tightened around my phone. "No. She won't. If she falls again, she could do serious damage to her brain."

Tuck groaned. "Please tell me you didn't buy her a car already."

I hadn't. If I thought there was any chance of her accepting it, I would've. But if there was one thing I'd learned about Kennedy over the past couple of months, it was that she was stubborn when it came to her beliefs. And she didn't want a damn car. "I'll be driving her wherever she needs to go."

A grin stretched over Tuck's face. "Can't wait to hear what she thinks of that. Should we start taking bets on how long it takes for Kennedy to throw his keys in the lake?"

The laughter that escaped from Walker made me want to deck them both. "You can kiss my ass. Both of you."

That just made them laugh harder. I waited for the words of warning. Similar to what Walker had said that first night I'd met Kennedy. But they didn't come. Both he and Tuck kept right on wearing those shit-eating grins.

Walker did his best to get his under control. "Okay, okay. In all seriousness. What can we do to help?"

I thought about it for a minute, fought the urge to take care of everything myself. It would mean a lot to Kennedy to know that she had a whole support system behind her. I pulled out my wallet and handed a scrap of paper to Walker. "Could you get that prescription filled? Maybe pick up some ginger ale and crackers in case the meds make Kenz nauseous?"

"You got it. I think Jensen and my mom were baking her cookies, so I'll bring those over, too." Walker guided the bike over to the side of the house. "Don't give in to temptation and throw this in the lake."

The guy was a damn psychic. That was exactly what I was considering. "Fine." I'd just hide it from sight. Maybe Kennedy would forget she ever had a bike to begin with.

Walker gave me a chin jerk as he headed for Tuck's truck. "We'll be back as soon as we've picked everything up."

"Thank you." Something tickled the back of my throat as I spoke. A flicker of emotion. Walker and Tuck had been through so much with me. And every time I needed them, they were there. They were my family now. "I mean it," I said, my gaze focusing on Tuck and then Walker. "Thank you. For everything."

I wasn't sure I'd ever properly thanked them for what they'd done for me in college. I'd done so through my actions, always having their backs, but words were important, too. Sometimes, you needed the damn words.

Tuck cleared his throat. "Anytime. You know it."

I nodded, watching as they climbed into the truck and headed for the gate. When the vehicle disappeared, I turned back to the house and made my way in, fighting the urge to dropkick the bicycle I could still see.

The house was quiet. Still. I walked down the hall and slowly pushed Kennedy's door open. Chuck raised his head from the foot of her bed, standing guard over his mistress. Kennedy slept peacefully, her mouth falling open just slightly in a way that made me stifle a laugh. She was gorgeous, even banged-up and turning black and blue, she was still so beautiful, it almost stole my breath.

That vise was back, squeezing the life out of my chest. One wrong move, and I could've lost her today. She could've gone tumbling into traffic instead of that field. Too many close calls. I rubbed the space between my pecs, trying to get the pressure to ease.

I forced myself to look away from her. To leave the room. I had work to do. I headed for my bedroom, going for the safe and keying in the security code. I grabbed my laptop, but my movements stuttered. I lifted a couple of files, searching for the thing I rarely brought out anymore. My fingers hit glossy paper, and I pulled out the photo.

I wandered over to my bed on autopilot and sat. She'd been so beautiful. Gleaming, dark hair, skin that was tan from the summer, and a smile that was so very Kiara. Bright and full of life, with a hint of mischief thrown in.

My jaw clenched as my eyes burned. There were days where it seemed impossible that she wasn't still here. Like my phone would ring at any moment, and it would be her, talking my ear off about the stray cats she was feeding behind the house, or some ridiculous girl drama at school, or the new band she'd fallen in love with. Those days, it was as if someone had punched a hole straight through my chest when I realized I'd never hear that voice again. And that hole...I didn't think it would ever close.

I squeezed my eyes closed for a brief moment. When I opened

them again, I slipped the photo into my nightstand. Locking away the memories, trying to shut off the pain. I needed to focus on the here and now. I pulled out my phone and hit Rachel's contact.

She answered on the second ring. "Cain."

"Hi, Rachel."

"It's good to hear your voice. How is everything?"

I scrubbed a hand over my face. "Things are fine, but I need your help on something."

"Anything, you know that."

A flicker of guilt swept through me. Rachel worked her ass off for me, and I wasn't always the most appreciative. It was probably time to think about another raise. "Thank you. I need you to look into getting a health insurance policy for someone. The same one I have."

The sound of fingers flying across a keyboard came over the line. "All right. I'll need a full name, date of birth, and a social security number."

"The name is Kennedy Charles. I'll email you the birthdate and social as soon as I have it."

There was a brief moment of silence. "The woman you brought to the gala?"

"That's her. How long do you think it will take to get the ball rolling?"

Another beat of silence, this one longer. "Cain, are you sure that's wise? That she's not taking advantage of you? Those policies are expensive…"

I tightened the grip on my phone. "I didn't ask for your opinion, Rachel. I asked for your help. Can you do it, or do I need to call someone else?" The accusation had my blood heating.

"I'm sorry. I'm just trying to look out for you, someone has to."

"I'm quite capable of looking out for myself."

"Understood. I'll get right on this."

"Thank you, Rachel." I hung up without a farewell. She didn't deserve my anger, but I couldn't seem to hold it in. I couldn't seem to hold *anything* in when it came to Kennedy. She was the one thing that could snap my carefully crafted control in a heartbeat. I let out a long breath. She was safe now, and I would do everything in my power to make sure she stayed that way.

CHAPTER
Twenty-seven

Kennedy

MY EYES FLICKERED OPEN. THEY WERE GRITTY, AS though the sandman had been extra thorough with last night's visit. I felt as if I'd slept forever. Still, I had the vague recollection of Cain waking me throughout the night, asking me simple questions and inquiring if I needed another painkiller.

I eased onto my side, there was pain, but it wasn't awful. The sight that greeted me was too adorable for words. Cain was reclined in an overstuffed chair, his head drooping to one side. And behind him, sleeping on the back of the chair, was Chuck, his little head resting on Cain's shoulder. Snoring away, of course.

The laughter flew out of me before I had a chance to consider that the action might hurt. The quick flash of pain had me gasping for air. Cain shot up in his chair, making Chuck let out a little growl. "What's wrong? What happened?" He was over to me in a flash.

I breathed through it, as shallowly as possible. The ribs were killing today, and my head wasn't far behind. "I'm fine."

"Would you stop saying that? You're obviously not fine. Tell me what's wrong."

"Someone's not a morning person." Cain only pinned me with a stare. "Okay, okay. I just laughed, and it hurt. My ribs."

Cain pulled back the covers and, before I could protest, lifted the t-shirt I'd slept in. He hissed out a breath as he took in my side. It was an assortment of purple and blue. *Shit.* "I'm going to make you some breakfast, and then we are going to get some pain meds in you."

I nodded, pulling down my shirt, desperately trying to ignore the little sparks that had danced across my skin when Cain's knuckles had grazed the flesh there. Electricity that had nothing to do with pain. "I'm going to take a shower and get ready."

Cain's body gave a little jolt. "I don't know if that's such a good idea. You haven't eaten yet. What if you get light-headed?"

I reached out and laid a hand over his. "I'll be okay. And I need to feel human again."

Cain's Adam's apple bobbed as he swallowed. "All right, but let me at least get you some juice first. It will get your blood sugar up."

"Fine."

He scowled at me. "That's becoming my least favorite word, you know." He headed for the door but paused, turning back to face me. "Why is my shoulder soaking wet?"

I pressed my lips together as tightly as possible to hold the laughter in. "Please don't make me laugh."

He looked over to the chair he'd slept in, his eyes narrowing on Chuck's snoring form. "That damn dog has to have some sort of condition, it's not natural to produce that much drool."

I grinned up at Cain. "It just means he likes you."

"Well, maybe he could like me a little less."

"You really are an amazing cook, you know that?" I was cuddled under a million blankets on the couch as I licked a drop of cheese sauce off my finger. "I think that's the best mac and cheese I've ever eaten."

A flush crept up Cain's neck. "I'm glad you liked it."

I lifted the remote and pointed back at the television. "Ready for another episode?"

Cain groaned. "What is it with your obsession with *Murder, She Wrote*?"

My eyes narrowed in his direction. "Are you going to insult the magical and insane genius that is Angela Lansbury and a dreamy coastal town in Maine?"

"Maybe." My eyes narrowed further, and he held up two hands. "Okay, okay. Angela Lansbury can do no wrong." He stayed silent, studying me for a moment as I hit buttons on his fancy remote. "It's just that it's not a television show you think of women in their twenties connecting with."

I paused my scrolling, tilting my head to face Cain. "When I was in fifth grade, I got pneumonia. I was out of school for six weeks and bored out of my mind. There was a station that had reruns of *Murder, She Wrote* on all day long, and I got hooked."

What I didn't share was that as soon as my brother got home from school each day, he'd race to my room and climb in on the opposite side of my bed and watch with me. It didn't matter what my mom threatened him with, he stayed with me as much as he could. He didn't complain about what we were watching and always played along, trying to guess the killer with me. Mom would only stand in the doorway and ask if I needed anything, while she sent our housekeeper in with soup.

I swallowed down the memories. The sweet ones were that much more painful. Knowing I'd lost that, and I'd never get it back. But I had *this*, this unidentified pseudo-friendship with Cain. A friendship that included some handholding and lips on my forehead and the best mac and cheese I'd ever tasted. I wasn't going to take that for granted.

"You look a little lost in thought."

I brought myself back to the present moment, to Cain, and smiled. "Just thinking about how I'm lucky."

The look that flashed across Cain's face said he thought I was just a little crazy. "Lucky?"

"Yup," I said, popping the p.

"How so?"

I couldn't give him everything, not my whole truth, but I could give him some of it. "That I have you in my life. Someone who will watch *Murder, She Wrote* with me even though he hates it, ensures I don't faint in the shower, and makes the best mac and cheese that has ever graced these lips."

"Well, good." There was a gruffness to Cain's tone, as though my gratitude made him uncomfortable.

"You need to get used to people appreciating you. You're a good man, Cain Hale, and you're just going to have to put up with people telling you so."

He turned his gaze back to the laptop in front of him. "Didn't you want to watch more of your inspiration, Angela Lansbury?"

I hit play on an episode I'd seen at least three times before. "All right, I'll let you off the hook." I tried to focus on the show, but my gaze kept being pulled back to Cain. He was intensely focused on the screen. His fingers would fly across the keyboard for a minute or so and then freeze, his eyes tracking back and forth, taking in whatever it was he'd done.

I cleared my throat. "Are you making progress?"

Cain's gaze flicked to me. "For the first time since I moved here, yes. I think I finally figured out the missing piece I needed." As he said the words, an expression that was nothing less than child-like glee filled his face.

"That's amazing. Must be the genius that is the murder-solving Angela Lansbury rubbing off on you."

Cain's smile turned gentle, his eyes roaming over my face. "Or maybe you're my good luck charm."

CHAPTER
Twenty-Eight

Cain

"YOU'RE CHEATING. YOU HAVE TO BE CHEATING."

Kennedy arched a single brow in my direction as she counted the brightly colored Monopoly money. "And just how would I be cheating?"

"You stole extra cash from the till when I got us drinks. Or you're using weighted dice. I don't know. But there's no way you've won three games in a row by this much." I glanced down at the board, my poor little shoe game piece sitting on the Boardwalk space Kennedy owned with two hotels. That move had wiped me right out. "It's just not possible."

Kennedy laughed and, for once, it wasn't followed by a wince. Just a couple of days of rest and healing, and she was doing so much better. But it was that sound, given so freely, that was music to my ears. "You're just going to have to live with the fact that I could probably run your empire better than you."

I scowled. She wasn't wrong. "Stealing the food right out of my mouth, I tell you."

The color drained from Kennedy's face, and I could've kicked myself. She cleared her throat, placing the money back on the couch cushion between us. "I probably got a little more bloodthirsty than I needed to." She laughed again, but this time, it *was* forced. I hated the slightly jagged edges of the noise. And the absence of the lightness that I'd grown addicted to.

"Kenz."

"Hmm?" She didn't look up to meet my eyes.

"I know."

"Know what?" She stayed staring at that damn game board as though it held the answer to climate change, world hunger, and everything in between.

I moved the board from the couch to the coffee table. "I know who your father is."

"Oh." Her voice was so damn small. Apologetic. Unsure. "I wondered when you didn't ask any questions after the gala."

"I wanted to give you time. That scene with your brother was intense. And I hoped you'd open up to me on your own."

She nibbled on her bottom lip. "But I didn't. So, you went looking."

I lifted a shoulder in a shrug. "I did."

Kennedy let out what sounded like a cross between a growl and a sigh. "Nothing's private anymore, is it? I'll never get that fresh slate I want because there's Google and YouTube, and my worst moments are just there for anyone to see. They can watch them on repeat if they want to." She blew out a breath, sending the wisps of hair that framed her face fluttering. "But I guess I've bought that."

Guilt churned in my gut. I didn't think I'd ever had a second's remorse for digging into someone's past. It was how I armed myself. Protected myself. I could control almost anything when I had enough information. But this felt all sorts of wrong, to know so much about Kennedy without her permission. Things she'd rather I not know. "I'm sorry."

She leaned back against the pillows behind her and pulled her knees up to her chest. "Why?"

"It hurts you. I never want to be the cause of your pain."

Her gaze locked with mine and held for several seconds before she looked away, out the window at the lake. "Can we go out to the dock?"

I'd tried to restrict Kennedy to the living room and her bedroom, with one brief hour on the back deck yesterday. But I knew she was getting antsy. "Sure." I pushed to my feet and reached out a hand to her. She paused for the briefest of moments before slipping her palm into mine. I pulled her to her feet. "Go slow, okay?"

"I'm not going to try and run a marathon. Just go to the backyard."

"All right, smartass."

Her lips tipped into a small grin, but she said nothing. The late-afternoon air was pretty much perfect, and I kept Kennedy's hand in mine as I led her down the steps, across the grass, and onto the dock. I told myself it was in case she lost her footing, but even I didn't believe the lie. Her hand felt too good to let go of. Too warm and vital and real.

Kennedy slowly eased herself down onto the dock. The movement was a bit jerky, and I didn't miss the twist of pain on her face. I wanted to bundle her up and carry her back inside, but it wasn't what she wanted. She needed this right now, and it was within my power to give it to her.

She stared out at the sun lowering in the sky, just beginning to paint the horizon with different colors. "It does hurt me that you know."

That truth was more of a blow than I thought it would be. That I'd caused her pain. That she wanted to hide from me when I wanted to know everything about her.

"I just—I—" She let out a long breath. "I want to be known by who I am now. Not who I once was."

I laid my hand next to hers on the dock, just my pinky

overlapping with hers. I knew she didn't want my embrace in this moment, but I needed to touch her, to have that point of contact. "I think most people feel that way. But we can't erase our pasts. They make us who we are. And, often, it's the ugly parts that lead to the most beauty."

"But is the beauty worth all that pain and suffering? And not for me. I would take the pain of losing my family, of knowing the destruction my father caused, over and over again if it meant getting to who I am today. I like that person. But it's not worth the suffering of all those innocent people."

I pressed my palms into the rough wood of the dock, the bite of pain from the planks a welcome distraction. "It's almost never our choice, though. I know it wasn't yours. That choice was taken away from you."

Kennedy tipped her face towards the sun, closing her eyes for a brief moment. "Jensen said the same thing."

"You told her?" I didn't want to admit to the flare of jealousy that had taken root in my gut.

"She deserved to know who was working for her, who was living in her space. She deserved the truth. The opportunity to ask me to leave if she wanted to."

I blinked rapidly, trying to make sense of what Kennedy had just said. "You thought she'd ask you to leave?"

Kenz turned back to me. "I thought it was a possibility. Come on, Cain, can you honestly tell me if you'd found out the truth about me before you came into the Kettle that first time, that you wouldn't have encouraged her to kick me to the curb?"

I winced. She wasn't wrong, but it was only because I would've been looking at it through the wrong filter. Because I looked at everything that way. *Identify the potential threat.* But Kennedy was showing me that some things were more important. "But I would've been wrong. And I would've missed out on knowing one of the most incredible women I've ever met."

Kennedy scoffed. "The most incredible thief, you mean."

"Oh, bullshit. You haven't stolen a damn thing in your life."

"You're wrong." The fire blazed in her eyes now. "Every five-course meal, five-star vacation, every single thing I was ever given by that man was stolen from someone else."

All of the puzzle pieces slipped into place. "You're punishing yourself."

Kennedy reared back as if I'd struck her. "What are you talking about?"

"Kenz, you work yourself to the bone and have almost nothing to show for it. You never allow yourself a single luxury, not even a damn bottle of Perrier, and give everything you can away." I pushed on when Kennedy opened her mouth to argue. "Anna told me what you did for that little girl at your dance studio who couldn't afford classes anymore. I have no idea how you even afford to eat."

"I have plenty to show for how hard I work. It might not be private planes and million-dollar mansions, but it's better than that to me. It's having self-worth for maybe the first time in my life."

I gripped the edge of the dock, trying to keep my temper in check. "I'm fucking thrilled you've found that, but is it worth putting yourself at risk? Not even having health insurance? No backup, nothing?"

"It's worth everything!" She screamed the words so loudly, it left her chest heaving. "I could barely look at myself in the mirror for an entire year after it happened. Couldn't bear the sight of my own face. My family hated me, those who'd invested with my father hated anyone associated with my family name, strangers on the street probably wouldn't have spit on me if I was on fire." She sucked in air. "I live with so much guilt. The only way it quiets down is when I give more than I take. When I give, and when I'm grateful."

God, I knew what it was like to live with guilt, to try and battle that five-ton monster that never seemed to leave you alone. I just had different coping mechanisms than Kennedy. My drug of choice was pushing myself to the point of exhaustion at the gym or work or wherever else I could find that release. So, who was I to judge how Kennedy operated? We were both just trying to cope, to hold on to the little bit of control we could.

"I get it. More than you know, I get it." I couldn't hold back from her any longer. It was as if her soul called to mine in a song only the two of us could recognize. A broken siren's song. And it was the most beautiful thing I'd ever heard.

I slipped my hand under the fall of Kennedy's hair, sliding my palm up the side of her neck, tipping her head back so I could take her mouth. The move wasn't as gentle as it should've been, but it wasn't as rough as I wanted it to be either, it was caught somewhere in the middle, just like we were caught between the past and the present.

Her lips parted on a small gasp, and my tongue slipped in, gliding, teasing, testing, waiting for any hint that she wanted me to stop. It never came.

CHAPTER
Twenty-Nine

Kennedy

I WANTED TO COMMIT HIS TASTE, HIS FEEL TO MEMORY. THE bite of lime from his earlier drink. The warmth of his tongue teasing mine. The pressure of it all. The hint of desperation. Of need. I didn't want to forget a single thing.

He pulled back then rested his forehead against mine, the only sound that of his breathing and my own heartbeat hammering against my chest. I could feel the battle that warred inside him in how he gripped my neck, how he occasionally forced himself to loosen his hold. But I didn't want that. I wanted him to hold me tighter. I wanted that wildness he tried to lock away.

I tilted my mouth to his, nipping his bottom lip. Cain groaned. "Take me to bed."

"I don't know if that's a good idea, Kenz. The way I'm feeling right now, I could hurt you. You're just starting to recover and—"

I pressed a single finger to his lips. "You won't hurt me. I want this. Do you want to touch me?" I trailed that finger from his lips down the column of his neck and let it dip into the opening of his shirt. I unbuttoned the first button.

Cain hissed out a breath. "You're a temptress. You know that?

From the second I laid eyes on you, I knew you could undo me." In a move that took me by surprise, he jumped to his feet, pulling me up with him. My legs wrapped around his waist as he picked me up. The small twinge in my ribs barely registered. He began striding towards the house.

"I can walk, you know."

Cain didn't meet my gaze. He was singularly focused now. "But then I wouldn't have your body pressed against mine."

That was a good enough argument for me. He jogged up the stairs, pulling the door open and letting it slam behind him. His strides were long, powerful, and the friction they caused had my core tightening. "Hurry," I breathed.

His pace quickened. Soon, we were in his room, in front of his massive bed. He slowly lowered me to the floor. My center pressed against the bulge in his shorts as he did so. I couldn't hold in my moan.

Cain let out a curse, quickly pulling off his shirt. I took in the sea of bronze skin over tightly honed muscle. So smooth, so tempting. I let a finger trail over his pec, down to the ridges of his stomach. "Off." He uttered the single word as he pulled my t-shirt over my head. He sucked in a sharp breath. "No bra? You've been walking around my house all day with no bra?"

I couldn't help the laugh that escaped me. "We weren't going anywhere."

He shook his head and cupped my breasts, his thumbs running over my nipples, circling, teasing. They beaded under his touch. Tightened almost to the point of pain. "You're perfect."

I wasn't. No one was. But I would take that look in his eyes anytime I could get it. One that said he'd never seen anything as beautiful as what lay before him. He sank to his knees, his hands going to my waist. Cain bent forward, trailing his lips lightly along the healing bruises of my side. My body shuddered slightly, but I didn't say a word. The gesture was so tender, I couldn't.

Cain's fingers slipped into the sides of my sweats, hooking them and my panties, and slowly, oh so slowly, pulling them down. His knuckles skimmed the sides of my legs, sending goosebumps skittering across my skin. He released the material to the floor, guiding one leg to step out and then the other.

He turned back to me, his face level with the most intimate part of me, but I didn't squirm or try to hide. This man knew it all now, all the ugly parts of my past, and he wanted me anyway. I wasn't going to shy away.

Cain's hands gripped my thighs. "You're bare."

I swallowed against the dryness in my throat. "Dance. I had to be. Leotards don't exactly hide much."

He leaned forward, pressing a kiss to my pubic bone. "I think I'm going to have to come to one of these dance classes." Another kiss just a breath lower. "Or maybe I can convince you to give me my own private performance." Lower still, he inhaled deeply. "You smell so fucking good."

Somewhere deep inside me spasmed at his words. Without warning, his tongue flicked out, delving in and circling my clit. I had to grab Cain's shoulders to steady myself. Sensations rolled through me, waves of tension, and sparks of pleasure. His mouth latched on to the bundle of nerves, and he sucked deep. "Cain." The word came out as a half-whisper, half-moan.

It only spurred him on. He alternated sucking with quick flicks using the end of his tongue. I needed more. That something extra to push me over the edge. I needed him. "More." I couldn't put my thoughts to words, could only get out that single plea.

"I've got you." Cain slipped a finger inside me, and I wanted to weep. He stroked me from within, driving me higher and higher until I thought I might burst. His lips latched on to my clit, and when the slightest hint of his teeth grazed those nerves, I went spiraling. My knees began to buckle, but Cain held me up with a single arm, pressing me to his face, wringing every last ounce of pleasure from my body.

I couldn't control the shudders, didn't want to stifle the electric pulses that danced through my muscles. As they eased, Cain lowered me to the bed, his fingers slipping out of me. I watched as he sucked them clean, his eyes flaring. "Never tasted anything so sweet."

I lifted a leg, my toes pulling at his shorts. "Off." I wasn't nearly done. I wanted to know what it felt like to have him moving inside me. To experience the dance that would be uniquely ours. The way our bodies came together.

Cain shucked his shorts, his cock springing free and jutting out. He was breathtaking. Just the sight of it had saliva pooling in my mouth. He strode to his nightstand, pulling out a small foil packet. He tore it with his teeth, rolling the rubber over the tip and down his shaft. I'd never thought the sight of putting on a condom could be such a turn-on.

Cain paused, looking pained. "I don't want to hurt you."

"Trust me, you won't." I had enough endorphins running through my system to fight off any pain.

He studied my face carefully, then sank to the mattress, rolling me on top of him. He lifted me so that I was straddling him, hovering just above where I wanted to be. "Ride me."

I wiggled my hips so he would loosen his hold, Cain got the message. I lowered myself, slowly taking him in. Each minuscule movement, stretching and creating a delicious pressure. I moaned as I took all of him. Cain cursed, his hands going back to my hips. I began to rock, small, testing movements that stoked the embers within me back to life.

I rolled my hips and sucked in a breath as he hit a spot inside me that no one had ever touched before. Cain's grip on me tightened. "Are you okay?"

My teeth sank into my bottom lip, and I nodded. I was so

much better than okay. I picked up a new rhythm, and Cain's hips rose to meet me, each of our bodies speaking without words, telling the other what we wanted, what we needed.

The end of each thrust caused contact that teased my clit, that spike of sensation tightening the cord within me a little tighter each time. Cain's strokes grew deeper. How, I didn't know. Hitting that spot inside with each thrust. "Dig deep, baby. Find it. Find it with me."

I sucked in a breath as I arched my back, seeking, searching. I found it. My walls clamped down around him as my body shuddered. As Cain thrust up, so damn deep, I knew it was a claim. I rode out the waves of trembles and sparks of pleasure, not wanting to miss a thing. And Cain rode it out with me until I stilled, collapsing onto his chest, heaving.

His fingertips trailed up and down the ridges of my spine. I relaxed into him. "Not sure I'll ever recover from that."

Cain chuckled, the action causing my core to tighten. "Fuck. You're going to kill me, woman."

I laughed. "It'd be a hell of a way to go, though."

"That it would." He pressed his lips to my temple. "I have to get rid of this condom." Cain eased me off him, and I rolled to my back, wincing a bit at the loss of him.

Cain was back in a matter of seconds, pulling back the covers and ushering me under. As soon as I obeyed, he pulled me to him so that I was lying on my unbruised side, head resting on his pec. "Do you feel okay?"

I let out a bark of laughter. "I feel like a noodle."

"Is that a good thing?"

"Oh, it is definitely a good thing."

Cain ran his hands through my hair. "Glad to hear it." He paused for a moment. "This changes things. You know that, right?"

"How so?"

The smooth strokes of his fingers through my hair took a stutter-step. "This thing between us, we're going to explore it."

I tilted my head back so I could see Cain's face, those beautiful, storm-blue eyes. "Are we now?"

"We are."

My lips twitched. "Is that your way of asking me to be your girlfriend? Are we going steady?"

Cain scowled. "I'm not fifteen."

"Aw, shucks. I was hoping for your Varsity letterman's jacket."

Cain shook his head. "Do I need to fuck you again? You have entirely too much sass for someone who just had two orgasms."

I grinned. "Give a girl a second to catch her breath, would you?" I laid my head back on his chest. "Did you play sports in high school?"

Cain's body locked under mine as his hand froze in my hair. The fingers began moving again. "Nope. Not really an organized sports kind of person."

"What kind of person were you?"

The tension in Cain's muscles wasn't going away. "Just not into a lot of group activities."

Something about this was all wrong. It wasn't like I was asking for state secrets, just a glimpse of who Cain had been at fifteen. I risked a push. "What were you into, then?"

"Nothing, really. Just your average high school guy stuff, I guess."

It was a brush-off, and I knew it. I had laid myself bare for this man. Physically, emotionally. And he couldn't even tell me what his hobbies were. As my mind ran through the time I'd known him, I realized something. Cain only shared personal tidbits on his terms. What I knew about him would barely fill two pages in a notebook.

He knew everything about me, but I knew almost nothing about him. But, somehow, it felt like my soul recognized his.

Was that a lie? My brain tricking itself because there was burning chemistry between us?

No. I knew him. Enough of him, anyway. I'd seen the kindness in him when he played with Lizzie. The generosity of his spirit in everything he gave away. The protectiveness in how he cared for the people who were important to him. I knew the important things. But I'd thought I knew the important things about people in my life before. People I loved. And in a blink of an eye, they'd turned into strangers capable of destroying everything we held between us.

CHAPTER
Thirty

Cain

KENNEDY LET OUT A LITTLE MOAN AS SHE STRETCHED, her perfect backside pressing against me. "Careful," I warned, palming a breast in my hand. "You might not be ready for what that action could bring."

She turned her head to look up at me, her eyes executing a slow, sleepy blink. "Morning."

"Morning, baby." I swept my lips across hers, but she pulled back. I scowled.

"Morning breath."

I didn't give a fuck about morning breath. I wanted her lips. Having a taste of her had only made the cravings worse. I dove in, taking her mouth with no apologies. Slipping my tongue inside, stroking, teasing, demanding. When I released Kennedy, she looked a little dazed. "How's that for morning breath?"

She grinned. "I guess I don't mind it so much, after all."

"Good." I tucked a strand of hair behind her ear. "What do you want to do today? More *Murder, She Wrote,* or are you going to cheat your way to victory in Monopoly again?"

Kennedy rolled her eyes. "Who knew you were such a sore

loser?" I nipped at her earlobe, and she squealed. "Okay, okay, I promise not to embarrass you in Monopoly again." She paused, pressing her lips together briefly. "I was actually thinking it might be nice to get out of the house a bit. Maybe go into town. Do you know if Walker got my bike when he picked up your car? I need to take it to a bike shop and see what happened to the brakes."

I stiffened. That damn bike. I wanted to run it over with my SUV.

"What? You just got all scowly."

"I don't want you riding that damn bike."

Kennedy pushed up in bed, the oversized t-shirt she wore slipping off one shoulder. "Excuse me?"

"It's a death-trap. You could've been killed."

"Which is why I want to take it to a bike shop and have some-one look it over. They'll know what went wrong."

I ran a hand through my hair as I pushed up against the pil-lows. "Even if they can fix it, it's not safe."

"Cain, you're being ridiculous. People ride bikes all the time. I had an accident. That's all."

I turned to face Kennedy. Her auburn hair was in wild disar-ray from sleep, her green eyes flashing. Nothing could happen to her. "I need you safe."

Kennedy's expression softened, and she scooted closer to me, placing both palms on my chest. "I am safe. What is this really about?"

My chest tightened. "You know what it's about."

"But can you tell me a little more? So I can understand better?"

I opened my mouth to say something, anything, but I just couldn't. The idea of recounting every painful detail of Kiara's death was too much. I couldn't do it. I'd never actually had to say the words before. Walker and Tuck had been with me when I'd gotten the call, they'd spoken directly to the police. And they had been the ones to bring Dr. Murphy up to speed when I'd started seeing him. We'd talked about Kiara, sure, what had happened, but I'd never had to tell the tale from beginning to end. I never wanted to. Something about saying the words aloud made me fear I would break.

I swallowed against the cracking dryness in my throat. "I can't talk about it. I'm sorry. I know that's not fair. I just—I can't."

Kennedy pulled her knees up to her chest and curled into herself. "It's okay. You don't have to. I'm here whenever you're ready." There was a hint of hurt in her tone, one that had me kicking myself. She deserved more. I would give her everything I had to offer, but I wasn't sure I'd ever be able to give her this.

I pressed my lips to the crown of her head. "Thank you."

We were quiet for a while, both lost in our own thoughts. My phone buzzed on the nightstand. I reached over and picked it up. It was a text from my assistant.

Rachel: *Health insurance for Kennedy Charles is all set up. I'll have them send the card directly to you.*

I typed out a quick reply.

Me: *Thanks. I appreciate you moving so quickly on this.*

Rachel: *Whatever you need.*

"Is that Walker?" Kennedy asked, pushing off my chest.

I cleared my throat. "Um, no. It was my assistant. I asked her to get some health insurance set up for you—"

"What?"

I let out a little cough. This would not be good. "I had her set up some health insurance for you."

That fire was back in Kennedy's eyes. "I appreciate that you covered my hospital bill, but I will be paying you back for that. It might take me a while, but I'll do it." Like hell, she was. "But I didn't ask you to get me health insurance. I don't want you to get me health insurance. I already talked to Jensen about getting me an affordable plan through the Kettle so I'm covered in emergency situations."

"Kenz, things have changed. We're together, figuring this thing out. I want to take care of you. Why won't you let me?"

She swung her feet off the bed and stood, beginning to pace. "Did it ever occur to you that I don't want someone to take care of me? That I can take care of myself?"

I got to my feet. "Oh, you take such good care of yourself that you were begging me to send the ambulance away because you had no health coverage? You can take that good care of yourself?"

Kennedy glared at me. "It was an oversight that I've now corrected. Jensen has already submitted an application for me."

"Yeah, for some budget plan that will have crappy coverage. I have the means to get you the best. Why won't you let me?"

"And what happens when you leave, huh?"

My body jolted. She thought I was going to leave her. That as soon as this nasty business with my company passed, I'd be gone for good. Even if things didn't work out between the two of us, I'd never cancel her health insurance. Was that seriously what she thought of me? When my eyes really took in her face, I saw it, the fear, the uncertainty. She'd opened up to me completely, given me everything, and I was still holding back. Like I always did. I crossed to Kennedy, pulling her into my arms and resting my chin on her head. "I'm not going anywhere."

"You live in Portland."

"I live here."

"But you'll need to go back there eventually."

The idea of going back to Portland, a city I'd always thought I wanted, didn't hold the same appeal anymore. There was something special about Sutter Lake, the energy that flowed through the town and the wilderness surrounding it. This place was good for me. Being surrounded by people I trusted, who I knew cared for me, not for what I brought to the table, but because I was family to them. There had to be a way for me to stay on permanently.

I pressed my lips to the top of Kennedy's head. "I may have

to go back occasionally, but I like it here. And when I go, you can come with me." Already, I couldn't imagine leaving her here, spending a night without her. I'd slept better last night than I had in almost two decades.

She pressed her face harder against my chest as if she were trying to burrow inside me. "My name is death for any business. When the truth of who I am gets out—and it will if we're ever photographed together—it could ruin things for you."

"Kenz, if anyone doesn't want to do business with me because I'm with a woman who was so brave, and cared so much about doing the right thing that she helped the FBI arrest her own father, giving up every privilege she'd been raised with in the process, then I don't want their business anyway."

Kennedy seemed to sag against me. "You say that now, but it might be different when half your clients walk."

They wouldn't. She overestimated how hated she was. Her brother was at work for another financial firm already. Time dulled people's memories. I rubbed a hand up and down her back. "It'll be okay. I promise."

"I want to try. But we have to find a way to meet in the middle."

I pulled her back to the bed, sitting and tugging her into my lap. "What does that look like?"

She nibbled on her bottom lip. "I'll ask Jensen if there is a better plan I can get under her insurance. You can pay the difference in plan prices until I can handle it on my own. Fair?"

I wanted to argue how ridiculous this was, that the price of the premium plan I'd gotten her was mere pocket change for me, but I held those thoughts back. What was important was that she was protected, would have no reason not to go to the doctor. "Fair. What about the death trap?"

Kennedy sighed and rolled her eyes. "I want to keep riding my bike." My muscles tensed. "But I know my body needs some recovery time. Could you give me a ride to ballet and the shelter for a couple of weeks?"

I hated that she was already planning on going back to work. That she wasn't asking for a ride to the Kettle because she was planning on staying in her studio. Well, that was fine, I'd just stay there with her. "I can do that. Will you avoid that hill from now on?"

"There's another route I can take. It's just a little longer."

"Thank you." I brushed my lips against hers. "I have one more request."

She studied me. "And what's that?"

"You let me stock your fridge with Perrier."

Kennedy burst out laughing. "If that will make you happy, go right ahead." She gave a happy sigh. "It has been nice to have my Perrier again."

She'd been drinking it like crazy since she was at my house. It was such a tiny thing, but it brought a smile to her face, and Kennedy had been depriving herself of those little things for far too long. I could see clearly that it was some messed-up form of atonement for a situation that wasn't hers to assume. I was going to do everything in my power to get Kennedy to let herself enjoy the simple pleasures in life again. Giving her endless Perrier wasn't enough, but it was a start.

CHAPTER
Thirty-One

Kennedy

"YOU CAN TAKE ME TO WORK, OR I'LL WALK. AND think of all the bandits who could get me then." It had been a week since the relationship between Cain and me had changed since we'd had our meeting of the minds—and bodies. And things were good. Mostly great, actually.

We spent our days, tangled together on the couch. Cain worked while I watched *Murder, She Wrote*, and I'd even gotten him to try and predict who the killer was with me. He was also trying to teach me to cook. So far, I'd mastered scrambled eggs without setting fire to his kitchen.

We spent the nights tangled together in a whole different way. I'd never had someone light my body on fire the way Cain did. It was as if he knew the exact map of my nerve endings and took great pleasure in tracing every single one.

The only hitch had been when he'd insisted on accompanying me to my follow-up doctor's appointment. He'd basically bullied the doctor into agreeing that I needed another week's rest. I think he'd scared the older man, actually. But I was done.

There was only so much Angela Lansbury and Cabot Cove a girl could take.

In an attempt to appease me, Cain had loaned me his fancy tablet so I could work on research for the shelter and the community center. I had a few ideas for programs that I thought would be perfect. One was bringing in horses and a therapist to work with residents who had been through trauma. Another was getting someone like Cain to offer free classes on working with computers, everything from the basics to programming. Those skills were things the job market was desperate for, and it would set the shelter residents and the community members up for success. But now that my wheels were turning, I was even more hungry to get back to work and Hope House.

"Kenz, the doctor said—"

I held up a hand to stop him. "Cain, you basically threatened to sue the man if I went back to work and got so much as a headache. Of course, he said I needed another week off." I crossed to Cain, gentling my tone. "Baby, I need to go back to work. I'm going stir-crazy. If I start to feel bad, I promise I'll call it quits and go upstairs to rest."

Cain huffed out a breath. "Fine. But Chuck's staying with me."

I let out a laugh, and Chuck raised his head from where he lay on the couch, his gaze going back and forth between us like a tennis match. Chuck had started following Cain around like he was his new best friend. I knew it was because Cain slipped him bacon every morning, the cheater.

"Fine. Chuck can stay here today." We hadn't talked much about me returning to my apartment over the Kettle. I needed to, but I wasn't quite ready to say goodbye to the routine I'd built here with Cain, either. *Stand on your own two feet*, I reminded myself. It was important. I'd fought so hard for so long to build the independence I had. I didn't want to lose it.

"All right, go get ready. I'll fix us breakfast for the road."

I chuckled and kissed Cain's cheek. "Don't sulk, it's not very manly."

"I'll show you manly." Cain took my mouth in a bruising kiss that had me panting when he pulled away.

"Much better than sulking." Cain smacked my butt as I walked away, and I couldn't hold in my laugh.

"You're back! Ohmigosh, I didn't think you were going to be back for three more days. Get over here." Jensen wrapped me in a warm hug. "Missed you."

"I missed you, too, J. Sorry I left you high and dry."

She released me. "It's not your fault." She looked behind me to Cain and burst out laughing. "I take it someone isn't too happy you're returning to work."

"She's supposed to take another three days off." Cain had been full-on pouting since we'd pulled out of his driveway.

"I promise I'll make her take it easy. Frequent breaks. And she can always lay down upstairs if she needs to."

Cain nodded and crossed to me. "I'll see you in a couple of hours." He cupped my face with his hands and took my mouth in a slow kiss that lit a simmering fire in my blood that would burn for hours. "Call me if you need me."

I nodded, watching him leave. When I turned back to Jensen, her mouth was hanging fully open. She closed it and opened it a few more times before she got any actual words out. "What? When? Tell me everything!"

I laughed. "Come on, I'll fill you in while we prep for the lunch rush."

Jensen and I spent the rest of the day catching up as we worked. I hadn't realized just how much I'd missed her. My body held up pretty well. My ribs began to twinge towards the end of my shift, but Jensen picked up on my awkward movements and put me to work in her office, adding receipts to a spreadsheet. Before long, Cain was knocking on the open office door. "How are you feeling?" The look of concern in his eyes had me melting just a bit.

"I did great. Thanks for picking me up." I pushed to my feet and went to grab my bag.

"Are you sure you're up for ballet, too? This is a lot for your first day back."

"It's just one class, and then I want to go by the shelter for a little while, too."

"Kenz." My name was a low warning.

"Just for an hour. I haven't seen Anna or Lizzie in too long."

"Fine. But then straight home to rest."

"Sir, yes, sir."

Cain grabbed hold of my hand and tugged me to him. "Why is it that the sass always makes me want to fuck you?"

My breaths started coming a bit quicker. "That's really just encouragement for me to be more of a smartass."

Cain chuckled and nipped my bottom lip. The move sent an electric hum straight to my core. My hands fisted in his shirt, and I pressed my mouth to his, my tongue darting in, hungry, searching. Cain cupped my ass, pulling me flush against him.

A throat cleared behind us. "Uh, this is a place of business. Children come here. Take it upstairs, would you?" Jensen then burst into laughter.

My cheeks were on fire. "Sorry, J."

Cain scowled at her. "Like you and Tuck are any better."

"Fair point, well made."

I glanced at my watch. "Shoot, we gotta go, Cain. I can't be late." Seraphina hadn't exactly been happy when I'd told her that I needed almost two weeks off work. If I was late my first day back, I might have to kiss my dance job goodbye. "I'll see you tomorrow, J. What time do you need me?"

"Not till ten."

My brows rose. That was a lot later than usual.

"I'll fill you in tomorrow."

I nodded and tugged Cain out the door. We made the drive to the dance studio in a matter of minutes, and I was inside with more than ten minutes to spare, but Seraphina was waiting. "Cutting it a little close, aren't we?" she asked with a huff.

"Sorry, my other job ran a little over." I felt Cain at my back, but Seraphina barely spared him a glance.

"It's clear this job isn't very important to you. Maybe it's time I start looking for a new teacher."

My stomach sank. As much as I hated dealing with Seraphina, this was my favorite of all my jobs. Getting to introduce little ones to dance, seeing them gain strength and confidence, it was the best feeling in the world. "Please, don't."

Cain stepped forward, his face hard. "I'd hate to think that you were threatening an employee for taking a medical leave of absence. I'm fairly certain the court system would have something to say about that."

Seraphina's mouth fell open. "Excuse me? And who are you?"

"I'm her boyfriend. Someone who also happens to have the top law firm in Portland on retainer. So, just go ahead and try me, lady."

Seraphina sucked in a sharp breath. "Well, I never." Her head whipped in my direction. "This is who you choose to associate with, Kennedy? I'm disappointed. Though I guess I shouldn't be surprised." She jerked her chin up and turned for her office.

Cain turned back to me, carefully assessing my reaction. I let out a long breath before I spoke. "I can fight my own battles."

He took a step towards me, brushing the hair from my face before cupping my jaw. "That doesn't mean you should always have to."

A burning sensation started up along my sternum, but it was

different than the usual fire I felt there. This was a mixture of pleasure and pain. It had been so long since I'd had someone fight for me. Maybe Cain was right. Perhaps it was okay to set down my sword for a little while and rest. Let someone who cared for me take up the mantle for a minute.

This man was slowly slipping behind every defense I had. And as much as he seemed to care for me, I knew I cared for him more. But *care* wasn't the right word. It wasn't strong enough. I was dancing closer and closer to the strongest word there was. I was falling in love with Cain Hale. And I was absolutely terrified.

CHAPTER
Thirty-Two

Cain

I WATCHED HER THROUGH THE STUDIO WINDOWS AS I listened to the phone ringing on the other end of the line. She was grace with a little bit of whimsy thrown in. Kennedy's arm arced, and her back bowed, curving into a shape that seemed to defy logic, but then she threw in a funny face at the mirror where her students could see when she came out of the move.

"Cain."

"Doc," I greeted.

"Haven't heard from you in a couple of weeks. How are things?"

And wasn't that a loaded question? So loaded, I wasn't exactly sure how to begin its answer. "Kennedy was in an accident."

The sounds of leather squeaking came across the line, and I saw Dr. Murphy in my mind, straightening in his chair behind the desk in his office. "Is she all right?"

"I'm watching her teach ballet to about a dozen six-year-olds right now." She was more than all right. She was perfect.

Murphy sighed. "I'm glad to hear that. How'd you handle it?"

I thought about it for a moment. There had been bone-deep

panic for sure, but I hadn't lost it. I didn't tear apart a hospital room or require sedation. I made sure that Kennedy was taken care of. Safe. I hadn't thrown that damn bike into my lake, even though I still wanted to. I was showing restraint. Maybe I could do this. "I slept with her." The words tumbled out before I could stop them.

Murphy chuckled. "Kennedy was in an accident, and you slept with her?"

I rubbed a hand over my jaw. "Not right after she was in the accident, like a week later." It had probably been too soon, but I hadn't been able to hold myself back from her. Not for a moment longer.

"Ah. That makes a bit more sense. And how is the relationship progressing?"

"We're finding our way. I'm trying to compromise." But I knew there would always be the cloud of my past hanging over us. Things I wouldn't—no, *couldn't*—talk about. "She wants to know why I am the way I am."

"Why you're fixated on her safety?"

"Yes." I watched as Kennedy led a line of little girls and one little boy across the floor in a series of jumps. The sheer joy on all their faces was something to behold.

"And what did you tell her?"

I focused back on Murphy's voice. "She knows I lost someone. I just can't give her more. I can't go there." I squeezed the back of my neck. "And that makes me feel like a grade-A asshole because she's shared some pretty personal stuff with me."

Dr. Murphy was silent for a moment. "It may not feel like it. But this is progress."

I grunted in response. Claiming my victories in this area had never been my strong suit. Maybe because I still felt so weak. So out of control whenever memories of Kiara hit. There was nothing I hated more than that feeling.

"It is. You're letting someone new in. There's a part of you that wants to share more with her."

"No, there's not." I couldn't allow even the smallest piece of me to want that. Because if I let something slip, and I broke, I wasn't sure I could climb back out of that hole.

"Cain, there's no rush. Keep Kiara off the table for now. Have you shared other parts of your life with Kennedy?"

That vicious vise-grip on my chest eased a bit. "Yeah." I told her about my company, the bullshit and betrayal I was dealing with, the project I was working on. I'd told her more about that than I'd told anyone else.

"Good." I could hear the smile in Dr. Murphy's voice. "New assignment for the week."

I groaned. "Enough with the fucking assignments."

"Just bear with the torture a little longer. This week, I want you to mark the things that go right. You're too focused on the negative. Try to pay attention to the positive. Write down three things every day that you're thankful for."

"You sound like Kennedy." She was in the process of hugging all her little dancers before they ran off to meet the parents who'd come to pick them up.

"How so?"

"She has this thing about gratitude. She has these jars, and she writes down things she's grateful for each day and puts them in there."

"I like her already. Maybe you can make your own jar."

"Don't push your luck, Doc." I couldn't exactly see myself painting and decorating a jar and putting it on my bookshelf.

Murphy chuckled. "Fine. I'll settle for you writing down three things a day. You can burn it after if you want."

Now there was an idea. Kennedy bent to grab her bag and rubbed her ribs where the bruising was. "I gotta go."

"Talk to you soon, Cain."

I didn't even say goodbye, just hit end on my phone. I met Kennedy at the door, pulling it open. "You overdid it."

She looked up at me with a puzzled expression. "What are you talking about?"

"I saw you rubbing your ribs. Do you want to go home and take a painkiller?"

Kennedy's puzzled expression melted into amusement, and she pushed up on her tiptoes and brushed her lips against mine. "I'm fine. I promise. I still want to go to the shelter for just a little bit."

I let out a growl of frustration, grabbed the bag from her shoulder, and started towards my SUV. "Fine."

"There's no need to pout, grumpypants."

I froze, turning in place. "Did you just call me grumpypants?"

Kennedy's lips twitched, and her eyes danced. "I could call you Mr. Grumpypants if you're feeling fancy."

I strode towards her, cupped her jaw, and pulled her to me for a hard kiss. "You're going to pay for that later. That orgasm you want? I'm going to make you beg for it."

"We'll see who's begging," she challenged, stepping out of my hold and giving my ass a little slap as she headed for my SUV.

I shook my head and grinned up at the sky. The woman was going to kill me.

"Kennedy, I'm so glad you're all right." Doug pulled Kenz into a hug that went on for far too long. My eyes narrowed on him until he released her.

"I'm fine. I think I'll be back to regularly scheduled volunteering by next week."

I pulled her back against me, wrapping an arm around her and pressing my lips to the crown of her head. Doug's eyes narrowed at the action, and I grinned. *Starting to get the picture, buddy?*

"Are you sure you're okay? You got some scratches on your

face." Lizzie nibbled on her thumbnail as she spoke, and the fear in her voice had my chest clenching.

I released my hold on Kennedy and crouched down so I'd be eye-level with the little girl. "I promise you, Kennedy is okay. You know when you fall down and scrape your knee when you're playing?" Lizzie nodded. "That's what happened to Kennedy."

Lizzie didn't look like she completely believed me. "I think it would hurt lots more if you fell on your face."

Kennedy chuckled. "It wasn't fun, but Cain's been taking good care of me. He even made me the best mac and cheese I've ever tasted."

Lizzie's eyes widened. "Ever?" Kennedy nodded, and Lizzie looked back to me. "Will you make me some?"

I grinned. "I'd love to. How about next week?"

Lizzie nodded enthusiastically.

"Well, it's about damn time." Anna strode across the rec room floor and pulled Kennedy into a hug. "I'm so happy you're okay." There was a hitch in Anna's voice as she spoke.

Kennedy squeezed her back. "I'm feeling so much better, there's no need to worry." Anna released her. "Thank you so much for helping out at the Kettle while I was laid up."

I knew that having Anna take on some of her duties at the Kettle had made Kennedy feel less guilty for taking time off. Time that she had definitely needed.

Anna smoothed out her apron. "No problem, girl. It actually worked out perfectly." A smile stretched across her face. "Jensen offered me a job. Said she needs help with all of the baking."

Kennedy grinned. "I was hoping she might because we all know that isn't exactly in my skill set."

Everyone laughed, but as Kennedy joined in, she winced. I'd had enough. "Baby, we need to get you home. You've had enough for one day."

She sighed. "Okay, you're probably right. I'll see you guys next week."

"*Baby*, huh?" Anna smirked at us.

Kennedy blushed. "Things might have changed since the last time I saw you."

"Oh, I just bet they have. Good for you. Get you some of that pretty boy."

I chuckled. "Why do I suddenly feel like a piece of meat?"

Anna's gaze flicked to me. "I don't think you mind our girl here treating you like a piece of meat."

I shook my head. No, I didn't. Lizzie was looking between us like she was trying to figure out exactly what was going on, but it was the look on Doug's face that almost had me choking with laughter. He looked as if he were sucking on a lemon and had smelled something bad all at the same time.

I wrapped an arm around Kennedy's shoulders and guided her towards the doors. "Let's get you home."

"We have to go pick up Chuck first. I left him at your place."

My steps faltered. When I'd said I wanted to get her home, I'd meant *my* home, the place that was quickly becoming ours in my mind. "You don't want to stay at the lake house?"

Kennedy rolled her lips together. "I've been at your place for almost two weeks. Don't you think I should stay at my apartment tonight?"

"No." I didn't want to spend a single night without her.

Her lips quirked. "Cain, I can't just move in with you. We haven't even gone on a date."

"I'll take you on a date, then." Usually, my encounters with women had plenty of that. The best restaurants and wine, followed by five-star hotel rooms. None of that was Kennedy. I'd never even taken a woman I was romantically involved with to my home, and here I was, wanting nothing more than to move Kennedy in. It was too fast for her, but I saw that flicker of desire underneath. She didn't want to leave.

I brushed my lips across hers. "Let's make a deal. Stay at my place tonight. Tomorrow, we'll go to yours."

"We?"

"Yes, we. I'm not spending the night without you."

A smile stretched across Kennedy's face. "That sounds like a plan I can get behind."

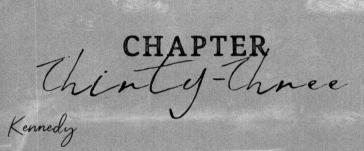

CHAPTER
Thirty-Three

Kennedy

I MOANED AS MY PHONE RANG AGAIN FROM WHERE IT SAT ON the nightstand and reached out a hand to grab it. It took a few tries for my fingers to find it.

Cain cursed and rolled to his back. "Who the hell is calling at six in the morning?"

I blinked sleep out of my eyes. "Jensen." My stomach dropped. She wouldn't be calling this early unless something was wrong. "Hello?"

"Hey, I'm so sorry to wake you up."

I sat up in bed. "It's okay. What's wrong?"

Jensen groaned. "There's a gas leak at the Kettle."

"Ohmigosh, is everyone okay?"

"Everyone's fine. It smelled like crazy when I opened the back door, so I called Walker, and then the gas company. They're here trying to figure out what happened. But it looks like there might have to be some repairs."

I looked over at Cain, who was wide-awake as soon as I'd asked if everyone was okay. I gave him a reassuring smile but continued talking to Jensen. "I'm so sorry. Can I do anything?"

"Well, you'll have a few days off, at least. Do you think you could stay with Cain for a while longer? It looks like the leak was centered under the apartment, so I think they'll be doing the most work there."

It wasn't exactly a hardship, having an excuse to stay with Cain longer. Chuck crawled up from the foot of the bed and laid his drooling face on Cain's naked chest. Cain shook his head but scratched behind Chuck's ears. "I don't think that'll be a problem."

Jensen laughed. "I didn't think so. They said you can come pick up some of your belongings if you need to. Just give them another hour or so."

"That would be good." Some things in that apartment were precious to me, and I didn't want to lose them if something happened while they were making repairs.

"Okay, see you in a bit."

"See you. Just text me if you need me for anything."

"Thanks, Kenz."

I hung up and turned back to Cain. "There was a gas leak at the Kettle."

Cain straightened. "What? How?"

"I don't know. Jensen just smelled it when she opened the back door this morning. There's a crew at the shop assessing the situation, but I guess there's something that needs to be repaired."

"You're not staying there."

I rolled my eyes. "No, I'm not staying in an apartment that is leaking gas."

"Smartass." Cain pulled me to him, sending Chuck back to the bottom of the bed. He nipped at my bottom lip. "Where are you staying, then?"

"Hmmmm. I don't know...Do you know anyone who might take me in?" I brushed my mouth against his. "I always pay my debts."

"Temptress." Cain rolled his hips, his hard length sending a trail of sparks across my center.

I straddled him, pulling my t-shirt over my head. We had an hour to kill, and this was a hell of a way to do it.

I hopped out of Cain's Range Rover as soon as he parked. My eyes were locked on Jensen, who was huddled talking to Tuck, Walker, and an older man I didn't recognize. She nodded and rubbed at her temples before the older man walked away, heading back into the building.

"J, are you okay?" I wrapped her in a big hug. "I'm so sorry you have to deal with this." There was a flicker of guilt at spending my morning wrapped up in Cain while my friend was worried and stressed.

She squeezed me back. "Thank you. It'll be fine. It shouldn't take longer than a week to fix, so we won't have to be closed long. It's just so weird…"

"What is?" Cain asked, coming up behind me.

I released Jensen, and Cain wrapped an arm around me, pulling me to his side. I loved the feeling of his warmth. His comfort. Just the pressure of his body against mine gave me peace. I hated and loved it at the same time. Because what happened if he decided that small-town life wasn't for him? *I* wasn't for him? What if he left and took my peace with him? Or worse, what if all those things he locked away reared their ugly heads? What if he betrayed me just like everyone else I'd loved? I shook my head, trying to clear my thoughts to focus on J.

Tuck cleared his throat, a muscle in his cheek popping. "They found that a few of the pipe fittings on the gas lines under the apartment were loose."

I looked between Tuck and Jensen. "Is there a reason that's weird?"

Jensen glanced back at the building. "All of that stuff was re-done when I renovated five years ago. I can't imagine those guys being careless enough to leave pipe fittings loose. And I'd have thought we'd have a problem before now if that was the case."

Tuck reached out and grabbed J's hand, tugging her to him. "We'll figure it out. Maybe someone was messing around in there and screwed something up."

"Maybe…" Jensen's eyes widened. "My deep-clean crew came in last night. Maybe they were wiping down the pipes and acci-dentally loosened something. Oh, God, Tuck, they could've been hurt."

Tuck rubbed a hand up and down J's back. "Everything's okay, Wilder. We'll fix it and make sure nothing like this happens again." His eyes met Cain's and then Walker's. They shared a look I couldn't quite read.

The older gentleman I'd seen earlier appeared in the doorway. "You can come in now and grab whatever you need."

Jensen straightened. "Go ahead, Kenz. I'm so sorry I'm kick-ing you out of your home."

Walker coughed. "I don't think she or Cain mind too much."

My cheeks heated, and Cain smacked Walker upside the head. "Watch it."

"Come on." I tugged on Cain's hand. "I want to get my stuff." We headed inside, side-stepping various crew members as they assessed pipes and took readings. As soon as we were safely in my apartment, I turned to face Cain. "What was that about?"

"What was what about?" He seemed genuinely confused.

"That look Tuck gave you and Walker when we were talking about what happened."

Cain's jaw tightened. "You're too observant for your own good." I made a gesture for him to continue. Cain sighed. "A cleaning crew couldn't accidentally loosen some fittings, not if they were installed correctly. They're too tight."

My brows pulled together. "So, what do you think happened?"

"I have no idea. It's possible there was an error during installation, someone was lazy." But something in Cain's tone told me that he wasn't totally convinced of that.

I nodded. Hopefully, they'd find some answers when they made the repairs. "I just want to grab a few things."

"Here." Cain laid the duffle bag he'd brought with him down on the bed.

"I really just want my jars, a couple of books, and this." I reached up to my bookshelf and pulled down the photo of Preston and me. That flare of familiar pain danced along my sternum. This had been the best day. Some girls at school had been picking on me, so Preston had decided I needed a break. We'd both skipped classes, and he'd taken me into the city to the Central Park Zoo. We'd walked around and talked for hours. About what was going on at school, and about things that were of no importance.

No one had understood me better than my brother. But now…How could he not understand that I had to turn our father in, that I was trying to protect him? I knew, at his core, he wasn't a greedy man. Sure, he enjoyed the privileges we'd grown up with, but he was also caring and incredibly generous. Tears stung the corners of my eyes.

Cain wrapped an arm around me, pulling my back to his front. "Why do you keep it out?"

"Why?"

"Yeah. It hurts you to look at it. Why do you keep it out? In a place where you see it every day."

I traced Preston's and my faces with my fingertip, both of us grinning so hugely in front of the polar bears. "Because I don't want to forget that my brother loved me once. I don't want to forget that I had this one magical relationship growing up, someone who laughed and teased, who supported and encouraged, someone who understood me. Just because it's painful now, doesn't mean I want to forget."

I turned in Cain's arms, and the pain I saw in his eyes stole my breath. "Cain, who did you lose?" It was impossible for me not to ask the question. I couldn't see the depth of his pain and ignore it, even though I knew he wanted me to.

His Adam's apple bobbed. "I can't talk about it."

"Why?" The one word was a plea. *Tell me. Show me. Trust me.*

Cain released me. "I don't want to. Don't go there, okay? I've shared what I can."

The words stung, invisible barbs coating my skin. "Maybe you should paint me a roadmap of what I'm allowed to ask about and what I'm not."

His gaze met mine, and he nodded. I'd said the comment in anger, but he was taking it practically. "Anything after college is fair game. And I won't talk about my family. Ever."

I blinked up at him. I could have his present, maybe even his future, but I could never have his past. I wanted Cain, but I was selfish, I wanted all of him—the way he had all of me. My gaze skimmed over his face, the raw pain in his eyes, the hard set of his jaw. I couldn't let him go, even if it hurt every day for the rest of my life not to have it all, *some* would have to be good enough. "Okay."

Cain's shoulders sagged, and he pulled me to him, wrapping both arms around me and pressing his lips to the side of my head. "I'm sorry."

I was, too. I hurt for him, for myself, and for whomever it was that he lost—the person I'd never know, who would always be a part of him. The present. The future. I had to stay focused on that. It was more than so many had, and I needed to be grateful.

I shrugged out of his hold. Even his hug was painful. "I need to see if Jensen wants to get rid of any stock that will go bad in the next few days, and then we can take it to Hope House. That okay with you?" I looked up at Cain but couldn't quite meet his eyes.

"Of course."

We gathered everything Jensen wanted to part with, which turned out to be quite a bit, and headed for the shelter. The drive over was quiet, both of us lost in our thoughts, my heart squeezing in a painful rhythm. As soon as Cain came to a stop, I hopped out of the SUV, grabbing a bag from the back.

Cain's hand came to rest on mine when I tried to take a box, as well. "I can get the rest."

I nodded, and we headed inside. I waved to a couple of residents who were seated at tables in the rec room. Jay looked up from the cards he held. "Need a hand, Kennedy?" He seemed to eye Cain suspiciously.

"We've got it. Thanks, though."

"I don't like that guy," Cain muttered as he pushed open the door to the kitchen.

I let out a laugh. "That's because you're paranoid. Should I get you a tinfoil hat in case he's an alien?"

"Hardy har har."

Doug appeared in the hallway, looking a bit startled. "What are you guys doing here in the middle of the day?"

I set my bag on the counter. "There was a gas leak at the Kettle. It's going to be closed for a few days, so Jensen thought we might want the stock she can't use."

Doug nodded. "That was generous of her. Please, thank her for me."

"I will."

His gaze jumped from me to Cain and back again. "Actually, do you have a minute? I wanted to discuss something with you."

I paused in unpacking the bag. "Sure. What's up?"

"Can we chat in my office?"

"Of course." I looked back at Cain. "Can you unload this stuff? I'll be right back."

A muscle in his cheek fluttered. "Sure." His eyes narrowed on Doug.

Oh, boy.

I sighed and started for the back office. As soon as we made it inside, I sank into one of the two chairs opposite Doug's desk. He took the other.

"How are you feeling, Kennedy?"

"So much better. Thanks for putting up with me missing so many volunteer days."

Doug waved a hand in front of his face. "You don't need to thank me, I'm just glad you're okay." He began to fidget in his seat. "That's actually what I wanted to talk to you about." My brows pulled together in confusion. "I'm worried about you, Kennedy."

I gave him a gentle smile. "I promise, I'm fine. You can call my doctor if that'll make you feel better."

Doug's Adam's apple bobbed as he swallowed. "It's not that. I'm concerned about your involvement with Cain. He doesn't seem like the most stable fellow."

My mouth opened, then closed, then opened again, but I struggled to find the right words. "Doug...I really appreciate you wanting to look out for me, but Cain is a good man. He's just a little overprotective. That's all."

Doug snorted. "A little? He practically threatens anyone who goes near you."

"I think that's a bit of an exaggeration." My temper pricked. I wasn't a child. I could make decisions regarding my own life.

He reached out and grabbed my hand. "Kennedy, please. Just think about his behavior. It's not normal."

I pulled out of Doug's grasp. "Our relationship is my business. We're friends, Doug, but I didn't ask for your opinion. I'm a grown woman who can make choices for myself."

Doug's jaw tightened. "Of course. Just know I'm always here if you need to talk."

I rose from my chair. "Thank you. I need to get going, but I'll see you later this week."

I strode down the hallway, the weight of a day that wasn't even half over seeming to feel heavier with each step.

Cain straightened from where he leaned against the counter. "What's wrong?"

I shook my head as Cain pulled me into his arms. I let my forehead fall against his chest. "It's just been a no good, very bad day. Can we go home and forget about the real world for a little while?"

"Of course, we can." He pressed his lips to the top of my head. "I'll even give you a foot rub."

I lifted my face up to meet his gaze. "Sweet-talker."

"Always."

Cain led me out of the kitchen, our fingers intertwining. Just being with him, having that simple touch, gave me such peace. I only hoped he wouldn't rip it all away one day.

CHAPTER
Thirty-Four

Cain

"I BELIEVE YOU HAVE OFFICIALLY MASTERED SCRAMBLED eggs."

Kennedy beamed as she took a bite of egg and toast. "With *cheese*," she said around chews.

I chuckled. "The cheese is the most important part." Kennedy lived with a joy I didn't think I'd ever witnessed before. It was the simple things that gave her the most pleasure. Mastering a new dish, drinking a Perrier in the evening as we watched the sunset, watching her dog chase after his ball for the millionth time. The kinds of things I had been taking for granted for the past decade. She reminded me of what was important. And I had hurt her.

Kennedy tried to hide it. Still, there was an underlying sadness just below the surface, almost as if she were mourning something. And I knew I had put it there. By holding back. By not telling her everything. I was a bastard for it. Asking her to give me everything but not doing the same in return. I would do everything I could to make up for it.

I cleared my throat. "Sooo…"

"Yes?"

"I finished the program."

Kennedy shot up from her stool and launched herself at me with such ferocity, I had to hold on to the counter to keep us both from tipping over. "Cain! That's amazing! When?"

"Last night." I hadn't been able to sleep, so I'd pulled out my laptop and worked while Kenz slept peacefully next to me.

The wide smile faltered a bit, and she released her hold on me. "Does that mean you'll be heading back to Portland soon?"

I pulled Kennedy back towards me so she was tucked between my legs. She still didn't believe me, that I wanted a life with her here. "I've been thinking about building a headquarters in Sutter Lake." There was an office park on the outskirts of town that I'd seen on my way to pick up food the other day that would be perfect. I'd done a little research, and it was just lying vacant because the last company housed there wasn't large enough to keep it afloat. Halo was. And I knew I had more than enough employees who would love to make the move with me. To have a chance to work for a company at the top of the game but raise their families in an idyllic small-town setting. It really was the best of both worlds.

Kennedy studied my face, her hands resting on my shoulders. "Is that really what you want?"

I brushed the hair back from her face. "I want you. I want the life I'm building here. A future that is full of you and that tiny terror." I inclined my head towards the living area where Chuck snored away.

The corners of Kennedy's mouth tipped up. "I want that, too."

"Good." I brushed my mouth against hers, cupping her ass and pulling her flush against me. I let out a groan. "But first, I have to deal with my company."

Adorable little worry lines appeared between Kennedy's brows. "How are you going to do that? You still don't know who the leak is."

I kissed the tip of her nose. "I've got a plan." I let out another groan as I stood. "One that unfortunately doesn't include taking you on this counter right now." The flicker of heat in Kennedy's eyes told me she wasn't opposed to the idea. Shit. I had to focus.

She gave my chest a little shove. "Go. Do what you need to do, and then we'll celebrate."

"I'm holding you to that." I headed back to my bedroom to get my computer and make some calls. I'd finally come up with the perfect plan to smoke out the traitor in my midst. I'd created a dummy program. One that would run for weeks before anyone knew something was wrong and that it wasn't doing what it was supposed to. But once it was uploaded to a new computer and running, it would send me a new notification, and that notification would have a piece of code that was specific to whomever I'd given the program to.

I would know if anyone gave it away. And I was starting at the top. The two people who knew the ins and outs of Halo better than anyone. If I could clear them, I'd breathe just a little bit easier. I reached for my cell and sent a text.

Me: *Not a word of this to anyone, but I finished the program. I think it's going to take us to the next level.*

Within seconds, I had a reply.

Jake: *I'm in my office now. Can you encrypt and send?*

Me: *Give me five.*

I got to work sending him the program while I tapped out another text.

Me: *Keep this between you and me, but I finished the program.*

Two minutes later, my phone rang.

"Cain, that's amazing! You must be so proud," Rachel whispered, likely trying to avoid any listening ears.

"Thanks. I want to get you a copy to upload to your company laptop for safekeeping."

She cleared her throat. "Why don't I take the jet and we can do the transfer in person? You know how I feel about you sending that stuff. I don't want to be blamed for something getting out." I was silent for a minute, trying to read her reaction. She pushed on. "I have a bunch of documents for you to sign, as well."

Whether we did this in person or not, the test was the same. "All right. Have Vince accompany you. There are loaner cars at the airport he can use."

"Okay. I'll be there tomorrow." She paused for a moment. "It'll be good to see you, Cain. Things haven't been the same around here without you."

A trickle of guilt slid through me. I was a bastard for putting them all through this, but there was no other option. If I wanted to build a headquarters here, it had to be with people I trusted. I cleared my throat. "It'll be good to see you too, Rach. Fly safe."

"Will do."

I hit end and stared at my phone. This time next week, I'd have my top two team members cleared, and I could start convincing Kennedy that I was here to stay.

CHAPTER
Thirty-five

Kennedy

CAIN WAS TRYING. I KNEW HE WAS. THAT KNOWLEDGE ignited something in me. Excitement. Hope. Maybe I could have a family again, one of my own choosing. But there was also a healthy dose of fear coursing through me. I kept waiting for the other shoe to drop. I hated it, but the fact that Cain wouldn't tell me about his past, said that he didn't completely trust me yet.

But I had to hold on to that sliver of hope that, over time, he would. That he would fully let me in. It seemed like this was new for him. As if sharing even the mundane things about his days was a habit that had grown rusty over time. I wanted him to feel safe, accepted, loved. Even if I wasn't ready to say the words yet. And that meant no more pushing.

It went against my nature. If I saw something was wrong, I wanted to fix it. If someone was hurting, I needed to help heal them or at least bring comfort. It took everything in me not to dig, but I was holding strong.

I keyed the code into the gate and waited while it swung open. I'd convinced Cain to let me borrow his car. I wanted to do something special for him, a real celebration of him completing the program he'd worked on for months. Something from the heart, something that would mean more to him because he knew me.

A smile curved my lips. That was the ultimate gift, to have someone know you, all of you, the good, the bad, the ugly, and the beautiful, and love you because of the unique mix it all made. I just wished Cain could see that I wanted to give him the same.

I pulled the Range Rover to a stop in front of the house and hopped out. Popping the trunk, I moved around to grab my two bags of groceries. The sound of tires on gravel had me turning around. An unfamiliar SUV with tinted windows appeared at the bend in the drive. It had to be Cain's assistant. He hadn't shared much of his plan to trap whoever was selling his company's secrets, just assured me that, within a few weeks, he'd be able to start putting the pieces in place for an office here.

The thought had more warmth spreading through me than I wanted to admit. This was just our beginning. A door slammed, shaking me out of my daydreams.

"Hello," I called as Rachel crossed to me, her mouth pressed into a tight line.

"Hello, Callie." Rachel's gaze traveled the length of me, seeming to assess and find me lacking.

"It's Kennedy." It was awkward, but if I didn't correct her, I would come across as a timid mouse she could scare off. This was a different woman than the one I'd met briefly on the ride to the gala. That woman was professional and polite. This one was...not.

She scoffed. "I can't be bothered to learn all the names. You'll be gone before I can blink, and I have more important things to focus on. More important things *Cain* wants me to focus on."

So, that's how it was. I bit back the smile that wanted to surface. I didn't blame her. Working around Cain twenty-four-seven for years, I'd want him, too. I knew Cain didn't see her that way. The way he talked about her was the same as you'd discuss any colleague.

I shrugged. "Sounds good. I'm just going to unload these groceries because I've got a celebration planned."

Her eyes narrowed on me. "And what exactly are you celebrating?"

"Cain finishing the program."

Rachel's jaw fell open. "He told you that?"

"Yup. It's amazing news, right?"

Her cheeks began to redden. "I can't believe he trusted a…a gold-digger like you with that information."

"Rachel…" The low warning came from Vince.

I grinned at him, ignoring the heat coursing through me at her accusation. "It's okay, Vince. I don't blame her. Cain's hot and kind and a million other things she doesn't know about. That'd make me cranky, too."

Vince chuckled, but Rachel's spine shot straight. "You're the one who doesn't know him. You've been around for…what? Two-point-five seconds? You think you've caught him because he's fucking you? You couldn't be more wrong. I'm the one he turns to. The one who's been there from the beginning. The one who knows all his secrets. Knows why he built this company. The pain he's trying to escape. Do you even know about Kiara?" She scoffed. "Of course, not. All you know is the shape of his cock."

"Rachel!" Cain strode from the house, anger seeming to tinge the air with each step. "What the fuck did you just say?" His words were slow, deliberate, and filled with so much fury I couldn't help but take a step back.

The problem was, his anger didn't change the truth. One that might as well have been a barbed stake to the heart. Apparently, other people could know about Cain's past. It was just *me* who couldn't. I took another step back. I needed away from this. Space to let out the tears I was holding so tightly to at the moment.

"Don't." The single word was a whip as Cain's head snapped in my direction. "Don't you move. The only one who's going to be moving is Rachel. After she explains the bullshit that was coming out of her mouth."

Rachel's face screwed up into a mix of hatred and longing. "I spoke the truth. It's not my fault if she can't handle it."

Cain's jaw went to granite. "We are colleagues. We have only ever been colleagues. You don't know the first thing about my personal life."

"Really? Who deals with your flings when they do everything they can to get a second or third go? Who stays until midnight when you're working on a project just to make sure you remember to eat? Who has been with you from day one, giving everything? Just waiting for you to notice that the perfect woman is right next to you?"

I felt bad for her then. She was a bitch, but so was unrequited love.

Cain's mouth fell open. He was totally and completely clueless. "Rachel...I'm sorry, but I don't feel that way about you..."

Rachel held up a hand to silence him, her face going red. "Shut up. I don't want to hear it." Maliciousness filled her features, and I knew that whatever she was about to say, it would be meant to cause the maximum amount of damage, to hurt Cain the way he'd hurt her. "Didn't know there was a traitor under your nose just like you didn't know there was one in your family. Isn't that right, Cain? What does it feel like to know you couldn't protect your sister then, just like you can't protect your company now?"

Cain's eyes narrowed, a coldness I'd never seen before slipping over his features. "Have you been selling access to our servers, Rachel?"

She let out an ugly chuckle. "I might not be a CEO, but I'm

not an idiot. I'm not telling you shit. But you should've realized how much the people around you have grown to know about the programs you designed."

I didn't think, I just lunged. This greedy little—She'd stolen Cain's blood, sweat, and tears and sold it to the highest bidder. "You bitch!"

Cain caught me around the waist. "Don't. She's not worth it."

I tried to shake loose, but Cain's hold was too strong. "She stole from you!"

"I know. Calm down, baby. Calm." I stopped my thrashing as Cain pressed his lips to my temple. "And that's why she's fired." He looked to Vince. "Confiscate her company phone, computer, and tablet, and escort her back to Portland."

"Of course, sir." Vince held out his hand to Rachel. "Ma'am."

Rachel threw the phone at Vince's chest. "Fuck all of you." She stormed back to the SUV and got inside. Vince raised a brow at Cain.

Cain released me and pulled out his phone. After a minute of typing on the screen, he looked up. "She's locked out of the system."

"You going to press charges, boss?"

Cain looked to the SUV, and that's when I saw it. Pain. He hadn't expected the traitor to be Rachel. Someone who had been with him since day one. Someone he'd thought had his back. "I need to get in touch with my PI, see if we can figure out just how much damage she did."

Vince nodded. "I'll put a tracker on her car. Just in case."

Cain chuckled. "Thanks." He watched as Vince strode back to the SUV and climbed in. He kept watching until the vehicle disappeared from view. Then he turned to me.

"I'm so sorry, Cain." I didn't go to him, didn't reach out. Because it felt like a step in any direction was a step into quicksand.

He took two steps forward. "I'm not."

"You're not?"

Another two steps. "Nope."

I licked my suddenly dry lips. "Why?"

Another two. He was just a breath away, but he didn't touch me. "I'm free. I can start a life here without looking over my shoulder."

"Are you sure you want that?"

Cain's jaw clenched so tightly there was a faint clicking noise. "Why do you keep fucking doubting that?"

I looked over his shoulder, not able to meet his gaze. Rachel might be a bitch and a traitor, but she knew things about him that I didn't. Things I might never know. And that burned.

"Please tell me the lies Rachel spewed didn't get to you."

My gaze flicked back to Cain. "You shared things with her that you won't with me."

"I did fucking not. I've told her nothing about my past. Anything she knows is because she snooped where she had no business. The person I've shared the most with in the past decade is you." Cain reached out, grasping the end of my tank top and pulling me gently to him. "You are the one I want a future with. I never thought I'd say that. But I am." He brushed his mouth against mine, soft and strong. "Is my future enough for you?"

"Yes." I breathed out the agreement. It was instinct. There was no other answer. I loved this man, and I wasn't letting him go. "You're enough. Always."

"Thank fuck." Cain lunged, tossing me over his shoulder and startling a laugh out of me.

"Cain! My groceries."

He growled but turned back to the Range Rover, grabbed the bags, and shut the back hatch. "Groceries aren't exactly my priority right now."

"I need them for later." I had a surprise in store for the man who held my future, and I didn't want some wild animal to steal it out of his SUV.

Cain jogged up the steps as if I weighed nothing. Pulling the door open, he tossed the bags on the floor and headed towards his bedroom.

I pinched his butt. "It's a good thing there wasn't anything breakable in there."

"If there was, we could always buy more."

I groaned. I didn't think I'd ever be able to get this man to be practical.

Cain flipped me off his shoulder, sending me sailing through the air and landing on his bed with an *oomph*. He grinned wickedly at me. "Now, that's better."

I smiled back. "Better would be naked."

"That can be arranged." Cain tugged the tee over his head, and I followed suit, pulling off my tank and slipping off my shorts. Cain cursed. "Seriously, no bra again?"

I bit my lip, staring up at the gorgeous man in front of me, a picture of smooth, tanned skin over hard, lean muscle. I wished I had a lick of artistic ability in me. I wanted to immortalize him just like this. "I'm kind of anti-bra when I can get away with it."

Cain stepped closer to me, reaching out a hand and swiping a thumb across my nipple. It beaded under his touch. "You know that means I'll constantly be staring at your tits from now on, wondering if you're bare under there. People are going to think I'm a pervert." I couldn't hold in my laugh. "Oh, you think that's funny, do you? That I have zero control when it comes to you? That you make me lose all common sense?" He gave my nipple a light pinch, twisting as he went.

I sucked in air. "Cain…" My voice was breathy, pleading.

"You like that?"

I nodded.

He pinched both nipples, a little harder this time, and sparks danced through my nerve endings as heat flooded my core. Cain slipped a hand under my hair, tugging my head back to grant him better access. He took my mouth in a slow assault. Stoked the fire that had been lit when he pinched my nipple and driving it higher.

I reached out, making quick work of the button on his jeans and pulling them down. With a dexterity I certainly didn't possess, Cain kicked his pants aside. I grasped his cock and he sucked in a sharp breath. The smoothest silk that seemed to grow impossibly harder as I stroked. My fingers wandered. I wanted to know every inch of this man's body, inside and out. He may not be able to give me his past, but I could have this. And I wanted to know it all. What turned him on, what drove him higher, what made him absolutely lose his mind.

I cupped his balls, tugging just slightly, and Cain tore his mouth away from mine, eyes blazing. "Are you trying to make me lose it?"

I grinned. "Maybe."

"Fuck. I need a condom." He strode towards the nightstand, starting to open it.

"I'm on the pill now. And I got checked."

Cain's head jerked in my direction. "When?"

I licked my lips. "When I had my follow-up at the doctor in town."

Cain's eyes turned molten, the dark blue in them seeming to almost glow. "I'm clean. I've never gone without a condom."

"Take me."

There was the briefest moment of hesitation before Cain lunged, covering my body with his. I knew how much this meant. He was giving me a piece of his trust. It wasn't everything, but it was more. And all I needed were little pieces of more along the way.

Cain's cock bumped my opening as his lips trailed up my neck to my ear. "Are you sure?"

"I'm sure."

He didn't hesitate this time. With one slow thrust, he was inside me, bottoming out and stealing my breath.

"Cain." It was a whisper and a plea. For what, I wasn't exactly sure. But Cain seemed to know somehow. The pace he set was deep and slow, as if he were trying to fill all of me, imprint himself on every last cell of my body.

He cupped my face with one hand as he moved, his thumb brushing back and forth across my cheekbone. The movement stilled for the briefest moment, and he held my gaze with his, so much passing between us. "You're everything to me."

Tears welled in my eyes. A feeling of belonging overtook me. Of being cherished. I hadn't felt anything close to it in so long. We weren't the perfect people, but we just might be perfect for each other. "You're everything to me, too."

It was all he needed. The slow strokes were gone. In their place was a punishing pace that seemed almost feral, as if Cain needed to be closer, deeper than ever before.

I moaned, arching my back and granting him access. Hooking my legs around his hips, I dug my heels into his ass, spurring him on. The feel of him with nothing between us was everything. My fingers dug into his shoulders, my nails biting into his skin.

Cain cursed and thrust even deeper, the movement sending the room spinning. As if everything I could see or feel cracked like frozen glass. One more stroke and the glass shattered. My world came apart around me, and I knew things would never be the same.

CHAPTER
Thirty-six

Cain

"WHERE ARE YOU GOING?" THE BED DIPPED AS Kennedy rolled away from me, disrupting my light snooze. A nap that was needed because she had drained every ounce of energy from my body.

She grinned at me over her shoulder as she picked up the shirt I'd hastily discarded on the floor. "Stay where you are. I have a little something in store for you, but I want it to be a surprise. So, no peeking."

I watched her body bend and twist, graceful even while just getting dressed. "I've got all the surprise I need right here. Except you keep covering up my view." I leaned forward and grabbed the corner of the t-shirt she'd just put on, pulling her towards me.

Kennedy bent, brushing her mouth against mine. "Behave."

"Now, why would I want to do that?"

She grinned. "Because good boys get rewards later."

I pulled a full-on pout that had Kennedy cackling as she headed out the door. I didn't like her away from me. I wanted to touch her anytime I damn well pleased. Having her near meant breathing easier. I needed to get a grip. This was getting ridiculous.

I pushed out of bed, pulling on a pair of boxers and grabbing my laptop. I needed to get some things in play for Halo. I booted up the computer and reached for my phone, hitting Jake's contact.

He answered after only two rings. "Hey, man. The new program looks great. Not that I'm as well-versed as you are, but from what I can tell, it does everything we were hoping for."

My gut clenched. I really hoped my number two didn't up and quit on me. "About that. There's something I need to tell you."

"Okay." The sound of a door closing came over the line. "Sounds serious."

"It is." I picked up a coin from my nightstand and flipped it over and over between my fingers. "I found the leak."

Jake was silent for a moment before clearing his throat. "Who?"

"You're not going to believe this. It was Rachel."

Jake sucked in an audible breath. "No, shit? How'd you find out?"

"She as much as admitted it, but there's more." I set the coin back on my nightstand. I could get away with not telling Jake what I'd done with the dummy programs, just send him a new one and say I'd updated a few bugs. He'd never have to know that I doubted him, that I had tested him. But that wasn't fair. I owed him the truth.

So, I spilled it all. The list of people I'd narrowed things down to, my plan to cross him and Rachel off my list first so they could help ferret out the culprit, Rachel's nasty explosion at Kennedy. I told him everything.

Jake was again silent, and it lasted longer this time. "So, you gave me a program that sends you an alert as soon as it's uploaded to a new computer?"

"I did." The program has to run for at least twenty-four hours, but he didn't need to know the ins and outs, just that I'd tested him. And for that, he deserved an apology. "I'm sorry, Jake. I needed to know I could trust my people at the top. But I'm sure you're pissed as hell right now. And that's fair. If you don't want to work for me anymore, I'll understand, but I hope we can get past this."

There was more silence, then the shuffling of papers and the sounds of Jake rising from his chair, pacing maybe? "I get why you did what you did, it just sucks to be on the other end of it. I need a couple of days to wrap my head around this."

"Take all the time you need." It was the least I could give him.

"Thanks."

Jake hung up before I could say goodbye. I had a feeling I'd be looking for a new second in command before long. Jake and I had never been friends exactly. But I'd destroyed the little bit of trust between us, and that was almost impossible to rebuild. Maybe it would be better to part ways, start fresh with someone new. I'd give Jake a more than generous severance package. He'd earned it.

The sounds of a mixer whirring wafted in from the kitchen. I winced. Kennedy was cooking. She'd mastered scrambled eggs and a few other things, but she'd never ventured out on her own, making something from scratch. Hopefully, she wouldn't start a fire. Or cut herself. The possibilities for harm were endless, and my chest began to constrict, the panic setting in.

I took a slow, deep breath, in through my nose, and out through my mouth. She would be okay. I was right here if anything happened. She needed her freedom, even in something as simple as cooking, and I had to give it to her. I never wanted to clip her wings, I wanted to help her fly.

I forced myself to relax against the pillows. I could focus on work. I'd ignored my email inbox for far too long, getting sucked into finishing the new Halo program and being distracted by all things Kennedy. And it wasn't a distraction that I thought would fade with time. Kenz was endlessly fascinating. Hell, I'd been transfixed just watching her get dressed. I'd never tire of just watching her move through space, through life.

I shook my head. She was distracting me even when she wasn't here. I zeroed in on my laptop screen. "Work. Emails. Kennedy later." I lost myself in proposals and inquiries, sending a message to HR that I'd need a new assistant. I politely suggested a male this time.

Time flew by in a blur of reading and typing as I remembered why this company was so important to me and got excited again about what I could make it into.

"Cain." Kennedy's voice calling from the kitchen jolted me from my thoughts.

"You ready for me?" I called back.

"Yup, come on out."

I closed my laptop and set it on the bed. Rising, I threw on a pair of sweats and a tee. As I opened the door of my bedroom and stepped into the hall, the scent of something sweet—and distinctly not burned—filled my senses. I grinned wide as I headed for the kitchen. My girl had done it. She needed this win.

Kennedy beamed as I walked into the kitchen. She threw her arms wide. "Ta-da!"

I looked down at the creation in front of her and froze. It was one of those rainbow chip cakes. The ones with the multi-colored sprinkles in the frosting and in the cake itself. Just the sight of it, sent me hurtling back in time.

"Cain?" Kiara looked up from where she was coloring.

"Whatcha need, princess?" I set down my pencil next to my math book.

She rolled her lips together the way she always did when she was nervous. "Do you think maybe this year I could have a cake?"

My chest tightened the way it always did when it was so damn obvious that Kiara didn't have the same life as other little girls. Then heat seemed to spread through me. Our good-for-nothing mother sure as hell wasn't going to get her a cake. It was four o'clock, and she was already at the bar, drinking away the little money we had. Good thing I lifted cash from her purse whenever I could. If I didn't, Kiara and I would probably starve.

I looked at Kiara's hopeful face. Turning six was supposed to be fun. I forced a smile. "I think I can figure something out." I'd make sure I did, even if I had to beg one of the neighbors to help me.

She smiled huge. "Maybe I can get one of them rainbow cakes!"

My brow wrinkled. "A rainbow cake?" Shit, I didn't even know what that was.

Kiara's head bobbed up and down. "Yeah! You know the ones that have all the sprinkles in the frosting and in the cake, and they're all different colors?"

The tension in me eased a little. That was a cake from a box. I could handle a cake from a mix. I would make it every year for her if it put that kind of smile on her face.

"Cain?"

Kennedy's voice shook me from the memories. I had made the rainbow cake for Kiara that year. For her sixth birthday, and every birthday after until I'd left for college. Until I'd left her alone. Abandoned her to a woman I knew wasn't any kind of mother.

"I can't." My voice was hoarse, even to my own ears.

"Cain." Kennedy's voice was so incredibly gentle. There was no anger, not even any hurt, just concern. "What's going on?"

"I'm sorry. I just can't." I turned on my heel and fled.

CHAPTER
Thirty-seven

Kennedy

WHAT THE HELL HAD JUST HAPPENED? I LOOKED down at the cake I'd worked so hard on. I'd read the instructions half a dozen times, just to make sure I got it right. But this wasn't about me. There'd been pain in Cain's eyes. So raw, it seemed to claw at my chest, tearing at the flesh there.

How did so much pain come from me making him a cake? Cain hadn't trusted me with his pain. Would every step I took forever mean guessing where the landmines lay? Hoping I didn't step wrong and get blown to bits? Because as much as I knew his reaction wasn't about me, it still hurt. No, it killed.

I wasn't sure I was strong enough to withstand a lifetime of that. Of rejection for no discernible reason. Of thinking I was helping, only to hurt instead and then be punished for that pain.

I gripped the granite counter, the edge of the stone cutting into my hands. I welcomed the bite of pain and pressed down harder. I'd spent most of my life walking on eggshells, attempting to avoid my mother's disapproving judgment, making sure I didn't disappoint my father with dreams that differed from his.

The life I'd built in Sutter Lake was my first taste of freedom. I didn't want to lose that, couldn't. But I didn't want to lose Cain either. I took a slow, steadying breath and released my death grip on the granite. He had to talk to me. Let me in. At least, tell me why a damn cake had sent him running, and my heart breaking.

My heart hammered in my chest as I headed for the bedroom. Walking inside, I could hear the shower running. Good. Maybe that would cool Cain off, calm him down, help him to see reason. He couldn't lock some huge part of himself away from me and expect us to build a life together. It would be impossible.

I lowered myself to the bed, facing the bathroom door. I could wait. I twisted the hem of Cain's t-shirt I wore, rubbing the soft cotton between my thumb and finger. The shower continued to run. I released my hold on the tee and studied the room around me.

Cain's house was beautiful, but it had a coldness to it. There were no personal touches. No photos, keepsakes, or art that seemed to mean anything to him. If you walked through this house, you'd learn nothing about the man who lived in it. But that's exactly how he liked it. He kept everyone at arm's length, including me.

My gaze swept over his nightstand, catching on the drawer that was slightly ajar. A pop of color had caught my attention. Snagged it because the rest of the house was all muted tones. Grays and blues, greens, and shades of white.

I pulled the drawer open an inch. Glossy paper. A photo. My fingers moved without my mind agreeing to it. It was one of the most beautiful young women I'd ever seen. Glossy, dark hair, flawless, tanned skin, a smile that you knew would light up a room, and eyes that I knew almost as well as my own. Irises so dark blue, you'd practically think them brown.

"What the hell are you doing?"

I jolted at Cain's voice. I'd never heard it sound fiercer, holding

248 | CATHERINE COWLES

tightly to rage beneath the surface. "I'm sorry. I-I-I just. The drawer was open, and I saw a photo. I grabbed it before I really thought it through. I'm so sorry."

Cain's bare chest heaved. He wore only low-slung sweats, ones that had been my favorites until this moment. The way he studied me, analyzed every micro-expression my face made, said he didn't trust me one bit. It was another slice to my already shredded chest. "You were fucking snooping. I open up my home to you, and you betray that?"

I pushed to my feet, my hands trembling as I laid the photo on the bed. Cain did not get to pull this on me. I was not going to let him twist this into something it wasn't. Twist me into something I wasn't. For the last two and a half years, I'd let the world paint me into a monster. I'd never defended myself. I'd allowed my own brother to twist my motives, my soul, into something ugly. I hadn't wanted to let anyone close enough to feel that betrayal again, but I had. And I wasn't going to allow Cain to get away with doing what Preston had. I was done letting the world decide who I was.

"You don't get to pull that card, Cain. I wasn't tearing apart your room, trying to uncover your secrets. But maybe I should because you won't tell me anything. I never know what's okay to ask you about. I made you a fucking cake that I was so proud of, and you looked like I handed you a live grenade. Why?" My heart hammered against my ribs as I waited. Cain said nothing. Silence had never hurt so much. Tears stung the backs of my eyes, but I forced them down. "I've laid myself bare for you, and you won't tell me a single personal thing about your past. Do you know how that feels?"

Cain's eyes blazed now. A deadly, blue heat. "What do you want to know?" He growled the words low, just as dangerous as the fire in his eyes. "That my mom was always drunk? That I took care of my sister from the time I was five?" My heart seized as I pictured tiny Cain trying to care for a miniature version of the girl in that photo.

"That I left her because I had this great opportunity to go to college, and while I was gone, my mom got hooked on oxy. That her dealer broke into our house when my mom wasn't home and decided to take his payment by raping my sister? Or maybe that when she wouldn't stop screaming, he strangled her? Is that what you want to know?" He spun around, reaching for the decorative ceramic bowl on the dresser, a piece in those same muted tones as the rest of the house, and hurled it at the wall, shattering it into a million pieces. "Fuck!"

I didn't even flinch when the bowl hit. Didn't twitch at Cain's shouted curse. I was numb. His sister. Oh, God. His sister. Cain. My gaze met his, and it was ravaged. I thought I'd known what guilt felt like. I knew nothing. "Cain." His name was a cross between a whisper and a prayer, maybe it was a plea.

"Get out." His body trembled as he released the words. "Get the fuck out of my house."

That had me jerking. "What?"

"I'm getting some air. When I get back, I want you gone." He strode right out the door. Didn't glance at the destruction he'd created, didn't look at the wreckage in his wake. Just left.

My body shook as I tried to get it to move. It took a couple of tries. Finally, my limbs obeyed my brain. I pulled out my phone.

Me: *Can you come pick me up at Cain's?*

I had a response within seconds.

Jensen: *Sure thing. Now?*

Jensen: *Wait, is everything okay?*

I wasn't sure everything would ever be okay again. Not for me. And definitely not for Cain. He'd let that pain fester, and it had turned septic. It was eating him alive from the inside out.

Me: *I'll explain when you get here. I'll be by the gate.*

The last thing I needed was to be accused of giving out gate codes to Cain's house. Not that it mattered. I was sure he'd change all the security as soon as I was gone. I wasn't trustworthy, after all.

Jensen: *On my way.*

I let out a shaky breath and hurried to stuff my belongings into the two duffle bags I had. *Jensen. A place to live. A job. Chuck.* I paused, trying to think of one more gratitude. I let out a choked sob. "I'm alive."

I glanced down at the photo on the bed. I was alive, and the beautiful girl in that photo...her life had been cut short in the worst way imaginable. In that moment, I would've traded my life for hers. I would've done anything to protect Cain from the pain he was feeling now. But I couldn't. And he wouldn't let me help him bear it.

I slung a duffle over each shoulder and headed for the living room. Chuck snored away on the couch. His deafness finally came in handy. That scene in Cain's bedroom would've scared him. I hooked the leash onto his collar and scratched his ears. "Come on, buddy."

Chuck's eyes flew open, and he took in my face. Like always, he immediately knew something was wrong. He lapped at my cheek. I picked him up and sat him on the floor. "I've still got you. You and me against the world."

I headed for the door. My heart lurched as I reached for the handle. The tears I'd been holding at bay finally spilled over. This was it. I glanced over my shoulder, through that wall of glass, to the lake. The man that would probably always hold my heart stood on the dock, hands in his pockets, staring out at the water as if it held all the answers in the world.

He looked so very alone. My chest spasmed again. I wanted to run to him. To throw my arms around him and refuse to let go, no matter what ugly accusations he hurled at me. But I couldn't. I had to save myself first. Even if it meant that my heart would never be whole again.

CHAPTER
Thirty-Eight

Cain

I WATCHED THE WATER RIPPLE AND FLOW. I WAS JEALOUS OF it. How no matter what was thrown its way, it stayed intact. It simply changed shape, form to adapt, but it always returned to its rightful resting place.

I couldn't roll with whatever life threw at me that way. No. I bent, broke, shattered. Just like that bowl I'd thrown at the wall. Tiny, irreparable pieces lying on the floor.

"Fuck." I'd thrown a bowl at the wall. I'd done that. It had been nowhere near Kennedy, but I'd still probably scared her. And then I'd left her, told her to get out, with no way of doing so. I was scum.

I turned and strode back to the house. I couldn't be with her, that much was clear, but I could make sure she got back to town safely. To her life. Without me.

Just the thought had my chest seizing. A life where someone safe, like fucking Doug, would come along and scoop her up. Someone who didn't have demons. Someone who didn't lose their shit because she'd simply looked at a photo.

I looked up at the house as I climbed the stairs. I deserved the emptiness that awaited me. Beautiful, empty rooms. No soul. A home that would remind me every day how empty my life had become and whose fault that was.

My phone buzzed in my pocket, and I pulled it out.

Jensen: *Not sure you give a shit, but I picked Kennedy up.*

The cavity around my heart spasmed. Pain and relief all at once. She was gone. And she'd never come back. It was how things needed to be. For her protection, and mine. The safest thing for us both, even if it was the thing that would rip away my last shot at feeling again.

Me: *Thank you.*

I paused for a moment, couldn't help needing to know more.

Me: *Is she okay? Where is she staying?*

I knew Jensen would take care of her, but I needed the details. The things that would hopefully help ease the painful vise on my chest. The invisible beast that liked to steal my breath and send my mind spiraling.

Jensen: *No. She's not. And I should let you stew and wonder, but even though you're a total dipshit moron, I love you, too. The Kettle was cleared to reopen, so she's back in her place.*

I needed to call Walker and Tuck, see what they'd found out about the gas leak. Make sure everything was fixed. My hands cramped as I realized I had no excuse to make sure Kennedy was safe. I couldn't give her rides or drop by her work or go with her to the shelter. She was going to be alone.

I couldn't seem to fill my lungs fully as I ran back outside and around the side of my house. She'd taken the damn bike. Of course, she'd known where it was all along. She'd been humoring me. Letting me protect her because she knew it eased something in me. But that was done, over.

I opened and closed my fists, trying to get blood to flow there, trying to urge the muscles to release. My breaths came quicker, and the cramping only got worse. No. I wasn't going to give in to this again. Wasn't going to let that invisible beast control my life. Dr. Murphy called it anxiety, PTSD, but I knew the truth, it was a monster. One that would destroy everything.

She's safe. Everything is fine. I repeated the words over and over in my mind until my heart rate began to slow, my breaths becoming more even. The world around me came back into focus. But I knew that at least half of what I'd chanted over and over was a bald-faced lie. Things sure as hell *weren't* fine. They probably never would be again.

I'd lost half my heart when Kiara was killed, and I was fairly certain Kennedy had taken the other half when she walked out that door. I'd just have to figure out how to exist without it. I didn't want it back. I wanted it where it belonged. With Kenz.

My phone buzzed again in my pocket. At least, I'd put it back in there and not dropped it on the cement in my panic. I pulled it out, expecting to see Jensen's name and maybe some more of her colorful cursing. But it wasn't. It was an alert.

My dummy program. My brows furrowed. It had to be an error. A glitch in the code. I tapped on the notification, quickly scanning through the text. My gut twisted. Jake. The program I'd sent to Jake had been uploaded to a computer outside of our network yesterday, one hour after I'd sent it to him.

Blood pounded in my ears. None of this made sense. Unless... my mind circled back to the encounter with Rachel. There'd been something in her eyes that'd told me she was hiding something. I'd just assumed it was the extent of the damage she'd done to Halo. Or maybe that she'd been embezzling, and we just hadn't caught it yet. But what if all of it was a lie?

An image of the pain that shone in Rachel's eyes flashed in my mind. I'd hurt her, and if there was one thing I knew about Rachel, it was that she had a vindictive streak. I'd seen it more than once in her decade working for me, but it had always been to my advantage. Now, it had been turned against me. I

254 | CATHERINE COWLES

knew without a shadow of a doubt that, after the other day, she would've sold anything she could get her hands on to my competitors. She would've done anything she could to cause me pain.

I hit the contacts icon on my phone and dialed Jake. "You've reached Jake. Leave a message." That twisting in my gut intensified. Rachel hadn't sold a damn thing. She'd lied to hurt me, knowing I counted on her and Jake most of all, maybe hoping it would give the real culprit a chance to cause more damage.

It had been Jake all along, and I'd given him a head start by coming clean to him earlier. I hit another number on my phone. Two rings, and someone picked up.

"Dante."

"It's Cain." I hoped he was in the country and could drop everything to hunt down the son of a bitch who'd thrown away everything I'd ever given him, who was so greedy that the millions I'd paid him over the years weren't enough. "I need your help."

Dante, always on alert, always ready for what a client might lay at his feet, said only one word. "Talk."

I filled my PI in. I'd used Dante on various things over the years. While we hadn't opened up and shared life stories, which would be difficult given the fact that the man barely talked, I knew he always got the job done. "I need you to find him. I'm filing charges. I want that fucker in jail." I sucked in a breath. "He'll go low-tech. He knows I can track him if he touches his bank accounts or credit cards. My guess is car travel and cash."

Dante grunted. "I'm on it." He said nothing else. Simply hung up.

My feet automatically began moving me back to the dock, to the water, the one bit of peace I had left. All I'd ever have. It would have to be enough.

CHAPTER
Thirty-Nine

Kennedy

"ALL RIGHT, IT'S TIME FOR WINE." JENSEN HURRIED past me and pulled open the fridge door, pawing through its contents until she found what she was looking for and emerged with a bottle. "You get the glasses."

The pouring of wine meant I was no longer off the hook. We'd spent the day readying the Kettle to open again. I'd helped J prep dough for tomorrow's baked goods, sorted teas, and wiped down tables. She hadn't asked one question, just let me sort through my feelings in silence.

Except I wasn't sorting. I couldn't. Because I was numb. It was as if everything inside me had simply turned off. It was a self-protection mechanism. Because if I let myself really feel the depth of losing Cain, I worried I'd fall into a pit that would be impossible to climb out of.

I pulled two glasses from a shelf. They were designed for juice, but beggars couldn't be choosers. Jensen inclined her head to the front of the shop. "Come on." She led me towards the two overstuffed chairs in the back corner. I set the glasses down, and she gave us both a healthy pour. "Hit me with it."

I settled into the chair, slipping off my shoes and pulling my knees up to my chest. I needed the comfort. The points of contact. The pressure to hold me together. "I don't really know." Jensen simply arched a brow at me. "He wouldn't talk about his past. All he'd say was that he lost someone. It was clear he was hurting. There's so much pain in him, J."

She nodded, concern flashing in her amber eyes.

I studied her face. "You know."

J took a sip of her wine. "Only the broad strokes. That he lost his sister in an incredibly violent way. That he takes it on himself. Takes responsibility for everything. It's why he was so overprotective of you."

"I'm getting that." I twisted the glass of wine in a circular pattern on the table between us. "Him keeping something from me, something that I knew was hurting him, was hard for me. I told him everything. About my family. My shame. I laid it all at his feet, but he couldn't trust me to let me in even a little."

"I don't think it's about trust, Kenz. It's just too painful for him to go there. I don't know a lot about that time in his life, but I overheard Walker talking to my dad one night when he was home from college for a weekend. Cain lost it when he found out. Took a swing at a cop. He was admitted to the hospital on an involuntary hold."

I sucked in a sharp breath. Images of my beautiful, strong, kind Cain, restrained. Sedated. Those invisible claws dug deeper into my chest. I could only imagine how alone he'd felt. I wanted to wrap my arms around the image in my head. "I hate this for him. All of it. I'd do anything to take it all away." I swallowed, tears brimming in my eyes. "But I also can't walk on eggshells for the rest of my life, wondering what random thing might set him off."

Jensen's brows pulled together. "What happened?"

I told her about the cake, now realizing it must have somehow reminded him of his sister, then about going into the bedroom, finding the photo. "I wasn't trying to snoop. I swear. I just—there aren't any photos in his house. So, when I saw that one…"

"You were naturally curious. I get it. Kenz, you were pretty much living there, I don't think you're evil for looking at a photo that was sticking out of a drawer."

But guilt churned in my stomach, its choppy waves making me feel just a bit nauseous. "But I invaded his privacy. I get him being mad. I do. The thing that absolutely kills…" A burn started up in the back of my throat. I swallowed it down. "I was starting to feel like we were a team, like maybe, just maybe, I could build that family I'd always wanted. But in that moment, I was on the outside looking in. We weren't a team anymore. I was the enemy." My breath hitched. "I don't think anything has ever hurt that much, not even losing my brother."

That was the thing about starting over, about moving on. When you took a chance, knowing how much it could hurt when you lost someone, the risk was that much greater. The fall, when everything came apart, so much more painful. I rubbed at the place between my breasts. Even now, knowing how much this hurt, I missed Cain. I craved that feeling of safety, comfort, and peace that came when I was wrapped up in his arms.

"I'm so sorry, Kenz. Give him some time to come around." Jensen gave me a gentle smile. "I think this is the first time he's attempted a real relationship since college. He needs to adjust to letting someone in."

I shook my head. I'd seen the ferocity with which he held onto his demons. The memories that haunted him. He'd never let me in there, and I was no longer sure we could make it work if he didn't.

I looked down at my still-full glass. "I'm sorry, I don't think I'm up for wine, actually. I'm just going to go upstairs, take a long, hot shower, and try to get some sleep."

Jensen stood, pulling me to my feet and wrapping me in a hug. "I love you, Kenz. You have a family here. It's me and Tuck and Noah and all of my nosy, intrusive, well-meaning relatives. You're not alone."

I let out a hiccupped sob. "Thank you."

"Always." She gave me one last squeeze and released me. "Get some sleep."

"I will." I climbed the stairs, pulling open the door and pausing briefly as my hand hovered over the security system keypad. I'd have to deal with the reminder of *him* as long as I lived here, but I didn't have to set the dang thing. Maybe I could hang a picture over it or something. I sighed, bending to scratch Chuck's ears. He only raised a single eyelid. He was mad at me. He missed Cain, too. "Sorry, buddy."

I shuffled to the bathroom, stripping off my clothes and stepping under the hot spray. It didn't matter that it had been in the eighties today, there was a chill in my bones that I couldn't escape. I turned the water up to scalding. It still didn't cure the cold.

I turned off the tap, climbing out and toweling off. I pulled on pajamas and forced myself to blow-dry my hair. Waking up to a rat's nest wouldn't make anything better. I sighed and glanced at the time on my phone. 8:13. Maybe I could find a Tylenol PM to take and force sleep.

Chuck barked from the other room and let out a low growl. *Had I forgotten to feed him?* I didn't think so. I pushed open the door. "Bud, what's with the barking?"

A hand tugged sharply on my long hair, yanking me back into a solid chest as a hand covered my mouth. I was stunned into frozen silence for the briefest of moments before I began to thrash. I slammed my elbow back into the man's gut, and he grunted.

I raced for the door, but he caught my hair again, this time pulling it so hard I lost my footing and slammed into the wood slats of the floor. The world swam around me, everything a picture of rippled blurs. "Shit! Why'd you have to run? I didn't want to have to hurt you."

I couldn't see the face, but that voice. It didn't make sense. He shouldn't be here. My mind tried to put the pieces together, but before I could, I slipped away into a sea of black.

CHAPTER
Forty

Cain

"**Y**OU'RE BEING A DUMB SHIT."

"Tuck," Walker warned as he filled his coffee mug.
Tuck cut his gaze towards Walker. "What? Someone
needs to tell him the truth. He's used to living surrounded by yes-
men, we're not that."

As Tuck and Walker continued bickering about how to handle
me and the clusterfuck I'd made of my life, I reached for a donut.
They'd shown up at my gate before six a.m., so they were damn
lucky they'd brought food. I took a bite of the chocolate old fash-
ioned. The taste barely registered.

"Well?"

I turned my attention from the pastry back to the guys at the
sound of Tuck's question. "Well, what?"

He groaned. "Are you going to fix this? Jensen came home last
night and wouldn't stop talking about it. One minute, she was
bitching about you being an asshole. The next, she was worried
about your heart. I don't like my woman upset, Cain. You need
to fix this."

My lips gave the barest flicker of a twitch. The man who couldn't get enough of different women was now fully dedicated to one. I was happy for him. I rubbed a spot on my chest where the slightest twinge had made itself known. Okay, maybe I was a little jealous, too. That sensation grew as Kennedy's face flashed in my mind. I hadn't slept more than a fitful hour or two last night, questions running through my head. *Is she okay? Crying? Can she sleep? Will she try to make eggs without me in the morning?* It was endless.

I set my donut down on a plate. "I'm not sure it's fixable."

"Why the hell not?" Tuck asked.

The sweet cake turned sour in my gut. "I just…there's too much I can't talk about with her. And that's not fair. She wants to know it all."

Walker pulled out a stool at the counter and sat. "I know that it's not easy for you to go there, but Cain, it's one difficult conversation for a lifetime of happiness."

But it wasn't. The fucking cake had been evidence of that. There were a million and one things that had the potential to send me spinning back in time. Triggering memories I wanted to keep safely buried in the past. I knew what each of those things was, but no one else did. I couldn't explain that to Walker and Tuck. They'd had their fair share of shit in their lives, but nothing that was their fault. "It's not that simple."

Walker sighed, setting down his mug of coffee. "I get it. You know I do." His gaze met mine in a hard stare, but even in that, there was an edge of sympathy. "It might be the hardest thing in the fucking world. But, man, if you get even a sliver of what I have with Taylor, that battle will be more than worth it."

His words sliced at my skin, barbs that dug in and tugged. Because he wasn't wrong. When I tried to picture a life without Kennedy, it was empty and dull, a gray-scape. She painted my existence with the most vivid splashes of color. I'd lived too long with the gray. I wanted the color.

Life with Kenz meant the simplest things being full of joy.

There might be pain, but there was also laughter and love and so much passion, it scorched my skin. Was I really ready to numb everything, even the good, so that I didn't have to remember the bad? The bad was still there. Haunting. Dogging my heels everywhere I went. Life with Kennedy just meant I'd have to expose it to the light. "I'm an idiot."

Tuck threw up his hands. "Praise, Jesus, he has a brain in there, after all."

Walker chuckled. "I knew he'd come around."

My phone buzzed in my pocket, and I pulled it out.

Dante: *Found your boy trying to cross the border into Canada on a fake passport. Border Patrol has him and will be sending him back to the cops in Portland. Need anything else?*

I let out a breath. At least one problem had been solved.

Me: *Nope. Just send me a bill.*

Dante: *I always do.*

I slipped my phone back into my pocket. My company was cleansed. I could start the next phase of programming without having to look over my shoulder. So why wasn't I more relieved? Because everything was just a little empty without *her.* I wanted to build that headquarters here in Sutter Lake, but I wanted to do it with Kennedy by my side.

I ran a hand through my hair and stood. I needed to fix this. And that could only be done face-to-face. If I had to haul every skeleton out of my closet, I would. Hell, I'd fly us to Portland and take her to Dr. Murphy with me if I had to. I just needed to make this right.

Tuck's brows drew together. "Where are you going? Don't you want your donut?"

"I need to fix this."

"That's what I've been saying!"

Before I could tell Tuck that he was an idiot, Walker's phone rang out in the mostly silent kitchen. "Hey, Little J. What's up?"

The sounds from the other end of the line were so loud, Walker had to pull the phone away from his ear. "Slow down. What's wrong?"

My body locked, but Tuck went absolutely wired. "What's going on?"

Walker held up a hand to silence him as his eyes hardened. "Okay. Everything's going to be all right. We're on our way. Stay where you are."

We were already moving. This brotherhood didn't need to know exactly what had happened to show up for one another, we only had to know there was a need.

As soon as Walker hung up, Tuck was on him. "What's going on? Why didn't Wilder call me?"

Walker pulled the front door open. "Because I'm the deputy chief of police in this town, not you." His gaze flicked to me. "Something happened to Kennedy."

My steps stuttered as we hit the stairs, my blood turning to ice. "What do you mean?"

"Get in my truck."

I didn't argue, I wanted to get to Kennedy as fast as I could, and Walker had a siren on his rig. We all piled in. "Talk."

Walker turned over his key, and the engine roared to life. I was already keying in commands on my phone to open my gate so we didn't have to stop. "When J got to the Kettle, Kenz wasn't waiting for her in the kitchen. She just figured she'd overslept because she'd been upset the night before." My chest burned at his words. Upset because I'd hurt her. Caused her pain because I was a coward.

Walker pressed down on the accelerator as soon as we cleared the gate. "But then she heard Chuck whimpering." My gut twisted to the point of pain. "She went upstairs to check on them and found the door wide open. There'd been a struggle. Chuck's hurt." He paused, and I kept staring straight ahead, willing the truck to go faster. "Kennedy's gone."

I didn't say a word. Couldn't. They wouldn't form on my tongue. She was gone. Someone had hurt her. Because, yet again, I was selfish. I hadn't been there, and now she was gone.

My mind raced in circles, chasing down every possibility I could drum up, but I kept coming back to the same thing. It had to be something to do with her father. An angry past client, maybe. A family member of someone who had ended their life. I needed to get in touch with the agent who'd been in charge of that case. I searched the recesses of my brain for his name, but for the life of me, I couldn't remember it.

"Cain. You hanging in there?" Tuck gripped my shoulder from the backseat. I gave a small jerk of my head. "We're going to figure this out. We'll find her."

We would. There was no other option. I would burn the world down around me until we did. And whoever had invaded Kennedy's home. Scared her. Hurt her. Took her. I was going to rain hell down on them.

Walker screeched to a stop behind a patrol car, and we all jumped out. Jensen was holding Kennedy's dog in her arms, tears streaking down her face while Taylor rubbed a hand up and down her back. Taylor took Chuck from J as we approached, knowing Tuck would be on the warpath.

He pulled Jensen into his arms. "Wilder, you're okay. Everything's going to be okay."

Walker wrapped an arm around Taylor, pressing his lips to her hair. They had their women safe in their arms. Mine had never felt emptier. My skin burned with the memory of how Kennedy felt wrapped in my arms, flush against me.

Taylor kissed the bottom of Walker's jaw. "I'm going to take Chuck to the vet. We think he might've broken his leg."

Fuck. That would kill Kenz. That dog was like her child. I swallowed against the emotion building in my throat. "Take him to the best one. Here, let me give you my credit card."

Taylor shook her head. "No. I've got this. I'll take care of this little guy." Her voice hitched. "You just find Kennedy."

Emotion burned a fiery trail up my throat, and I knew I wouldn't be able to hold it in for long. Where was she? What was happening to her right at this very moment? Was she breathing? *No.* I wouldn't go there. Couldn't. I refused to think of a world without the light that was Kennedy.

My phone buzzed in my pocket. *Unknown Number* flashed across the screen. A chill skittered down my spine. I showed it to Walker, who was instantly on alert. "Step away from the crowd and answer."

We headed back towards his truck, and I hit accept. "Hello."

"Cain Hale." The voice was one of those automated deals, and the ice was back in my blood. "We have Kennedy. If you'd like her returned to you breathing and unharmed, we'll require payment. The details have been emailed to you. You have twelve hours."

The call ended. Twelve hours. Payment. My heart was at war with itself. Part of me was relieved. I had money. I could pay whatever they asked. But the other was stuck with the worst fear I'd ever felt. Because once I paid that ransom, what reason would they have to keep Kennedy alive?

CHAPTER
Forty-One

Kennedy

"**F**UCK, FUCK, FUCK!"

The curses were a drumbeat assault against my skull as if each one might cause the bones to fracture. The pain radiating out from my head seemed to make my entire body throb. I groaned and tried to roll over, away from the noise and the light and everything.

"Kennedy. Kennedy, are you okay?"

I groaned again. That voice. Why was he talking to me? And why did everything hurt?

"Kennedy, open your eyes."

My lids fluttered, catching only snatches of images. A blurry figure standing over me. A man rubbing the side of his face. "Can't. Hurts." My voice was scratchy, my mouth felt like cotton. What had happened?

"Shit. I'm so sorry. I didn't mean—fuck!"

I winced at the volume of his voice. "Doug. Quiet." He stilled and, in that moment, so did I. I searched my memory. Glimpses flickered through my mind. Wine with Jensen. Going upstairs. Showering. Someone grabbing me. My eyes flew open, and I tried to scramble away, but the movements were jerky at best because my hands and feet were tied with rope. My head jerked as I tried to take in my surroundings.

The movements turned the dull pain into sharp ice picks. I was on a bed. That knowledge alone had my stomach roiling. But my clothes were still in place. I wasn't sore in that way. I swallowed against the dryness in my throat as I took in the man I'd trusted, one who I'd thought had nothing but good in him.

Doug held up both hands. "I'm not going to hurt you. I mean, I didn't mean to hurt you—shit. I'm sorry, Kennedy."

"What's going on? Why am I here?" My voice was barely audible. Still raspy.

He reached for a bottle of water on a nightstand. "Here, drink some of this." I shook my head. How would I know if he'd drugged it? Doug seemed to guess my train of thought and took a sip himself. "It's fine, I promise."

I hated the idea of drinking after him, but I was desperate. My throat felt as if I'd gone days without water. I nodded, and Doug helped me take a few sips. The liquid felt like heaven. "How long have I been here?"

He sat in a chair near the bed. "Just since last night."

"Why am I here?" It was always the why that mattered most, and nothing I could think of was good.

Doug picked at the label on the bottle of water. "You won't be here long. As soon as we get the money, we'll be gone, and then we'll send the police your location."

My stomach pitched. Money. As soon as he got the money. Was this about my father? "Doug, I don't have any money." Panic started to set in. If he'd made a demand of my family, they sure as hell weren't going to pay any ransom for me. My brother would probably tell them to go ahead and kill me.

Doug's grip on the bottle tightened as his mouth pulled into a thin line. "Not you. Your boyfriend." He said the term as if it were a dirty word.

Cain. He'd made the demand of Cain. A man who'd sent me packing less than twenty-four hours ago. A man who wanted nothing to do with me. But he was a good man. He'd probably pay them anyway, and then I'd owe him even more than I already did. "We're not together anymore."

Surprise flickered in Doug's eyes, maybe even hope, before he shut it down. "It doesn't matter. He'll pay."

Tears burned the back of my throat. "Why?" I couldn't stop myself from asking the question again. I never could wrap my head around people's desperate need for more. How someone could hurt another human just to raise themselves up.

Doug didn't meet my eyes. He was weak, unable to look at the truth of what he'd done. "I got an offer that was too good to say no to." His gaze flicked up for a brief moment. "No one's going to get hurt."

I let out an ugly laugh, the action sending shooting pains through my head and down my spine. "No one's going to get hurt? What about stealing money from someone who's worked hard for it? What about me? Do you really think whoever you're working with is just going to let me ride off into the sunset after seeing your face? They're going to kill me." My voice hitched on the word because it wasn't until that moment that I knew my fate. There was no way these people, whoever they were, would just let me go.

Doug's face hardened. "Cain has more money than he deserves. It's not like he's going to miss a few million. And no one's going to hurt you. I made them promise."

I wanted to laugh. He'd made them promise. Like the word of a kidnapper and extortionist could be trusted. We were both going to end up dead. As soon as whoever this was got their money, we were done for. Tears filled my eyes. It wasn't even about being scared of the pain that was surely coming. It was about what was being stolen from me. The possibility of life that was mine and mine alone. One that I could shape into whatever I wanted it to be. One where I shared a moment in time with a beautifully broken man, even if I didn't get to keep him. I'd always take those beautiful moments, despite the pain they left in their wake. I'd hold on to their memory as long as I could.

"Please." I sat up, inching towards Doug. "Please, don't do this. Whoever is in charge is going to kill us both. You have to let me go."

The bedroom door swung open. "Really, Kennedy. Stop being so dramatic."

No way. There was no possible way that voice belonged to who I thought it did. I had to be hallucinating. Maybe I'd fallen and hit my head and was still unconscious. But as the figure stepped into the room, I knew I was wrong. The betrayal sliced bone-deep. I didn't think my family could hurt me any more than they already had. But I was wrong. So very wrong.

CHAPTER
Forty-Two

Cain

MY FINGERS FLEW OVER THE KEYBOARD AS THE CHATTER around me dulled to a low hum. There was only one thing that mattered now. Finding out who had Kennedy. Tuck was the tracker on land, but I was the tracker in digital space. And I was going to chase this bastard down with keystrokes. I'd use the same to dismantle his life once I found out who he was.

"What's he doing?" Tuck's voice permeated my haze.

"Trying to trace the email," Walker answered. He cleared his throat, and my gaze flicked briefly in his direction. "We've got a trace on your cell and landline. If they call back, try to keep them on the phone, talking. Ask for proof of life."

"They won't call." I kept typing. The call I'd gotten was a recording, nothing more. The email demanding money transferred to an account in a country that had practically zero banking laws had told me almost nothing. "I asked for proof of life when I emailed back."

"You sent an email back?" Walker clasped my shoulder. "Would you stop what you're doing and look at me? You can't correspond with the kidnapper without running it by me first."

The hell, I couldn't. I wasn't waiting on Walker to get what I needed, and what I needed more than anything right now was the knowledge that Kennedy was safe. "Check my phone. You can see what I wrote." I went back to typing.

Walker strode to the counter and started tapping the screen on my phone. "Cain. You can't give them the money. They'll kill her. We need to buy some time."

I shot to my feet, the chair I was sitting in at the kitchen table flying back and toppling to the floor. I fisted Walker's shirt, practically lifting him off the ground. He did nothing to fight it. "Don't you say that. She's not fucking dying. She's going to be fine. We're gonna get her back."

Firm hands gripped my arms, pulling them back. "That's enough, Cain." Tuck squeezed harder, and I released my hold. He clapped me on the back. "We are. We're going to get Kennedy, and whoever the fuck is responsible is going to pay. I promise you that."

I nodded, then headed back to my computer to get back to work.

Tuck spoke to Walker in hushed tones. "Watch your word choice, would you?"

There was silence for a minute before he answered. "We might have to put him down when we figure out where she is. He's one second away from losing it. He could compromise everything."

Like hell, he would. If he stood in my way, I'd tear him apart, brother or not.

Jensen called out from the foyer of the house. "Walker?"

"In here, J."

Jensen appeared with Anna, who twisted and untwisted her fingers in front of her body, looking around the room before her gaze landed on me and caught. She was ravaged, too. Anna loved Kennedy, and this was killing her.

Jensen eyed me and then turned to her brother. "One of your

officers went to the shelter to ask some questions, and Anna says he didn't really listen to what she had to say. We wanted to tell you directly."

Walker straightened. "Which officer?"

Anna stilled her nervous movements. "Officer Matthews."

"I'll have a word with him about taking statements. What did you think was important for us to know?"

Those fingers of Anna's started tying themselves into knots again. "It might be nothing, but I wanted to tell you, just in case." Walker nodded, and Anna took a deep breath. "Doug called in sick the past two days. He's only called in once the entire time I've been at Hope House. And this time, he didn't sound sick. The past few weeks, he's been acting weird. At first, I thought he was sulking because Kenz was dating Cain. But I don't know, maybe it's more?"

My muscles locked the moment Anna had spoken his name, and as soon as she was finished, my fingers began flying. Within minutes, I was in his bank accounts. I scanned the deposits, looking for anything out of the ordinary. His salary was direct-deposited each month, almost always the same. Then my eyes caught on something. I was aware that Walker was talking, assuring Anna that he'd look into it, but I didn't care. "There's a deposit in his account for ten grand from three days ago."

"Fuck, Cain. You can't just hack into his accounts. I can't get a search warrant with that."

I stood, managing not to topple my chair this time. "Do you think I give one shit about warrants or procedure or any of that?" My voice was a low growl as I stalked towards Walker. "The woman I love is in the hands of someone who plans to hurt her for money. For *money*, Walk. Her life means *nothing* to him. I am going to do whatever it takes to get her back. And if you even think of trying to put me down, I will take you out. You know I can."

Walker was strong, but I had feral rage on my side. He knew he couldn't compete. "You love her?"

I blinked. "That is what you heard out of everything I said?"

Tuck chuckled. It was forced, an attempt to clear some of the tension in the air, but it was there. "Well, we did have it on pretty good authority that you'd never let yourself go down that road again."

"That's not important right now—" My words cut off at the ding from my computer that alerted me to a new email. I turned back to the screen. It was from the kidnapper. A photo appeared.

Kennedy. Pale. Eyes stricken. And the side of her face swollen and battered.

He was hurting her. And I would end him for it.

CHAPTER
Forty-Three

Kennedy

A FLASH WENT OFF IN MY FACE. IT WAS A SMALL CELL phone one, but it was enough to have me wincing and shielding my eyes. A throb reverberated in my skull, the pain sharp and stabbing as my vision began to blur again. But none of that distracted from the pain dancing across my chest, the vise that seemed to grip my heart.

"Mom?" My voice was raspy as though I'd smoked a pack a day since birth.

She typed out something on her phone and then placed it in her pocket. "Hello, darling. You're looking a little shabby." A flicker of annoyance passed over her face as she glanced at Doug. "Was that really necessary?"

Doug's face reddened. "I didn't mean to. It's just—she was getting away."

My mother's hand fluttered across her face as if flicking away a gnat. "It is what it is. Have you given her water?"

"Yeah, she just had some."

My eyes followed them as if watching some sort of twisted tennis match. It was as if they were discussing the weather, not their kidnap victim. I swallowed, but my throat didn't seem to want to obey, the motion sticking. "Why?" I was a broken record. I didn't even care about the how. How she'd found me. How she'd orchestrated this whole thing. I only wanted the why. But at the core of it was only one question. Why did she hate me so much?

My mother scoffed, lowering herself into a chair opposite my bed. "Because my dipshit husband and son couldn't be trusted to handle anything."

I blinked rapidly. I didn't think I'd ever heard her curse before. I didn't recognize the woman in front of me. She'd always seemed so weak, almost fragile. Forever going along with whatever my father wanted. Doting on my brother. Tolerating me.

I searched my memories, my mind reeling, trying to find any hint of that in this person I saw before me. Snatches of moments flashed. She had always gotten what she wanted. Somehow, every year, we vacationed at her preferred destination, ate at the restaurants that were her favorites. My father had hated the house we lived in, but my mother loved it, so we stayed.

I studied her carefully, and the truth of our relationship hit me with the force of a freight train. She'd hated me because she couldn't manipulate me. I never seemed to bow to her will quite enough. Wouldn't date the sons of her friends she deemed eligible. Wouldn't starve myself into that size two. Avoided her ladies' lunches at the club like I might catch a plague. They'd all seemed like little things at the time, but they were the types of things my father and brother always acquiesced on. I never did.

"You knew what Dad was doing?" The smoker's rasp was still there.

My mother scoffed. "Of course, I did. I told him to be cautious, to cover his tracks better, but the man's ego never could be tamed." I guess even she didn't have total control over him. She pulled out her phone, checking the screen. "It shouldn't be long now. I'm guessing that photo will encourage your beau to move more quickly." She glanced up at Doug. "Maybe your beating the hell out of her face wasn't so bad, after all. Might have to do a little more of that if he dawdles."

Doug stiffened. "I didn't hit her. She fell. And I'm not hurting her. You said no one would get hurt."

"Oh, shut up." In a movement swift and surprising, Mom pulled a gun from the purse in her lap and fired twice. Doug slumped to the floor.

I screamed, jolting back in surprise. The movement had my vision blurring again, and my head pounding. This had to be a dream. A nightmare.

My mother rolled her eyes. "Oh, please, like you care whether the man who beat you to shit is killed or not."

But I did care. I might've wanted to give Doug a swift kick to the balls before sending him to jail for a decade or so, but I didn't want him dead. But the thing that sent ice sliding through my veins was the absence of emotion on my mother's face. She was totally and completely numb. How had I missed that all these years?

"You really should be thanking me. The original plan was for you to come to an unfortunate end."

"W-w-what?" I hated the tremor in my voice.

Mom chuckled and placed the gun back into her purse. "You've had quite a few near-misses lately, haven't you?"

"What are you talking about?"

She grinned, and it was a bit feral. "Your bike. The gas leak at that shitty little apartment of yours." She took a moment to examine her manicure as if checking to see if shooting a man had chipped her polish. "I made the mistake of hiring out on that. And you know what they say. If you want something done right, do it yourself."

My head spun. She could've killed Jensen—my stomach pitched—or even Noah with that gas leak. One glance at the woman who'd been my mother for decades, and I knew she wouldn't care. But it didn't make sense. Killing me would get her nothing.

She rubbed her thumb along the edge of her nail. "I see you trying to put the pieces together, but you're missing the key one." She paused, her lips pursing. "Your grandmother died. She left everything to you, your brother, and an assortment of charities."

My jaw went slack. Helen Barrington had never been warm and welcoming to me. She'd always kept me at arm's length. I didn't think I'd ever seen her hug another living being. But she had always kissed my father's cheek whenever we went to her home. She'd seemed to love him in her own way. Her leaving him nothing, even after what he'd done, didn't compute.

Mom straightened in her chair. "Charities, when her own daughter-in-law was being thrown out of her home. Did she have no family loyalty?" My mother might've lost her twenty-million-dollar home, but I knew she had a trust fund from her own parents that paid out a yearly sum that was more than enough for a comfortable existence. Just not one with caviar and couture.

She brushed a strand of hair back that had fallen free of her perfect chignon. "I'll admit, I was understandably upset at first. I shouldn't have looked to end your life when there were obviously other options, but I was hurt that you'd betrayed us so." The woman was deranged. It was as if she were apologizing for raising her voice, not trying to kill me. "But you've done so well for yourself, finding an almost suitable match." Her nose scrunched. "His family is abysmal, but he's made up for that with his tenacity and business sense. He won't even miss the piddly amount I'm asking for. And then we'll all go our separate ways."

Tears welled in my eyes as waves of nausea swept through me. This is what I came from. Manipulation. Greed. Selfishness. "Please, don't." I awkwardly scooted myself towards the edge of the bed, swinging my bound legs over. "Please, don't do this. You can have Gran's money. I'll sign it over to you."

Mom removed the gun from her purse. "That's close enough. And what do you take me for? A fool? Like that signature would stand up in court. You have two choices. You can play along like the obedient girl you always should've been, or"—she flipped the gun over in her hand—"I can kill you. And all that money will go to the person who's named in the will I had drawn up." She grinned. "Don't worry, I signed it for you, so it's all official. Now choose. Behave, or die."

CHAPTER
Forty-Four

Cain

I STRODE TOWARDS MY BEDROOM.

"Cain! What the hell do you think you're doing?" Walker called after me.

I went straight for the safe, keying in my code and placing my finger on the scanner. It beeped as it opened, and my hand made a beeline for the metal box in the back. My fingers were the only thing needed to unlock this case, their prints the only code. I lifted the Glock out, checked the magazine and chamber.

"Oh, shit," Tuck mumbled.

I hated guns. Anything that could cause death and destruction, really. But I also understood better than most that you never knew when violence would show up at your door. The deeply rooted need I had to prepare for that possibility meant that I'd logged more than enough hours at a shooting range to be proficient with the weapon in my hands.

Walker grabbed my shoulder in a grip meant to stun. "What the hell do you think you're doing? Are you just going to knock on Doug's door and pull a gun on him?"

I pushed to my feet, pulling a holster from the box and

clipping it to my jeans. I slid the gun in. "I wasn't planning on knocking."

"Do you want me to arrest you?" I ignored Walker's words and headed for the door. "Do you want to get Kennedy killed?"

That stopped me in my tracks. I turned slowly, facing Walker and Tuck head-on. "What do you want me to do? You have nothing. Not one thing that could get you a warrant. The time on their deadline is running out. I'm not going to stand by and let them keep hurting her. *Did you see her face?!*" The ferocity in my words grew with each sentence until I was yelling. That image of Kennedy's bruised and swollen face would haunt me forever. My chest heaved, but I lowered my voice. "They're going to kill her."

Tuck took a step forward. "You're not going in alone." Walker cursed, and Tuck turned to face him. "You know he's right. We have to go in now. Get creative. Find a reason."

Walker ran a hand through his hair. "Fuck. Okay. This is what we're going to do. Vest up. We are going to Doug's because he's the one person we haven't talked to yet to see if he's seen or heard from Kennedy. When we get there, if we hear a scream, sounds of imminent danger, Tuck and I breach. You,"—Walker pinned me with a stare—"stay the fuck outside."

Like hell, I would. But I nodded. Walker would forgive the lie later on.

"Let's go. I've got gear in my truck." Walker strode out of the room, only to come face-to-face with Jensen.

"What's going on?"

Tuck pulled J to him, kissing one temple, the other, and then her forehead. "We're going to go ask Doug a couple of questions." Jensen opened her mouth to say something, but Tuck silenced her with a kiss. "Please, just this once, do what I ask without fighting me on it. Go back to the ranch. Take care of Noah. Let me rest easy knowing you're safe."

Jensen's eyes reddened. "What about you? Are you going to be safe?"

Tuck hugged her tighter to him. "You know I always am, Wilder."

Fuck. Jensen had almost lost Tuck once, and here I was, bringing him into more danger. "Tuck, why don't you go with J?"

His head jerked in my direction. "Don't say stupid shit. We're in this together."

Jensen straightened from Tuck's hold. "No, you're right. You need to go with them." Her gaze traveled over us all. "*Please*, be careful."

"We will." Walker pulled J in for a quick hug. "Tell my girl I love her, and I can't wait to marry her." Jensen nodded, and we all took off, piling into two separate vehicles. Jensen and Anna on their way to the ranch, and Tuck, Walker, and I headed for Doug's.

Walker pulled the address up on his navigation system as Tuck studied a map. "He rents an old cabin at the base of the mountains. It borders national forest land, so no one's around."

My jaw tightened, that familiar click sounding in my ear. "The perfect place to hold someone."

Nothing else was said as we curved our way up the mountain roads. The only thing running through my mind was a chant. *Be okay. Be okay. Be okay.* As if I could will Kennedy's state of being into reality with my mind alone.

We pulled to a stop at the base of a steeply inclined drive. Walker turned off his truck. "We go on foot from here." We climbed out, and Walker handed out Kevlar vests.

I slipped the weighted material over my head, tightening the straps. I looked up, watching as my friends checked their weapons and vests. They always had my back. No matter what. No questions asked. "Thank you." Two sets of eyes met mine. "You're my brothers."

We stood in a circle, gripped each other's shoulders. No other words of affirmation or gratitude were necessary. We knew we were each other's chosen family.

Walker released the hold first, starting up the side of the gravel drive, sticking to the tree line. "We play this smart. Tuck and I take point. Cain, you remain outside until we've cleared the building."

I grunted in response. Tuck eyed me and shook his head. He knew there was nothing in this world that could keep me out of this house. And if Walker was honest with himself, he knew it, too.

As we crested the hill, a cabin and two cars came into view, an SUV that looked to be on its last legs, and a Mercedes. Walker held a finger to his lips and inclined his head towards the vehicles.

I took in the cabin, searching for any signs of movement. There was nothing. If not for the cars, I would've thought there was no one inside.

Walker and Tuck arranged themselves on either side of the door, Walker motioning for me to stand behind him. Gun gripped in two hands, Walker nodded. Tuck took two strides up onto the cabin steps. "Sutter Lake police." With a swift movement I'd only seen on the screen, he kicked the flimsy door open, wood shattering around the busted lock.

My friends cleared the door in seconds, making their way through the space in a choreographed dance that only came with hours of training and practice. I followed behind, doing everything I could not to get in the way. The only sounds were the occasional "clear" from Tuck or Walker. Until I heard a strangled scream.

My chest seized as Tuck and Walker rushed towards the sound, careful to clear any doorways before passing by. It was taking too long. Kennedy was screaming, and anything could be happening to her. I pushed out every dark and disturbing image that tried to fight its way into my mind. I had to stay focused on Kenz. She was the only thing that mattered.

Tuck pushed a door open as Walker held his gun ready and halted as soon as he crossed the threshold. "Sutter Lake police. Put the weapon down, slowly."

The air in my lungs disappeared in an instant. There was only Kennedy. My Kenz. My wild dancer. Perrier-obsessed, joyous spirit. And she had a gun to her head. The woman who held it looked vaguely familiar, but I couldn't place her.

"I don't think I'm going to do that." The voice was calm. Far too composed for the situation.

"Ma'am, the only way out of this is for you to let Kennedy go. Releasing her will make the courts lenient." Walker's negotiator hat was on now.

The woman laughed, sharp and ugly. "So polite, with the *ma'am*. Kennedy, you've made such proper friends. It's a shame you couldn't do that growing up."

What the fuck? Who was this woman?

"Oh, screw this," Tuck muttered. There was a pop and, suddenly, the woman was down. Down and convulsing, wires seeming to come out of her chest. I didn't care what had happened, I only cared about Kennedy.

I rushed to the bed, grabbing her face as gently as I could. "Kenz. Where are you hurt?"

She winced at the sound of my voice. "I'm okay. Really. Can you untie me?" Her voice started to almost slur as she asked, and her eyes rolled back in her head. Kennedy's body stiffened, falling to the bed and then seizing.

What the hell? Had Tuck tased her accidentally? I checked for wires. There was nothing. Panic dug its icy claws into my chest. "Help! I need help!"

Walker rushed to my side. "What happened?"

"I don't know." My hands frantically skimmed over Kennedy's

body as she convulsed. "She said she was fine, but her words were slurred, and then her eyes rolled back in her head."

"Help me get her on her side." We rolled Kenz to her side as she shook.

"What's going on?"

Walker glanced quickly at me before returning his focus to Kennedy. "She's having a seizure. Could mean trauma to the brain."

"Ambulance and backup are on the way. ETA, five minutes," Tuck called from the floor where he was cuffing the woman.

My muscles were wound so tight, it seemed they might snap. *No. No. No.* This could not be happening. I would not lose her. Kennedy's body stilled, and Walker rolled her to her back, placing his cheek next to her mouth. "She's breathing."

My muscles didn't relax. I circled around Walker as he moved to her wrist, trying to take her pulse. I brushed the hair back from Kennedy's face. She was so pale, her freckles standing out in dark contrast. "Kenz. Please open your eyes."

Tears filled my eyes. I couldn't hold them back. Didn't want to. I hadn't cried since the day we'd put my sister in the ground. But these tears, they were filled with all the words I hadn't said. Things I hated myself for holding back. "Kenz." It was a plea. "Don't leave me." My voice broke. "I love you." A single tear spilled over, splashing on her cheek. She didn't answer.

CHAPTER Forty-Five

Kennedy

BEEP. BEEP. BEEP. THE SOUND WAS THE FIRST THING I became aware of. Then came the pain. A throbbing that seemed to engulf my entire body. I let out a small moan. Or what should've been a moan but was more like a croak.

A hand spasmed in mine. Warm. The skin rough. Everything about it was familiar somehow. "Kenz? Can you open your eyes?" The voice. It was tough and gentle all at the same time. I wanted to crawl inside it and stay there forever. "Please, Kenz. Let me see those beautiful green eyes. Please."

I wanted to give the voice what it asked for. My lids fluttered, but I couldn't quite seem to force them open. It was as if each eyelash held a weight, keeping them down.

The hand squeezed mine. "That's it, baby. You can do it."

My eyes flickered and then opened. The light in the room was low. The figure hunched over my bed, almost in shadow. Scruff covered his jaw, and his eyes were full of pain. He took my hand and brought it to his lips. Warm, soft skin pressed into my own. "Cain." My voice was barely audible, and the single word burned my throat.

Cain instantly turned to grab a cup from the table. "Here. They said you could have a couple of small sips as soon as you woke up." He guided the straw between my lips. They felt dry, cracked, but the water was heaven on my tongue and throat. I swallowed eagerly. Cain removed the straw. "Okay, that's enough. We don't want you getting sick."

I let out a sound of protest, but the moment I tried to lift my head off the pillow, pain shot through my skull. I gasped.

"Shit. Let me get a nurse." Cain rose, crossing to the door and calling out into the hallway.

The loss of him, his closeness, was worse than any pain coursing through my head. My breaths picked up speed as panic set in. He couldn't leave me. I wouldn't be able to handle it.

Worry etched lines in Cain's beautiful face as he returned to my bedside. "Baby, breathe. What's wrong?"

"Don't leave." I wasn't above begging. Any bits of pride had long since fled. Tears filled my eyes.

Cain's jaw hardened as pain, raw and deep, filled his gaze. He gently cupped my cheek. "I'm not going anywhere. Not ever again. You have me."

I opened my mouth to respond, but a woman in scrubs bustled in, ending the moment. "Hello, Kennedy, we are so glad to have you awake and with us." The woman was beautiful. Smooth, brown skin, and amber eyes, hair piled on her head in a bun. She eyed Cain with a smile. "And I'm pretty sure your fella here is glad, too. I'm Dr. Andrews. How are you feeling?"

Cain answered before I had a chance. "She gasped in pain when she tried to lift her head off the pillow, and her throat hurts."

The doctor nodded. "For now, let's try to stay still. I'm going to do a quick exam, and then we'll get another dose of pain meds in you. Sound good?"

"Yes. Thank you." I licked my lips. "What happened?" Everything was hazy. I wasn't even sure what the last thing I remembered was.

Dr. Andrews pulled a small penlight out of her pocket. "We'll fill you in on the whats and hows a little later, but you hit your head." She flashed the light over my eyes. "There was enough force that it caused a bleed in your brain that required surgery to relieve the pressure in your skull." I tensed, and Dr. Andrews patted my hand. "You're going to be just fine. We're taking good care of you, and if all goes well, you'll be out of here in just a few days." She pulled on a pair of gloves. "I'm just going to check your incision quickly."

In a matter of moments, she was peeling back what felt like gauze and then putting it back in place. "Everything looks great. The nurses will be in to check on you every thirty minutes or so for the next few hours, but we'll try to let you get some sleep tonight." Dr. Andrews glanced at Cain. "Should I let everyone in the waiting room know the update?"

Cain scrubbed a hand over his jaw. "Yeah. That would be great. Thank you. For everything."

Dr. Andrews beamed. "Of course. I'm glad everything's going so well. I'll give you two some privacy." She winked at me and headed for the door.

I looked at Cain. "Brain surgery?"

His hand clasped mine again, bringing it to his mouth and merely holding it there. He whispered words against my skin. "I've never been more scared in my life. I-I—" Tears filled his eyes. "I thought I was going to lose you." He moved my hand to his cheek and pressed it there, the stubble pricking my palm. "I thought I was going to lose you, and that you'd never know how much I loved you."

I sucked in a sharp breath. "You love me?"

"I didn't want to." The words stung, but I didn't want pretty lies, I'd had that all my life, I wanted the ugly truth. The truth that was beautiful in its ugliness because it was raw. Real.

Cain pushed on. "I wanted easy. Predictable. Numb. I didn't want someone who would make me feel. I wanted someone I could place in a carefully constructed box. That was never you, you could never fit into some small sliver of my life, you snuck into every last piece of it. The scent of you lingers in every room, your touch burns my skin long after you take your hand away. You crawled into my fucking heart, and I know I'll never get you out. I never want to try. I love you, Kennedy. And I'll work for the rest of my life to atone for hurting you. I'll tell you every last detail of my past. Show you any picture you want. Take out every last skeleton. You have me. All of me. Even the demons."

Hot tears spilled over my cheeks. "I love you. I'll love your demons, too. Just don't hide them from me."

Cain shook his head, keeping my hand pressed to his cheek. "Never again. I love you." He chuckled, dropping my hand to the bed but keeping it firmly between his. "I was terrified of those words, and now I can't stop saying them."

I grinned, not caring that the motion made my head throb. "I'll never get tired of hearing them."

There was a knock on the door. Cain scowled. "Hold on." He released me, but the fear of him leaving didn't return this time. He pulled the door open a crack and spoke in hushed, angry tones. "Wait." He shut the door in the person's face.

Cain turned and strode back to the bed, a scowl on his face. "Preston's here."

The sound of my brother's name had memories flooding back. Doug. My mom. Her plan. The pain. My hand shot to my mouth as tears filled my eyes again. "My mom."

Cain gently pulled my hand away from my face. "I know, baby. I'm so sorry."

"H-h-how could she do that?"

He pressed his mouth to my hand, lips skimming over my knuckles. "I don't know, baby. I don't know how evil can root itself so deeply in some people."

I hiccupped. "Preston's here."

Cain tried his best to hide his scowl but was only partially successful. "The cops had to call him to question him. He hopped on a plane the minute he heard." Cain glanced at the door. "I don't trust him…but he seems pretty wrecked. Do you want him to come in?"

My chest constricted and released. I wanted my brother back. It didn't matter how many past hurts lay between us. I'd forgive it all if I could just have him in my life again. "Please."

Cain nodded and slowly turned back to the door, releasing my hand. Opening the door, he growled out a warning. "You say one thing that upsets her, and you're out."

Preston nodded. No snide or pissed-off response, just quick agreement. Cain stepped out of the doorway, and Preston gasped. I was sure I looked awful, but he didn't appear much better. His hair was a tumbled mess as if he'd run his fingers through it hundreds of times, and his eyes were swollen and red. He shuffled his feet but never took his eyes off me. "Twinkle Toes."

The two words had my eyes filling. "Pres."

He rushed to my bedside, reaching out to take my hand but stopping short. He swallowed. "Can-can I touch you?" I nodded, and he scooped up my hand, squeezing it gently as he sat in the chair next to my bed. "I'm so sorry. I didn't know. I swear I didn't know."

"I know you didn't." My brother might've lost his way, said things that cut deep, but I knew he'd never physically try to harm me. He didn't have that kind of meanness in him. I looked from my brother to Cain. "Where is she?"

He knew exactly who I meant. "In jail." His Adam's apple bobbed as he swallowed. "Where she belongs."

Cain leaned against the wall on the opposite side of my bed. "And she will be there for a very long time."

Preston squeezed my hand again. "I know Dad screwed up. If I'm honest with myself, I know you did the right thing. But I was just so mad that you didn't come to me first, let me try and fix it—"

"It wasn't fixable, Pres. It was too far gone."

He winced. "You might be right about that. But I was hurt. And I couldn't let go of that anger." Tears welled in his eyes. "And now I'll never be able to take back all those horrible things I said."

My fingers dug into the back of Preston's hand, my heart at war with itself. He'd hurt me so badly, but under all the pain, one thing was true. I wanted my brother back. "I won't pretend there's not a lot of hurt lying between us, Pres." He blinked back tears, and I hurried on. "But I want you in my life." His hand spasmed in mine. "I think we can build a relationship again, don't you?"

He nodded as he wiped away a single tear that had escaped. "I missed you so fucking much, Twinkle Toes."

"I missed you, too." I looked up at Cain with what I knew was a watery smile. "I've got my family now."

Cain's returning smile was gentle. "Now, and always."

"Can you get me a piece of paper and a pen?"

Cain nodded. "Sure. Why?"

"I want to write down exactly how this feels right now. How grateful I am." It was maybe the most important slip of paper that would ever go into my gratitude jar. The thing I had always hoped for. A family who loved me just as I was.

TWO WEEKS LATER

"If you don't let me off this couch, I'm going to bean you with my bottle of Perrier."

Cain snickered and didn't look the least bit scared. Apparently, my sense of gratitude for my newfound family had been short-lived. Because they were all hovering like crazy. Sarah brought over food what seemed like every other day. Walker had personally taken my statement at the lake house so I wouldn't have to venture into the police station. When Tessa and Liam had returned from the most recent leg of his tour, she had brought Liam over to play me my own personal concert because she had read that music was helpful to those recovering from brain injuries.

The girls had taken pity on me last night and came over with spa supplies in tow. They painted my nails, and we did face masks. It almost felt normal, except that Cain appeared every twenty minutes *just to check on me.* Jensen had finally threatened that the next time he came into the living room, she'd put a mask on his face and glitter polish on his toes.

I loved them all. But they were driving me batty. My doctor had given me the go-ahead for moderate activity, and Cain was still trying to keep me couch-bound for twenty hours a day. I let out a growl that only had Cain laughing harder. "Come on, Kenz. I haven't seen this *Murder, She Wrote* episode yet, and I think I've got the killer figured out."

They were going to need to figure out who killed Cain in a minute. I scowled at the screen. I'd even hit my Angela Lansbury limit, which was saying something. I glanced over at Cain, who was refocused on the screen. His dark blue eyes shone in the afternoon light. The stubble he often wore now, dotted his jaw. He was so damn handsome, it stole my breath.

My lips twitched. Slowly, so he wouldn't notice, I slipped off the boxers I was wearing under the blanket before moving the cover aside. Cain's t-shirt hung low on my frame, covering everything yet slipping off one shoulder. I moved swiftly, throwing a leg over Cain's lap and straddling him.

"What are you doing, Kenz?"

I nipped at his chin. "What does it look like I'm doing?" The doctor had said that sex, as long as it wasn't too rough, was totally fine. Cain had ignored the decree. He touched me plenty, but it was all gentle and loving and not sexual at all, yet it still managed to drive me crazy.

"I don't think this is a good idea." His hand slipped under the hem of my shirt, finding me bare. "Fuck! Where did your shorts go?"

I giggled. "Oops. Must've lost them somewhere."

Cain let out a litany of curses, but his fingers dragged lower, delving into my center. I pressed up on my knees, granting him better access. He teased and toyed, stroking in lazy circles, but not venturing where I needed him most. "What do you need, Kenz?"

"You." It was a breathless plea, and I didn't even care. I tugged at his sweats until he lifted, helping slip them down around his knees.

Cain's eyes met mine and held. "Slow and easy. Promise me."

"Slow and easy."

His mouth took mine as I lowered myself onto him. I almost wept at the feel of him. Stretching, so full. God, I'd missed this. Cain broke the kiss, cupping my face. "I love you."

My breath hitched. "More than I can say." It was true. I couldn't put into words how much I loved this man. So, I'd show him. I began to move, slowly rolling my hips, exploring the dance that only the two of us would ever have. Testing movements until I found that perfect pace.

Cain tugged at my shirt, pulling it over my head. He leaned back against the couch, taking in all of me. His breaths were coming faster now. "You're the most beautiful thing I've ever laid eyes on." His words had my core tightening. "Fuck. I'm not going to last. It's been too long since I've been inside you. Find it, baby."

My back arched as Cain palmed my breasts, teasing my nipples. He gave one a gentle pinch. It was all I needed to go tumbling over the edge, taking him with me.

I collapsed onto Cain's chest. "Thank you."

He chuckled, sending delicious sensations through my over-sensitized body. "You never have to thank me for that, baby."

"I like for you to know I'm grateful."

He nipped at my ear. "There's nothing in this life I'm more grateful for than you."

Epilogue

Kennedy

TWO YEARS LATER

LIGHT HANDS. WHISPER-SOFT. TRACING OVER MY FACE. "Mmmmmm." My response was part moan, part complaint. "Sleeping."

A deep chuckle sounded beside me. "I know, but you need to wake up. We've got a big day ahead of us."

I cracked open a single eyelid. "What time is it?"

Cain sat propped up against the pillows, all the glorious tanned skin of his chest on full display. "A little after six."

I burrowed my face back into the pillow. "I can sleep for another hour."

"If you open those eyes, I'll give you a present."

"Your cock is not a present," I mumbled against the pillow.

Cain grunted. "That's not what you said last night."

My eyes flew open, then narrowed. "Careful, if you want my mouth anytime in the next month."

He scoffed. "Please, you couldn't stay away from my dick for longer than a day or two."

He wasn't wrong. I had an addiction to the man that was

unrivaled. I pushed myself up and leaned against the pillows. "All right, I'm awake. What's my present?" I eyed his flannel pajama bottoms.

"Eyes up here, baby." Cain's voice was low but held a hint of humor.

I shrugged. "Your choice."

Cain reached over to the nightstand and handed me a jar. It was breathtakingly beautiful. It looked like intricately blown glass, a swirl of blues and greens. "It's gorgeous." I studied it more carefully, turning it in the light. As I did, I caught an etching on its surface. *Forever grateful.*

My gaze flicked up to Cain. "A gratitude jar for me?" I'd kept up the process, even though life was easier these days. I never wanted to lose that sense of appreciation or wonder. We had an entire bookshelf in the living room dedicated to my jars.

The lake house was full of a lot more mementos like those. The walls housed photos, new and old. We'd brought Kiara out of the dark and into the light. Into our lives. Cain didn't shy away from her memory anymore, he embraced it. The journey hadn't been an easy one, but he'd taken it and never once pushed me away through it all.

Cain tapped the lid of the jar. "I don't know. It looks like it might already be full."

I took in the slips of paper I'd missed on my earlier inspection, too distracted by the shimmering glass in its beautiful colors. I unlatched the lid and pulled out a scrap of paper. It was filled with Cain's sloping scrawl.

The way you take care of everyone in your orbit.

My brows pulled together as I glanced quickly at Cain. He motioned for me to pull out another. I did.

The look on your face when I make you come.

My cheeks heated as I reached for another.

How you love my demons.

My heart clenched. I did. I loved every last piece of Cain. And now I knew them all. It had only made my love grow deeper, rooting itself in me in a way I knew would last forever.

Cain tucked a strand of hair behind my ear. "It's all the things I love about you. All the things I'm grateful for." My eyes flew up to meet his gaze. "Well, not all the things. One jar wouldn't be enough. But I promise, I'll keep making you these, so if you ever need reminding, you'll only need to pull out a slip of paper."

My breath hitched as my eyes welled. "Just when I think I can't love you more."

His face softened. "Do me a favor?" I nodded. He reached into his pocket, pulling out a small box. "Be my wife."

I didn't wait to see what the box held, I launched myself at him, sobbing into his chest and nodding.

"Is that a yes?"

"Yes! Of course, it's a yes."

Cain stroked a hand down my back, pulling my hair away from my face. "You haven't even looked at the ring." It could've been made of barbed wire, and I still would've said yes. But, of course, it wasn't. Cain slipped the ring onto my finger. It caught the light, sending rainbows dancing on the wall.

"Cain…" It was breathtaking. Too large, but I knew better than to argue the point. I had to let him have his way here. Compromise. I looked up to meet his gaze. "It's perfect."

He let out a breath. "I thought you might fight me on it."

I laughed. "I'm getting better. I did get a car."

Cain rolled his eyes. "One of the cheapest you could find."

I pinched his nipple. "A Jeep isn't cheap. It's practical." I was never going to be into all the fancy gadgets he was, but I also wasn't punishing myself for someone else's deeds any longer.

He grinned and placed my jar back on the nightstand, then rolled me to my back. "I'm glad you're reasonable, Mrs. Hale."

My eyes welled again. "I can't wait to make it official."

His mouth swept across mine, tongue darting in. "Let's do it soon."

"Next month?"

Cain pulled back. "You sure?"

I nodded. "Something small. Simple. Just our family." Our family was one and the same already. Our perfect small circle of loved ones. "Chuck can be the ring bearer." A snore of agreement sounded from his bed on the floor.

Cain shook his head as his mouth lowered to mine again.

"Hey, guys. You up? I'm going to make breakfast."

Cain scowled. "You have got to be kidding me."

I dissolved into laughter. "You're the one who decided to propose when you knew my brother was here."

"He's such a cock-block."

I kissed Cain slowly. "I'll make it up to you, future husband. I promise."

"Damn right, you will." He groaned as he rolled his hips against me, just once. "We could always take a shower…"

"A really long one."

In a flash, Cain was up and had me thrown over his shoulder. I shrieked as he headed for the bathroom.

Cain lifted one of the half-dozen cakes out of the trunk. His eyes traveled over the rainbow sprinkles dotting the frosting. I wrapped my arms around his waist. "Do you think she'd like this?"

Cain's voice was thick when he answered. "Kiara would love that we're celebrating her birthday this way."

I squeezed his waist. "She'd be so proud of you."

He nodded, shifting the cake to one hand so he could wrap an arm around me. "I know she would. And this place, it's keeping a piece of her alive."

I looked up at the brand-new building where the community center used to be housed. After the dust had settled from my mother's attack, I'd found out that my grandmother had indeed left me an exorbitant amount of money. More than I had any need for. I'd struggled with it at first, but Cain had been there, helping me process it all and deciding what to do.

My brother and I had decided to give the vast majority of our inheritances to create a fund to help reimburse the victims hit the hardest by my father's crimes. Because while my mother had gone to prison, my father had toed the line of his parole and remained free, making no attempts at restitution. But I'd kept a few million of my inheritance aside for a very special project.

I'd approached the city and asked to buy the community center, with an agreement that I'd build a new one in its place. The buildings that lay before us now were so much more than that. Hope House had its own separate space with a cafeteria, a rec room, and apartments for families needing a place to stay until they got back on their feet again. Another building held a multi-level gymnasium complete with a gym, pool, and studio space for classes. Any member of the community could take any assortment of sessions for free. And I got to teach as many ballet classes as I wanted.

Lastly, there was the Kiara Center. A building that housed social workers, therapists, and an after-school staff. It was a safe haven for anyone who needed it. It was a place for kids who needed somewhere to go after school because no one was home. A place to help and support when the world hit especially hard. It even had a food pantry and a kitchen where anyone could come by for a warm meal. It was our dream to prevent the violence that had cut Kiara's life short by providing the support any family might need. The help Cain and Kiara had needed.

"I'm so damn proud of you." Cain pressed his lips to my temple.

I looked up. "I'm proud of us both." While the project was mine, Cain had helped me every step of the way. He was my supporter, sounding board, and of course, he'd installed all of the security—at his expense.

"All right, already. Enough with the mushy stuff. We've got work to do." Anna strode towards us, clapping her hands.

I grinned. "Good thing the head of Hope House is on top of things." I'd given Anna the title she always should've had, and she was thriving here.

"They've been doing this all morning," my brother groused as he trailed behind Anna.

Cain handed Preston the cake he held. "You could always stay at a hotel."

"Boys," I warned, holding up a hand.

"Holy shit!" Anna grabbed my hand. "You're engaged?!" She pulled me in for a hard hug before I could answer. "Oh my God. Congratulations! Of course, he'd put a monster rock on your finger."

I laughed. "Thank you."

"I'm so glad you got your happy, girl."

"Me, too."

"What's going on?" Jensen called as she crossed the parking lot, hand to her swollen belly, trailed by Tuck and Noah.

"Cain put a ring on it," Anna called.

"What?!" Jensen shrieked. "Taylor, Tessa, hurry up! Our girl's engaged!" She started speed-walking.

"Wilder," Tuck warned. "Slow down."

"Oh, calm down. The baby's not going to just pop out."

I stifled a laugh as Jensen pulled me in for a hug. This pregnancy had her snapping at Tuck a little more than usual. "You're going to give the man a heart attack."

"He needs to relax." She pulled out my hand to examine the ring and grinned. Her gaze flicked up to Cain. "You do good work. Why am I not surprised?"

The next few hours were spent doling out congratulatory hugs, setting up for our grand opening, and finally seeing the space I'd worked so hard on come to life. By the time the doors opened, I was exhausted. Cain grabbed my hand and tugged me outside, leading me towards an Adirondack chair in the shade and pulling me into his lap. "Time for you to take a break."

"But I—"

"Nope. No arguments. You've been going flat-out for the past week with all the last-minute prep. Sit back and soak it all in."

I eased back against Cain. He was right. I didn't want to miss the joy of the moment because I was too busy running around trying to make it all perfect. I sighed as the summer breeze ruffled my hair and carried with it the sounds of laughter and happy shouts.

I'd decided that a carnival setup would be the perfect way to bring people to the center, to make it a place that was fun and welcoming, not scary or just a place of charity. I wanted this to be a place where everyone felt welcome, no matter who they were or where they came from. It had worked like a charm.

My gaze caught on Walker and Taylor, their son toddling between them, holding onto each of their hands. The way they met each other's gazes over his head, I wouldn't be surprised if number two followed shortly behind.

Kids ran from one ride to the other, pausing to stare up at the Ferris wheel that reached high into the sky. Liam had Tessa wrapped in his arms, his hands resting on her belly that was just starting to show. They had one at home, but she was now expecting twins, much to Liam's delight. Tessa had always wanted a big family, and he was determined to give her one.

Tessa reached up a hand to wave at Noah, who bounded over, parents, grandparents, and great-grandmother in tow, pointing up at the ride. "Hell no, Wilder." Tuck's voice carried on the wind as he stalked behind Jensen. "You are too pregnant to go on that thing."

Jensen whirled on him. "Are you saying I'm fat?"

"Boy," Irma said with a shake of her head, "did someone hit you with the stupid stick this morning?"

"Oh, shit," Cain whispered in my ear. "He's in for it now."

Tuck's mouth opened and closed a few times before words came out. "Of course, not. I—"

Jensen's hands whipped out and grabbed Tuck's arms. "Uh-oh."

"What do you mean, uh-oh?"

Jensen glanced down at the ground and then back at Tuck. "I think my water just broke."

I got to my feet, Cain hot on my heels.

"Your water just broke?" Tuck's eyes widened. "You're having the baby now?" She nodded. "Shit! We have to go. I have the bag in the car, and we need the pre-filled paperwork. I have that in the—"

Jensen pulled Tuck to her in a swift move, silencing him with a kiss. "We're going to have a baby."

Tuck framed her face in his hands. "Love you, Wilder."

"I love you, too."

I twined Cain's fingers with mine. "You guys are really sweet and stuff, but I'm thinking your water breaking means it's time to hit the road."

Tuck jolted. "She's right. We have to go."

Irma beamed at them both. "I'll gather up the rest of the hooligans. You two get going."

I grinned. "I just have to tell Anna what's going on, and then we'll head to the hospital."

Jensen shook her head. "No, Kenz, this is your big day. You can't leave."

I wrapped my arms around J and whispered in her ear. "You

are my closest friend in the world. You made me feel safe when it felt like the whole world was against me. If you think I'm missing you bringing this baby into the world, this little one has pickled your brain."

She sniffled. "I love you, Kenz."

"Love you, too, J."

"We gotta go. Now." Tuck tugged on Jensen, breaking our hold.

"We'll be right behind you." I turned to Cain and leaped on him. Thankfully, he caught me. I brushed the hair back from his face and pressed my mouth to his in a searing kiss. I pulled away slightly breathless. "Today is the best day of my life."

Cain's smile was soft, that adoring one he wore only for me. "The first of many best days, baby. The first of many."

THE END

BONUS SCENE

Want a little peek into Cain and Kennedy's life a few years from now? By signing up for my newsletter, you'll get this bonus scene. Plus, you'll be the first to see cover reveals, excerpts from upcoming releases, exclusive news, and have access to giveaways found nowhere else. Sign up by going to the link below.

www.subscribepage.com/BBCbonus

ENJOY THIS BOOK?

You can make a huge difference in *Beautifully Broken Control*'s book life!

Reviews encourage other readers to try out a book. They are critically important to getting the word out about a novel and mean the world to every author.

I'd love your help in sharing *Beautifully Broken Control* with the world. If you could take a quick moment to leave a review on your favorite book site, I would be forever grateful. It can be as short as you like. You can do that on your preferred retailer, Goodreads, or BookBub. Even better? All three! Just copy and paste that baby!

Email me a link to your review at catherine@catherinecowles.com so I can be sure to thank you. You're the best!

ACKNOWLEDGMENTS

Now, to my very favorite part...the acknowledgments. Since you've read Kennedy and Cain's story, you might have guessed that I have a thing for gratitude. I love shouting out to the universe just how much I have to be thankful for. And with each book, there are a whole lot of people to appreciate. Here we go...

The first thank you always goes to my mom. She gave me my insatiable love for books and is my biggest supporter. Thank you for everything, Mom!

Writing can be lonely at times, but the internet can be a beautiful place. If you're lucky, you'll meet some of the most amazing women you can imagine. Those who encourage, share wisdom, and generally keep you from rocking in a corner when things get tough. Thank you to all the wonderful authors who have been supportive in every way possible. An extra special thank you to Meghan, Emma, and Grahame...I'm so grateful to have you in my life!

To my fearless beta readers: Angela, Emily, Ryan, and Trisha, thank you for reading this book in its roughest form and helping me to make it the best it could possibly be!

The crew that helps bring my words to life and gets them out into the world is pretty darn epic. Susan and Chelle, thank you for your editing wisdom and helping to guide my path. Julie and Janice, for catching all my errors, both big and small. Hang, thank you for creating the perfect cover for this story. Stacey, for making my paperbacks sparkle. Becca, for creating trailers that give me chills. And my team at Social Butterfly: Jenn, Sarah,

Shan, and Brooke, thank you for believing in me and working so hard to get my books into as many hands as possible.

To all the bloggers who have taken a chance on my words... THANK YOU! Your championing of my stories means more than I can say. And to my launch and ARC teams, thank you for your kindness, support, and sharing my books with the world.

Ladies of Catherine Cowles Reader Group, you're my favorite place to hang out on the internet! Thank you for your support, encouragement, and willingness to always dish about your latest book boyfriends. You're the freaking best!

To my personal cheering squad: the Lex Vegas ladies, Lyle, Nikki, Paige, and Trisha, thank you for endless encouraging conversations and lots of laughs. So grateful to have you in my corner.

Lastly, thank YOU! Yes, YOU. I'm so grateful you're reading this book and making my author dreams come true. I love you for that. A whole lot!

ALSO AVAILABLE FROM
CATHERINE COWLES

Further To Fall

Beautifully Broken Pieces

Beautifully Broken Life

Beautifully Broken Spirit

ABOUT
CATHERINE COWLES

Writer of words. Drinker of Diet Cokes. Lover of all things cute and furry, especially her dog. Catherine has had her nose in a book since the time she could read and finally decided to write down some of her own stories. When she's not writing, she can be found exploring her home state of Oregon, listening to true crime podcasts, or searching for her next book boyfriend.

STAY CONNECTED

You can find Catherine in all the usual bookish places…

Website: catherinecowles.com

Facebook: facebook.com/catherinecowlesauthor

Catherine Cowles Facebook Reader Group: bit.ly/ ccReaderGroup

Instagram: instagram.com/catherinecowlesauthor

Goodreads: goodreads.com/catherinecowlesauthor

BookBub: bookbub.com/profile/catherine-cowles

Amazon: https://www.amazon.com/author/catherinecowles

Twitter: twitter.com/catherinecowles

Pinterest: pinterest.com/catherinecowlesauthor

Printed in Great Britain
by Amazon